WHISPERS

OF

SHADOW

&

FLAME

EARTHSINGER CHRONICLES BOOK TWO

Also by L. Penelope

Song of Blood & Stone
Breath of Dust & Dawn

WHISPERS

OF

SHADOW

&

FLAME

EARTHSINGER CHRONICLES
BOOK TWO

L. PENELOPE

ST. MARTIN'S GRIFFIN   NEW YORK

First published in the United States by St. Martin's Griffin, an imprint of St. Martin's Publishing Group.

WHISPERS OF SHADOW & FLAME. Copyright © 2019 by L. Penelope. All rights reserved. Printed in the United States of America. For information, address St. Martin's Publishing Group, 120 Broadway, New York, NY 10271.

www.stmartins.com

Designed by Steven Seighman

The Library of Congress Cataloging-in-Publication Data is available upon request.

ISBN 978-1-250-14809-4 (trade paperback)
ISBN 978-1-250-14810-0 (ebook)

Our books may be purchased in bulk for promotional, educational, or business use. Please contact your local bookseller or the Macmillan Corporate and Premium Sales Department at 1-800-221-7945, extension 5442, or by email at MacmillanSpecialMarkets@macmillan.com.

First Edition: October 2019

10 9 8 7 6 5 4 3 2 1

For my mother, who started it all

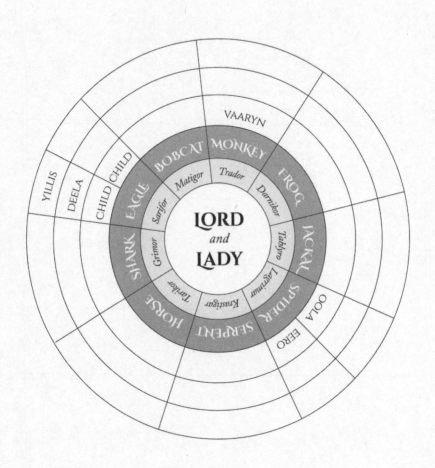

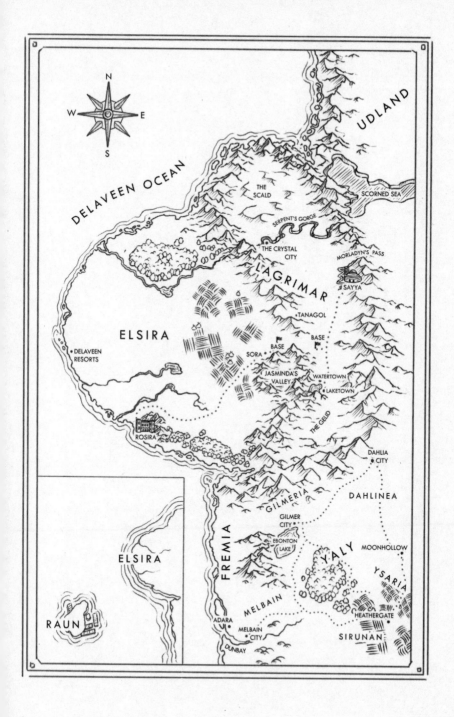

WHISPERS

OF

SHADOW

&

FLAME

EARTHSINGER CHRONICLES BOOK TWO

PROLOGUE

The earth holds its breath as the young Queen falls to the ground. The jeweled handle of her betrayer's dagger protrudes from her side.

The valley shudders as a great swell of Earthsong is pulled from the source. The spell is cast, the barrier erected, unseen by any eye but felt by all.

The Mantle.

This valley, these mountains, will divide the people forevermore. Wives and husbands are separated, brothers and sisters, parents and children, Songbearers and Silent.

The Queen does not awaken, but neither does she die. Her limp form hangs like a doll from the arms of her lover. He carries her away, for her long slumber.

The Queen's betrayer compels the people to sing cities from sand, to spell barren land until it is fertile, to bring dry riverbeds back to life. They transform the desert the way their ancestors did, but may not speak of them.

The betrayer has outlawed history, leaving only myth.

He creates a new language and forces the people to use it. He changes the names of their foreparents, changes his own name, demands the land be known as his. He calls it the Fatherland and he must be known as the father, not just the king. The True Father.

Some,

many,

almost all,

will buckle.

Will watch those who fight against the True Father be cut down like trees. Will fall in line to preserve their meager peace. Will have their Songs ripped out and pretend they are whole without them.

But hope comes in the words of a promise from across the mountains. The promise is whispered in secret, passed down through generations, believed only by a few.

It is a promise to never accept that this life is forever, to never forget there was once another way.

The Queen still lives, sleeping in another land, and those who sleep must one day

Wake up.

—EARTHSINGER CHRONICLES,

AS TOLD TO MOORIAH BY THE MOTHER

CHAPTER ONE

My purpose is to set it all down right
And let not fear nor anguish stay my hand
For one day when my bones have turned to ash
I do not want my soul to roam this land
So though I be a poor historian
Pray let my words be writ stentorian

—THE BOOK OF UNVEILING

Two and a Half Weeks Before the Fall of the Mantle

"I-I'm sure we can come to some kind of understanding."

The man before Kyara ul-Lagrimar scrambled backward, slamming his back against the wall, shaking the tapestry hanging next to him. The scent of his fear was rancid, filling the

room. The stench overpowered the savory aroma of the freshly
roasted goat laid out on the table behind her. His whimpers
drowned out the weeping of the woman cowering across the
room.

Kyara judged the distance between them and determined the
wife was far enough away to remain safe but only if Kyara stood
very close to her target. Close enough to feel his sour breath on
her skin.

Her stomach clenched at the thought; however, she forced
herself forward, erasing the few paces between them. The finely
woven rug swallowed the sound of her boots. Now added to
the room's collection of odors: the scent of piss. The dark stain
spreading across the front of his trousers was proof enough that
the fellow knew who she was and why she was here.

"W-we can negotiate. I'm sure there must be something you
want." Beads of sweat punctured his forehead, and the thick
vein at his neck jumped with his rapid pulse. "I have money,
enough grams to make you a wealthy woman. And jewels, trunks
full of them. The finest s-silks." He spread a shaking hand, pointing to the wealth on display in his home.

Delicate crystal and china graced the polished table, ornate
tapestries hung from the walls, and electric lamps brightened the
space. Kyara had noticed it all in one sweep of the room when
she'd first burst in the front door, brushing past the weary maid.
The house: three levels of sandstone within view of the glass
castle, spoke for itself. This man—a payroller most would call
him—had been very useful to the True Father for some time.
And had been paid well for his trouble. But now his usefulness,
and his trouble, were at an end.

"I am not here to negotiate with you." Kyara's voice was paper
thin.

The man's eyes widened. He spread his arms, attempting to press himself into the wall. Kyara didn't move from her position a hairbreadth away. She didn't need to touch him, but he didn't know that.

"Whatever transgression His Majesty believes I've made, I will redress, threefold. I am but a simple man. A husband and father." He waved a pudgy hand at the shaking woman in the corner. "I give tribute for all I collect, I pay on time and . . ." His pleas became a drone in her ears, mingling with those of a hundred other men who had begged for their lives over the years. Other men in other homes like this, flaunting their wealth while so many starved.

Rugs and tapestries and real glass in the windows. The enticing fragrance of meat, fresh vegetables, and butter tickled her nose. Some unidentifiable spice hung in the air. All this, while most of the city found ways to make their meager rations last far longer and feed more mouths than intended. And those in the Midcountry scraped by with even less.

Kyara's mouth watered at the dinner she'd interrupted, but she never ate the food of the dead.

The heat in the room became oppressive. She wasn't sure if it was the fear or the piss or the meal, but nausea overwhelmed her. If she didn't end this quickly and get out, she would be sick, right here on this beautiful rug.

Her warped Song prowled inside her, restless. It wanted to launch itself into the maelstrom of source energy, to ride the brutal currents of the force like a kite in a violent wind. She shuddered and reined in her power. Instead of giving in to the despised urge, she opened her mind's eye. The world fell away, leaving only a field of black. She spread her senses, shutting out the energies of the overcrowded city and focused on this home, this room. Moving arcs of white light burst across her vision, like the undulating waves of brightness produced by a fire dancer swinging a torch.

This was Nethersong. Her gift and her curse.

Just as all life carried energy—Earthsong—so did death. And while an Earthsinger may grow crops from seeds or feel the pulse of life moving in the plants and animals around them, Kyara did the opposite.

In her vision, the light of the man before her pulsed brightly. His death energy was a cyclone spinning out of control. Judging by the strength of Nethersong within him, he had not been kind to his body—a feat much easier when you were on the True Father's payroll and could afford an abundance of rich food and drink. If the immortal king were a patient man, Kyara wouldn't be needed at all. This payroller would die from his dissipation sooner rather than later.

In the corner of the room, the wife's light was dimmer. She was younger and healthier than her husband. A barely there glow several paces away from the wife indicated a faint trace of Nethersong, which surprised Kyara. There was a child hiding under the table. She had been careless not to notice.

"You two. Out." She didn't turn from the payroller, merely pointed behind her, ignoring the shuffling and desperate whispering that ensued. There were others in the house as well, but all were far enough away to be safe.

The mangled skin on her chest began to ache. She must act soon or the pain would intensify. Her orders were clear, and she would have no peace until they were carried out.

She shuttered her extra sight, bringing the man's jowly face back into focus. A silent apology cramped her heart. Yes, this payroller had sinned, had contributed to his people's poverty and strife, but no judge or jury had convicted him. He had merely chosen to align himself with a mad, immortal king who was as capricious as he was powerful. And the payroller's time had run out.

The executioner had been sent for him.

She released the tight hold she kept on her Song. The beast leapt forward eagerly, darting into the deluge of primordial energy that was Nethersong.

Ydaris had once told her that pulling from Earthsong was like turning on a water spigot. Weaker Singers could use a trickle. Stronger Singers a gushing torrent. Nethersong was nothing like that. There was only one setting: flood. Opening her Song to the energy was like walking through a raging sandstorm. Howling gales of power assaulted her, batting her to and fro like a wildcat with its prey.

She steeled herself against the forces pummeling her and wrangled her Song back under control. Then she flooded the man before her, turning his light from bright to blinding.

He clutched a hand to his chest and gasped. The Nethersong within him grew, rapidly increasing the damage to his body, accelerating whatever ailments or diseases he already harbored. What would have taken months on its own, Kyara forced to occur within seconds.

She pulled back from the tumult of Nethersong, once again caging her Song, ignoring its protests. The pain in her chest faded, and she nimbly stepped out of the way as the man slid to the floor in a flaccid heap. He died with his eyes open, the whites swiftly darkening to black. Black eyes and black gums were the signature all her victims bore.

A movement to her left caught her attention. The wife. She'd made it only to the doorway. Now the poor thing was on

her knees, emptying the contents of her stomach onto the polished floor.

She had been far enough away to avoid suffering any lasting
damage but had not been left unscathed. That pulse of Nethersong would leave her feeling queasy for several hours. Kyara bent
to peer under the table and found a pair of dark brown eyes, one
lighter than the other, trained on her. Caught between wonder
and terror. At least the young girl's lack of Nether left her virtually immune.

But another wave of loathing rolled through Kyara's belly.
Control of her ability had always been tenuous at best, and she
could never manage to stop the wild expression of the energy.
Even her most focused pulse would radiate, affecting those it
wasn't meant for.

When the wife finished retching, her panicked gaze locked
onto her husband's killer.

"Come, child," the woman hissed, but the girl did not move
from her hiding spot.

Kyara crouched, bringing herself down to the child's level.
Fear shone in the girl's bright gaze. The eyes of another young
girl came to mind. Fierce and fearless and kind. But gone now.

She pushed away the old memory and tore her attention from
the girl to look at the mother. "The True Father has no qualm
against you and your child." While no child was ever truly safe
in Lagrimar, Kyara had never been ordered to kill one. A small
mercy.

"Sh-she's not mine," the woman whispered, almost inaudibly.

Kyara looked back at the girl, who bore no resemblance to
the woman. She shrugged. "Regardless, you should get far
away from here. Everything your husband owned is forfeit to the

king, and the sackers will likely arrive before the Collectors do. Have you a family? Anywhere to go?"

The woman nodded. Light glinted off the silver pendant she wore at the base of her throat.

Kyara squinted. "The House of Serpents?"

The woman's hand flew to her necklace and fingered the metal nervously. She nodded again. The family sigil was tarnished but the image of a tangled snake biting its own tail was still clear.

Kyara sighed, a trickle of envy running through her. She tried to put the woman at ease. "I am *ul-nedrim*," she said, referring to her status as harem-born. "But I always wished to be of the House of Serpents. It is a noble lineage."

"As are they all," the woman whispered.

"You follow the old ways?"

"I honor the ancestors."

Kyara had met many in her travels who kept to the tradition of revering the original nine Earthsingers from whom all Lagrimari were descended. As it was not truly a religion, and no ancestor had ever intervened when called upon, the True Father had no laws against it. Still, it was considered out of fashion, especially among the elite, and she was surprised to see a young woman—she appeared in her late twenties—keeping up the practice.

A two-way radio crackled to life in the opposite corner of the room, breaking the quiet. Kyara stood and walked over to it. Static-filled chatter crossed the airwaves between lackeys of the True Father. She detached the large battery from the radio, and the machine went silent.

Above the table holding the radio, shelves had been built into an alcove settled into the wall. More of the payroller's finery was on display: a gold-trimmed clock, a dagger with a jewel-encrusted handle, and several rather ancient books.

Almost without her bidding, her fingers rose to run along the spines of the bound volumes. One in particular caught her attention. It was slim, its leather cracked and worn, but burned onto the front was another family symbol—two birds curled around one another—the House of Eagles. The pages inside were somewhat brittle, covered in fading, handwritten script. She flipped to the first page.

The Book of Unveiling
Keep the secrets, spread the lies, remember the truths.

Alarmed, she closed the book with a snap. "Is this yours?"

The wife shook her head with a wry look that suggested very little in this house had been hers.

"Just another trophy then," Kyara said. Books were rare and precious commodities, further evidence of the payroller's status and not an indication of scholarly pursuits. It would be a shame for the sackers to get their grubby hands on it. Kyara tucked the volume into her tunic so it lay against the bandages covering her upper chest and ignored the twinge of pain.

She turned to regard the dead man on the floor. His wife shouldn't have to stare at her husband's bloated face one moment longer.

A tapestry hung askew on the wall depicting the True Father constructing the glass castle when the capital city had first been founded. Though the workmanship of the art was fine, she felt no qualms about pulling it down to cover the body.

"May you find serenity in the World After," she mumbled, then turned to leave.

"Is it true?"

The girl's voice was so small that Kyara almost hadn't heard her. She paused and looked back, one eyebrow raised.

The wife had almost folded in on herself, shaking with fear, but the little girl was lionhearted. "You're the Poison Flame?"

A lump lodged in Kyara's throat. She considered the child, who peered at her with such piercing, oddly colored eyes. Kyara had been not too much older than her the first time she remembered killing. Now, at twenty-one, she felt ancient. Life spent in service to a madman would age anyone.

"I am. And if you aren't naughty, you'll never see me again."

The girl took a step back.

As quickly as she'd arrived, the deadliest assassin in Lagrimar left the payroller's home. The book shifted, pressing against her breasts, grazing the bandages covering the tender flesh of her breastbone.

The Mistress of Eagles, head of that ancient house, was the bearer of prophetic knowledge and a messenger to the other houses. Something about the little book had called to Kyara, waking a hope that had lain dormant for so long.

Though she could not say why, the writer's mention of secrets, lies, and truths had sparked the old craving for the impossible, a longing she had pushed away as year bled into year with no change. But somewhere out in the world there had to be some way to rid herself of the burden of her deadly Song.

Ulani counts to twenty after the strange woman disappears into the night. Only then does she move.

Her stepmother stands frozen in place, staring at the lump on the ground that used to be Papa, but Ulani doesn't waste any time. She runs up the two flights of steps to the cramped closet where her older sister has been locked away. A loose brick at the base of the wall holds a tiny space where they'd hidden the extra key.

Ulani unlocks the door, and Tana looks up from her spot on the floor, confusion on her face.

"Papa's dead."

Tana stands up quickly, a wild look on her face.

"The True Father sent the Poison Flame." Ulani's voice is clear and strong. Already, the sight of her papa being murdered in front of her fades like mist into the place she puts bad memories. When she thinks about it later, she might feel bad that she never mourned the man.

Tana searches Ulani's face, as if trying to determine if she's telling the truth. But Ulani never lies. Whether Tana believes her about the details doesn't matter, the older girl obviously can tell something has happened.

She leaves the closet to head down the stairs. "And Stepmother?"

Ulani shrugs, following her. She cares about her father's wife a little less than she cares about the neighbor's howling dog. The woman has been about as useful.

Tana doesn't seem to spare much thought for their father's wife, either. "Doesn't matter. Go and pack some food. I'll get our things. We're leaving."

She races to follow her sister's instructions. The kitchen staff has already vacated the house. They left so fast, they didn't even steal anything. But the Poison Flame was right, sackers will come to loot the place once word gets out.

She stuffs everything she thinks will keep into a sack and then waits for Tana. Ulani doesn't know where they will go or how they will get there, but she understands they can't stay here. Doesn't even want to. Their home was barely safe while Papa was alive—not safe for Tana at all—now that he is finally dead, it's a tomb.

As if on cue, the dog next door gives a keening cry. He's tied to a pole in the tiny space out back, probably hungry. Ulani thinks of the Poison Flame showing up. She'd been there less than ten minutes and changed everything.

She wonders if the woman's words are true. Will their paths never cross again?

CHAPTER TWO

Pay heed to the tale of the Scorpion
The Spider's heir she is, a legacy
And though she soars so high on Eagle's wings
The sky is not her realm, nor is the sea
In darkness did she first open her eyes
In darkness still she waits, one day to rise

—THE BOOK OF UNVEILING

Darvyn placed the portable radio receiver back in its cradle with a shaking hand. He leaned back to rest his head against the rock behind him. Wind flew across the mountain, chilling him. Those last words, heard through a haze of static, reverberated in his mind.

A man he hadn't seen in years had located Darvyn through the nested tangle of secret communications frequencies used by the Keepers of the Promise to alert him of the sighting of a woman in Checkpoint Seventeen. A woman matching the age and general description Darvyn shared with trusted contacts. A woman searching for her long-lost son.

He squelched the hope that rose inside him. He'd been disappointed before.

In the desert valley below, soldiers marched, drilling their formations over and over again. Hidden in the mountains above them, Darvyn grasped the bit of metal strung on a leather cord around his neck. The pendant bore the image of a jackal, really just a head and a mess of limbs since it was only half of a whole. This woman in Seventeen was probably nobody. But what if . . .

The crunch of gravel on the rocky path tore him from his thoughts. Though this section of the mountain was well monitored, his guard remained raised until uneven steps signaled Meldi's approach. She limped toward him, favoring her right leg. The left one was a wreck of twisted scar tissue, courtesy of the fire that had nearly killed her as a child.

Darvyn rose and reached out to brush her forehead with his fingertips in greeting. She smiled and returned the gesture.

"How fares the Elsiran?" She motioned down to the uniformed men walking in unison far below.

Of the soldiers gathered, one was distinctly unlike the rest. He had the same general features shared by all Lagrimari with hair and eyes dark as midnight, but only one week ago the man's hair had been its natural ginger color and his golden eyes had glittered with mischief. Jack had gone through the transformation from Elsiran to Lagrimari without complaint. Darvyn admired his friend's courage even as he feared for his safety.

Darvyn glanced at her, surprised. Only the elders of the Keepers of the Promise were supposed to know of Jack's undercover mission.

Meldi shrugged. "Voices carry." The braids twining around her head formed a crown, making her look wise beyond her years. She was only a year older than he, but had a maturity only suffering can bring.

Darvyn reckoned she was right. That particular conversation had grown loud since the elders had not approved. At all. Fortunately, Jack wasn't a Keeper, and Darvyn didn't allow a lack of permission to stop him from using Earthsong to transform the man.

He sighed. "His squad has just returned from their supply run. He appears to be doing well. I feel no suspicion toward him from the others. They all seem to believe he is who he appears to be."

"Do you think he's found what he seeks?"

Darvyn shrugged. "I don't know what proof the Elsirans will need in order to believe another breach is coming. But if anyone can find it, Jack can."

Two weeks ago, Darvyn had sneaked into the neighboring country of Elsira, disguised as a local, to bring High Commander Jaqros Alliaseen a warning. The Mantle—the magical barrier which separated the two lands—was failing. It had stood for five centuries and only been breached seven times, each one resulting in war between Lagrimar and Elsira. But its magic was running out. The next tear would bring it down completely.

Jack had been shocked, but when Darvyn told him the information had come from the Queen Who Sleeps, the young man had leapt into action. Five years ago, the two had met in the aftermath of the Seventh Breach, Darvyn a recently released prisoner of war and Jack a soldier. Darvyn knew he could trust the young commander who treated the Lagrimari trapped in Elsira as men, unlike most of his countrymen.

But the Elsiran government hadn't trusted Jack when he'd passed on Darvyn's warning. They could not fathom that their goddess would speak through a lowly Lagrimari. Five years was too soon for another breach, they'd said, so it must've been some sort of trick from the enemy. Only if someone they trusted gathered evidence with his own eyes would they take any action. And so Jack had asked Darvyn to take him through the crack in the Mantle and disguise him so he could go undercover in the Lagrimari army.

It was madness. Reckless and foolhardy. Dangerous and desperate.

Darvyn wished he had come up with the idea himself.

Jack had been playing his role for a week now. They had agreed two weeks was enough time to gather suitable information to convince the Elsiran government that it was the truth. Darvyn was ready to pull Jack out if anyone caught wind of the deception, but Jack was apparently a terrific actor.

"You didn't climb up here just to check on him, did you, Meldi?"

She shook her head and smiled. "Grandfather has summoned you." Her voice was playful, but when Hanko ol-Darnikor called, it was usually a summons. "Your radio was busy."

When he started his apology, she waved it off. "Besides, I needed the fresh air. I've been cooped up in the safe house for weeks now. I wish I could be off doing something useful." She bent down to pick at a leaf on a nearby saltbush. Her olive-colored tunic and trousers blended into the desert landscape.

"What you do is valuable, Meldi. Without the safe houses being manned and stocked, none of the rest would mean anything."

She shook her head, visibly uncomfortable with the praise,

then turned to stare at the army base in the distance. "More troops arrive every day."

Darvyn nodded grimly. Soldiers were being called to the border from all over the country, amassing the entirety of the force. The last stand for the Mantle was coming soon, and they needed to be ready.

He gathered his pack and followed Meldi back down the path, slowing his pace to ensure she could keep up. When they were children, she had been taller than him, but as an adult, she only came up to Darvyn's chest. With her shorter legs and permanent injury, it was slow-going. He scanned her body with Earthsong for the millionth time, hoping he would one day discover some way to help her, but the old wounds could not be healed.

They approached a crumbling stone shack that backed up to the mountain. It was too small to hold more than four men standing shoulder to shoulder, and the narrow entrance gaped open, dark and uninviting. But any visitor would pass no fewer than three watchpoints and be prevented from entry before they took a step inside. And if they managed to make it in, they would see nothing more than the tiny, shadowed interior barely able to protect them from the wind.

But a Keeper of the Promise would know that things aren't always what they appear, and the presence of a wall would not deter him. Darvyn and Meldi passed through the barrier, a simple spell Darvyn was nonetheless glad not to have to maintain.

The safe house was cavernous, not naturally created, but cut into the mountain at some point in the past by an ancestor with the aid of Earthsong. From this location, the Keepers could monitor the army base at the edge of the Breach Valley undetected.

Hanko greeted them as soon as they entered the main chamber, smiling warmly at his granddaughter and less so at Darvyn. Behind him, half a dozen men and women pored over maps and other documents spread out on a table of pounded tin. Meldi disappeared into one of the side rooms; Darvyn regretted that she would not be a buffer between himself and the older man.

Nothing in the elder's appearance was severe; his bald head with unruly tufts of white hair clinging above his ears gave him an avuncular quality. His dark eyes were not steely or unkind. Yet disapproval wafted from his very pores.

"The Elsiran has not betrayed us yet?"

Darvyn ground his teeth. "He risks much for his people, the same as we all do. Why would he betray us?"

"Because he is Elsiran," Hanko said simply.

Darvyn took several slow breaths to calm his temper. "And yet we need them and their country, do we not?" He looked to the group around the table consumed with their plan making.

Lizana, a towering woman with a short puff of hair, pointed to one of the larger maps. "The places on the border with known cracks in the Mantle have been marked. The Singers assigned to each group will be able to feel them; there will be a disturbance in your Songs."

"You'll have to pay close attention," Darvyn added, walking up. "They're easy to miss."

Friendly welcomes echoed around the table as the other Keepers made room for him.

"Nice of you to join us," a burly, bearded man said. Darvyn merely smiled at Aggar, who scowled in return before turning his attention to the map. "These mountain paths will be treacherous.

Can we really expect groups of women and children to make the trip?"

"Our people are strong," Hanko replied. "They've endured much worse for far longer."

"I still say it's too big of a risk." Aggar tugged at his beard. "Perhaps we should wait, consider other options."

Darvyn shook his head. "We don't have any more time. The troops are gathering in preparation for the breach. We're days away, not months, from the Mantle coming down. We need to act now."

"It is not for you to decide." Aggar narrowed his eyes, the challenge evident.

"The elders have decided." Hanko's voice had an air of finality.

"And the Queen set this in motion," Meldi said, walking up to stand next to Aggar. At her gentle voice, the furrows smoothed from the man's brow, and the rough edge of his glare softened. "Has She offered no further guidance?"

Seeing the larger man's reaction to Meldi stole some of the rancor from Darvyn's anger. There would never be anything but enmity between he and Aggar, but he was grateful his old friend could soothe some of the man's beastlier qualities.

The others looked at him expectantly. "My dreams have been quiet," Darvyn replied softly. Murmurs of disappointment met him, but he was relieved from the reprieve of the Queen's other-worldly communications.

"Then we must do what we can," Hanko said. "We will trust in Her guidance."

"Yes, and hope that Her goals and ours are the same," Darvyn mumbled. Hanko's sharp glance indicated he'd heard the comment. Darvyn dropped his head, willing himself to keep the rest of his thoughts about their precious Queen to himself.

"So what now?" Lizana asked. She and Navar were the only other Singers present. The only ones who had managed to avoid the tribute and retain their Songs. Lizana, with her long limbs and leonine features, was far stronger physically than she was with Earthsong. Navar, who usually kept to the background, was a Singer of medium strength. He had been rescued by the Keepers when he was a teen in the army slated to join the Wailers, the regiment of soldiers allowed to keep their Songs for use in battle. Fortunately, they'd been able to get to him before his initiation. No fully indoctrinated Wailer had ever survived a rescue attempt.

"Now, we begin spreading rumors," Hanko said. "Talk will travel of cracks in the Mantle and seeking safe harbor in Elsira. I have no doubt that people will take the bait. We should be ready to begin leading asylum seekers over the border by the end of the week. And the special contingent of Keepers following the Queen's instructions will conceal themselves among the others entering Elsira."

"Will the Elsirans be ready for the influx?" Meldi asked.

"They will harbor us as refugees," Darvyn said. "Perhaps not well, but it won't be any worse than life here." His time as a teen in the Elsiran prisoner of war camps—a result of another one of the Queen's schemes—had taught him that. The Lagrimari would be considered second-class citizens, eking out a meager existence on the other side of the Mantle.

"Let us recall our vow," Hanko said.

Darvyn fisted his hands and pressed them together, old resentment bubbling to the surface. As one, they spoke the words of the ancient promise that all Keepers held sacred:

*"While She sleeps this promise keep
That She dream of us while for Her we weep*

May She comfort, counsel, guard, and guide
Those whose love will never die
And when Her betrayer pays for his lies
And finally the World After occupies
May love's true Song with Her remain
And awaken Her that She may rule again."

The meeting concluded and Darvyn waited impatiently for Hanko to finish a conversation with one of the safe house radio operators. As soon as the operator moved away, Darvyn pounced.

"I need to go to Checkpoint Seventeen," he said in a low voice.

The old man raised an eyebrow.

"I've gotten word that there may be . . . That is, it's possible . . ." He shook off the discomfort and powered on. "A woman fitting my mother's description was spotted there. I have to go investigate."

Hanko sighed deeply and pulled him into a corner away from the others, placing a gnarled hand on his shoulder. "It has been nearly twenty years since she disappeared, *oli*."

He bristled at the endearment, one generally used for a small child, and pulled away from the man's touch. "I know it's unlikely, but it's not impossible. And as long as there's some hope . . ." He trailed off, shaking his head. His finger moved to the pendant around his neck, the metal warm from his chest.

"Your mother is gone, boy. She left you in our keeping and hasn't been seen since." Hanko's severe expression mellowed. "As hard as it is to stomach, it was for the best. She gave you up to keep you safe, knowing how valuable you would be to our cause."

Darvyn's jaw set. Hanko closed his eyes for a long moment. "If you want to go to Seventeen I suppose I cannot stop you. But—" His stern look cut off Darvyn's growing smile. "There is an urgent matter that has just come to my attention that must be seen to first."

Hanko turned back toward the table, still holding onto Darvyn's shoulder. "Aggar, Lizana, Navar."

Meldi stood next to Aggar, looking hopefully at her grandfather, but he merely shook his head. When the others approached Darvyn and Hanko, she turned to limp down a corridor.

Hanko cleared his throat. "I've just been alerted that our Watchers have located the nexus of a network of nabbers. This group may be responsible for the staggering increase in kidnappings over the past weeks."

Lizana's eyes widened. "When I was in Sayya last week, word was that workers at the mines and camps are disappearing at unusual rates, too. The nabbers may be meeting the demand for new labor with these children."

Hanko nodded, his expression grim. "We need a team to monitor the activities of these nabbers and rescue any children they are keeping at this location. Disrupting the flow of labor is more necessary than ever with the impending breach. Aggar, you will lead the effort."

"I'll need a few more men."

"Gather who you'll need, but we cannot spare any more Earthsingers from the Mantle crossing."

"And where were these nabbers sighted?" Aggar asked.

"Checkpoint Six, headed east."

Darvyn's heart sank. That was hundreds of kilometers from where he wanted to be and going the wrong direction. "Am I truly needed for this mission?"

Aggar rolled his eyes.

"Start your preparations and keep this confidential," Hanko

ordered; the others moved away once again leaving the two of them alone. "Darvyn—"

"Lizana and Navar are very—"

"They're good and loyal Keepers," Hanko said, "but there are children to be saved. The Shadowfox could make the difference here."

"The Shadowfox cannot be everywhere." Darvyn crossed his arms.

"And so should he be at Checkpoint Seventeen where the need is smallest? Or will he rise to the task at hand, defending young ones from tribute and lives of toil and slavery?" Hanko lifted a shoulder. "You are your own man. I cannot tell you what to do. But our people suffer every day under the thumb of the immortal king. Our lives are spent in service not to ourselves but to others. Many have sacrificed so that you may stand here today to make this choice."

The old man bowed his head and walked away.

Darvyn rubbed the back of his neck, squeezing it tight enough to crack his knuckles.

The metal of the pendant felt cool now. Just like his hopes of finding the woman who had given it to him.

CHAPTER THREE

Before the first breath that she ever took
A cunning hand had cleaved the land in two
'Twas jealousy that dealt the final blow
But that sad state strikes more than just a few
A sorrowful, bankrupt inheritance
Unfortunately met with acceptance

—THE BOOK OF UNVEILING

Tarazeli crossed the courtyard of the grand estate, pausing for a moment to let the sun warm her face. She smiled, enjoying the gentle breeze that ruffled the braids gathered at her neck. A breeze was a thing to be cherished, rare as they were here in Laketown. She shook her head; she really had to stop using that provincial name, even in her mind. The town was properly called Lower Faalagol, known as Laketown by everyone but the elite. The Magister hated that term, and if Zeli ever wanted to be more than a servant, she had to change even the way she thought to match those of her betters.

Footsteps raced up behind her, causing her heart to race. She turned sharply. One of the little page boys skidded to a stop, barely missing crashing into her legs. "Devana-mideni is looking for you," he said, breathlessly.

Zeli sighed, hoisted the basket of laundry higher on her hip, and changed directions. She thought she'd have time to squeeze the laundering in while her mistress was out shopping, but Devana must have returned early.

When she noticed the boy lingering beside her she asked, "Was there anything else?"

His gaze flicked to her wrist and then away, his face taking on a sheepish expression.

A grin split her face. "Would you like a good luck charm?"

He pressed his lips together and nodded rapidly. Zeli chuckled and set her basket down so she could remove one of the half-dozen woven bracelets on her arm. She motioned for him to hold out his hand and then wrapped the bracelet around twice to fit on his skinny wrist.

The bracelets were as wide as her fingernail and made of ash-gray leaves from the hispid blade plant that grew on the banks of Lake Faala. Zeli had learned to weave them long ago at her mother's knee, where she'd listened to tales of how such a charm would bring luck to those who wore them, as long as they'd been woven with love and hope.

She swallowed as she tied the knot. The bracelet hadn't done her mother any good.

But the old tales were still believed by little ones with open hearts, and as the skill of weaving them had fallen out of fashion, Zeli was the only one on the estate who made them. The leaves would stay strong and supple for about three months, then they would rapidly deteriorate and the bracelet would fall off. Zeli wore several at a time though they hadn't brought her any luck yet . . . but she was patient.

"Thank you, Zeli-deni," the boy said, beaming at his new prize, before scampering back in the direction of the stable. Zeli picked up her basket and headed toward Devana's wing, mouth curving at the child's excitement.

The central courtyard connected the four wings of the estate with shaded pathways, but Zeli preferred to walk in the sun with the mossy grass underfoot. The double doors leading to Devana's sitting room were open, in deference to the breeze, and her mistress sat at her vanity table, studying her face for imaginary imperfections.

When she caught sight of Zeli in the mirror, she turned around, waving her forward. "Oh, there you are, Zeli-deni. Come here!"

Devana leaned forward and cupped her hand to her mouth, preparing to whisper, though they were currently alone in the spacious room. Her long lashes were coated in mascara imported in from Yaly, making them dramatic. They framed wide, doe-like eyes set in a heart-shaped face. Devana's beauty was known throughout the west and few could match it.

"Do you know what I just learned?" she said, trying and failing to hide a grin.

"What is it?" Zeli whispered, catching on to her mistress's excitement.

Devana scanned the room again, her eyes twinkling. "The guru is going to be nearby. Well, fairly close at least. He's leading a revival outside Checkpoint Eleven the day after tomorrow."

She leaned back, obviously elated at this news, but Zeli's heart fell.

"Even if your father would let you go, you wouldn't make it in time," Zeli said, frowning.

"We would if we travel by coach."

Zeli shook her head. "The Magister would never let you travel by public coach all the way to Checkpoint Eleven! He would never let you attend an Avinid revival at all."

Devana crossed her arms. "The guru Waga-nedri is a great man. Surely Father would be interested in me educating myself as to the mysteries of the Void."

Zeli raised a skeptical brow. Waga-nedri. The man's self-styled honorific was an endearment customarily used for fathers or father figures. It made her bristle.

"And besides, I wasn't planning on telling him." Now Devana was making more sense.

She perched on the edge of the cushion. "I'll say that I'm going to visit that horrible, spoiled cow over in Upper Faalagol, and I'll be gone for three days. He'll be delighted. He's convinced her father is responsible for the blight affecting the goshi fish and has been after me to visit her and see what I can find out."

Upper and Lower Faalagol, more commonly known as Watertown and Laketown respectively, had a rivalry that went back as far as anyone could remember. The Magisters of both cities each thought he should rule the entire Lake Cities region and thus control the lake that separated them, but were forced to play nice by the True Father. Their daughters were encouraged to maintain a relationship that was one part friendship, two parts jealousy, and thirty parts spying-for-their-fathers.

Zeli chose her words carefully. "I think it's wonderful that you want to better yourself, but traveling such a long way alone seems . . . unwise."

Devana pouted, crossing her arms. "Sacred seeds, I'm not going alone, silly. I'm not some witless fool. You're coming with me. I can't very well travel without my personal maid. Honestly, I thought you'd be more excited. We get to see the Midcountry and have secret identities." She grasped Zeli's hands in her own. "It will be an adventure."

Zeli remained unconvinced. "But why don't you ask Kerymmideni?"

Devana sighed wistfully. "Kerym-mideni cannot know. Promise you won't tell him. He doesn't think much of the Avinids, and has never said a kind word about the guru."

Zeli had a feeling that Devana's fiancé would not be left in the dark for long, but she kept the thought to herself. "I just . . . I still think . . ."

"Zeli-denili." Devana's voice hardened and her eyes turned flinty as she made their difference in rank clear by her choice of suffix. Zeli lowered her eyes.

Devana was usually very generous with her, calling her Zeli-deni—with the informal honorific used by equals in High Lagrimari speech—but Zeli had fallen out of line. She swallowed and nodded.

"All right. I won't say anything." Her throat thickened, hating the censure.

When she looked up again, Devana was beaming. As if a switch had been flicked on her mood, the change was so sudden it would have been alarming if Zeli hadn't known the girl so well.

Devana stood suddenly, motioning for Zeli to rise. "We need to be on the five a.m. coach tomorrow. You must go down to the depot and get the tickets. And Zeli-deni?"

"Yes?"

"I promise this will be fun."

Zeli rubbed one of the bracelets on her arm, hoping for an infusion of luck right now. But the leaves had gone brittle and the tie snapped, causing one of the charms to fall from her wrist and onto the carpet.

On her way to the marketplace, Zeli passed through the kitchen, where she'd left her shoes for one of the footmen to mend. She usually roamed the estate barefoot, but a trip into town would require footwear.

The warm space was busy as the kitchen staff prepared for dinner. By virtue of the sheer quantity of food being chopped, sautéed, baked, and boiled, it looked as if the Magister would be entertaining that night.

She paused by the pantry, finding her shoes there in line with several others that had been newly patched, and noticed Gladda, the staff matron, filling a large, painted basket with items from the shelves.

The woman was middle-aged and had worked for the family for decades. She'd known Devana since the girl was born and was perhaps the only one, aside from the Magister himself, who had any sway with her. Maybe Gladda would know a way to persuade Devana not to go through with her foolish plan.

But Zeli had been sworn to secrecy and couldn't betray Devana's confidence, much as she wanted to. She slipped her shoes on and when she looked up again, the pantry door was closed.

With halting feet, she left the estate and walked down the winding road leading to the heart of Lower Faalagol. The Magister's sprawling home sat on a hill overlooking the lake to the north and the city to the south. It was a twenty-minute walk to the nearest market square, which was where the closest public coach staging depot was.

The air was thick and heavy as the red days came to a close. Though she loved the cooler, crisp weather of the yellow-orange days, she did not mind the heat, though perspiration quickly dampened her skin. She felt no hint of the earlier breeze as she wound her way down the hill, but still found cause to delight at the sight of the wildflowers blooming on the side of the road. They would be gone in a few weeks.

As the buildings she passed grew more dense, the plants grew more sparse until she was in the city proper, roads paved with stones quarried from the mountains that loomed over the Lake Cities. Upper and Lower Faalagol battled for the distinction of which was the second largest city in Lagrimar. Zeli happened to believe that Laketown was the larger and finer city of the two, though she'd only been to Watertown a handful of times to compare.

Horses, wagons, carriages, and the occasional diesel contraption clogged the street, creating a cacophony that vibrated through the soles of her feet. She fought her way through the crowded sidewalks until she reached the northern market square that served the upper-class neighborhoods where the favored lived.

The public coach depot was a one-story stone structure attached to a stable. A large coach sat unhitched on the side of the building; Zeli shuddered at the thought of riding on the thing. The coaches were notoriously cramped and uncomfortable and often beset by bush wranglers who robbed the travelers. But once Devana's mind was set on something it was nearly impossible to turn her away. A byproduct, no doubt, of always getting her way.

Zeli approached the ticket window and got into line behind a half-dozen other customers. She'd only moved forward one spot when she felt a tingling at the top of her spine like she was being watched. Clenching her limbs and holding her breath, she turned to scan the area. A wave of relief was followed instantly by a quickening in her chest when she observed Devana's fiancé, Kerym, striding toward her, a questioning smile on his face.

"Zeli-deni?"

She tried to respond, but her mouth wouldn't cooperate at first. When Devana used the informal suffix on Zeli's name, it was out of kindness and denoted a level of familiarity between mistress and servant. It encompassed the fact that they'd known one another for a decade, since they were both seven-year-old girls who'd lost their mothers and clung to one another in grief.

However, when Kerym used the term, the politeness inherent made Zeli's knees weak. There was little familiarity between the two of them, and yet . . . She traced the edge of one of her bracelets and took a deep breath before addressing him. "Good afternoon, Kerym-mideni."

His grin was the sunshine. Not for the first time she wondered if his short beard was soft. If it tickled Devana's cheeks when they kissed. If he—

"Are you going on a trip?" He motioned to the line she stood in and all her dreaminess fell away. Apprehension seized her belly.

She clasped her hands in front of her. Here stood one of the five Ephors of Lake—she shook herself mentally—of Lower Faalagol. The man who would one day be Magister. If she hoped to have a future in his and Devana's household, she couldn't very well lie to him. But she couldn't betray Devana, either, especially since her mistress had specifically not wanted Kerym to know about their trip.

Zeli cursed silently. She should have gone to another coach depot. Though this one was closest, it was right in the middle of Kerym's territory—why hadn't she thought of that before?

She tugged at the sleeves to her tunic and swallowed, but remained silent, looking everywhere but at him.

"Sworn to secrecy are you?" he said, amusement in his voice. "How about I guess? I heard a rumor that a certain withered old man would be holding some kind of hootenanny in the bush outside of Checkpoint Eleven. Blink your eyes if I'm getting close."

Zeli couldn't very well not blink. She lifted her gaze to meet the dark ebony of his eyes, so warm and captivating, and blinked. Then dipped her head again.

But she peeked up through her lashes to see his smile.

"And my lovely fiancée has no doubt enlisted her faithful maid to procure tickets on the coach without her father's knowledge so that she can witness the legendary 'wise man of the west' in all his wrinkled splendor."

Zeli held back a smile and blinked again.

Kerym sighed. She wasn't quite sure what would happen next. Would he order her to leave and not allow Devana to do something so silly? Would he tell the Magister? Have Zeli punished? She was merely following orders; could she be sent away to the camps or worse for trying to trick the master?

But Kerym just shook his head and stepped into line beside her.

"W-what are you doing?" she asked.

"Well, I know I can't convince her not to go because she's one of the most stubborn women to ever grace the Fatherland, so I suppose I'll just have to go with you."

Zeli gasped, her mouth hanging open.

Kerym shot her a careless grin and tossed a coin in the air before catching it. He, too, wore several bracelets, but his were made of gold and other precious metals. They denoted his status as Ephor, one of the right hands to the Magister, and represented his other duties, all important and necessary to the running of the city and its surrounding region.

"Are you sure?" she managed to get out.

"Well, I can't just let you go alone. The Great Highway is a dangerous place. You don't mind if I accompany you, do you?"

He looked at her intently as if her answer mattered. As if he may change his mind based on the word of a maid—a plain, short girl who still looked far younger than her seventeen years and was no match for Devana's beauty and poise.

"I-I don't mind," she said through quivering lips, and Kerym chuckled, the sound rich and sweet, like the melted chocolate crèmes the cook served on Mercy Days.

Zeli's face flamed. Her breathing came in short spurts—sacred seeds, he was standing so close. His tunic untied at the top, showing off the powerful muscles of his chest. Her gaze kept darting there and then away, but getting caught at his lips or his hands. Finally, she closed her eyes and squeezed them shut until she could exert better control over her senses.

The rustling of fabric and shuffling of feet indicated the line was moving. She pried open her eyes, forcing them to stay on the braided head of the woman in front of her. Before she knew it, the woman was walking away and they were at the front of the line, standing before the stooped old man selling tickets.

Kerym ordered three round trips on the coach and paid out of his own change purse, holding a hand up when Zeli tried to contribute the money Devana had given her.

"Keep it," he said, as the cashier handed over their tokens. His gaze roamed over her, assessing. "Buy yourself something nice."

She kept herself from looking down at her clothing. Her tunic and trousers were clean and in good repair. Her shoes freshly mended, but nothing she owned could truly be called nice.

She would have to give the money back to Devana, but the mere fact he'd suggested such a thing warmed her heart. Her mistress was truly lucky to be betrothed to such a man. Zeli cut off the urge to drift into her own dreams of love and partnership. Later, she would review every aspect of this meeting.

"Come now," Kerym said, striding away from the depot on long legs. Zeli raced to catch up. "I think it's time I had a word with my dear fiancée."

Dread mixed with anticipation as Zeli followed him back toward the estate. Kerym was going with them. Perhaps this trip wouldn't be such a disaster after all.

CHAPTER FOUR

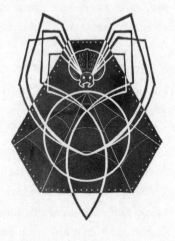

The Scorpion entered a world adrift
Bonds forged in unity now rent by war
This misery would one day be eclipsed
By conflict on a scale not seen before
A seer blinded by the days ahead
Consented to a deal he'd come to dread

—THE BOOK OF UNVEILING

Red-orange light filtered in through the translucent glass wall in Kyara's room. The red days were nearly complete. Over the next couple of months, the glass castle of Sayya would slowly shift its tint to a yellow-orange color, marking the time of harvest in the farming camps.

The light was enough to read by—she'd already used up her

ration of lamp oil, and electricity was reserved for those far more important than she—though the red glow made the pages of the little book she'd taken from the payroller's home appear angry. She had not gotten very far in her reading when the quiet was interrupted by a soft rattling. With a groan, she closed the book, slipping in a dagger she'd been meaning to sharpen to serve as a bookmark.

She rolled off the thin mattress of her bed to retrieve the jiggling object from the washbasin tray. The tiny red stone was warm to the touch and didn't stop shaking until she'd pricked her finger with the much sharper blade kept in a loop attached to her boot, and touched a drop of blood to the stone.

"Kyara-denili!" A shrill voice rose from the little stone. "Come here immediately." The stone grew cold, ending the communication.

"Mercy forbid she send a pageboy with a message," Kyara grumbled. But Ydaris preferred the magical to the mundane, and another scar added to Kyara's collection would mean nothing to her.

As she walked swiftly down a side corridor toward one of the main halls, a tense hush lay over the castle. The ringing of a bell made her stop short, just shy of the intersection of the two walkways.

The True Father's retinue padded along the wide passage from the grand entry. Three dozen people moved silently, the loudest sound coming from the swishing fabric of their clothing. Guards, advisers, high-ranking servants, and several harem women all wore garments dripping with jewels of every color. In the center of the group, the immortal king stood tall. His gemstone-encrusted mask was multicolored today and covered his face and hair. White, diamond-studded gloves graced his hands. His tunic was similarly arrayed with precious stones. She held her breath, shrinking against the wall as he passed.

As a child, growing up in one of the harem's cabals, Kyara had heard whispers from the women that the type of jewels in the mask from day to day hinted at the king's mood since no one had ever seen his face. However, she had seen him wearing rubies, emeralds, sapphires, and various combinations of gemstones, and had never discerned any difference in his disposition.

The quiet he surrounded himself with was unnatural. Only the bell ringer walking far ahead announcing the king's path could be heard. Kyara stood stock-still, her gaze on the ground until the sound of the bell faded. The True Father's very presence was a force that sobered everyone in the vicinity. In the wake of the royal company, the thick tension slowly eased from the air and she was on her way again.

She steeled herself before pushing open the heavy, ornately decorated door and entering the library of the Royal Cantor. The massive space was two stories tall and set high within the castle. Books lined the shelves from the floor to the ceiling. Rolling ladders hung from each wall, and everything was made of dark, polished wood from no tree native to their barren land.

The Cantor herself sat fiddling with the knob of the radiophonic in the corner, trying to get a clear signal. Snatches of orchestral music filtered in through the static. A deep baritone crooned a sultry tune in some language Kyara couldn't place.

The sole sanctioned channel broadcast only official news reports—which droned on and on—and endless recorded speeches by the True Father. Never music. But on days like today, in the calm hours after a desert windstorm, the airwaves sometimes carried a weak pirated signal originating from somewhere in the city. A rebellious act that would result in the death of whoever was responsible, if he or she was ever found out.

Ydaris swayed in her seat to the rhythm and hummed along with the melody. Moments ago she had sounded irate, but music always soothed her mistress's mercurial temper. Kyara hated to interrupt the calm by calling any attention to her presence, but the woman made no move to acknowledge her.

Kyara cleared her throat. "You called, Ydaris-mideni?"

Ydaris shot an annoyed gaze over her shoulder, then stood and crossed the room, her embroidered gold skirts swishing as she walked. A head taller than Kyara, Ydaris was statuesque and imposing. The fabric wrap twisted elegantly around her hair made her appear even taller.

"Why must you constantly make me wait? I have entirely too much to do as it is. The True Father hoards his magic like a miser does coins, leaving all the heavy lifting to me." She shook her head and began to mumble. "Faster, he says, as if I wasn't already taxed beyond belief."

Speaking like this, especially out loud, was grounds for death. But Ydaris appeared unconcerned about the treason she was committing. "Your mission was successful, I trust."

"Of course," Kyara gritted out.

Ydaris's smile was tight. Her unusual jade green eyes seared Kyara with their intensity. "Of course," she repeated. "The Poison Flame never misses her mark, does she?"

Shame flooded Kyara. She endeavored to push it away—now was not the time for weakness, or regret, or feelings of any kind.

Ydaris's eyes narrowed as though she could see the struggle taking place within Kyara. "I do believe I heard an old griot crooning in the marketplace an ode to our dear, deadly Poison

Flame. Though the tales of your exploits have become quite
overblown, have they not?"

Kyara's lips sealed in a grim line.

"He claimed the king's assassin has killed a thousand men."
Ydaris gave a dry chuckle. "'From Laketown to Checkpoint
Eight to One and back again' was the verse, if I'm not mistaken."

She pinched Kyara's chin between her thumb and forefinger,
tilting her head up. Those eerily colored eyes peered down at her.
"You've certainly captured the public's imagination."

A note of jealousy laced her tone. "And when you've completed your next task, they will be talking once more. I cannot
wait to hear the songs they'll sing then."

Ydaris released Kyara and moved to sit at her desk in the center of the room. It was the one pristine space amidst the wooden
tables covered with overflowing stacks of books and ledgers and
scattered parts of mechanical contraptions. Everything in the
Cantor's library was oversized, as if made for giants; the tables
and desk stood nearly waist high, and the chairs were high off
the ground. Everywhere else in Lagrimar, cushions and low
stools made up the bulk of the seating, but Ydaris did everything
a bit differently.

Kyara's gaze landed on the stone table at the edge of the
room, then skirted away, also passing over the bench directly
next to it that featured a wide array of knives and other sharp
instruments.

She approached slowly, as Ydaris shuffled through sheafs of
paper. "The True Father has handed down your next assignment.
Apparently, he believes he has cultivated an informant within
the Keepers of the Promise."

Kyara's eyes widened; the Cantor waved her hand. "No
doubt a trick. The Keepers are notoriously loyal. But he feels the

information is worth following up on. The informant claims to know the next assignment of the Shadowfox."

Speaking of a figure who'd captured the public's imagination. Many a song had been written of the exploits of the Shadowfox. Altering the weather, transforming desiccated soil into lush farmland—to hear some tell it he could practically raise the dead. And the True Father had been after him for decades.

At first the king had sought to capture the rebel and drain him of a Song said to be more powerful than any other Singer alive. But then, when the legendary Keeper continued to elude his pursuers, the goal became to kill.

"Mideni, no assassin has ever gotten close to the Shadowfox."

"No other has had information about his whereabouts beforehand. Up until now, we've only known where he's been."

Kyara blinked rapidly. "But even knowing where he will be, won't he sense my intention using Earthsong long before I get close enough to . . . remove him?" A sickening apprehension filled her. Kyara did not need to be close to kill, though she could reduce collateral damage that way. She sank into a chair as fear welled. Her range could encompass an entire town, and Ydaris knew it. How many souls could she be ordered to sacrifice just to kill one man?

"The king does not want the Shadowfox dead any longer. You're to bring him back here for questioning."

Kyara closed her eyes as relief filled her lungs. But then the realization of the order took shape.

"Bring him back? Surely others would be better suited. I have never . . ." She hesitated to say that she had never been instructed to leave one of her targets alive. "Besides, if I cannot get near the Shadowfox, I cannot capture him. He will still read my intent."

"That isn't precisely true." Ydaris tapped a finger to her lips, giving Kyara a sidelong glance. "Do you know why I prefer blood magic to Earthsong?"

"Because blood magic can be done by anyone. It doesn't require an inborn Song."

"True enough. It is a way of balancing the scales, shall we say. The universe demands balance. Nature is balance. And do you remember what I told you all those years ago, when you first came into my library?"

Kyara shivered, not willing to think on that meeting. She had languished in the dungeon for days waiting to be executed before the guards had dragged her here. Once again the wretched stone table on the other side of the library commanded her attention. She refused to look. Instead of the punishment she'd expected that day, she'd received one far worse.

"Nature always wins?" Kyara whispered.

Ydaris chuckled. "Nature always wins. And yet . . ." She paused, stroking the delicate gold chain encircling her throat. "You, my dear assassin, are decidedly unnatural. But perhaps you will prove an exception to the rule. Perhaps you will win against all odds."

Kyara's chest tightened as she struggled to follow the conversation. "I don't understand."

"Earthsong is life energy. We gamble when we use it for battle. Hurling fireballs or icicles, opening sinkholes and creating earthquakes. We make educated guesses using probabilities about what will cause damage, but we cannot target our kills. Life energy prevents it." Ydaris shrugged. "But Nethersong was made to kill and so were you."

The old shame could not be ignored forever. Kyara crumpled inside at the reminder.

"Your Song is a blessed symphony of death." The music from the radiophonic underscored her words. "And Earthsong cannot touch you."

"Wh-what do you mean?"

Ydaris gave an exasperated sigh. "You are immune to Earthsong. Unlike blood magic, Earthsong glides off you like oil."

The song ended and dull static buzzed from the speaker before the next one began. The hissing silence matched her disbelief. "Immune? Why?"

Ydaris spread her arms. "The universe still nurtures its mysteries."

"But why did you not tell me before?"

"Why should we have? It was irrelevant until now. What difference could it possibly have made?" Ydaris's bafflement seemed genuine. Kyara's mouth opened, but nothing came out.

"So you see, you are quite the perfect candidate for this mission, should this 'informant' be real. You are to head to Checkpoint Five immediately. The Blackheart squadron of the Golden Flames will assist you."

The last part cut through Kyara's haze of astonishment. "Aren-deni's squad? The Golden Flames will draw too much attention. They may make the rebels scatter."

"They've been instructed to be discreet. They won't do anything to endanger the mission."

The bars of Kyara's prison closed in around her. She was prohibited from harming anyone in the castle, nor could she injure any of the elite military force known as the Golden Flames. Not for any reason, even self-defense.

Ice gripped her heart at the thought of working with Aren. She opened her mouth to plead for flexibility in her instructions, to at least be allowed to protect her own safety, but Ydaris was already speaking. Turning the lock on her chains and swallowing the key.

"Kyara ul-Lagrimar, your mission is to ascertain the identity of the Keeper known as the Shadowfox and bring him back to Sayya, alive, for questioning."

Under the bandages that she'd reapplied regularly for nearly ten years, the unhealing wound on her chest delivered a pulse of excruciating pain. Only the fact that she'd borne the weight of the blood spell for so long made her able to merely grit her teeth and not scream in agony as the directive was sealed. The commands were locked in, her obedience assured.

A knock sounded at the library door. Upon the Cantor's command to enter, two guards dragged an emaciated, chained man inside.

"Strap him to the table," Ydaris called out, standing and stretching her back. The guards headed for the stone table.

Kyara got to her feet, nearly toppling her chair in her haste to leave. She did not want to see any more, but could not avoid hearing Ydaris's words to the prisoner.

"I'm sorry, but we must skip the pleasantries. I simply haven't got the time."

Kyara burst into the hallway and raced around the corner. Just before she'd run out of earshot, the screaming began.

CHAPTER FIVE

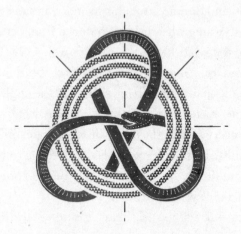

A jealous man sought wisdom beyond bound
To learn the secrets time had hidden well
And open up his mind and teach his mouth
To craft the workings of the perfect spell
And much to history's misery and woe
A pact was made, seeds of the future sewn

—THE BOOK OF UNVEILING

Darvyn had been nursing the same mug of beer for the past hour. The pub was half-full of regulars, villagers whose nightly ritual consisted of dampening the sting of lives bursting with misery. They sat on cushions around low tables of pounded tin balanced on knee-high stacks of mud bricks. Each patron hunched over glass mugs of beer or copper cups of potent moonshine.

Out of habit, Darvyn scanned the faces of every woman appearing more than twenty years older than he. In truth, he wasn't exactly sure what he was looking for. His mother's face had long since blurred and dimmed from his memory. It had been so long and he was so young when he'd been ripped from her arms.

Outside, the wind howled, eerie as a wolf's cry. Light from the oil lamps cast menacing shadows on the pub's interior. Darvyn took a sip of beer, cursing silently as the unpleasant taste hit his tongue. Bitter, vile stuff this Midcountry brew.

Though every soul in the dimly lit room appeared engrossed in their drinks, tension fogged the air. Both patrons and staff alike were studiously ignoring the table in the corner and the promise of trouble wafting from it like smoke.

Five men—all with cruel, blunt features—sat drinking and laughing raucously, oblivious to the anxiety around them. Darvyn had followed them here to monitor them. The two wagons the men had arrived in sat in the stable along with the horses. Half an hour ago, Darvyn's friend Zango entered and folded his massive limbs onto the cushion across the table, whispering that the covered wagons were empty. Each held nothing more than a dozen manacles chained to bolts in the floor. The men were definitely nabbers.

Since then, Darvyn had rarely let his eyes stray from the table. The desire to provoke some kind of confrontation was strong, but that would have run counter to his mission. He needed to be inconspicuous and stealthy to continue tracking them unnoticed. Eventually, they would lead him to wherever they had stashed the children.

Nabbed children fed a black market for domestic servants, factory workers, and occasionally something even viler. It was a fate children should never be subjected to, yet wealthy payrollers seeking to mimic the True Father's harems often turned to the nabbers as suppliers. And unlike when a child was called for service to the government and sent to the mines, the work camps, the army, or the king's harem, the parents of nabbed children received no extra rations in exchange for the loss of their sons and daughters. The rations were a poor replacement, but at least they allowed the parents to feed their other children until their time came to be taken. The population of the Midcountry dwindled further with every generation.

The pub door opened, letting in a blast of wind that caused the lamps to flicker. A sandstorm was brewing tonight. In his peripheral vision, Darvyn saw the newcomer enter but didn't pay any mind. He only turned his gaze away from the corner table when a cracked, reedy voice rose above the din.

"Kind villagers, if I could have but a moment of your time. The night is cold and the sands wild. Allow Grimmar ol-Grimor to warm your evening with a tale. Or a song if you prefer. Only ten grams to be transported to another time and place. Perhaps the Creeping Gardens of Lumina or the savage wilds of Udland? I have many stories to tempt you with at a very affordable price."

The gnarled man wore a long, frayed cloak that had faded to a dull gray. His silver hair was twisted into thick, matted coils, reaching his midback. A bushy beard framed his mouth, but sharp, intelligent eyes glinted brightly in the lamplight.

"I could spin you a tale of the ice monsters of the Gelid or the pale creatures that live below the earth in the north to escape the burning sands of the Scald."

Darvyn was glad he offered no tales of the Shadowfox. He had no wish to hear exaggerated stories of his own exploits. A hum of mumbles flowed through the pub, but no one was willing to spend ten grams on the old griot. The nabbers in the corner were quiet, their attention momentarily captured by the storyteller who had a quality about him that was difficult to ignore. A tin cup shook slightly in his hand as he shuffled between the tables, offering it to the patrons, seeking someone willing to purchase a story. It seemed there would be no takers tonight.

Darvyn focused on the table of nabbers when a clink indicated someone had placed a coin in the man's cup.

"And what type of story would you like, young miss?"

"I would like to hear a tale of the Mistress of Serpents." The voice was clear and feminine.

Darvyn's head shot up. The speaker sat at the bar, wedged between two old cottagers who looked like they'd been attached to their cushions since the town was built. A hood hid her face, and Darvyn got only a glimpse of her in profile. The tip of a nose. A flash of cheek.

"The Mistress of Serpents," the griot said, appreciatively. The cup disappeared beneath the folds of his billowing cloak. "Have you heard about her quarrel with the Master of Spiders?"

The young woman shook her head, and the griot smiled, revealing a spate of missing teeth. He sat at a nearby table and pulled the *luda* off his back, strumming the strings of the instrument softly and bringing it into tune.

A melody emerged. Darvyn thought the man would sing, but instead, he began his tale in a singsong voice much smoother than the tones he spoke with.

"Of all her siblings, the Mistress of Serpents was considered the bringer of justice. Petty disputes and squabbles among all the houses were brought before her. While the Master of Sharks was known for his wisdom and the Mistress of Eagles for her prophetic knowledge, all agreed that it was the Serpent who best put wisdom into action. And so one day, the Master of Spiders came seeking his sister's help.

"The Spider had twin children, a boy and a girl whom he loved very dearly and wanted to ensure were left a grand legacy. However, vanity and greed had impoverished the House of Spiders. The great wealth the Spider had been born with had been squandered on foolishness, and none of his brothers and sisters would trade with him to allow him to rebuild.

"*What can I do,* he entreated his sister, *to leave a suitable inheritance to my son and daughter?*

"The Serpent considered this and knew the answer would not be to her brother's liking, but it was the fair and just response. *It is unfortunate that your mistakes have affected your children's birthright, but it is already done. They will have ample opportunity to build their own fortunes through their efforts.*

"The Spider was predictably displeased. *Why should my children suffer when you and the others have so much? Share it with me, and all will be well, sister.*

"*Why should any of us share our wealth when you have so diligently squandered yours?* she replied. *Your children will be well taken care of. They will not starve, nor will they lack shelter or other necessities.*

"However, this was not good enough for the Spider. He thought and thought, and decided to propose a bargain to his sister. If she would share her fortune with him so that he may gift it to his children, he would spin a web so beautiful that it would stand forever as a tribute to her generosity and goodness.

"But the Serpent did not wish for a web in her honor and refused him. And so it was that the Spider planned to steal his sister's riches and hide them away in a cave until his children came of age. But the Serpent was wise and knew her brother's heart. She gathered their siblings together, and when the Spider came to steal her treasure, they were all there to stop him.

"As punishment, the Serpent decreed that the Spider would spin a web with the symbol of the thief embedded within it. When the Spider's children saw this, their shame was deep. The twins swore off spinning and never truly recovered from the humiliation their father had wrought. They made their way in the world and earned their own wealth, but both agreed the House of Spiders would end with them. The grand legacy their father had sought ended up being one of thievery, and neither twin had any wish to perpetuate it.

"When the twins passed into the World After at the end of their long lives, the House of Spiders was no more."

The griot ended his tale and looked around the room. All who listened had been drawn into his telling and sat rapt. Darvyn shot a glance to the corner to ensure his quarry was still there. Even the hardened nabbers had grown quiet for the story and with good reason. It was a subversive story to utter aloud.

To spin a tale of the Master of Spiders was dangerous, especially an unflattering one. While in the story, the House of Spiders supposedly ended, in reality it lived on in the sons born in the True Father's harems. The king himself was now the master of that fateful house.

The *ol-nedrim*, as the harem-born sons were known, filled the army—why recruit when you could kidnap girls and force them to bear offspring designed for only one purpose? And none knew of the fates of the king's rare daughters or why he sired boys almost exclusively. No one Darvyn knew had ever met an *ul-nedrim*.

But at least the True Father's vile seed spread no further. All of the *ol-nedrim* in the army were sterile.

The griot took his life in his hands to trust that no payrollers were among the pub's patrons. Tyranny existed because of the willingness of many to inform on their fellow man to try and curry favor from those known as the favored of the Father.

Darvyn scanned the room with Earthsong to gauge whether any here had intentions of betraying the elder. The tension and malice from the nabbers made things cloudy, but admiration and fear were the primary emotions in the room.

"Thank you, Griot-deni," said the young woman who'd requested the tale. Darvyn strained to see more of her face. She spoke with the peculiarities of High Lagrimari, which meant she spent a great deal of time in the cities. Something about her voice was very pleasant, but the hood still hid her from view. The other patrons were already turning away, getting back to their forgotten drinks. The griot rose, and the woman reached out as if to stop him.

A glass crashed to the floor in the corner of the room. The serving boy hovered at the nabbers' table, eyes wide, gripping a tilted tray. The nabber nearest him rose, and a chorus of shouts rang out. Another man banged a fist and the table upended, clattering to the ground. Darvyn and Zango both stood to face the commotion.

"You bloody fecking whore's daughter!" A nabber vaulted himself across the overturned table, scattering glasses across the floor, to throttle the neck of his companion. The serving boy nimbly skirted the violence as the two men fell to the ground, knocking over the table next to them.

The other three nabbers stood. Two tried to pull the fighting men apart, but an elbow to the nose enraged one and he began throwing punches as well. Soon all five were in the midst of it, trading wild, drunken blows. One nabber picked up the square of tin comprising the tabletop and slammed it against two of the others.

The crowd scrambled to get out of the way, and jammed the single door in their rush to exit. Zango stood tall next to Darvyn, large fists curled and ready. A former mine worker, Zango was a fearsome fighter, though he'd lost his Song before joining the Keepers. His bald pate rose two heads taller than anyone else, and his size was often enough to dissuade men from violence.

A nearly empty bottle of moonshine shattered against the opposite wall. People ducked as the glass rained down. Darvyn sang a silent spell to redirect the shards so they wouldn't slice anyone. Other than him and Zango, standing in the center of the pub, the only other person not retreating or cowering in fear was the woman.

She'd pulled back her hood, and neat rows of braids lined her head. Darvyn was surprised by how young she was. Younger than her voice sounded, at any rate. Her hands hung loosely at her sides. She eyed the fight almost with an air of boredom, but shielded the griot as he hunched down behind the crowd of panicky customers.

Who was she? Darvyn could see only her profile—a straight nose, slightly upturned at the end, gave her an impish quality. Her eyes narrowed at the scene before her.

Her boots were sturdy, her trousers and tunic well made. A thick, warm coat graced her back. There was nothing fancy about her attire that would identify her as a payroller, but the quality of her clothing and her confidence made her stand out. As did her lack of alarm.

If he didn't know better, he'd say she had the bearing of a soldier. Not just in the self-possessed way she carried herself but in the set of her jaw and the wariness of her eyes. Even from here he could tell those eyes had seen much. Perhaps nearly as much as his own.

The body of one nabber flew through the air, taking out the table right in front of her, sending cups clattering to the ground. She didn't flinch.

The crush of bodies blocking the door began to thin; the place was nearly empty. The old bartender stood at the end of the bar, gripping an ancient musket. He didn't seem overly concerned about the brawl, but did appear ready to fire his single shot if the fight threatened the costly bottles of liquor.

The young woman stayed until the other patrons had left, her eyes never straying from the fight. And then, with a brief, frowning glance to him and Zango, she was gone.

Darvyn released a pent-up breath. Their eyes had only connected for an instant, but her gaze was a hot desert breeze that left his skin tingling. Pins and needles prickled all over him before he could shake off the feeling.

He'd been waiting for her to leave so he could stop the fight, but now that she was gone, he wished he'd been able to talk to her. Find out something about her. Everything about her.

Another body slammed into the table directly in front of him. Zango raised an eyebrow, and Darvyn responded with a grin, cracking his neck as he reached for his Song.

Whenever possible, it was best not to sing obviously in front of witnesses. You never knew who you could trust to not inform on the Keepers and he had no desire to call attention to himself. At his age, to still be in possession of his Song was rare and would bring heavy suspicion upon him. However, the bartender was a friend to the Keepers, and with no one else around, Darvyn opened himself to Earthsong, allowing the stream of power to connect with his inner Song. He focused on the life energy of the nabbers, blocking out everything else. The energies of all within range faded from his senses, from the children sleeping in the bedroom above, to the wild dogs prowling the edges of town, to the wildness of the bush beyond.

The five heartbeats of the brawling nabbers raced. The one sprawled out in front of him got to his feet, fists raised. Darvyn felt the men's pulses, sensed the very life flowing through their veins, and could heal them if they were ill. Not that he wanted to. But he did need these men to lead him to the children. However, that would have to wait, at least for a few hours. Now they needed to sleep.

In a feat of strength no other Singer he knew could have accomplished, Darvyn pulled from the ocean of energy, filling himself, and then sped up the breakdown of the large quantities of alcohol the men had consumed. Accelerating any system of the body so quickly generally led to almost-immediate sleep. The men dropped, one by one, to the ground, each snoring softly.

Darvyn sagged back upon his cushion. He felt the connection to Jack's disguise spell as he released his grasp on Earthsong. Performing so many delicate spells at once was tiring even for him. Affecting these five simultaneously, plus maintaining Jack's spell, left him breathless, like he'd run a long sprint. He rested his aching body for a moment while Zango knelt before the dozing men, checking their pockets.

The bartender placed a cup of water on the table in front of Darvyn.

"Thank you." He drank it down greedily.

"Nay, thank you, *oli*. My livelihood thanks you, as well."

Zango stood. "Nothing on them to tell us about their hideout."

"That would have been too easy, huh, mate?" Darvyn rose to his feet, fighting a wave of dizziness.

His friend approached, concern etched in his face. "How are you feeling?"

"Fine, fine. The nabbers shouldn't wake for a couple of hours."

"I'll get them out of here," Zango said. "Let them sleep it off in their wagons. Wouldn't want them waking up in here and causing another ruckus. I'll set young Farron to watch over them so we can follow in the morning." With each of his hands holding onto an ankle, Zango dragged two of the nabbers out the door and into the night.

Darvyn sighed. He hadn't wanted to bring Farron on this mission, but Aggar had insisted. At sixteen, the boy was young for a Keeper recruit. But he'd been the only other Singer Hanko had allowed to join them since he couldn't be trusted with leading a group over the mountains. At least watching sleeping nabbers wasn't very dangerous.

Darvyn's eyes drooped. Rest was the only way to restore his Song, but he had not used so very much that he should be sleepy. Still, he realized he must have dozed, at least for a few minutes, when the door crashed open and his head popped up.

Farron rushed in, breathing heavily. The teenager's lanky form stumbled over the cushions on the floor.

"What's happened?" Darvyn asked.

"There's something out there you need to see."

CHAPTER SIX

All knowledge was not meant for men to find
Though seeking hearts will rarely rest unsure
And when the hunt for that which lays concealed
Leaves seekers worse off than they were before
Wise is the student of self-discipline
Who finds his answers by searching within

—THE BOOK OF UNVEILING

"Griot-deni," Kyara called, following the old man out amidst the fleeing crowd.

"Yes, *uli*?" His kind face set her at ease. His story had brought her back to her days in the harem, where the younger girls would sit some evenings listening to tales told by the old *ulla*, the head of their cabal. But the little book Kyara had taken days earlier held a tale she'd never heard before.

"Have you ever heard of the Scorpion?" she asked.

The griot frowned, leaning on a staff she hadn't seen him holding before. "As in a House of Scorpions?"

"Perhaps."

"There is no House of Scorpions." He eyed her curiously, his eyes flashing. Jackal, Serpent, Monkey, Bobcat, Eagle, Shark, Horse, Frog, and Spider—all Lagrimari children knew the nine houses.

"Perhaps an heir to the Spider? I'm not sure. It's just . . ." She took a deep breath, unsure even of what she was asking. But the griots knew all the stories. He must be able to shed some light on what she'd been reading.

He looked around, but they were alone in the street. Still, he pulled her to the side and stood just beyond the pool of light from the nearby shop. "What is it?"

"I found a book. It mentions a scorpion. But . . . it's not like the stories I've heard before."

"A book?" He eyed her clothing. "And you can read it?"

Where she would expect suspicion, the griot sounded merely curious. "Many girls in the harem learn to read," she said. A true statement, though not for her. But telling him the Cantor had taught her to read would absolutely make him suspicious.

If he wondered how she'd left the harem, he did not ask and she was grateful. He tapped his staff twice before looking around again. Then he pitched his voice very low.

"The griots preserve the tales in our memories. Listening ears may repeat what is said, but the surest way to prove wrongdoing is to have printed evidence." He tapped his nose knowingly, and she felt a surge of affection for him. He was subversive in his daily life; the tale he'd told virtually spat in the eye of the True Father.

"So if there was a book, what would that mean? Who would have written such a thing?"

He frowned, thinking. "Only someone either with no fear of being caught or with information so dangerous it could not be risked in the minds of men."

Keep the secrets, spread the lies, remember the truths. The book certainly felt dangerous.

"As for the Scorpion . . ." He looked around again and sighed. "My great-grandfather broke stones in the mines as a child. Back when the True Father tried to mine the western mountains. Eventually they abandoned the effort; their Songs would not work in the west. But my ancestor claimed to have met a man there who spoke of the legend of the Scorpion."

Kyara leaned forward.

"Everyone thought the man mad, but my great-grandfather, the son of griots, listened to his tales and committed them to memory. They were stories of a great darkness that was prophesied to sweep the land and only the Scorpion could bring the light."

"A darkness greater than the True Father? I've never heard anyone speak of this before."

"Some stories are lost to time. My father had the telling of it, but didn't pass it down. It made the people nervous. Gloom and doom doesn't fill the belly." He smiled sadly. "Most want to hear accounts of their own house. Who wants to hear tell of a ghost?"

A chill went through Kyara. The old man grasped his staff with both hands. "I must be on my way. The road at night is seldom safe for man or beast."

Kyara forced a smile, though her gratitude was real. "Thank you."

He nodded and touched her forehead in leave-taking. She stood, mulling over his words. Just as she'd been drawn to the book for reasons she couldn't explain, the tale of the Scorpion was one that reeled her in. Perhaps one deadly creature called to another. Though she had little hope the book would offer a way to remove her Song and make her no longer useful to the True Father, its mystery intrigued her. Would she be able to make sense of it?

The quiet darkness was pierced by the wail of wild dogs in the distance. The pub was located toward the outside of the spiraling main road in the town of Checkpoint Five. In the Midcountry towns, the more prosperous folk lived in the center of the spiral, protected from the harsh winds that raced across the flatlands of the bush and battered the outer buildings. Center homes were also at lower risk from the random attentions of bush wranglers—marauders who roamed the highway looking to torment and rob—and wild animals. Attacks from beast or bandits made the nights perilous, but Kyara had nothing to fear from any of them. She shrugged into the warmth of her coat in the cold desert evening and turned to go.

A sound behind her made her whip around again. That enormous, bald man from the pub was dragging two unconscious men out the door. He hauled them by their ankles and dumped them at the mouth of the adjacent alley.

Had he and that other one taken on five rowdy nabbers on their own and knocked them unconscious? The huge man certainly looked capable; still, it was quite a feat.

Kyara had wanted to step in, as well, but it was not her business. And she'd needed to speak to the griot. Yet, she could not get the image of the second man out of her mind. He wasn't as tall or wide as his huge friend, but his body looked efficient.

Strong and lean and unafraid. She'd only had the briefest glimpse of his face, but his eyes had burned their way into her memory. *Intense* was not the word. They were almost *overpowering*.

A chill ran through her, and she pulled her coat closer. She was tempted to go back into the pub just to relieve this curiosity that had sprung up within her, when footsteps stomped along the tightly packed dirt road. Kyara's blood chilled. Those were the precise steps of soldiers, their heavy boots much sturdier than what most villagers could afford.

Four men appeared from around the corner, marching directly underneath a hanging lantern. The black uniforms with gold edging marked them as Golden Flames. Technically, she was a member, as well, but her status as the Poison Flame set her apart. She worked alone and wore no uniform.

Aren, the captain of the squad, squinted into the darkness as the men came closer. Kyara stood in shadow, hoping it would protect her from his perusal, but his gaze went immediately to her, like iron to a magnet. He frowned and motioned to his men, who hung back, then approached her alone. She retreated a few paces so she could keep the entire street in view. This felt too much like an ambush.

"Were the Keepers inside?" His voice was monotone, his stance stiff. In the dark, his eyes were obscured, the waxing moon giving off a weak glow that barely lit the street. She was grateful for the reprieve from his cold gaze.

"Hard to say, but the nabbers certainly were. Follow them and I'm sure the Keepers won't be far behind."

He sniffed and tossed her a canvas bag. "The collar for when you capture the rebel."

Kyara scanned the empty street before opening the bag. She pulled out the collar, once a strip of curved metal now encased in the hard, red stone of a caldera. Blood magic. She suppressed a shiver and tried not to wonder whose blood had been spilled to make this.

Calderas were special containers for magic. Much of Ydaris's work for the True Father depended on them. Major calderas, the most powerful kind, required more than just blood. Death was necessary, but for minor calderas like the collars, some poor soul would have been dragged onto the stone table and sliced into while the Cantor whispered a string of words in a foreign tongue. Kyara had witnessed the ritual too many times to count, and when no one else was convenient, her blood was used.

She ran her thumb across the two metal loops that stuck out on either end so that a padlock could be affixed. The collar's spell blocked its wearer from connecting to Earthsong. The thing was warm to the touch and made her skin crawl. She dropped it back into the bag, then confirmed that both the lock and key were also inside. The only other item was a sheaf of paper, but it was too dark to make out the writing.

"What's it say?"

"The location of the warehouse where they're keeping the children. A dilapidated structure about four kilometers south, out in the bush."

Kyara stuffed the entire bag into the traveling pack slung across her shoulders. "You do realize that showing up here in full uniform is not exactly discreet. The whole point is for the Keepers not to suspect me. Or are you trying to sabotage me?"

Aren shifted into a patch of light, and the cold mask of a hardened soldier thawed a few degrees. A flash of desire lit his eyes. Kyara wanted to step away, but the wall behind her gave her nowhere to go.

"After you've completed this mission, we need to talk." His

palm rose to cup her cheek. She held herself very still, muting her instinct to recoil at his touch.

"Talk about what?" She breathed in through her nose, wanting to steady the beat of her heart. Inside, her Song awoke, taking note of the danger present.

"You know what."

Kyara shifted her head, pulling away from Aren's touch. "I said all I needed to. It was one time. Weeks ago. And it was a mistake. It won't happen again."

She slid to the side, seeking more distance between them, but he grabbed her wrist, holding her in place. He leaned in so that his lips hovered over hers. The tobacco on his breath filled her nostrils. "And *I* think we should talk about that." His thumb slid up the sleeve of her coat, caressing her skin. "I think you will reconsider. Do you know the other men are disgusted by you? Do you think anyone else but me will ever have you?"

A deep hurt threatened to swell at his words, but she pushed it back. He had been her first, her only. He had pursued her for weeks, breaking down her resistance, that feeling she should have listened to that told her he was a bad idea. But loneliness had won out. Handsome and strong, Aren's chiseled face and accepting smile were a far cry from the frightened looks most of the men gave her. She'd been curious, wanted to know what it felt like to be touched by a man.

But Aren hadn't been gentle. His rough fingers had abraded her skin, and his single-minded focus on his own pleasure had soured the experience for her. It had been more painful than pleasurable, and she'd kicked herself for not listening to her instincts.

It was only when she'd declined his continued advances that she began to be truly afraid of him. Fortunately, he had been out on a mission for the past few weeks. She had hoped that time would lead him to a new obsession, but Aren was nothing if not tenacious.

She firmed her voice so there would be no misunderstanding. "It. Is. Over. It was a mistake that I don't care to repeat."

He tightened his grip, crushing her beneath strong fingers. Kyara gritted her teeth and leaned forward, unwilling to give him the satisfaction of seeing her pain. When she longed to strike him and defend herself, her chest wound flared in warning. She could not harm any member of the Golden Flames, for any reason.

"Get your hands off me," she said flatly.

"I've been patient with you, but you're going to have to see reason eventually." He twisted so hard she thought he might mean to break her arm. Her Song surged, wanting release, but it was met with the resistance of a burst of agony from the wound. If she could have endured it, she would have struck Aren anyway, the wound be damned. But years of torturous training made her respect the pain. It ruled her. It owned her, just as much as Ydaris and the True Father did. She was not strong enough to fight against it, and so she could not defend herself from Aren's cruel turn.

"If you would only see the light, Kyara-deni, see how good we are together, all that we could accomplish . . . Together, we could be the king's right hand."

Her knees buckled, but she ground her teeth again to withstand the pain. "His right hand? So that's what this is about? You think the True Father favors me in some way? You think that favor could extend to you?" She almost wanted to laugh.

"You're his prized assassin. Of course he favors you," he rasped into her mouth. She pressed her lips closed in case he thought about trying to kiss her. Perhaps that was what it looked like to the soldiers on the other side of the street. Kyara wondered if the wound would stop her from biting Aren's tongue off if he tried anything. That pain would be worth it.

A commotion across the street finally made him release his grip. Footsteps approached and Kyara nearly sagged against the wall, keeping her eyes on the Flames.

"What is it, Dalgo-deni?" Aren asked as his lackey came closer.

Dalgo's gaze flicked to Kyara and then back to his captain. "It's them, sir." The other three Golden Flames had finally noticed the prone forms of the brawlers at the mouth of the alley. "They are part of the crew of nabbers."

Aren's gaze moved from the unconscious men to scan the empty streets. "The Keepers must be nearby monitoring them."

Kyara thought back to the two men in the pub watching the fight. She had suspected they were two of the Keepers she was looking for.

Aren appeared to have come to a similar conclusion. "Your first undercover mission," he said, his icily handsome face breaking into a scary grin. "You asked if I was trying to sabotage you. I'm just as invested in this assignment going well as you are. And my orders are to help however I can. We can't have the Keepers thinking you're in league with the Flames, now, can we?"

All emotion drained from his expression. He became a total stranger as he took a step away and then launched a kick to her midsection. Her ribs exploded in pain and she fell onto her back.

Aren grabbed her by the ends of her braids and dragged her up to a standing position. "I don't think I heard you quite right. Did you just tell me to feck off? I think you need to be taught a lesson," he called out loudly, then smashed his fist into her face.

Her Song mushroomed within her, seeking to retaliate. The

more she longed to fight back, the worse the wound hurt, keeping her in check. The coppery taste of blood filled her mouth and her vision swam.

Aren punched her again, this time in her abdomen, and she fell down. Another vicious kick sent her sliding across the ground. She sucked in short breaths, trying to supply oxygen to her lungs. He said something else in a mocking tone, but the words were lost to the roar in her ears. Then everything went black.

A yelp sounded from somewhere nearby, and Kyara realized she hadn't blacked out. She just couldn't see anything. Had Aren beaten her so badly she'd gone blind? A head injury?

The sounds around her were confusing, but it seemed as though a scuffle was taking place. Her fingers dug into the dirt around her.

"Why can't I fecking see anything?" someone cried. It could have been Aren or one of his men. That made her pause. She wasn't the only one blinded? But that didn't make any sense. The blackness was perfect, complete, as if the candle of the world had been blown out. Though her body cried out with each movement, she crawled until her hand reached the hard surface of a wall.

The sound of wind rushed her ears, and an incredible gust blew across her back. If she hadn't been lying flat on her stomach, it would have blown her over. Sandstorms came up quickly, but not this quickly. And while the wind beat against her, none of the flying grit she would expect filled her nose and mouth.

As quickly as the storm came, it was gone, and the blackness retreated, leaving the natural darkness of the night, bright as midday in comparison to what had come before it.

Kyara rolled over, pain coloring her every movement. The

unconscious brawlers still lay there, but Aren and his men were gone. The only person visible was a teenage boy walking toward her. His hair was shaggy and unkempt, but his clothes fit well and seemed in good repair. He crouched before her and peered into her eyes.

"Are you all right? I have my Song. I can try to heal you."

"No," Kyara said. "Save it. It's not as bad as it looks."

The boy pursed his lips and looked her up and down. She struggled to a seated position with her back against the wall and attempted a smile to put him at ease. What would happen if he tried to heal her? Would he immediately recognize that she was resistant to Earthsong? He might be a Keeper, as well, considering he had his Song, though he was young.

"What just happened?" she asked.

The boy looked away and shrugged his shoulders. "Midcountry weather is unpredictable this time of year."

She narrowed her eyes, at least the one that wasn't nearly swollen shut. "Did you do that? With your Song?"

"I wish. No, it wasn't me." The tone of his voice indicated he knew who it had been, though.

Could it be the Shadowfox, or was it another Keeper who'd managed to avoid the tribute? Serendipity had brought her so close to the one she was seeking, but she refused to credit Aren's sadism.

"Well, whoever it was, I'd like to thank him or her," she said.

"What did he want? That Flame?" The boy spat out the word.

"Oh, the usual thing. He didn't believe I wasn't a whore."

He scowled. "The Flames are a menace."

Kyara snorted. She couldn't disagree. "Don't say that too loudly," she warned. "You know what happens if someone hears you." This boy could be an ally if she approached this correctly.

She took a deep breath and rolled to her knees, then stood. The boy held out a hand to help stabilize her, and she took it gratefully.

"What's your name?"

"Kyara. And you?"

"Farron." He looked about sixteen or seventeen.

"Well, thank you, Farron-deni. I'm all right."

He made a face. "Just Farron is fine. No need for High Lagrimari around here."

Mentally, she kicked herself. She had to be more careful. Subterfuge had rarely been required of her before, but watching how she spoke and acted was more important than ever for this mission.

"Do you need help getting home?" Farron asked.

"No, I'll be fine."

He nodded, and she felt his gaze on her as she slowly walked away.

If the Keepers were watching the nabbers, they would find their way to the warehouse. Kyara was in no shape to head there now, however. Finding an inn for the night was the first order of business. None of her bones were broken, and a good night's sleep would do much.

In the morning, she would resume her mission. She suspected she would be seeing Farron again very shortly. And hopefully she'd find out who the mysterious Singer was who had helped her—and had dispatched Aren—so mysteriously.

CHAPTER SEVEN

A seer cannot act for tomorrow
Without heeding the impact on today
To lose sight of the road on which you walk
Will often cause your feet to go astray
But some truths die swift on the teacher's tongue
As elders say, youth's wasted on the young

—THE BOOK OF UNVEILING

"Just stay calm and everything will be fine." Zeli said the words without moving her lips, a frozen smile plastered on her face. She glided down the pathway behind Devana, who, judging by the set of her shoulders, was working herself into a frenzy of nervous energy.

Soft chatter and lilting music from the dining hall filtered its way through the courtyard as they approached. The dinner the

Magister was holding that evening was even larger than his usual shindigs. One of the kitchen maids had told Zeli that they'd roasted two pigs. And temporary horse stalls had been erected to accommodate more animals than the already large stable could on its own.

It would be an evening of food, drink, conversation, and cunning that would last into the wee hours of the morning. Giving them little time to sneak away to catch their coach.

Much as Zeli relished this turn of events, she still needed to reassure Devana—it was one of her primary roles in addition to dressing her, cleaning her clothes and room, organizing her cosmetics, braiding her hair . . .

"I *am* calm," Devana said. "I just don't understand why he didn't give me some kind of warning. Usually a dinner this large would be planned for weeks in advance."

True. The kitchen staff had been scurrying around to make the preparations in record time. Zeli nodded in commiseration as a footman rushed by with a soiled tablecloth in his arms.

"Perhaps this is really a gift. Your father will likely drink too much and sleep so deeply that he won't awaken until tomorrow afternoon. He may not even notice you're gone until you return."

The words felt hollow, but Devana's shoulders relaxed. The girls paused at the threshold of the dining hall, where the guests were being seated. The low tables were set up in a U-shape, with the Magister at the short, head table. Seating, on plush embroidered cushions brought out specially for the event, was arranged in order of favor, with the highest ranking guests closest to the Magister.

When it was her time to be seated, Devana took her usual place at her father's left side. Kerym sat on his right, with the other four Ephors next to him. Though his late father, from

whom he'd inherited the position, had held the highest rank of
the five, Kerym as the youngest had the least. However, his be-
trothal to the Magister's daughter had skipped him above the
others, rank-wise. Zeli had no doubt there were hard feelings
surrounding that, ones only voiced well out of earshot of the
city's ruler.

The Magister took his place last. He was a tall, broad-
shouldered former warrior only just beginning to thicken around
the middle. His dark hair was graying at the temples and even
the wicked scar bisecting the right side of his face did little to
detract from his rugged appeal. The thin mark was several shades
lighter than his skin and ran from his hairline, through his eyebrow, and down his cheek. It was a miracle he hadn't lost the
eye. Word was an Earthsinger had saved it, but had stopped
short of healing the injury that had eventually scarred so badly.
Since then, the Magister hated Earthsingers and made sure all
of his staff gave tribute as early as possible. Even the youngest
page boys had been shipped off to Sayya to be drained of their
Song by the immortal king.

Zeli herself had made the trip at seven—far too young to
travel so far alone. She remembered nothing of the actual tribute.
Vague images of a carved door and a hard, cold table on which
she'd lain, and then . . . nothing. She'd opened her eyes a time
later with a hole in her heart the size of her Song. The emptiness
still echoed within her. That sense that some important part of
her was missing.

She shook off the lingering sensation. It was far better to be
employed by the wealthy Magister than starving somewhere in
the Midcountry, or being a broodmare in Sayya in the True
Father's harem, or any number of other fates that could have
befallen her.

With Devana seated, Zeli positioned herself in the line of servants standing at the ready against the wall. She ladled soup and poured wine. Removed dirty plates and replaced them with clean ones. Picked up discarded napkins and brushed away crumbs.

Gladda bustled up to her during the final course. "Yalisamideni requires her special tea. She said you'd know where she keeps it in her room."

Zeli nodded, excited for the task. She glanced toward the end of the table where the Magister's mistress, Yalisa, sat. The elegant woman caught Zeli's eye, a small smile on her lips. Zeli returned it, then dashed off on the errand.

When Zeli had first come to the estate, Yalisa had been a lady's maid. She'd served the Magister's late wife and after her death became Devana's personal servant. Yalisa had trained Zeli and been her mentor in all areas of life. She'd taught her when to speak and when to stay silent, how to manage her monthly courses, and she had been the one to comfort Zeli after her return from that fateful tribute trip to Sayya.

After a year of mourning his wife, the Magister had been beset by aristocratic women hoping both to comfort him and secure their own futures. But somehow, he'd found solace in the arms of his daughter's maid and soon elevated her from servant to favored. Though she was of low rank, she could come and go as she pleased, wore gowns of the finest fabric, and rubbed foreheads with the upper class. She'd even met the True Father on the king's last visit to the region.

She was everything Zeli wanted to be.

Zeli raced into Yalisa's room, which always smelled of vanilla, and went straight to the clay jar in which the woman kept her tea. The special blend soothed her throat, and her need for it indicated she expected to be called to sing at the party. Yalisa's voice was pure honey. Zeli despaired that she herself could not sing—was it Yalisa's voice or her beauty that had endeared the Magister to her? And what sort of future could Zeli hope for without either?

She sped back to the kitchen and prepared the tea, then served it to Yalisa.

"How are you enjoying the evening?" the woman asked as Zeli poured. Even before her first sip of the sweet-smelling brew, her voice was a throaty purr.

"It's quite a large dinner on short notice. Do you know what the occasion is?"

Yalisa's painted lips firmed. She shot a glance at the Magister before recovering her smile. "All will be revealed, never worry."

Zeli looked in the direction of the head table, only her gaze was caught by Kerym as he gave a full body laugh at something the Magister had said.

"Be careful, little swan," Yalisa said. "Your eyes give you away."

Zeli dropped her gaze, chastened. It would never do for her to reveal the crush she had on her mistress's husband-to-be. On the Magister's other side, Devana laughed as well. A pretty, feminine sound that trilled across the room. Zeli wasn't sure what she looked like when she laughed, but it was certainly not so sweet and winsome.

She had begged Yalisa to teach her the other things a mother taught a daughter. Lessons on how to attract and keep a man. Not Kerym, of course, but perhaps she could catch the eye of another of the favored. Perhaps she, too, could be elevated and have her own room, finely appointed, no longer having to share a straw mat with three other girls. But Yalisa had so far demurred with one excuse or another. Now, Zeli was determined the press the issue at the next opportunity.

Yalisa patted her hand. "Go. Your mistress looks like she needs you." She winked at Zeli before stirring her tea.

Zeli hurried back to the front table to switch out Devana's dessert for one with fewer nuts.

"So," the Magister said, patting his belly as the final dishes were cleared. The chatter in the room silenced as if someone had turned the volume down on a radiophonic. "Nothing like a gathering of friends and neighbors, is there?"

The quiet seemed somehow unnatural, like the hush before a Midcountry sandstorm. It was as if, on a subconscious level, those gathered somehow knew what was coming. Zeli held her breath.

"I would hear, if I may, of the triumphs and troubles of my dear friends." He turned in his seat toward the end of the table. "Ogus-deni, please, tell us about your jewelry shop. I'd heard the production out of the mines has been down quite a bit this year. Has this affected you greatly?"

Ogus, a rather short, rather squat man of middle years looked up, surprise sharpening his features. He was of low rank, one of the people it seemed the Magister invited just to fill the available seats.

"Oh, well, mideni, yes, that's true. Over the past few months raw materials have been a bit scarce, but we've made do with what we have. It's the Lagrimari way." He chuckled nervously. Did he feel the strange tension in the air like the prescient echo of a coming storm?

"Indeed." The Magister's voice rumbled. Beside him Devana looked bored, but Kerym leaned forward, intrigue evident on his face.

"So please tell me, in these times of retrenchment, how is it that your house staff has been seen carting in bushels of food into your home?"

Ogus's deep skin tone turned ashen. He swallowed several times. "Mideni, I'm not sure where these reports have come from, but I assure you they're entirely false. We have our rations, and what extra provisions you yourself have chosen to supply in your generosity, and that is all." He spread his hands apart to indicate the meager quantities he had.

The benefits of being one of the favored were the gifts allotted to them by those of even higher rank. Their wealth, extra provisions, and supplies set them apart from a populace living off what the government provided in the way of food.

The Magister smiled, his expression now edging on the feral. Zeli leaned back against the wall, instinctively trying to get as far away as possible from what was coming. Even Devana perked up, no doubt sensing the blood in the water.

"I'm quite sure that you're not doubting the efficacy of the intelligence personnel who I myself handpicked?" The Magister's voice never lost its pleasant edge.

"Oh, certainly not," Ogus stammered. "It's just that, perhaps there's been a misunderstanding. That's all I . . ."

"I find it very interesting," the ruler continued as if the other man hadn't spoken, "that a craftsman, highly skilled as you are, would think to outsmart those ranked above him. The True Father has divisions for a reason. He is ever wise, our king is."

Ogus bobbed his head up and down. "Yes, he is, mideni."

"Ever wise and ever watchful." The Magister tapped the insignia on the sash tied across his tunic, the all-seeing eye of the Father. The motto was one of the first things a Lagrimari child learned. The immortal king, it was believed, saw all and knew

all, in no little part due to the extensive network of people willing to report on their neighbors. The Magisters, the Ephors, anyone with even a modicum of power—derisively called "payrollers"
by those without status—had earned it by virtue of the intelligence they provided the king, or anyone above themselves.

The Magister leaned back. "I'd thought better of you, Ogus-
denili. I never dreamed a man who had been welcomed into my
home on many occasions and shown every courtesy would try to
cheat the True Father."

"B-but, I . . ."

"Guards."

The guards appeared out of nowhere and lifted poor Ogus
from his seat. He was still denying and sputtering, tears running
down his face as he was dragged out.

Zeli clenched her jaw and widened her eyes so as to show no
visible reaction. Anyone displaying too much sympathy for an
accused would have suspicion cast upon them. She didn't know
why it had to be this way. The True Father demanded loyalty, she
supposed that was the right of any king, but to require the elite
to keep their positions by having an endless network of spies
whispering in their ears about their neighbors and countrymen?

If someone thought you had more food than you ought to,
finer fabrics than you should have been able to afford, or con-
versely, if they thought your clothing or shoes weren't fine
enough when you had been gifted fabric and leather enough that
you must be doing something nefarious with the excess—the list
of crimes was longer than her arm. Zeli didn't understand how it
all worked. It was the one part of being favored that gave her
pause. At least when you had no rank you knew where you stood.
You did what work you could, received your rations, and scrabbled along. The poor had no need to worry about their neighbors

informing on them, they could be "called into service" and sent to the camps, the mines, or the harems at any time for no reason at all.

She couldn't say she understood, but it was the way of things. It kept things orderly, she supposed, and was as the True Father wished it.

The rest of the party was silent until Ogus's screams could no longer be heard.

"Well." The Magister slapped his hand on the table. "How about some entertainment?"

CHAPTER EIGHT

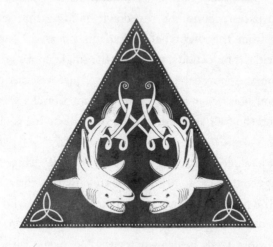

Hindsight's perception sharpens through the years
Especially when conscious of regret
A mind in turmoil wishes for reprieve
For what it cannot manage to forget
When wrongs well-meant cause suffering immense
A debt is owed to pay in recompense

—THE BOOK OF UNVEILING

"Your lack of curiosity is astounding, Farron." Darvyn shifted to the side to dislodge a stone that was poking into his abdomen as he lay between Zango and Farron, behind a cluster of coarse shrubbery.

The late-afternoon sun beat down on their backs. Every now and then, Darvyn would sing a cooling breeze to bring some relief, but he needed to conserve as much of his Song as possible for a confrontation with the nabbers.

Two other groups of Keepers were similarly positioned several hundred paces around the run-down building into which the nabbers from the night before had disappeared. Zango currently held the binoculars, watching the single door to the structure. The warehouse had no windows, just a series of round ventilation holes near the roofline. The mud bricks were crumbling, and the roof appeared on the verge of caving in at several places.

They had been watching the property all day, since the nabbers staggered back to it after waking in the early morning hours. The five from town had joined three more who Darvyn could sense inside. He also felt over three dozen children within. Most were healthy but two had been badly beaten. Darvyn had healed the children's fractured bones when he'd first arrived but left the more superficial wounds so the nabbers would not become suspicious.

It pained him to allow the children to suffer at all, but Aggar would not let them move into action yet, insisting on more surveillance. Darvyn felt they'd seen more than enough. Nothing had changed for hours. The Keepers numbered nine to the nabbers' eight, and with four Earthsingers, the odds were good. But of course, Aggar would not listen to reason, and so Darvyn had been distracting himself with thoughts of the night before.

"You have no idea where she came from or what she was doing in Five?" Darvyn asked Farron, incredulous. At least the teen had gotten the woman's name—Kyara. A shame he'd learned little else about her.

"She'd just been beaten. I didn't want to assault her with questions as well."

Darvyn tore his gaze away from the building to glance at Farron. "And yet you let her just leave and disappear into the night?"

"She said she was fine, and she was walking all right. If you were so interested in her, why didn't you go talk to her?" Farron raised his brows.

Zango snorted, his big body shaking in silent laughter. Darvyn elbowed his friend in the ribs.

The night before, Darvyn had rushed out of the pub to find a Golden Flame beating the woman who'd captured his attention. Instinctively, he'd sang a cloak of darkness over the area. It was a simple but effective spell. The windstorm that had blown the soldiers off their feet had been satisfying. Perhaps he'd taken it too far, blowing them all the way down the street and out of the town entirely, but it had been worth it. He'd let Farron go after her so Darvyn could keep his anonymity, but now he regretted it.

"If the elders hear about you using Earthsong on a group of Golden Flames they'll be livid," Zango muttered.

"I won't tell them if you won't," he said with a wink. Zango shook his head.

It had been quite a while since any Midcountry girl had caught his eye. Usually those who avoided being called into service and stayed in their villages were married off as soon as their meager dowries could be scraped together. In Sayya and the Lake Cities, where better weather, soil, and more abundant food made life a bit easier, he could generally find a girl to regale with tales of fighting in the Seventh Breach or impress with tidbits about his time with the hated Elsirans. Somehow he doubted this Kyara would be awed by his stories. What would it take to dazzle her?

A nudge from Zango brought him back to the present. His friend passed the binoculars to him and pointed north. Darvyn brought the landscape into focus and spotted a cloaked, hooded figure on horseback approaching the warehouse.

Another nabber joining his companions?

Darvyn stretched his senses forward but could not read anything about the rider. Male or female, young or old, friend or foe—nothing was coming through his Song. They must be a Singer, and one with a particularly powerful shield if Darvyn couldn't sense anything.

"I don't think that's a nabber," he said. It was impossible to conceive of a nabber who'd avoided tribute. Plus, he couldn't fathom an Earthsinger being able to withstand the suffering nabbers brought upon the children.

"Who is it, then?" Zango asked.

"I don't know." Darvyn pulled the binoculars from his face to wipe away the sweat dripping into his eyes.

"What does he want?"

Darvyn shook his head. He raised the glasses again and peered through. The rider was nearly to the warehouse. Darvyn scanned the brush for the other Keepers. Another pair of binoculars peered his way—Aggar. Darvyn gave a hand signal indicating what he'd told Zango, that he knew nothing about this newcomer.

The rider alighted the horse and approached the entrance. Though he was too far away to hear, Darvyn imagined the rattle of the tin door as a fist pounded on the metal. The door didn't open, but the rider stood there for some time. It appeared he was talking to someone on the other side. Then the door slid open a fraction and the rider pulled a pouch from his belt. Were they exchanging money? Was this rider purchasing one of the stolen children?

Darvyn went on immediate alert. If the rider attempted to leave with a child in tow, Darvyn would have to stop them at the risk of exposing the Keepers and possibly endangering the other children. Aggar had not yet come up with a solid plan for saving the captives, and if he had any ideas, he hadn't shared them.

The door opened wide enough to reveal a tall, lanky nabber with scars marring his shaven head. His face screwed up, and he shook his head before slamming the door shut. The rider, still obscured in the hood, banged on the door again for several minutes to no response.

Darvyn hoped the man would get on his horse and go back to wherever he came from. Finally, it seemed he realized no one was going to answer. He approached the horse, but instead of climbing on, he pulled a container from the saddlebag. Then he returned to the warehouse and began pouring out liquid around the base of the structure.

"What is he doing?" Farron whispered.

Once again, Darvyn attempted to read the intentions and mood of the cloaked figure but could not. The substance that the rider was pouring on the tin and mud-brick structure he could sense, however.

"That's kerosene. He's going to burn it down," Darvyn said, dropping the binoculars and rushing to his feet. He raced across the flat ground toward the building. He had the presence of mind to sing a gust of wind to blow up a cover of dust in front of him, in case one of the nabbers peered out the door. It was poor concealment, but he had to stop the rider from burning the warehouse and all the children inside alive, if that was indeed the fool's intention.

Footsteps sounded behind him. He glanced over his shoulder to find Farron fast on his heels. He didn't have time to admonish the boy. The rider disappeared behind the back of the building, and Darvyn only hoped he could reach the idiot before he struck the match.

CHAPTER NINE

When thunder roars and lightning has her say
The clouds erupt, emitting fleeing rain
Who sees the sky at war without a thought
Of why such close kin ended up in pain
A tempest's fury views all men with scorn
Royals and rustic both revere the storm

—THE BOOK OF UNVEILING

Kyara was just considering whether to douse the four covered wagons parked to the side of the warehouse with kerosene, as well, when the odd cloud of dust reached her. A hand reached out of the swirling mass to knock the metal canister from her hands. The force was enough to cause her to stumble and fall to the ground.

Her hood fell away as she sprawled on her back. Her ribs, still sore from Aren's attack, protested harshly, but she held back a cry of pain. The teen she'd met, Farron, stood above her, his hair even wilder than it had been last night. Next to him, blocking out the sun, stood the man from the bar.

Though he was in shadow, his eyes blazed, as intense as the heat of the day. "You!" He crouched down, allowing her a closer look. "What in pip's name are you doing?" he whispered fiercely.

She froze, staring up at him. Those devastating eyes regarded her from an oval face; a dusting of stubble ran across his clenched jaw. When his eyebrows descended, she mentally shook herself, shocked at her reaction. Scrambling backward, she looked around, expecting the other Keepers she'd sensed in the area to emerge from their hiding places.

"There are children in there," the Keeper said through gritted teeth. Then he cocked his head to the side, as if listening.

Kyara opened her mind's eye, sensing the Nethersong of everyone inside the warehouse. The nabbers she could sense clearly, as well as the older children, but the younger ones were far more difficult. She could still not get a good count of them due to their weak Nether swirling together. Since when did nabbers start taking children that young?

The nabbers were moving around inside; one approached the door. Either the Keeper before her had his Song, or exceptionally good hearing, as his body suddenly went rigid.

"Hurry," he said, gripping her arm firmly. Kyara held back a wince. She healed quickly, but most of her was still sore from the previous day's beating. The Keeper frowned and released her. She stood on her own and followed him and Farron to the other side of the covered wagon, where they crouched and hid.

The metal door opened, and a new nabber poked his greasy

head out, looking back and forth. Kyara held her breath. The horse she'd bought that morning was tied around the corner, out of his sightline. The nabber sniffed the air. If he picked up the scent of kerosene, he apparently didn't find it odd. He retreated into the warehouse and slammed the door. With her other sight, she saw his light move deeper into the interior.

"All clear," she said.

"I know," the Keeper said, glowering. "Who are you and exactly what do you think you're doing here?"

"I could ask you the same." She raised an eyebrow and enjoyed watching his expression shift from fury to frustration and back again.

"We can't talk here."

Kyara shrugged.

"Come with me," he said, rising and peering at the still-closed door. He led her the long way around the back of the warehouse until they reached her horse. Farron hadn't said a word to her yet, but she looked over at him and smiled. He teetered somewhere between confusion and smiling back. The Keeper noticed and whispered something into the teen's ear that caused him to grimace. Then he ran off into the bush.

The Keeper mounted the horse and motioned for her to get on behind him. He was awfully bossy, this one. She clenched her jaw and complied. It was bad enough having to follow orders from Ydaris and the True Father. She had no desire to add this Keeper to the list, but she reminded herself that this was part of her mission. She had to gain their trust, at least for long enough to discover the Shadowfox's identity.

Once on the horse, she realized touching him would be necessary if she didn't want to go flying off. Reluctantly, she wrapped her arms around his middle. When her palms met the firm muscle of his abdomen, her temperature, already high from the desert heat, increased another few degrees.

They rode north for several minutes in silence until an almost imperceptible slope of the land and a cropping of high bushes hid the warehouse from view. The Keeper reined the horse to a stop, and they dismounted.

When he didn't speak immediately, she found herself once again lost in his features. His eyes were dark and fathomless, and the corners of his mouth naturally turned up, giving even his grimmest expressions a hint of levity. The bottom lip, fuller than the top, had a hypnotic effect on her.

The collar of his tunic was open, and around his neck he wore a thin leather band that disappeared beneath the fabric. Her gaze traveled down a well-muscled chest that piqued her curiosity before snapping back to his face.

Her cheeks heated. She hoped she truly was resistant to Earthsong. Not only did she not want this Keeper to read her attraction to him but he had to believe her lies, as well, and lying to an Earthsinger was normally impossible.

"Who are you?" he asked again, his voice tight.

She forced her gaze to his eyes, also distracting, and then decided to speak exclusively to his nose. "My name is Kyara ul-Krastigar," she said. A new surname had been necessary. For her story to work, she could not be ul-Lagrimar and give the surname of her father, the king, else she would have to explain how she had escaped the harem. What better choice than the House of Serpents?

"And what are you doing here? Why were you trying to burn down that building? Do you know there are children inside?"

"Of course I know! I wasn't trying to burn the children. My sister was nabbed a week ago. I suspect she's inside. I came here seeking to buy her back, but they refused. The fire was just a way to get everyone out in the open so I could see whether or not she's truly there."

The cover story was one she'd taken care in coming up with. It was a tale any Keeper of the Promise should be sympathetic to. Although rare, it was sometimes possible to buy back a nabbed child, though most Midcountry folk could never afford the cost.

"That's a terrible plan," he said, rubbing the back of his neck.

Kyara's eyes narrowed. "At least I was doing something. You're a Keeper, I take it?" He didn't respond, but it was obvious. "And what? Were you going to watch them all day?" She realized she wasn't doing much to make her sympathetic, but her plan *had* been good. It was just like a man not to acknowledge it since he hadn't thought of it himself.

He continued staring at her, frowning. "How is it you still have your Song?"

"What makes you think I do?"

"Your shield. It's virtually impenetrable."

Kyara shrugged her shoulders, glad for the years of practice at keeping her face emotionless. "My Song isn't relevant here. My sister is. Can you at least tell me your name?"

"Darvyn, and you've nearly undone quite a lot of work."

"I didn't see any *work* happening. I saw quite a lot of nothing, actually."

He sighed in frustration, his hand gripping the back of his neck again. The muscles in his forearm tensed, and Kyara looked down. Why was his *forearm* distracting her? She should only be thinking about one thing: her mission.

Could this Darvyn lead her to the Shadowfox? Was he one of the high-ranking Keepers who knew the identity of the Singer?

She wasn't really getting anywhere by antagonizing him, but being the sweet and gentle female wasn't in her nature. "Listen, I'm sorry if I interfered in whatever plan you all are cooking up. I just want to find my sister." If she could, she would have tried to force some tears out, but Kyara hadn't cried in years. And even without being able to read her emotions, she suspected Darvyn was too astute to fall for the simpering-woman routine. There was a keen intelligence shining in his eyes, and that was what she'd need to appeal to.

"Perhaps we could work together. Our interests are aligned," she said.

"Where was your sister taken from?"

He believed her. That was good. "Checkpoint Twelve. I arrived two days after and began tracking the nabbers, searching for a way to get her back."

"You tracked the nabbers?" His voice was skeptical, and his gaze roamed her up and down. Not in a lecherous way, simply assessing. She could not hide her clothing and boots, well-made but not fancy. She was not ostentatious enough to be a payroller, but she was no hardscrabble Midcountry girl, either.

She stood tall, straightening her back. His gaze dropped to her chest before locking in on her eyes. A wave of satisfaction swept her at the glance he'd tried to hide. The tale she'd practiced fell from her lips. "My father was a courier. We traveled so much that the Collectors never quite caught up to us so I was never called into service. When Papa passed to the World After, he left me his wagon and I took up the trade. But I sold the cart and all but one horse for the money to bribe the nabbers."

He gave her a look of begrudging respect. She wished that she could truly deserve it, earn it for something she had actually done instead of these lies.

"Why is my plan so terrible?" she asked. "What was *your* plan?"

He opened his mouth, then closed it and glanced away. He looked even more frustrated than before, if possible, as if he were about to burst out of his skin. Finally, he shook his head and chuckled. "Have you ever thought about becoming a Keeper? You'd make a good one."

She snorted. "You all are a bunch of dreamers. You may save a few here and there, letting some grow up with their Songs, but in the end, the True Father will always win."

His amusement faded. "If you think that, why try to save your sister at all?"

Her shoulders slumped. She'd forgotten herself for a moment, giving him a little too much truth. Foolish or not, this particular Keeper seemed kind. Good-hearted. He spent his life helping, not hurting people. She could admit her jealousy to herself, though she had no time to spend wallowing in it.

"Listen, we can work together or not, but unless you have something better to offer than what I've planned, I'm going back to get my sister." She turned back to the horse, but his voice stopped her.

"You said they wouldn't take your money? Why not?"

Kyara turned around and shrugged. "It seemed like they were waiting for something. Like they had a quota to fill. I can't imagine they'll be paid more per child than what I offered, but . . ."

That was the truth. The nabber she'd spoken to had seemed fairly antsy.

Darvyn gave her another assessing glance before stepping toward the horse. "I think we can work together on this, but I'm not the one in charge."

"Who is?" Kyara's pulse quickened. Surely the Shadowfox would be the one in charge.

"I'll take you to him." He climbed back on the horse. Kyara swallowed, the anticipation of touching him again thrumming through her veins. She mounted and settled behind him, once more feeling her heartbeat speed as she wrapped her arms around his firm body. They headed off into the bush with Kyara trying and failing to keep her mind only on her mission.

Darvyn sagged with relief when they finally got off the horse. Kyara's hands, once on him, hadn't moved, but he'd had a visceral reaction to her closeness and her touch. Her scent had assaulted him during the entire short ride, too. An intoxicating, gentle fragrance that reminded him of sandalwood. His mind filled with thoughts he couldn't stop but could not afford to have.

His reaction to her was overwhelming. There were female Keepers with whom he worked all the time. Attractive women, capable women, but none had ever affected him as Kyara did. Her spirit and self-assurance drew him to her, but something he couldn't define had hooked him.

He tied her horse with the others they'd left at their rendezvous point a kilometer south of the warehouse. They'd have to walk the rest of the way back to where Aggar and his team were positioned, monitoring the southern side of the building.

It was an hour until sunset, and the temperature was rapidly dropping. As he drew nearer to the rest of the team, Kyara close behind, Darvyn could feel Aggar's anger pulsing. The man had witnessed Kyara's "plan" from afar and would not be happy at having a stranger brought into the midst of their operation.

Distrust and wariness radiated from the two other Keepers of Aggar's watch group, Navar and Lizana, but those emotions were dwarfed by Aggar's own silent rage. It pounded against Darvyn's Song, nearly drowning everything else out.

The team leader marched forward to meet them, staying out of hearing range of the others. He rounded on the two of them, and Darvyn felt a small surge of respect when he saw Kyara square her shoulders out of the corner of his eye.

Aggar was nowhere near as physically menacing as Zango, but he had risen through the ranks of the Keepers due to stubbornness and determination. He and Darvyn were the same height, but Aggar was built more like a barrel where Darvyn was lean. The man shifted his weight in a way that seemed orchestrated to appear more forbidding. The permanent scowl etched on his face helped his cause.

"What is this?" he asked, not looking at Kyara or acknowledging her in any way.

"Her sister was nabbed. She believes the girl is inside."

Aggar let out a grunt that was more like a growl and spat into the dirt. "And?"

Darvyn's jaw tensed. "And we could work together to get those children out."

Finally, his eyes moved over to Kyara. "What makes you think we need any help from a civilian?"

She didn't shrink back, instead took a step forward and cracked her knuckles. A woman had to be made of tough stuff to drive the Great Highway for a living. There were unscrupulous toll takers, as well as the sackers and bush wranglers just waiting to steal any merchandise that came their way. Most couriers were former soldiers and traveled armed to the teeth. Kyara couldn't be a soldier, but she obviously knew how to handle herself if she'd survived for any length of time in her profession. It was also obvious that Aggar wasn't intimidating her in the least.

"It's nearly sunset. I'll wager you've been here all day and done nothing." Her voice was low and mean. "Do you think if you watch it long enough, the building will magically disintegrate around them? I'm pretty sure you can't do that with your precious Song."

She'd called them fools for opposing the immortal king, but antagonizing Aggar was not the wisest choice. Still, Darvyn enjoyed the steam pouring from the man's ears in response to her.

"Not all of us have Songs," Aggar growled, bitterness dripping from his voice. "And you are not welcome here. We do not need your help. Ride back to wherever you came from while you still can."

"Or what?" She took another step closer, a slightly deranged smile spreading across her lips. "I'm not leaving until I see if my sister is in that building, and I'm going to do what I need to do, unless you have a better alternative."

Aggar's jaw worked as his fury rose. "You are not one of us. We don't know who you are."

She stepped forward until she was mere inches away from him. "I am Kyara. And I am going to get every child out of that building while you all sit out here pissing in the dust."

Aggar's arm reached out, whether to grab her or strike her, Darvyn wasn't sure. Darvyn flooded himself with Earthsong, ready to ensure that Kyara would not be harmed by Aggar's thoughtless anger, but she darted away, sprinting across the bush toward the warehouse.

The shock of her action momentarily paralyzed Darvyn before Aggar's roar of outrage propelled him into action. She was fast and reached the warehouse well before he did. A lit match appeared in her hands. It looked as though she was going through with her original plan.

"Stop her!" Aggar bellowed from behind Darvyn. He felt obligated to comply. He didn't believe she'd thought through the risks a fire could pose, so he sang a strong wind to blow out the flame. Kyara struck another match; again Darvyn killed it. She shot an aggravated look over her shoulder and huffed out a breath as he reached her side.

None of the nabbers seemed to have heard the noise as no one inside was making any move to approach the door. Kyara had a faraway look in her eye that made him wonder if she was sensing the same thing he was. She must be. How strong was her Song?

She darted around him and went straight for the front door.

"What are you doing?" he whispered as Aggar reached them. The footsteps of the other Keepers, abandoning their hiding places, were coming up fast behind.

When Kyara wrenched open the door, they all froze. She shot Darvyn a hard glare. "Get the wagons ready," was all she said before disappearing inside.

He sensed Farron and Zango come up on either side of him, yet he couldn't pull his attention away from the doorway.

"Do as she says," he told them before following her into the warehouse.

CHAPTER TEN

The Scorpion was born from death's own hand
She clawed her way out of her mother's womb
And every breath she took a miracle
Though each and every one portended doom
To save them all she had to walk alone
Her path led to a mother made of stone

—THE BOOK OF UNVEILING

The warehouse is so hot, Ulani isn't sure whether she's conscious or not at any given moment. Papa used to threaten to send her and Tana to the Hollow Place—a realm like the World After, but full of endless horrors and torments. She'd thought the closet at the top of the stairs was such a place, but it pales in comparison to this sweltering prison.

If there is a real Hollow Place, then her papa is there now, and these nabbers will meet him soon, she hopes.

She is chained to a bolt dug deep into the ground with six other girls. Another few bolts hold other children as well, many curled up on the floor. A bucket in the corner overflows with filth and gives off a sickening stench. Slashes of light break up the darkness from hatches near the roofline, but nothing dims the heat.

A few minutes ago, the banging on the front door drew the men out of the back area and through the canvas curtains to the front. Ulani shudders, wondering who it could be. She doesn't know where they are, just that they're in the bush.

Next to her, Tana grips her hand and squeezes, sending a silent message that they are in this together—whatever this happens to be. Ulani never got a chance to find out what her sister's plan for them had been—before they even left the house, their stepmother had already derailed it.

The woman had taken a look at them, bags slung over their shoulders, dressed in their plain, traveling tunics, and suddenly grown a spine. Or so they'd thought. She'd insisted that they travel with her to her family's home in Checkpoint Four, where Papa had met her sometime after Ulani's mother had run off, and long after Tana's mother had died in childbirth.

They'd piled into a rickshaw drawn by a stoop-shouldered man and headed for one of Sayya's lesser used outer gates. Just outside the city, they were supposed to transfer to a carriage for the rest of the trip. But a large, enclosed wagon awaited them along with a grim-faced man whose eyes were even scarier than Papa's.

He'd tossed their stepmother a bag of grams and pulled the

screaming girls into the wagon, where they were bound hand and foot and tied to a bolt in the floor. The woman's first act of defiance against her dead husband was to sell his children. Tana had called it poetic.

Over the course of the trip, a few stops were made to pick up other children, then at some point when the sky was still dark, they'd been dragged here. To the Hollow Place.

Muffled whimpers and sobs keep up a steady rhythm. Ulani curls in on herself and places her thumb in her mouth—something she hasn't done in a long, long time.

Sounds of sickness rise from beyond the curtains toward the front of the space. Men coughing and retching. A woman pushes through the dirty fabric and stands there, light haloing her from behind. She looks like a warrior, face flushed, and breathing heavy.

Ulani sits up. She elbows her sister in the side. Tana rolls over and stares at the woman.

"It's her," Ulani whispers.

"Who?"

"*Her*. The Poison Flame." Her words are barely audible; awe steals her voice.

The woman disappears briefly, and Ulani wonders if she was real at all, then she's back with a ring of keys. More voices enter the warehouse—men and another woman.

The Poison Flame unlocks the shackles of the older children and then gives the key to Tana, instructing her to free all of them. When her chains come off, Ulani rubs her wrists, trying to bring feeling back into them.

She watches the Poison Flame carefully, but the woman doesn't seem to recognize her. Then she notices the others who came to save them. They must be Keepers of the Promise. A swell of hope rises.

The children are led into the sunshine, though it's already starting to lower toward the horizon. Still, the light feels good on Ulani's skin. Everyone blinks their eyes, taking in the endless bush around them and the wagons that had brought them here. Keepers watch over them, and a large woman with catlike eyes announces they're going to be taken to a safe house.

Ulani looks around, searching for the Poison Flame. She finds the woman at the edge of the group, talking to an angry man and another man who looks sort of familiar. She's sure she's never seen him before, but she can't shake the feeling that she knows him.

She elbows Tana again. "She must be a spy for the Keepers. Otherwise, why would she work for both them and the True Father?"

Tana squints and stares at the Poison Flame. "No, that's not possible. The king would know if she was spying. She can't be the same person who killed Papa."

Tana never believes her, but Ulani is sure. It *is* the Poison Flame. She had a feeling she would see her again.

As the children streamed out, Darvyn met Kyara's eyes. Her gaze was hard. She shook her head slightly, and his heart fell. Her sister was not here.

He couldn't say why he felt so much for a woman he did not know and wasn't sure was entirely sane, but she'd been effective. They cleared out the warehouse, captured all the nabbers, and saved the children without any bloodshed or casualties of any kind.

When he'd entered the sweltering space, he'd found four nabbers on their knees, vomiting into the dirt. All of the men here were either vomiting or had collapsed in pools of their own sick. What had she done in the few moments before he'd followed her inside, used poison? He wondered what was in her bag of tricks.

As the other Keepers were loading the children into the wagons, Kyara stood off to the side, peering at the faces of the young ones.

"We're going to question the nabbers," he said to her quietly. "Perhaps we can find out who may have taken your sister and where she is."

Her eyes were hollow when she looked at him, world-weary and bleak. She nodded slowly, then focused over his shoulder. He felt Aggar's approach and saw the warrior mask reassert itself on Kyara's face. Something in him wanted to reach out to her, to help console her. If he'd ever had a sibling, he would have done anything to keep them safe. Ironically enough, it was Aggar's parents who had made him begin to understand what a real family could be like, but that had all been stolen from him long ago. Like so much else.

Aggar's gaze was sharp when it landed on Kyara. "What did you use on the men to make them sick?"

She turned to face him fully, her stance proud and tall. "Special mixture of palmsalt extract and grimflour. When sprinkled on the skin or blown into the face it's not deadly, but it's enough to make a grown man wish he were dead—at least for a little while." She smiled secretively, and Aggar leaned back a bit.

"Do you have any more?"

"Why? Is something you ate not agreeing with you?"

Aggar spun on his heel and motioned for Darvyn to follow him. They walked a little ways into the bush to speak privately.

"I don't trust her. Are you sure she's telling the truth?"

Darvyn looked back to where Kyara stood with the others. Her eyes sparkled in the light from the fire that had been built just outside the warehouse. With full dark upon them, the chill of the night seeped into his pores.

"She's well shielded, so I cannot read her."

Aggar's nostrils flared. "Why did you not tell me before that she had her Song?" He whipped around to regard her again. "I think she's seen too much."

"And what do you propose we do? Interrogate her as we would a nabber?"

"She could be anyone."

"Like who? Aside from the Wailers, the Cantor is the only Earthsinger allowed to work for the True Father. I think it's safe to say she's not the Cantor, and considering she has all her mental faculties intact, she's not a Wailer, either." Darvyn shivered at the memory of the last time he'd gotten close to a Wailer. Those fully initiated into the regiment of Singers were little more than human puppets. They shuffled along mindlessly, stares vacant, every action controlled entirely by the immortal king. "The very fact that she has her Song gives us more reason to trust her."

"She's not one of us. Nor does it seem likely she's looking to join." Aggar spat.

"It's true she doesn't think much of us. But she's effective and capable. Not a drop of blood was shed. Wasn't that what you were afraid of?"

Aggar looked away, his brow pulling even farther down as his perpetual frown deepened.

"She's a courier by trade. Partnering with her means we can travel the highway and make better time than rumbling through the bush," Darvyn said. "She can get us through the checkpoints with less suspicion."

Aggar considered this. Without the proper licensing for transportation and travel, driving large wagons down the Great Highway would be quite an expensive proposition. They'd have to bribe each checkpoint guard to let them pass uninspected. They could use the nabbers' papers, which were obviously forged, but that would require even bigger bribes. The Keepers' funds were low due to many resources being diverted to supply those traveling across the mountain, but going off-road would be difficult and uncomfortable for the already traumatized children. A courier's license would make everything easier.

Darvyn saw the moment Aggar relented and agreed to keep Kyara with them. "Watch her closely. Don't let her out of your sight. And let me know the moment you feel something isn't right."

He nodded as Aggar walked away. Darvyn couldn't seem to stop watching Kyara, and letting her out of his sight was something he had no intention of doing.

CHAPTER ELEVEN

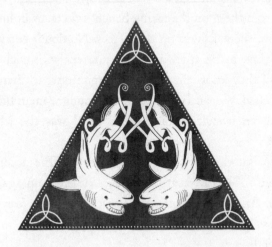

Abandoned out of love and out of fear
The Scorpion had not yet learned her sting
Her father, full of duty and remorse
Sought vengeance over every other thing
And so he left his only child behind
Tied to a world with blood and stone to bind

—THE BOOK OF UNVEILING

Zeli's mother had always told her that a tarnished mirror was still beautiful underneath, you just had to work a little harder to see it. It was her way of making sure Zeli didn't fall victim to gray moods and kept to the shiny side of life.

She'd always taken those words to heart, but even she was having a difficult time finding the shiny side to the public coach. She sat in the middle bench, facing backward, squeezed between Devana on one side and a portly cottager on the other, whose gender she couldn't determine from the cut of their mud-brown tunic. The individual was already asleep, snoring softly. Across from them on the facing bench, two teens in fine tunics looked on, silent frowns on their faces. No doubt cursing their poor fortune to be stuck in tight quarters with such riffraff. Little did they know that the young man next to them in the tattered cloak was an Ephor. And the young woman hiding her face with an oversized, olive-green hood was the Magister's daughter.

Kerym sat directly across from Devana. The accommodations were so narrow that their knees brushed up against one another's. And every so often, the coach would go over a bump and Zeli's right knee would tap Kerym's left.

Oh. Shiny.

Then she remembered Yalisa's words and focused on squelching the reaction that any sort of contact with him created. It helped that Devana was complaining. Well, she was usually complaining, but the cramped, jittery coach made it all worse.

"Why couldn't I have taken one of Father's carriages?" she lamented. "Or even his autocar." While Laketown had its share of diesel contraptions, the Magister had one of the finest horseless carriages in the west. He used it very little as fuel was in short supply and merely possessing the thing was more impressive than riding in it.

"You don't think he would have noticed if one of those had gone mysteriously missing?" Kerym asked, wryly.

Devana pouted. "Yes, of course he would. But still, facing his anger has to be better than this." She stomped her foot lightly for emphasis and banged Kerym's leg.

If Devana had ever learned to ride a horse, she could have easily bribed a stable boy for one. It's not like her father counted his horses with any regularity. And if that was truly a concern, they could have hired horses and ridden to Eleven. But that would be far less safe. No, sadly, though it was the least comfortable way to go, the coach was best. The trip would be just over twenty-four hours including horse changes. Still, as the wheels hit a particularly deep rut in the road causing everyone to jump, Zeli wished she were somewhere else.

Until Kerym's leg hit hers again.

They had just cleared the gate in the wall that surrounded and protected Laketown. Zeli peered around the snoring passenger and out the window at the land beyond.

The city itself was large and teeming with people, but outside its walls another world existed. This one, called the Snarl, was a community of tents, tarps, lean-tos, and hastily constructed shacks haphazardly erected. Once green fields stretching from the wall to the mountain were now just dirt, with muddy paths of no discernible organization separating one structure from another.

Zeli had grown up in the Lake Cities so it had been a shock when, at seven, she'd been sent on her first trip through the Midcountry and had seen what the rest of Lagrimar was like. Whether Upper or Lower Faalagol was the finest city in the west remained a subject for debate—what couldn't be argued was that both were virtual paradises in comparison to the rest of the land.

Everything to the east was a barren expanse of yellow-brown dirt, coarse shrubbery, rocky outcroppings, desolation, and despair. As a girl she'd traveled in the belly of a wagon and had only seen the surroundings during brief stops for food and to change horses. The difference had overwhelmed her then—

she'd been both enthralled and horrified by the vast and endless desert. No lake glittering with clear, blue water. No trees blossoming as the blue-violet days brought life back to them. No soft, mossy grass underfoot. No colorful birds singing merrily. No vines of plump grapes scaling trellises.

No food at all. Very little water. Ration tokens for meager meals that rarely filled any belly. Gaunt, desperate faces with hollowed-out cheeks and eyes. Those faces looked up now at the carriage as it passed.

These people had made the trek from wherever it was they'd come from to the Lake Cities for a chance at entering the hallowed gates. Access to both cities was tightly controlled. It made sense, Zeli thought, since the entire country couldn't very well live here.

The Magister made it clear that only those with particular and necessary skills could enter Lower Faalagol, those who were needed. However, every so often, whether due to death, arrest, or some other misfortune, space would come available for additional residents. A lottery was held and a handful of people from outside were admitted entry.

Everyone else was left beyond the gates to get on as they saw fit. A community had sprung up over the years. She heard tales of the Snarl from other servants. Crime was well managed inside the city, but the Snarl was lawless, having no Ephor managing it and falling outside of the purview of the Magister.

Though every so often, when things got truly out of hand—when crime affected one of the favored or if disease swept through the shantytown—soldiers would be sent to raze the place, tear down structures, burn the semipermanent buildings, kill indiscriminately, and force everyone away.

Afterward, a handful of the army's Earthsingers would be

dispatched to replant the grass, leaving the field beautiful and serene for a time. Then within a few months, a few stragglers would return, set up shop, and the whole thing would start all over again.

Not that Zeli knew much about the Snarl personally. She'd rarely had cause to venture outside of the wall. The Magister didn't like for Devana to travel; on her actual visits to Watertown, they used the lake's ferry instead of going the long way around.

It was just as well, for the sight beyond the coach's windows was miserable and depressing. Soon enough, the rabble surrounding the roadway faded into just a few sparse tents here and there and then nothing but the bush. Zeli sat back, looking straight ahead at the scowling face of the well-dressed girl across from her.

The public coach now rumbled along the Great Highway—the length of intermittently paved road which stretched the width of Lagrimar. Their first stop would be Checkpoint Fifteen, the next town after Laketown. There the coach would water the horses and let the passengers stretch their legs for a brief few minutes before continuing on.

Zeli let the vibrations of the wheels lull her into an almost trancelike state. Unlike the person beside her, she found sleep difficult. She turned her attention to the placard affixed to the interior next to the window.

The printed card bore pictographs spelling out the rules of travel since, with no formal system of schooling for the masses, much of the population was illiterate. The first rule was about drinking. The picture showed a bottle of spirits crossed out, and next to it two figures sharing it. If you bring alcohol, best be prepared to share.

The next was an X over a cigarette. No smoking.

Another image advised against using other passengers as pillows. And the last one portrayed a figure diving from the carriage as the horses run away and then being broken on jagged rocks.

Zeli turned away feeling sick to her stomach.

The journey was quiet, and soon enough they pulled up to the gate blocking the road at Checkpoint Fifteen. The driver slowed and paid the toll, then they crossed the gate and stopped at the way station.

All the passengers hopped out for a stretch and it was clear that several more people were waiting for the coach. Zeli found the outhouse and relieved herself. When she returned, Devana was locked in an argument with the driver.

"I'm sorry, miss, but when the coach is full, servants must ride atop."

Zeli looked carefully at the new passengers. Payrollers judging by the bright colors of their tunics and the fancy embroidering. They stood, turning their noses up at Devana's rough clothing meant to conceal her identity.

The girl was fuming. Normally, one word of who her father was smoothed out any opposition, but if she started throwing his name around then he would find out where she was and what she was doing.

Devana gave the driver her most imperious glare. "I've paid the full fare for all those in my party. I don't see why any of *my* people have to move when—"

"It's all right," Zeli said quickly. No need to make a scene. "I'll sit up top."

"On the roof of this horrid deathtrap?" Devana shouted, pointing. The roof already held several travelers, obviously poor and world-weary. "Up there stricken by the elements like a common knob?"

Zeli held back a smile at Devana's affront. It was kindly meant, at least for her.

"I can go up," Kerym said amiably. "I don't mind."

The horror Zeli felt was mimicked on Devana's face.

"You will do no such thing. You are—" She cut herself off and pursed her lips. Then turned to the driver. "I will have you written up for this. You'll be sorry you crossed me."

The driver didn't look cowed at all. But Zeli had no doubt that once the adventure was over and Devana was back home and had access to her vast resources, this man would be out of a job.

"I'm sorry, Zeli-deni. It's barbaric." Devana shook her head.

"I'll be fine, I promise." Though she was not enthused about what awaited her.

She approached the coach, not quite sure how those people had gotten all the way up to the roof area, which didn't have seats at all. Just a flat surface and an assortment of bags. It seemed you had to find a place among them.

A few metal rungs had been bolted to the corner of the carriage. As she was determining how best to reach them, warm hands engulfed her waist. Kerym's scent filled her nostrils as he gave her a boost so she could reach the makeshift ladder.

She sputtered out a thanks and clambered ungracefully onto the roof. There she settled on the hard surface, wedging herself between what looked like two mail bags. Once she'd gotten situated, she looked up. Three men, two women, and one little girl shared the roof with her. She nodded at them and then the coach was on its way again.

The adults turned back to their conversation.

"I've heard they're taking folk over the mountains," the white-haired man said.

"I don't believe it," replied a younger man, whose sparse beard barely covered acne scars. "You can't believe every fool rumor that comes your way."

"No, I've heard it from three different people, all hailing from different towns," a bony woman said through the gaps of several missing teeth. "Keepers will take those willing to risk it. There are cracks in the Mantle they say."

Zeli shivered as a warm gust of wind whipped through her.

"Pshaw." The younger man waved his hand. "How can magic have cracks? Besides, it's only been a handful of years since the last war. Not time for another yet."

"You've seen the factories ramping up, haven't you? Soldiers passing through, headed west. War is coming. And if there's a way to get out before then, best take it," the white-haired man said. "The Keepers are the best chance we've got."

Zeli tried to tune them out. Talk of the Keepers of the Promise always made her uneasy. There was no greater win for a favored than in exposing a Keeper. Forget being the mistress of a powerful man; revealing that one of your neighbors was a hated rebel? You could be set for life.

The chill running through her sank to her bones. A memory pushed its way forward—her mother, hair askew, only half-braided, shouting a warning. *Zeli, run!* Soldiers kicking down their flimsy door. Dragging Mama and Papa away, arms and legs bound.

She hadn't been able to run, so she'd been taken as well.

Her parents had been dubbed traitors, outed as members of the Keepers of the Promise, and then executed. After agonizing weeks of uncertainty as to whether she'd share their fate, Zeli had been sold. Indentured to the Magister who'd wanted a girl of about his daughter's age to keep her company and serve her.

She didn't know exactly who had outed her parents. Who had reaped the benefits of the knowledge? What had they received? A better home? Bushels of food? Fine fabrics? Perhaps they were even payrollers now, elevated enough to receive a salaried position in the government.

She swallowed. The Keepers had never let a few deaths slow them down. If these folk on the coach were to be believed, they were now taking people through cracks in the Mantle? It was preposterous. And even if it wasn't, what would anyone do in the land of the Elsiran pigs? A race who had committed so many atrocities in the Breach Wars.

No, Zeli would much rather stay here in Lagrimar. Life wasn't so bad if you followed the rules. Even if the rules tended to shift and change often, you just had to keep up. The True Father made them that way for a reason. That's what Devana and the Magister said at least, and Zeli had no reason to disbelieve them. Her parents had been misguided, and look where it got them. She wouldn't make the same mistakes.

The coach rolled on and the adults pulled out their rations and began chewing. Strips of tough jerky served as their protein accompanied by dried fruit and nuts.

Zeli fished out her meal as well, pocket bread filled with beans and pieces of real chicken. A bit soggy, but of better quality than rations. As the others ate, the little girl simply hugged her knees to her chest and looked away.

She was scrawny and dirty. About the same age as Zeli had been when her parents were taken. How she'd even afforded a coach ticket was a mystery. Zeli knew what it was like to be scared and alone on a long journey. She split her sandwich into two, wrapping half in the thin paper and handing it to her.

The girl's eyes widened and she took the food, gulping it down almost in one bite. Her eyes lost a fraction of their haunted expression and she gave a small smile that missed her mouth entirely.

Zeli nodded. She had once been young and hungry and far from home. And while she vowed to never be so again, she knew there were no guarantees.

CHAPTER TWELVE

Do deeds long done really stay in the past?
A secret locked away may seem secured
But time will play its games and play them well
The ticking clock reveals that which endures
A hidden tale is venom in the vein
A leech may bring relief and ease the pain

—THE BOOK OF UNVEILING

Kyara wasn't enthused about handing over her courier's license to Darvyn when he asked. They weren't easy to come by, even for agents of the True Father.

She used the document for the same reason the Keepers wanted it: passing through the gates was hassle free, and the toll takers waved them through without inspection. Since she wore no uniform, no one would give her the travel privileges of the Golden Flames, so she had always made her own way.

But she couldn't keep the license from him and so begrudgingly gave it up. The upside was, it allowed the caravan of wagons to travel through the night. Though taking the highway after sunset was often an invitation for trouble, blessedly they encountered no one else on the road.

Now dawn lit the bleak landscape in a cheery glow. Kyara rode next to Darvyn in the driver's seat of the second wagon. He hadn't told her where they were taking the rescued children. She suspected she had Aggar to thank for that. There wasn't much she could do about the man's suspicions—they were well-founded, after all. But his questioning of the nabbers had yielded information on another location where a group of children was being housed. Kyara had been allowed to accompany them to find her supposed sister.

She cringed to think about the lie. Deceit of any kind rankled her. When she walked through a man's door, after their shock subsided and they figured out who she was, there was no prevarication. They knew they were going to die. It was a dirty business, but all was done in the light. She never took a man's life without first looking him in the eye.

She'd managed to leave all the nabbers alive when she'd freed the children, thanks only to the presence of a desert sidewinder coiled unnoticed in the corner. Killing the snake with the most precision should could manage in such a short time had sickened the nabbers. But if one of them had died, explaining his black eyes and gums to the Keepers would have been difficult.

She may never truly gain the rebels' trust, but at least they didn't mean her any harm. Her Song always surged when danger was near and it was calm now. Enough so that she dozed off once or twice during the journey, much to her surprise.

The wagons clattered into Checkpoint Eight just as the town was waking up for the day. Eight was a large, prosperous town. It benefitted from being close to the Crossroads, where the Great Highway diverged, one branch leading southwest to the Lake Cities and the other continuing due west to the Breach Valley.

A hub for travelers and trade, Eight was still nowhere near the size of Sayya, but it was the closest thing this part of the country had to a genuine city. Even the outer spiral homes were well maintained and attractive. Real glass graced far more windows than not, and the people making their way through the streets in the early morning looked healthy and not half-starved. None of them paid any mind to the convoy of wagons, but as the Keepers approached the town's market, the reason became apparent. Dozens of vehicles lined the square, carts and wagons pulled by horses or mules and even a few diesel-powered contraptions, all homemade.

The buildings surrounding the market square were mostly inns and boardinghouses, but the curved dome of an Avinid temple was visible at the end of the row. Kyara wondered how much of the town actually lived here and how many were merely passing through.

The two-way radio pack sitting between her and Darvyn on the bench crackled, broadcasting Aggar's staticky voice. "We'll resupply here. Stay alert."

Once they stopped, Darvyn hopped down and was immediately accosted by two teenagers, a boy and a girl, who offered to guard his wagon for two grams. Kyara craned her neck to see that the other wagon drivers were being similarly propositioned by street urchins. Aggar, driving the lead wagon, waved off the children with an angry motion, but Darvyn dropped a gram into the outstretched hand of the girl with a promise of more when he returned.

"The wagon is locked, and there is nothing worth stealing inside," he told them. "You won't get the other gram if you try to thieve it." The teens nodded vigorously, then backed into the shade of the adjacent building to begin their watch.

Kyara did a double take at the girl. She could have been Ahlini's twin. Dark eyes glittered from a face far too hardened for her years. But Ahlini had smiled every day, including the day she died. This girl would likely never develop laugh lines. She caught Kyara's stare and scowled before turning away.

"Do you think they'll try to break in?" Kyara asked Darvyn.

A smile played upon his lips. "Lizana is in the back with the children. If those two try anything, they'll meet quite a surprise. She has an odd sense of humor." He motioned for Kyara to walk with him as he headed toward the outer market stalls.

"What do you mean?"

"I've never seen anyone use their Song quite so creatively for retribution as Lizana. I still get a pain on my— Never mind." He dropped his head, embarrassed, but still smiling.

A pang of jealousy shot through Kyara as she imagined the end of his story. It was a totally irrational reaction, and she tried to shake it away. Lizana was a stunning warrior with a deep, throaty laugh that had helped put the children at ease last night. She was in her early thirties and now on Kyara's shortlist of Shadowfox candidates. That wasn't the jealousy talking; it was just good sense.

Though the stories had always rendered the Shadowfox as

male, *he* could just as easily be a *she* as no one actually knew the powerful Keeper's identity.

Farron and Darvyn had admitted to having their Songs, but the Shadowfox must be older than both of them. The rumors of his or her exploits had been rolling around since the Sixth Breach, the year Kyara was born. Darvyn would have been just a toddler and Farron not even a gleam in his mother's eye.

Back then, the stories were of miraculous mass healings of villages that had been suffering from the plague. Women in her cabal of the vast harem had entertained the children with tales of strange occurrences in towns in the west. Lightning storms that created artistic designs in the sky. Dozens of tornadoes dancing in time to drumbeats in the bush. The normally destructive forces of nature being tamed into spectacles of great beauty. Nothing like that had been seen for years, and many didn't believe they'd ever happened. But no one could deny the Shadowfox's more recent exploits. Overnight a patch of sandy soil, from which nothing could be coaxed to grow, would be transformed into a field full of wheat or barley, ready to harvest.

Enforcers regularly roamed the bush, searching for illegal farms to salt and burn. But another would spring up somewhere else a few days or weeks later. The Keepers—and the Shadowfox by extension—opposed the True Father's ration laws and made it their mission to feed the near-starving Lagrimari people. That, plus their charge to save children from nabbing and tribute, caused another pang to go through Kyara. This one of regret. Yes, the Keepers were doing good for the people, more good than Kyara had ever done, but they were still delusional. They'd been fighting this fight for hundreds of years, and the True Father was no closer to losing power. In fact, he was very close to destroying the most powerful symbol of rebellion in Lagrimar.

The fact that she would be the one to bring down the mighty Shadowfox left her cold.

She rubbed the front of her tunic, skating over the wound that lay there. The bandages protected it from the fabric of her clothing. The wound did not bleed or fester, but it was a raw reminder of the power that controlled her. What could she do to fight against it? Her earlier thoughts of redemption were blasted away by a swift kick from reality. She would always be a monster, and capturing the Shadowfox would only cement that fact.

She and Darvyn met the other Keepers who gathered at the side of a row of vendors. Aggar stood tall, regarding the scene from beneath his furrowed brow. She suspected he wasn't as old as he appeared; the lines on his face were from frowning too much. Though he was in charge, his bitter reaction to being accused of having a Song had crossed him off her list of Shadowfox candidates.

The largest man, Zango, was still a possibility, but she had no idea if he still sang. Three other men and one woman completed the party. All were old enough, but flat-out asking them all if they had their Songs would be incredibly rude and raise even more suspicion.

Aggar shot a withering look in her direction before turning away. He spoke commands to the gathered Keepers too softly for her to hear and then they all split up. Again, she was left with Darvyn.

"Am I allowed to know what we're here to get?" she asked.

Darvyn's grin had her fighting to tear her gaze away from his lips once again. "My assignment is shoes. The children will need them."

Her next question died on her lips as she spotted a man walking through the market a few dozen paces ahead. Her Song surged, causing her to stumble to keep it leashed. Darvyn reached out to steady her. Even the tingle of his touch on her hand was not enough to warm her blood this time.

The man wore an orange tunic that fell to his knees with orange trousers underneath. The round cap perched on his head marked his profession as a physician. Unusual eyes of mossy green scanned the street in front of him as he approached. The urge to hide was strong within her, but she couldn't have moved her limbs if she tried. Her Song protested, thrashing, demanding release. She clamped down on it hard, afraid, for the first time in a decade, of truly losing control.

"Kyara, what's wrong?" she heard Darvyn ask, probably not for the first time.

Somehow her feet unlocked, and she turned toward him, keeping the physician in her peripheral vision. He had stopped at a stall and stood talking with the merchant. Her mouth opened and closed but no sound came out.

She focused on the feeling of Darvyn's hand in hers as he led her to a space between the market stalls where she could sit down on a discarded crate.

"I'll get you some water," he said and jogged away.

The physician's face was forever etched into her mind. She would never forget him or what he had done, even though she had not been able to prove it and no one had believed her.

Darvyn returned with a full canteen. She drank down the water quickly. He regarded her with concerned eyes while she struggled to get her breathing back under control.

"I'm sorry . . . I thought I saw someone." She shook her head, unable to think of what to say.

"Where? Who?" Darvyn's gaze roamed the area. His body was tense, as if ready to fight.

"The man at the cutler's stall. The physician," she said, keeping her gaze on Darvyn, unwilling to turn her head to see if the man in question was still within eyesight. "Though I'm not even sure if it was him, it's been a very long time. Sorry if I scared you." Her fear had been replaced by embarrassment at her reaction. It's not as if the physician could kill her right here in the middle of the market, could he? If he tried anything, she could defend herself. She had been given no orders to the contrary. In such a crowd, using her Song would be out of the question but she was still a Golden Flame and had trained in many forms of combat.

She chanced a glance to the vendor diagonally across from her. The merchant handed over a handful of grams to the physician, who pocketed them and walked away whistling, disappearing into the growing crowd.

Kyara sagged with relief. "We have shoes to purchase, right?" She tried to inject brightness into her tone, but by Darvyn's expression she wasn't doing a good job.

"What makes this physician so bad?"

Her mind raced to come up with a story, but in the end, the truth could do no harm. And she owed it to Nerys not to sully her memory with lies. "When I was a girl, I—I met a woman who was very kind to me." A weak smile creased her face as Kyara recalled. "The entire town thought she was crazy. She lived at the very edge of the spiral and often shouted nonsense in the streets about men made of light, but . . . when I needed help, she was there for me."

She took a deep breath as old pain squeezed her chest. "She was crippled from an old injury and walking was very painful. One day the physician came to town." Kyara froze at the memory of his bright-green eyes peering down at her. The only soul she'd ever encountered with eyes of that color had been

Ydaris. But the physician's smile had been kind, not cruel like the Cantor's.

"He had a way about him. A talent for making everyone in town fall under his spell. He was charming, mesmerizing. This woman, my friend, accepted his offer of aid gratefully. But I wasn't so sure—I didn't trust him." In fact, her Song had surged warning of danger once he began his "healing."

"He had a little wooden box carved with strange symbols I'd never seen before. Inside the box lay a thin glass tube and a long needle with a plunger in the back. The box also held a vial of amber liquid that he drew into the tube."

That's when Kyara's Song had begun buzzing in her chest. By then she had learned what it meant and ran out of the little cottage into the cold night to hover in the doorway. She'd wanted to be able to run off into the bush quickly in case she lost control.

"He injected the liquid into her body and the stuff did what he said. She walked pain-free almost immediately." Kyara's eyes focused; she looked up at Darvyn. "Though within a week, she was vomiting black bile and shivering with the chills."

"Plague?" he asked, voice pitched with alarm.

Kyara nodded. "Not just her. Everyone the physician visited and injected with his device was struck down. They died in days."

Despite the heat of the day, a chill ran through her, pebbling the skin on her arms. Darvyn stood straight, looking into the crowded marketplace, searching for the physician.

"He told us him name was Raal. He spoke like no one I'd ever met, with a strange way of phrasing his words. Even afterward, after he was gone and so many were dead, no one in the town believed he'd caused the plague. It's like he'd hypnotized everyone."

"Everyone but you." Darvyn's words snapped Kyara back to the present.

"Like I said, I'm not even sure it was him." She took a deep breath to calm her still-racing heart. "We had better get what's needed. I'm sure Aggar-*mideni* will want to be on his way again."

Darvyn smiled a fraction at her teasing use of the honorific, which perfectly matched Aggar's sense of self-aggrandizement. But he still looked around uneasily. "I'll go. Wait for me here. I'll see if I can find him again."

Raal had disappeared into the crowd and she had no desire to run into him. "All right, but don't—" She cleared her throat and looked away. "If it's him, he's very dangerous." She told herself that Darvyn's well-being was not her concern, but the idea of him coming to harm made her breath catch.

"I'll be careful," he said, a corner of his mouth raised in a grim half-smile. "You'll stay here and not go wandering?"

She nodded solemnly. "I promise."

Darvyn gave her an assessing look before turning and walking away.

Kyara dropped her head into her hands. She knew how little her promises were worth. The wound on her chest had stolen her will, but that was not why the vow she'd made to Nerys on her deathbed had gone unfilled. But that was long ago and there was nothing to be done about it now.

She counted to one hundred before standing and peering over at the stall the physician had vacated. Kyara may have broken her promise to a dead woman—but perhaps she could bring her some justice.

She crossed the row to approach the merchant. Technically she wasn't wandering, it was just a dozen paces or so from where she'd been sitting.

The cutler's table had finely crafted knives of all sizes on display. She examined the arrangement, and although she loved a good blade, the exhibit reminded her too much of the bench in the Cantor's library. Swallowing, she looked up to find a pair of hard eyes glittering at her from within a craggy face.

"Looking for something?" The vendor's voice was gruff. He crossed his arms in front of him as if annoyed. A thick scar encircled his neck and his hands were covered in tinier scars, each one sparkling in the light. A former miner, then. The miners kept their Songs during their service so they could use Earthsong to dig for the precious jewels lining the eastern mountains. They were chained while working and collared during downtime, and they were never able to get the glittery dust completely out of their skin—or lungs—no matter how long it had been. The merchant was old and must have survived three rounds of service in order to be released. That was quite a feat, and Kyara's heart softened a bit, forgiving his caustic attitude.

"The man who was just here. What did he sell?"

He raised an eyebrow before surveying the table and picking up a well-worn leather sheath. The knife was half the length of her forearm with a leather-wrapped handle. The vendor's twinkling hands pulled it from the sheath revealing a blade of white bone, with strange characters engraved into it. It was primitive but wicked looking, and the longer she stared at it, the more she wanted to run away.

"What kind of bone?" she whispered.

"Eh? What was that?"

She cleared her throat. "What kind of bone is it?" she asked louder.

The vendor scratched his head. "I didn't ask. Not sure I wanted to know. Though he was a nice fella, that one."

She picked up the knife and quieted the quivering of her Song. It warned her of danger, but she already knew.

The knife in her hands was familiar. Ydaris used one just like it in her blood spells, but hers bore different symbols. Kyara wasn't certain if it was her Song or some other inner knowledge that informed her, but she felt strongly that both knives were made from human bone.

"You interested?" the vendor asked, his tone skeptical.

She dropped the blade back onto the cutler's table, her fingers stinging from the contact.

"No," she said around the growing tightness in her throat and headed back across the way to wait for Darvyn.

She cursed herself for the fear spiking through her when she'd seen Raal. She was not that eleven-year-old girl any longer. She was the Poison Flame, and the next time she saw the physician, she would kill him.

CHAPTER THIRTEEN

A spirit made a body of red clay
With water flowing through to give it life
And for companionship a mate of stone
The blood a sacrifice to wed a wife
The Father and the Mother so were made
From their embrace, emerged Folk of the cave

—THE BOOK OF UNVEILING

Darvyn returned from the bootsmith carrying a sack filled with the smallest shoes he could find. Many were still too large for the children. The toes would need to be stuffed with fabric or straw, but at least they would have proper shoes on their feet when they crossed the mountain into Elsira. For many, it would be their first pair.

He spotted Kyara, sitting where he'd left her, and the coiling tension eased within him. He shouldn't have left her alone. Not just because Aggar would be furious if he found out, but because Darvyn had seen her fear. His Song wasn't required to sense her breath shortening or the anxiety invading her body. The desire to hold her, to pull her into his arms and offer comfort had been strong. He'd combatted it by searching for the physician—his orange tunic and distinctive hat should have made him stand out even in the crowd, but the man had disappeared.

He'd tried scanning the marketplace for threats as well, but nothing was amiss. There were, of course, the cheaters, the pick-pockets, thieves, and the like, their intent to do wrong almost tangible to his Song. Once upon a time he would have tried to catch them all and restore the victims' hard-earned money or possessions, but he had learned long ago both the impracticality and the danger of trying to help everyone.

Yet, if he could have located the man who'd struck such dread into Kyara's heart . . . He shook himself and forced his clenched fists to release.

When he reached her, she looked up, giving him a weak smile. He held his hand out, and she took it, gripping his fingers lightly as she stood. A riot of sensation cascaded over him from that one brief point of contact. She let go of him quickly, looking down as if embarrassed and focusing on brushing off the seat of her trousers.

She was still on edge, but much more of her confidence shone through now. Her eyes finally met his, and she gave a brief nod to indicate she was all right. He took a step back, flexing the hand she'd touched.

Farron ran up, out of breath, the portable radiotelegraph they'd liberated from an army supply truck slung across his body.

"You've got a message," he said, holding up a piece of paper with his scrawled writing on it.

"For me? Have you decoded it?"

Farron shook his head and handed over the message, exchanging it for the bag of shoes and headed back toward the wagons.

Darvyn studied the writing, decoding it in his head. It used a simple cipher, reserved for urgent, nonclassified messages. As he read, a pressure grew around him, making it feel like the air was constricting him.

"What's happened?" Kyara asked, squinting at the paper.

He crumpled the note and began walking toward the waiting wagons. She followed close behind. When they reached the one he'd been driving, he handed her up to the driver's seat.

"Wait for me here. I need to find Aggar."

She looked at him curiously, then nodded. Her gaze slid away, back to the busy market.

Aggar wasn't back yet, so Darvyn paced in front of the lead wagon. Finally, the man appeared with a bulging sack over his shoulder. Darvyn rushed up to him without preamble.

"Asla relayed a message from the school. The well's gone dry. They need—" He stopped short, noticing one of the street children hovering. The little girl headed toward the market, but Darvyn lowered his voice. "They need the Shadowfox to go there and rework his spell."

A flash of annoyance crossed Aggar's face, though it took years of knowing the man to distinguish it from his normal expression. "Asla will have to set some of those children of hers to digging."

Darvyn's own annoyance flared. Why did everything have to be a fight with him? "There are eighty-seven children there, plus the teachers. And the water in that part of the land is deep, too deep for them to dig for."

Aggar muttered under his breath, something about orphans and urchins. Darvyn was close to losing his temper. "You helped save many of those children from having their Songs stripped away, from being sent to mine or farm or breed for the rest of their lives. They are the future of Lagrimar, and they need help."

"We saved them from the tribute. You're telling me that with all those Earthsingers, not one of them can find water in the desert?"

"They're still being trained and the teachers aren't strong enough. Asla can teach them to pull a trickle of water from the plants, but that won't last very long."

The school was the largest Keeper compound and their greatest success. Darvyn had done much of the construction himself, singing the foundation and walls into place. He visited as often as he could, sometimes delivering a party of rescued children, sometimes to satisfy his curiosity and bear witness to the joys of childhood he'd never experienced.

Creating the well had not been easy, and if it had truly gone dry, then a new one may be needed. There was only one person capable of a spell that strong and Aggar knew it.

Aggar shook his head. "The elders would never allow it. With all the plans afoot, you're needed elsewhere. Hanko would have my hide if I let you go running around the bush following whatever fancy has caught your attention. Besides, how would you even get there?"

The school was well hidden, far enough out in the bush to never be discovered accidentally. And in four days' time, Jack was expecting to meet him at the army base to remove the disguise spell and help him get home. The trip to the school would take two days on horseback but far less if Darvyn had a motorized vehicle. If he could get his hands on a diesel contraption, he could make sure the children had water and be back in time to lead Jack home.

"I'll think of a way to get there. This is too important to ignore."

Aggar crossed his arms. "No. We'll find another way to help the school. You're not going. That's an order." He stomped off, leaving Darvyn shaking with anger.

The question of how to be in two places at once occupied Darvyn's thoughts as the caravan got back on the road. They were headed west to another safe house to drop off the rescued children. Some would be reunited with their families, but most would be headed even farther west, to Elsira, the safest option for them.

At the Crossroads, he might be able to acquire a diesel contraption capable of getting him to the school and back in time. He would have to defy Aggar to do it, but the man was simply too stubborn for his own good. And after the school and Jack were taken care of, he would head to Checkpoint Seventeen. Not only could he follow up on the lead regarding his mother, but that was where Kyara was headed as well.

Not that such a thing should influence his actions in any way.

They'd been traveling only a quarter of an hour when Kyara stiffened beside him and swung her head around, trying in vain to see behind them. Darvyn shook off his brooding, awakened his senses, and cursed aloud.

"Bush wranglers!" he cried out, tossing the reins to Kyara so he could pull the rifle from below his seat and check his pockets for extra ammunition.

The back door of the wagon in front of him opened, and Navar climbed out, balancing on the foot rack before closing the door. Darvyn couldn't see inside the darkened interior, but felt the children's fear. His warning gave the Keepers notice of about two minutes before a cloud of dust from the northeast approached the wagons from behind.

In broad daylight, a heist such as this one was gutsy but not entirely unexpected. Only the larger gangs would attempt to hold up four wagons at once. Darvyn sensed twenty men approaching—this was the largest group of bush wranglers he'd ever encountered. Many were on horseback, but nearly half of them approached much faster. The roar of engines pierced the air along with war whoops shouted by the thieves.

He glanced at Kyara. Her gaze was on the horses she now controlled. Her expression was pinched, more annoyed than frightened. She must encounter bands such as these all the time as a courier.

Sucking in a deep breath, he filled himself with Earthsong, allowing it to engulf his senses and take over his body. He almost never gave himself to the power so completely. He'd learned very early that strength was nothing without control. He'd always practiced excessive restraint, but the presence of so many bandits left him little choice but to gorge himself on the source energy.

The heartbeats of those around him pounded in his veins, his Song raging inside him. The distance between the thieves and the wagons was shrinking by the second.

Through the glut of Earthsong, he felt the energy of every living thing for kilometers. From the insects burrowing beneath the ground to the birds overhead. Every man and woman, every bush, every root. The whisper of the gentle breeze was a cyclone against his skin. He struggled to not be taken under by the myriad forces crashing into him. Instead, he sought to bend them to his will.

A bolt of lightning shot down from the clear, blue sky. Smoke rose from the strike location but didn't catch fire. Had that been him or one of the other Keepers? He tried to pull back from the deluge rushing through him but could not. It begged him to let go, to let it take over, but he knew better.

Discerning the positions of the bandits on horseback, he latched onto the horses. Their hooves ate up the ground beneath them. He didn't want to hurt the animals, just the men riding them. A nest of snakes nearby caught his attention. He urged them forward, propelling them to charge the approaching horses en masse. Animal suggestion was simple when it involved an action the animal was likely to take on its own. Pushing the snakes was no hardship.

Frightened whinnies from the horses filled the air as the ground before them became overrun with snakes. Darvyn pushed the reptiles to act like herding dogs, guiding the horses away, back into the bush. The horses complied, even as their riders tried desperately to beat them back toward the highway. Agitated by both their riders and the reptiles, the horses bucked sharply, throwing their riders off and leaving them amid the writhing horde.

Darvyn turned his attention to the other bush wranglers riding up alongside the caravan. Eight diesel crawlers roared, their engines deafening. Unlike most motorized contraptions found in the Midcountry, these crawlers weren't cobbled together from discarded parts. They were uniform and well made, likely imported straight from Yaly by the government. The bandits must have stolen them, but how could they have taken so many? And how was it possible they hadn't been caught yet?

Each man straddled a crawler, hunched low over the handlebars as the single caterpillar-like moving track churned the dirt of the road. And though they each dressed the part in leather riding clothes that conformed to their bodies, the men all appeared to be clean-shaven with closely cropped hair. Not the usual, ragged style of a bush wrangler.

A crawler approached Aggar's horses at the front of the caravan and was promptly enveloped in a cloud of dust. Navar, hanging on to the back of the wagon with an iron grip, was focused intently in Aggar's direction. His spell, then.

Darvyn glanced over his shoulder to find Lizana and Farron in the wagon behind him, pelting the thieves with rocks and mud and throwing small obstacles onto the highway. They held hands to link their Songs and combine their strength.

He didn't want to do anything that would cause the crawlers to lose control and crash into the wagons, injuring the children, but the thieves cut through the pesky obstacles created by the other Singers easily.

A gunshot rang out, from where he couldn't tell. Answering shots fired from in front of and behind him. Darvyn calmed the frightened horses with his Song, then stood in the driver's seat, his rifle loose in his hands, ready to use if necessary. A bandit pulled up beside him and lifted a shiny, new-looking pistol. Darvyn raised a wall of solid dirt, waist-high, directly in front of the crawler. The vehicle slammed into it, tossing the rider over the handlebars. Another wall of dirt on the side between the crawler and the wagon ensured the now-driverless vehicle veered off away from them, crossing the road and careening to the ground on the other side.

"Halt!" Darvyn screamed. All four wagon drivers slowed their horses, and Darvyn released another spell. The tightly packed dirt of the unpaved road rippled beneath them. He marked the position of the remaining crawlers and opened sinkholes under each one of them. The bandits' shrieks filled the air as they found themselves trapped in three-meter-deep holes in the ground where the road had been a moment before.

The wagons rumbled to a stop at the side of the road. Darvyn remained seated as the armed Keepers approached the sinkholes and peered down into them. One by one, Darvyn put the bandits to sleep, his body sagging from the effort of the past few minutes.

He surveyed the scene. None of the Keepers had been hurt. A scan of the wagons showed that the children were all uninjured, as well. He took a deep breath and sat back heavily, scrubbing a hand over his face.

"Well, that was exciting," he said, expecting a retort from Kyara, but she was strangely quiet beside him. He turned to her, a teasing question ready on his lips that died as he took in the sight before him. Blood seeped through her tunic where a bullet had pierced her stomach. Her lips curved in a sad smile before she collapsed into his arms.

CHAPTER FOURTEEN

That life must end in death is truth assured
As certain as the night shatters the morn
Birth and demise grace every living thing
But twixt these foes lies power lesser known
For no celestial force ever employed
Approximates the inscrutable Void

—THE BOOK OF UNVEILING

Zeli's body felt like a bag of marbles. She'd been thrown, jostled, and jerked to the point where everything hurt. Bones and muscles she hadn't known she'd had were achy and sore. Her shared straw bed at the estate had never been more welcome, and she whispered words of gratitude for everything she had awaiting her at home. When this trip was over, she'd try her best to never take her meager, but ever so shiny, accommodations for granted again.

Finally, as the sun cleared the horizon and dawn's light deepened into morning, the Checkpoint Eleven toll gate loomed ahead, marking the end of their journey. The town was visible over a rise in the earth.

Midcountry architecture consisted mostly of flat-roofed, boxy, mud-brick buildings, virtually all the color of sand. All except for the Avinid temple with its gleaming blue-tiled, domed roof glinting in the morning light.

Eleven was the home of the sect known as the Avinids, and the temple here was the first one ever built. What little Zeli knew of the group had come from Devana. Avinids were the only organization that could be called a religion in Lagrimar. Other small cults and sects had risen up over the years only to be wiped out by the True Father, but the king apparently had no problem with those who worshipped the Void. And apparently Avinids did not consider themselves to be a religion, merely a philosophy.

The story went that one night, a young, starving woman had wandered into the bush to die and instead had a vision of a vast, infinite emptiness. Zeli had no idea what a vision of emptiness would look like, but the woman, the first ul-Waga or daughter of the Void, had experienced an epiphany. Namely, that this earthly existence was merely a staging area and that man's real destiny lay in the space between something and nothing. Between life and death. In the Void.

She returned from the bush changed and began telling others of her insights. Early on, there were conflicts between believers and the True Father, but somehow the first ul-Waga convinced the immortal ruler that members of her budding organization were not disloyal to him. They could revere him as king while still worshipping the Void. Since this apparently made sense to the True Father, he never again bothered them.

And while Zeli reckoned there were probably still secret meetings of other sects and nascent religions, since people were far too stubborn to allow a little thing as annihilation to turn them off of doing what they wanted, the Avinids were the only ones who professed their beliefs out in the open.

The coach stopped at Checkpoint Eleven's depot, allowing the weary travelers to disembark. Only Zeli, Devana, and Kerym were getting off here, which was surprising considering it was obvious that Eleven had swelled far past its normal population.

Dozens of Avinids in their brightly dyed tunics, adhering to no pattern or style currently in fashion, moved through the street, shopping in the open-air market or gathered in small groups. A steady stream were headed down the spiraling road leading out of town.

Zeli stretched her throbbing legs before retrieving her and Devana's bags. As the carriage rolled away, she honestly hoped that when this day was over they would walk back home and not be forced to ride it again.

After a quick stop for hand pies in the market, the three of them joined the growing throng of people headed into the bush.

The pleasant morning air quickly burned away, leaving an oppressive heat. Devana's bag was an anvil on her shoulder. They were headed back home this evening; why in the Father's name had she packed so much? But even the desert temperatures didn't sour Zeli's love of being outside. She took a moment to enjoy the intensity of the sun on her face as she walked.

Also, the buzzing charge from the people around them was

energizing. It was almost as if the anticipation of the growing crowd restored her, dissolving her aches.

They walked for about two kilometers. Miraculously, instead of complaining, Devana chattered on about how exciting this was and what she hoped the guru would say.

The location for the revival was an amphitheater made out of a crater that had somehow formed in the land. It didn't seem entirely natural, though Zeli couldn't fathom how such a thing could have been dug—here in the middle of the bush. The ground sloped down to a large, flat rock on which a solemn figure sat, cross-legged, wearing the brightest clothing she'd ever seen.

Avinids had access to dyes that no other Lagrimari used or would ever want to, but the vibrant shades of orange, blue, green, and yellow on the guru's long tunic made the others pale in comparison.

From this distance, all she could see of the guru were the stripes of bushy, white hair on his cheeks—mutton chops, but no mustache—and the knit cap, pure white, which covered his head.

A crowd of mostly Avinids peppered with other, more dully dressed people, sat on blankets and cushions on the ground of the amphitheater. Devana announced that she wanted to sit near the front, and so they pushed and prodded their way through those gathered.

At the outer edges of the crater, vendors had set up their wares. The scent of sizzling meat and frying dough wafted down from portable oil stoves.

They found a good spot in what would be the fourth row, had the crowd been more organized. Zeli lay out the blanket she'd packed and they all sat, with her just behind Devana and Kerym.

All around them people streamed in and found seats. The Avinids generally maintained a solemn demeanor in opposition with their bright clothing. Others in the crowd chattered softly, curiosity flowing from them.

At the gentle strumming of a *luda*, a hush fell over the audience. At first, Zeli didn't see the musician, but a group of older Avinids appeared from behind the rock on which the guru sat. One played the *luda*, two others raised wooden flutes to their lips, a fourth kept the beat with finger cymbals.

They played a plaintive tune that seemed to drug the crowd. Zeli felt her limbs loosen, her attention focus, and her mind clear. Then the guru Waga-nedri began to sing.

His voice was just as calming as the odd tune. Neither high nor deep, it existed in a sort of space between. She couldn't quite categorize it. Soothing and haunting, it sent a chill up her spine even as it wrapped her in comfort like a warm hug.

The song had no words, just melodic vocalizations. And his singing made the heat of the day disappear, flowing a breeze over her skin. She nearly fell into a trance as if the wordless sounds were a lullaby.

Then the music stopped, and the crowd leaned forward as one, waiting for the guru to begin to speak.

"Children of the Void. It is well that you are here, as much as anything in this world of lies can be well. You have come to seek truth, but you have come in vain."

A ripple of unease went through the non-Avinids in attendance.

"I have no truth to share with you, for there is no such thing. These words we speak: truth, lies, good, evil, they are merely sounds on the breath." The acoustics of the amphitheater gave his words a slight echo.

He exhaled sharply. "Breath." He hummed. "Sound. That is all communication is. And yet we assign meaning to sounds and breath and think ourselves secure in this supposed knowledge."

He looked around the gathered throng. This close, Zeli could see that he was quite a bit older than she'd thought. His eyes had gone rheumy and clouded. His voice rose, punctuating each word. "There is no knowledge but the Void."

Devana nodded in agreement as did many in the crowd.

"You want meaning? Certainty? Purpose?" He spat the words out with disgust. "You search for diamonds in the mouths of swine. They are not to be found." Indignation colored his voice. "There is only one way—the way of the Void."

This statement was met by vigorous applause. Zeli looked around, dumbfounded. Devana's eyes were alight, an expression of serenity on her face. When Kerym turned to look at his fiancée, Zeli was delighted to note his expression mirrored hers—confusion.

The guru continued: "Life and death, the Living World and the World After are what most concern themselves with. But those with true understanding see the fruitlessness of worldly matters. The Void is all it needs to be, and in the Void, we truly are." He raised his arms above his head in a V shape. The Avinids in the crowd did the same.

Soon the non-Avinids followed suit. Zeli looked around and also raised her arms, receiving a sharp but wry look from Kerym, who finally did so as well.

The musicians, standing at the edge of the stage began playing again, an almost identical song to the first one, complete with the guru's chanting, or whatever it was.

Zeli's arms grew tired. She amused herself by tilting them forward, seeing how close she could come to brushing Kerym's arm with her fingertips without actually touching him. The song lasted several lifetimes, but as the last notes of the *luda* dissipated, everyone finally dropped their arms.

A drum had materialized in the guru's lap and he began softly tapping on it while one of the flute players began a strange little dance. Zeli blinked, wondering what exactly she'd gotten herself into. Suddenly Devana turned around. With a plastered smile, Zeli nodded encouragingly at her mistress. Devana seemed beside herself with joy. She held up her canteen and shook it slightly, indicating that it was empty.

Zeli grabbed it and surged to her feet, eager for a task that would save her from any more muscle burning postures. It took some time to maneuver through the large crowd to the edge where the vendors were. She only hoped she could find her way back again.

She wasn't sure if there would be a well this far in the bush, but quickly enough she found a woman with large barrels of water strapped to a mule cart and a small line of people queuing before it.

"How much?" Zeli inquired when she made it to the front.

"Twenty grams to fill your canteen," the woman said, showing off blackened teeth. Zeli hissed, that was highway robbery, but what else could she do?

Nearby vendors were doing a brisk business selling everything from food, to garishly dyed fabric, to empty, clay jars claiming to be samples of the Void. She snorted at that. Who would spend money on such foolishness? But just then a middle-aged woman walked up and bought a small jar.

Zeli shook her head and stoppered her full canteen. A group of young men stood off to the side smoking a sweet-smelling shuroot, passing it back and forth. The flavored tobacco lent a tangy scent to the air. When she passed them by, they began whispering.

She walked along the edge of the crater, trying to recall where she'd exited and what would be the best path back. As she scanned the area, she noticed the young men following her.

One of them, a dimpled boy of about her age, smiled. Zeli froze, flustered. Boys almost never noticed her since she was usually shadowed by Devana's beauty, or busy carrying out some errand, covered in dust or sweat. Truth be told, she was sweaty and dusty right now, but the dimpled boy eyed her with keen interest.

He was handsome, with a lean face and bright eyes. A red gem sparkled in his pierced ear. She smiled back then turned around, suddenly embarrassed. Flattered though she was, she had to get back. Devana was thirsty, and Zeli had no idea what to do beyond smiling.

She headed toward a gap in the crowd and stepped back onto the sloping ground of the crater. The guru was speaking again and everyone's attention was rapt. She excused herself as she picked her way through. A strange sensation prickled her skin and she looked over her shoulder to find the boy following her, his three friends at his heels.

It wasn't very often that she allowed herself to miss her lost Song, but now was one of those times. As a child she'd been especially good at sensing the emotions of those around her. Filtering through the energy that the disruption in their feelings created had been as easy as breathing. Now she was left to wonder whether this boy was so taken with her that he was following her to meet her, or was something else happening?

An icy foreboding snaked through her blood, and she

quickened her pace. The drone of the guru's voice was accompanied by the quickening of her heart.

She stepped around groups sitting on blankets and over outstretched legs. When she looked behind her, the boys were closer. The lead one's dimpled smile was still in place, but now that he was so near, she recognized the hardness of his eyes. Fear shortened her breath.

A cluster of closely grouped Avinids stalled her forward motion. She couldn't very well step on them, though part of her wanted to. As she stumbled, trying to find a way around them, a hand reached out to grab her ankle.

Zeli gasped as she was pulled down, landing roughly on her hands and knees. She opened her mouth to scream when a large palm covered it, muffling her sound. In an instant, the palm was replaced by a cloth gag and a hood was dropped over her head.

As her hands and feet were tied, she thrashed and fought. They were in the middle of a crowd, was no one paying attention? Heat and heavy cloth enveloped her as she was stuffed into some kind of sack. Her body left the ground, being carried somewhere. Out of the crowd and then what?

She should have known better. A normal, honest Midcountry boy would have no need of pierced ears or gem earrings. Such jewelry and flash belonged to the Sayyan payrollers; even the elite of the Lake Cities didn't favor that type of showy display. But the criminal gangs of bush wranglers and nabbers who roamed the Great Highway were said to.

Zeli continued to kick and fight until a punch landed in her midsection, stealing her breath. Then she quieted, unsure of what to do, crying silent tears in her dark prison.

CHAPTER FIFTEEN

The pulse leaps with the beating of the drums
A roar which thunders, seeps under the skin
The chanting of the Folk thrums through the veins
With force that flowed forth 'fore the world began
A power more sublime there never was
Than that provided to us from the blood
—THE BOOK OF UNVEILING

Darvyn cradled Kyara's limp form against him, straining to sense her injury. Without knowing the details he could not heal it, and her shield still kept him out. It couldn't possibly be as strong as all that, especially now that she had lost consciousness. He wanted to trust that her own Song would heal her, but without being able to sense anything, how could he take that chance?

He laid her flat on the bench of the wagon and lifted the

bottom of her tunic to inspect the damage. Blood gushed from the hole in her abdomen. The bullet had gone clean through, having hit her low enough to tear through her intestines, poisoning her from the inside. There was no sign of her body starting the healing process, and he could do nothing to help her.

Old scars across her torso caught his eye. One sleeve of her tunic had ridden up, uncovering more. He pushed it up to her elbow, revealing an assortment of lacerations, both old and more recent. Her other arm was the same. Dozens of cuts had punctured her flesh over the years. She could not still have her Song and retain this kind of damage. A particularly deep wound, healed by Earthsong, may scar, depending on the Singer's talent, but Kyara's cuts looked shallow. They would have been easy to repair. Who had done this to her and why? And if she had no Song, how could she shield at all?

Since Darvyn could not reverse the damage from the bullet and knit her torn flesh as he normally would, he tried flooding her body with Earthsong. Life energy always sought life and would work to enhance her body's natural healing factor. It was a far slower process, one he'd never really used before. An injury as grave as hers would require a steady stream of energy, if his plan even worked at all. He wasn't certain it would, but he routed more of the energy toward her until he felt something catch and take hold. His Song was the conduit through which Earthsong flowed and her body was not rejecting it outright; however, he would have to stay with her for hours in order to keep her from dying.

He whipped his tunic over his head and ripped it into strips to staunch the steady flow of blood gushing from her midsection. Footsteps rushed over, but he did not look up until the bandages were secure.

Farron sucked in a breath. "Kyara was shot? Why isn't she healing?"

"I don't think she has a Song. And I don't know what's shielding her, but it's also blocking me from healing her."

He finally looked over to Farron, wincing at the shock and disbelief etched on his face. Darvyn had seen his fair share of death. He had never been able to save everyone—often not even a fraction of those he'd wanted to. But it was not for lack of trying. He had exhausted his Song, drained himself dry over and over, requiring hours of rest before his power returned. But he had never hesitated to sacrifice a piece of himself to save a life. He would do no less for Kyara.

He explained his spell to Farron, how he was forcing life energy into her dying body. The teen remained quiet, his dark eyes watching Kyara's gentle breaths. Darvyn kept pressure on her wound, desperate for her to stop bleeding.

The noise of an engine made him glance back. The other Singers had filled in the sinkholes with dirt. Lizana and Zango pushed the diesel crawlers to the side of the road where the captured bush wranglers had been tied up.

"What's Aggar going to do with them?" Darvyn asked.

Farron scratched his head. "Leave them here. We need to get to the meeting place and hand off the children. We're going radio silent. He said something about these wranglers isn't right."

"Yes, I noticed. They're clean-shaven with all new gear. It's like they're only playing at being bush wranglers. I think they might be payrollers."

Farron frowned at the men again sitting in a line on the ground. "Why would a payroller pretend to be a bush wrangler?"

Darvyn shrugged. "Maybe it's some new scare tactic? Some new way to drive fear into the population?"

He extended his weary senses to the men, feeling out their dispositions. Resignation and satisfaction were the prominent emotions radiating from them. Fatigue was setting in, but their sentiments made no sense. It was as though they'd expected to be caught.

"Either way we don't have the time or manpower to interrogate them further," Farron said. "Aggar wants us back on our way in ten minutes." He tilted his head and frowned at Kyara. "Will she be all right?"

Another crawler rumbled to life as one of the Keepers revved the engine. With one of those, he could definitely make it to the school with plenty of time to fix the well and come back for Jack. But if he left Kyara, she would certainly die.

Some nagging doubt about the events of the past day dogged him. Was it a coincidence that the well-supplied group of bush wranglers had accosted them while Kyara was with them? Darvyn had believed her story about seeking her sister, but without being able to verify if she was lying with Earthsong, he had to entertain the possibility that she wasn't what she seemed.

Her breathing was steady, and the blood flow appeared to be slowing. Still, the only thing keeping her alive was the constant stream of Earthsong coursing to her. No other Keeper would be able to help her. No one else could use this much Earthsong without quickly exhausting their inner Song. If he left Kyara now, she would surely die. Until he had some proof that she wasn't who she'd said she was, he couldn't let that happen.

"Do you think they'll make an exception and let her in the safe house considering she's injured?" Farron asked.

Darvyn shook his head. "I'll have to take her with me."

Farron gave him an assessing look. "Does this mean you're *not* going to the safe house?"

Darvyn retrieved his spare tunic from his pack and slipped it over his head. "You had no idea what I was planning. You can tell him that and not be lying."

Bringing a stranger to the school was an even bigger risk than bringing one to a safe house. But Darvyn could ensure Kyara didn't know the school's location. And if it turned out he couldn't trust her . . . He shivered. He'd just have to climb that peak when it appeared.

Aggar was questioning the group of captured bandits. He was unlikely to get any answers, but his attention was centered on them. Lizana had just lined up the last crawler along the side of the road.

Farron said nothing, but his eyes implored Darvyn to change his mind.

"Safe travels, my friend," Darvyn said, touching Farron's forehead. Resigned, the teen mirrored the gesture, then stepped back.

Darvyn climbed from the wagon and lifted Kyara into his arms, then carried her down the road. Aggar hadn't noticed them, his focus aimed at the bush wranglers.

Kyara's body was slack. Darvyn settled her on the crawler farthest from the others and climbed aboard behind her. She slumped over the handlebars and nearly slid off. He tied the remaining strips of his ripped tunic together and looped it around both of their waists, staying clear of her injury, tethering them together so she wouldn't fall off. When he flipped the ignition switch, the metal beast roared to life.

Shouts came from behind him, but he pointed the crawler north and drove into the bush without looking back.

Kyara battled for consciousness, scrabbling her way out of the dark cavern that had closed in around her. She tore her eyes open and was momentarily confused to find a smattering of stars twinkling against a blue-black sky. She shifted, bracing herself for the pain she'd felt when the bullet had punctured her, but it never came. Her hands went to her abdomen and pulled at the hem of her bloodstained tunic. Smooth skin met her fingertips. She looked down and sucked in a breath.

A soft, orange light glowed next to her. She sat up and came face-to-face with Darvyn. They were camped, just the two of them, somewhere in the bush.

"How are you feeling?"

She pressed a hand against her stomach. "Better."

He barked out a dry laugh. "You actually heal rather fast."

She swallowed. "Did you . . . did you heal me?"

"Not exactly. I just kept you alive until your body took over."

The cold of the night broke through, causing her to shiver. She'd been lying on her coat and wrapped herself in it, relishing the lingering warmth of her own body heat.

The lack of scarring at the bullet site left her perplexed. Had her immunity to Earthsong been affected or was this something else? She had enough scars to know that even her own fast healing had never been so complete.

"Thank you," she said, wary. He hadn't smiled once since she'd awoken. In fact, his whole demeanor was careful, assessing. "Where are we? Where's everyone else?"

"I had to make a detour." He watched her intently. His stare remained even when she averted her own gaze. But she couldn't stay away for long. Glittering in the firelight, his eyes begged to be looked at, studied. She bet there were a thousand stories locked inside.

"A detour to where?" She forced the question out. Cold fear settled in her gut when he didn't answer. He knew. Somehow he'd found out who she was and why she was here. Now he was going to kill her.

Oddly enough, the thought calmed her. She would be grateful for death after so long. But just as quickly, her anxiety rose. If he knew, then why had he aided her in the first place? What was going on?

She sniffed the air but didn't smell smoke. For the first time, she peered at the orange glow she'd noticed earlier. It wasn't a fire. Instead it came from the boulder next to Darvyn, which radiated with heat like metal in a blacksmith's forge.

"We're off the highway," he said. "Something urgent came up, and I had to bring you along."

She hesitated to question him more for fear of what he may ask her in return. Could he sense her emotions now? Was that why he was looking at her so carefully?

The night sky gave no indication of their location. She stretched her senses, searching out nearby Nethersong. Kilometers of open desert surrounded them, the Nether bright in her mind's eye.

"The children are safe?" she asked.

"Yes."

"So, basically, you nabbed me?" He grimaced. "Why?"

"You were dying. I was the only one who could save you."

His words sent her pulse racing. She couldn't ask him why he was the only one. It wasn't possible . . . He was definitely too young to be the Shadowfox. Perhaps he was simply the second-strongest Singer in the group and the actual Shadowfox had to go on with the children, leaving her in the care of someone strong enough to help her.

Her wound throbbed with the need to stay on her assignment. Until she knew for sure that her cover was blown, she would stick with her story. She had to.

She wanted to ask how exactly he had saved her, but it didn't seem like something a normal person would wonder. Not unless she wanted to reveal her immunity to Earthsong—he obviously knew, but it was better not to discuss.

"This urgent matter of yours, I suppose it won't take us anywhere near Checkpoint Seventeen?"

He shook his head. "But it shouldn't take long. It can't. Then I can take you back to find your sister."

He turned to the glowing rock. On top of it sat a cooking pot. It was a nice trick, the heat and light of a fire without the smoke. A good cover for those seeking to hide their location. If Kyara had a normal Song, she would have done something similar.

"We would have been there tonight had the crawler not overheated," he said. "Once it cools enough, we can be back on our way."

"You stole one of the bush wrangler's crawlers?" She turned behind her to find the vehicle parked a few paces away.

"I don't think those were bush wranglers."

When she faced him again, the intensity of his gaze froze her in place. "I think you're right," she said. "Something about them was off." She suspected Aren had hired the men to attack the Keepers. Whether he thought he was helping the mission or merely antagonizing her, it was just the sort of thing she'd been afraid of when she'd found out he'd been sent to "assist."

"Was anyone else hurt?" she asked.

"No."

At least the children were safe, and hopefully off to somewhere better, though she could not imagine where that might be. She turned back to inspect the crawler.

"The headlights aren't very strong. I'm not sure how you would have made it."

The night suddenly brightened around her. She spun around, shocked to find a ball of flame floating in the air between them. Just as quickly, it was gone again.

"Handy," she said, catching her breath.

He shrugged and stirred whatever was in the pot. "Have you been injured much in your line of work?"

Icy fingers held her in place. Then she remembered that he believed her to be a courier. "Sometimes." Not since her training, though. Ydaris bleeding her for various spells didn't really count. Did he ask because he'd seen her scars? There was no good explanation as to why a courier would be a blood bank for a practicing blood mage. "It's dangerous work," she said simply.

"Do you enjoy it?"

She took a deep breath and stared out into the darkness surrounding them.

"I hate it with all my heart and soul." He straightened sharply, as if surprised by her answer. "But it feeds me, clothes me, keeps me out of . . . trouble." She shrugged.

"And you've never thought of joining the Keepers?"

She shook her head. "Do you really think you can win against the immortal king? His power is limitless."

"Everything has limits. If he were omnipotent he would be able to leave Lagrimar. The Mantle would be nothing but an inconvenience. But it keeps him in check. Even he has weaknesses."

"Well, good luck finding them." Her fingers worried a stone at her feet. She dug a small hole, creating a tiny hill of soil.

"Chip away at a mountain little by little and you'll dig a tunnel," he said.

"So that's what saving the children is? A chip of rock from a mountain?"

"We save who we can. Not nearly enough, but you can't save everyone."

Outrage snaked through her. She destroyed her little pile, flattening it with the palm of her hand. "And what happens when you die and the sum of your life is a pile of dust at your feet? The mountain won't even have felt it."

He leaned forward, forcing their gazes to collide. "Chip away enough and he'll feel it. When I'm gone, someone else will grab my pick."

Her anger dissipated. "You have purpose. Maybe that's enough."

"Everyone needs purpose. We all have our life's work."

"Do we?"

"Perhaps you were not meant to be a courier. Perhaps your life's work still remains to be discovered."

A pained smile tugged at her lips. She considered her actual life's work: dealing death. "Life's work is living until the end. Nothing more."

"Ah, so you're an Avinid." He sat back again, resting his hands on his knees. The position gave off the appearance of relaxation, but she felt he was always alert. Never truly relaxed. Much like her.

"I don't worship the Void like the Avinids, but I understand the desire. It's easier to believe that all this is for nothing than to try to assign some significance to the details of our lives. You Keepers worship some sleeping queen who is supposed to awaken and save us from the True Father. Five hundred years is a long nap. And those who follow the ancestors believe our long-dead foremothers will offer some comfort. That their animal spirits hold answers to life's mysteries. I've never seen a sleeping queen or a talking serpent. I am very familiar with the Void, however."

Those dark eyes penetrated her skin and filled her with a warm longing that gnawed at her insides.

"You are a very interesting woman, Kyara."

Her cheeks heated. "Let me take a look at the crawler," she said, rising, seeking to avoid further scrutiny. "I may be able to get it working."

The metal was still hot, but she wrapped her hand in her sleeve and popped open the side compartment to reveal the engine. The capital of Sayya was clogged with various motorized contraptions shipped in from Yaly or cobbled together by amateur mechanics. When not on assignment, Kyara liked to tinker with all sorts of mech from radio transmitters to rickshaw bearings. It was something she'd learned from Ydaris.

She peered into the recesses of the engine but couldn't see much with the dim light. Suddenly a small ball of fire appeared near her head.

She recoiled, then caught herself. "Thanks," she said under her breath. "Unless we have water to spare it will be several hours before the starter will catch again. The exchanger is clogged with dust. The fastest solution is to flush it. Otherwise, I can scrape it once it cools."

"Water isn't a problem," Darvyn said. He produced a metal canister and crouched near a saltbush, then snapped off a tough branch. Holding the canister under the broken branch, he waited. Kyara wasn't sure what was happening until water began to leak out of the branch into the waiting container. When the canister was full, the water shut off like a tap in the castle.

"Here you go," he said, handing her the container. She stared at the water for a moment, and a great thirstiness came over her.

As if he could read her mind he said, "Go ahead, take a drink. There's more."

She sniffed the water. Virtually all food in Sayya was produced at least indirectly because of Earthsong, but she'd never seen it done right in front of her. The water was clean and fresh, aromatic with the gentle scent of the saltbush about it, but not unpleasant.

She drank down half the canister, and Darvyn refilled it in the same way. Then she set about clearing out the engine clog.

Darvyn watched over her shoulder. She looked back a few times, but he remained silent, his steady interest covering her like a shawl.

"There you go. Should last another few hundred kilometers."

His eyes were wide. "Where did you learn that?"

She brushed off his apparent awe. "You come across lots of contraptions living on the road." Standing abruptly, she took a step away from him. The heat coming from his body was starting to scramble her brain. They were alone, truly alone, and her awareness of him was impossible to ignore. Fortunately, her stomach chose that moment to grumble.

"What are you cooking?"

Darvyn went to his pot and spooned some sort of mash into a metal cup and handed the concoction to her. It smelled bland but melted on her tongue.

"What is this?" she asked, scooping more into her mouth.

"Just a squashed tuber," he said, eating his more slowly.

"Where did you find tubers before harvest?" She'd burned her tongue in her haste but did not care.

Darvyn merely shrugged and offered her some more water, which she took readily.

When they'd finished eating, he packed up, and soon they were on the back of the crawler. Kyara sat behind him, forced once again to wrap her arms around his waist. She failed miserably at not allowing his proximity to affect her. She leaned in, sniffing his neck surreptitiously. His scent filled her nostrils, the sweet tang of oldenberry mixed with a smoky spice all his own.

They followed the ball of fire he spelled into existence as they raced off into the night. Fatigue soon enveloped her. The thrum of the engine beneath her and the firmness of Darvyn's body against her threatened to lull her back to sleep. She fought it as long as she could. Regardless of the way it felt to be this close to someone, she needed to remain alert.

"It's all right. You can sleep," he said over his shoulder. "It's natural to be tired after an injury like yours. There's no use fighting it."

As her traitorous body began to obey him, the doubts and fears once again crept in. Was she any closer to discovering the identity of the Shadowfox? If she had a god to pray to, she would beg to never complete her mission.

Darkness surrounds Ulani. She's light as a feather, floating through the night sky. Only there are no stars, no moon or clouds. Just darkness all around. But it's not the Hollow Place. She feels calm and patient. Expectant.

Someone is nearby. A warm presence wraps around her, and though she can't see anything, she knows it's a woman.

"Hello, little one," the woman says. Her voice is like a rainbow, colorful and bright. It shines over Ulani's floaty, feathery self and brightens the darkness.

"Hello," she replies.

"It's been a long time since you've come to visit me, Ulani."

She doesn't remember having been here before.

"Oh, you were a very little girl. Too young to recall. But I'm glad you're back. I don't know how long we'll have together, though."

Ulani's floaty self nods her weightless head. She's not sure if the woman can see anything, but she likes listening to her talk.

"Where are we?"

"Do you know where dreams take place?"

Ulani thinks hard. "The World Between, I think." She feels rather than sees the lady smile.

"Yes, you're right. We're in the World Between."

"How did I get here?"

"Dreams take people many places in this world. Some trips pass near enough to me so that I may converse with the traveler and some do not."

Ulani isn't sure she wants to ask the next question, but she does anyway. "And who are you?"

If voices can smile, the lady is definitely smiling. "My name is Oola."

"Are you dreaming, Oola-deni?"

Oola tsks. "How I wish my brother hadn't been so pedantic when creating your language. No need for all that, dear one, just Oola is fine. And yes, I guess you could say I'm dreaming as well. I've been dreaming for a very, very long time."

"Is it lonely here?"

Oola doesn't answer for a long time. When she speaks, it is very quiet. "Yes."

Ulani wants to hug her, but her floaty, feathery self doesn't have arms. "Sometimes, when Papa would lock my sister in the closet, I would sit outside and sing to her. That would make her feel better. Do you want me to sing to you?"

"I think I would like that, Ulani. Thank you."

She thinks of what she should sing and settles on her favorite lullaby. One of the only memories she has of her real mother, before she ran away from them, was of her singing at night. Helping her get to sleep. When her mama sang to her, she never had nightmares. Oola was already dreaming, but maybe she could still go to sleep and wake up to a new day full of light.

> "Rest now, little one,
> for the day is done
> Night crawls over everything,
> darkness now has won
> And if the light stays hidden
> and morning never comes
> On my heart your name is written
> I love you more than the sun."

She hears Oola smile again. "That's a lovely lullaby, and you sing it very well."

"Thank you." Ulani preens. "That's the only verse I know though."

"Would you like to hear the next verse?" Oola asks.

"Yes, please."

When Oola sings, her rainbow voice lights up the darkness. Ulani settles in to listen.

> "Don't cry, little one
> Save your tiny tears

They'll be needed one day soon
To wet the wasted years
So when the sky's distempered
And dry the rivers run
On my skin your name's remembered
I love you more than the sun."

Ulani likes listening to Oola sing. She likes it very much.

"You have to go now, Ulani, but I hope you will visit me again."

"I hope so, too." She doesn't want to wake up. She wishes she could stay here forever.

"You and your sister will need to stick together. You'll have to watch out for her. But don't worry, you'll soon have help."

The last time someone came to help them hadn't turned out so good in the end. But she trusts the lady with the rainbow voice. And she hopes to dream of her again soon.

CHAPTER SIXTEEN

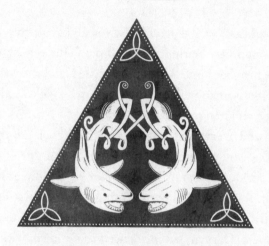

The Scorpion was reared by careful hands
But never did she feel a mother's kiss
The close-knit clans regarded her with fear
An outsider, from first she stepped within
The ravaged land beyond was not her home
Nor was the stone world where she walked alone

—THE BOOK OF UNVEILING

Little brown eyes blinked up at Kyara. First there was one pair before her, then two, then half a dozen. She stood rigidly, holding her breath, hoping they would grow bored and move along about their business. Some of the wild dogs she'd encountered in the bush were like that. They would sniff around for a bit and then retreat to other targets. If they weren't too hungry.

But Kyara didn't believe these little creatures had any interest in eating her, what with the delicious smell of freshly baked bread in the air; however, their stares were unnerving. Huge round eyes peered out of rounder faces, still bearing the baby fat of youth.

"Leave Miss Kyara alone. I know you all have better things to do than stand here staring at her all day." The schoolmistress's voice was firm but kind. Asla was her name, and she was a solid, no-nonsense woman with a huge smile she wielded indiscriminately. The children scattered at her words.

Kyara and Darvyn had arrived at the school late the night before. The barely there Nethersong of several dozen sleeping children inside the sprawling complex of buildings had surprised her. Asla, who had been waiting expectantly at the entry, welcomed them despite the hour and showed them to sleeping rooms to rest. Darvyn had introduced the women, with no further comment on Kyara's identity.

After sleeping during the journey, Kyara felt the need to stay awake the rest of the night. The little book and its strange, disturbing tale had kept her company as she monitored the surroundings with her Song. She had no idea where they were; several hours' ride into the bush would put them deep in uninhabited land.

Daybreak had brought a chorus of children's excited voices and the mouthwatering aroma of breakfast. But Kyara had been accosted in the hall by a gaggle of curious youngsters.

Even though Asla shooed them away, one tiny girl remained. The child crooked her finger at Kyara, beckoning her closer. Kyara looked to Asla for help, but the other woman only shrugged. Kyara crouched down to the child's height, and the girl leaned forward to whisper in her ear.

"Can I braid your hair?"

Reflexively, Kyara placed a hand on her head. Her rows of neat braids had grown messy over the past few days and she hadn't redone them.

"Ilynor loves to braid. She's very good at it. She did mine." Asla beamed and patted her intricately woven swirl of braids.

"She did that?" Kyara asked. Asla nodded and spun around to give a full view.

Kyara regarded the child, who looked no older than six. "All right. But only if you promise that it won't hurt."

Ilynor smiled bashfully and whispered something else.

"You must speak louder, child, if you want anyone to hear you," Asla instructed.

"It won't hurt," the girl said, a fraction louder.

"I hope not," Kyara said, suppressing the smile tugging at her lips.

And so, after a trip to the kitchen where a rail-thin man pressed a bowl of sweet-smelling porridge and a warm bun into her hands, the deadliest assassin in Lagrimar found herself sitting on the floor having her hair braided by a six-year-old girl sitting on a stack of cushions.

The great room of the school bustled with activity before her. A dozen large tables were scattered across the space, each filled with children grouped according to age. Two other women and three men visited the tables giving lessons, assisting the students with their schoolwork and playing games.

In a way, the place reminded her of the harem school. Though *ul-nedrim* weren't allowed to attend, Kyara had spent a considerable amount of time peering through the windows on her way to or from some kitchen errand. There, the classroom had been full of girls practicing a talent or skill and readying themselves to be called upon to perform for one of the True

Father's state dinners or Mercy Day holidays. Harem women were expected to provide all sorts of palace entertainment. Reading and writing were only emphasized insofar as they could amuse the king and his sycophants. Some girls learned to write plays or comic skits; others learned to read so they could perform in the productions. There was no learning for learning's sake, as was happening in this far-flung school.

Ahlini would have loved this place. Kyara's eyes stung from the unbidden thought. But it was true, her childhood friend had lapped up knowledge like a thirsty cat. Whatever she learned at school she would share with Kyara, though it wasn't allowed. Ahlini shouldn't even have spoken to a lowly *ul-nedrim*, much less befriended her and taught her.

And what did she get for her trouble and kindness? Though time and the imperfections of memory had blurred her friend's face in Kyara's mind, the image of her motionless body sprawled on the floor was burned into her brain. The whites of her eyes gone black as they stared sightlessly at the sky.

Ilynor's little fingers massaged their way across Kyara's scalp, rubbing away the past. All around her was a hope she had not imagined possible. A place for girls and boys to be children. She had never heard so many young ones laugh so much—not ever—and her eyes burned from the weight of emotion.

"I shouldn't be here," she whispered under her breath.

"What's that, miss?" Ilynor asked, her voice little more than a tickle against the air.

"Nothing . . . How long have you lived here?"

"Since the last red days."

About a year, then. "Do you like it?"

There was movement behind her, and Kyara craned her

neck to find the girl nodding enthusiastically. "Miss Asla and the teachers are nice. We have baths and dinner every night."

Kyara faced forward again, a smile pulling at her cheeks. "Baths are nice. I quite like them myself."

"Are you keeping Miss Kyara company?" a familiar voice asked from behind her, its timbre sending ripples of delight across her skin.

Darvyn sat on the ground next to her, propping up his head with a hand to his chin. "Ilynor here is a star student. She has the highest marks in all her classes, isn't that right?"

The girl giggled.

"And what she's doing to your hair is a work of art," he added.

Kyara longed to ask the girl where she'd learned to braid, but any questions about the past would likely only hold sad stories. The Lagrimari were not a people who looked backward. Survival meant moving forward.

"Is your urgent business complete?" she asked Darvyn instead.

"Just about," he said, looking out onto the classroom.

"The Keepers saved all these children from the tribute?"

"Yes. And now they'll be taught to use their Songs properly."

In the opposite corner, a teacher sat with a student, hand in hand, their eyes closed in deep concentration. Kyara guessed they were linking so the adult Singer could teach spells to the novice. A blade of jealousy speared her. If only she could have learned to control her Song in such a manner. But that would mean that someone else like her existed.

A conversation at the nearest table caught her attention. "But why did the Midcountry farms have to shut down?"

One of the teachers, a youngish man with a tuft of wisps on

his chin too sparse to be called a beard, sat with a group of older students of perhaps twelve and thirteen.

"The True Father outlawed private farming one hundred years ago. He wanted everyone to eat only from the officially run farm camps."

"But why?" a girl asked.

"No one knows why he does the things he does. But we can take a look at the results. Now that we all rely on Sayya for our food, we also rely on the ration tokens. So, if we break a law or anger someone in power, our rations and consequently our food is taken away.

"Before farming was outlawed, when a child was collected for service, the parents were paid in grams that can be spent at any merchant. Now, parents are only paid in ration tokens, making us even more reliant upon the government."

"If they're paid at all," one boy grumbled.

"Yes, Taron. This gave rise to the nabbers. They'd always been around, but their profitability soared around this time."

"That's why we need the Shadowfox," Taron said.

Kyara's ears perked up.

The teacher smiled. "The Shadowfox has helped many of our people survive. Did he ever come to your village?"

"Yes." Taron leaned forward, becoming more animated. "The town elders had convinced some of us older kids who hadn't been called for tribute yet to try to plant a farm. But there's always a snitch around. Someone told on us and Enforcement came and burned our field just as it was starting to bloom. A few weeks later, an entire crop of ripe tepari beans appeared. The Shadowfox did it in one night!"

The teacher turned the conversation back to his lesson on

farming techniques. Ilynor's little fingers moved quickly through Kyara's hair.

"I wonder what will happen when he's no longer around?" Kyara wondered.

"Hmm?" Darvyn said.

"The Shadowfox. He travels the country, bringing food to the hungry, healing the sick in secret. But he, or she, can't live forever; what will these people do then? It isn't like he can teach anyone how to do his miracles."

"I think 'miracle' is a strong word. He"—Darvyn gave her a sly look— "or she is just a powerful Earthsinger, there's nothing miraculous in that."

"A morsel of food is miraculous to a starving man. And besides that, what must it be like to know that some of the very people you are trying to save would just as soon report on you to the True Father?"

Darvyn shifted beside her, appearing uncomfortable. "If I were him, I think I would feel sorry for them."

Kyara snorted. "If you were him, you'd likely wish Earthsong could kill. Informers are the lowest form of humanity. They are little better than roaches, feeding from the trash. If they are not forced to it, if there is no knife to their throat as they spill their secrets, then they don't deserve any pity."

"And if there *is* a knife to their throat? If informing is the only way to keep themselves alive? What then, Kyara?" His eyes glittered with challenge.

She met his stare head-on. "Is their measly life worth more than someone who has saved so many others? Even if it were a knife to the throat of their child, unless that child could sing a crop of beans into existence, of what use are they? They are just another potential betrayer. Never trust a cockroach, Darvyn."

Ilynor gave a little tug, and Kyara faced forward again so the girl could continue.

Kyara wished she had never seen any of this. The simple joy of children laughing and learning in freedom. This was a fantasy, one that would soon be brought to an end by her own hand.

Zeli rolled over and opened her eyes. She thought she'd been in pain after the long carriage ride, but that was a gentle whisper compared to the angry way her body screamed at her now. She struggled up to a seated position, her movements hampered by the chain around her ankle and another on her wrists.

After they'd first taken her, the nabbers had thrown her into the back of a wagon, where she'd been for the Father only knew how long. When the hood and gag had finally come off, she'd been in this dark, stiflingly hot room, surrounded by children. She thought she might be the oldest one here, though she still looked young for her age. Others as young as five sat chained to bolts in the ground.

Tear-streaked cheeks mixed with hard-set jaws. Vacant, jaded stares came from faces too young for such expressions. All had accepted their fate and looked beaten down by their lives. A few had actually been beaten. Zeli looked at her chained hands and fought the urge to cry.

No one said a word.

Dim light filtered down from dirty windows placed high in the wall. The sky was overcast so she couldn't tell what time of day it was. The bolt she was attached to tethered half a dozen other girls. The child next to her was small and bony, her oversized tunic slipping off her shoulder to reveal old whip scars. She couldn't be more than eleven with short, bushy hair that had flattened on one side where she'd lain on it.

She sat hip to hip with a younger girl, maybe six. The two clung to each other like vines in a storm, trying not to be uprooted and blown away.

Sweat coated Zeli's skin, and she focused on breathing, lying back down, her cheek against the ground, searching for cooler air. They might be somewhere in the bush. She remembered the slow, bumpy wagon ride after it left the hard-packed highway.

The smaller of the two girls beside her began to shake. Her large, round eyes looked over at Zeli, who noticed one was just a shade lighter than the other. The older girl squeezed her tight, a scowl etched into her face. Were they sisters?

Zeli shifted to face them more fully, still lying on the ground. "What's your name?" Zeli asked the little one.

"I'm Ulani."

"Pleasant to meet you Ulani-deni, I'm Tarazeli, but you can call me Zeli."

The girl cracked a small smile, then the older one shifted, blocking her view. Zeli dragged her body over and Ulani shifted so they could maintain eye contact.

"What's her name?" Zeli whispered, pointing.

"That's Tana, my sister. She's grumpy."

"I'm not grumpy," Tana replied grumpily. "I'm chained to a floor in a warehouse, *again*, about to be sold. Should I be dancing a jig?"

Zeli snorted, recognizing an old soul in Tana. "We're alive and there's water." Zeli motioned to the bucket within arm's reach, a ladle handle sticking out of it. "It could be worse."

Tana gave her an incredulous look. "Are you daft?"

Zeli shrugged. "We could be in pitch darkness. They could not have given us any water. There could be rats." At Tana's glare, she smiled. "All worse."

Ulani nodded sagely. Tana shook her head. "You're crazy."

"All I'm saying is that while things are bad, they could get worse. That's all." She shifted slightly, trying to find a more comfortable position on the hard floor. One of the other girls chained to their bolt opened her eyes.

"What do you think they're going to do with us?" the girl whispered.

"Nabbers mainly provide labor for payrollers. Maybe for factories or sweatshops." At least, Zeli hoped that was where they were headed. There were more sinister fates a nabbed child could face, but she couldn't voice them.

She focused on the feverish gazes of the children around her. Most were ragged little things, but Ulani and Tana, even with the older girl's scars, were just a little too pretty for comfort. And for all Tana's bite, she still had a softness to her that the other children lacked.

Zeli had been here before. This prison was not so different from the one she'd been in after her parents were taken. That story ended happily enough; she wasn't sure how lucky she'd be again. All of her bracelets, save one, had fallen off at some point in the trip. And in the Midcountry there would be no hispid plants to make new ones. Was one enough to bring her luck now? She hoped so.

When someone in authority showed up, would they believe that she was a personal servant of the Magister of Lower Faalagol? Would it matter? At least while she could, she would try her best to look after these girls. For whatever it was worth.

"Where are you from?" Ulani whispered.

Tana groaned. "Does it really matter?"

But Zeli ignored her. "Lower Faalagol."

Squints and head tilts greeted her. She sighed. "Laketown."

The eyes of every child around her widened. "Laketown?" Ulani breathed the word like it was another planet and not just a city. "Is it as green and beautiful as everyone says?"

"Yes." Zeli nodded. "The lake is clear and blue and surrounded by flowers. The grass grows green, stretching out like a carpet and soft underfoot. There are fruit trees and little furry creatures we call shadow tails that race up and down the trees and chitter at you." Faces brightened around her.

"And everyone grows fat on roasted goose and oldenberry wine?" a boy a few paces away asked.

"Not everyone," Zeli said. "But the Magister there supplements the rations with food from his own stores. He owns farmland that stretches halfway around the lake."

The children hung on her words as she talked of the wonders of the Lake Cities. She embellished a little here and there, if only to keep their minds occupied and away from their present surroundings.

"Stop it!" Tana said, her voice a scythe cutting through the little bit of joy Zeli's story had managed to create. "What does it matter? None of us are going there."

"I'm going back," Zeli said, sitting up.

"Really? How?" Sarcasm dripped from Tana's voice.

"Not sure yet. But I am." She paused, choosing her words carefully. "Do you have somewhere to go back to?"

Tana looked away, but Ulani grew wistful. "We're from Sayya. Grew up in Windy Hill."

A boy leaning against the wall whistled. "You're a pay-roller?"

"Our *father* was a payroller," Tana said. "For all the good it did him."

"What do you mean?" Zeli asked.

"The True Father got tired of him. Sent the Poison Flame for him." Everyone bristled at the name of the famous assassin.

"I saw her," Ulani said.

"Her?" Zeli leaned forward.

The girl nodded. "She's pretty, but her eyes are . . ." She shook her head. "She saved us, you know." Tana rolled her eyes and Ulani grew indignant. "She did." The girl turned to Zeli. "After Papa was killed, our stepmother sold us to nabbers."

Zeli's heart broke into a thousand pieces.

"We were held in a place like this one, but somewhere else," Ulani continued, speaking faster now. "That's when the Poison Flame came again. She saved us. She was working with the Keepers of the Promise. She's really a spy, only pretending to work for the True Father."

Tana shook her head. "It wasn't her. In the warehouse. Couldn't have been."

"It *was*," Ulani said, but Tana only rolled her eyes. "You never believe me."

"Because the things you say you see are too fantastical to believe. The king's assassin is really a spy? Men made of light come to watch over us? Really?"

Ulani huffed and crossed her arms.

"So how did you end up here?" Zeli asked, hoping to diffuse the tension between the two.

Tana snorted. "After they saved us, the Keepers were taking us to a safe house, but their caravan was attacked. This time the so-called Poison Flame was nowhere to be found." She shrugged. "No one's coming this time."

That settled the mood down. Zeli couldn't think of anything else to say. All she knew was that Tana was right. Who would come to save them? Relying on the Keepers was obviously out of the question. Somehow, she would have to figure out a way through this. And get back home again.

CHAPTER SEVENTEEN

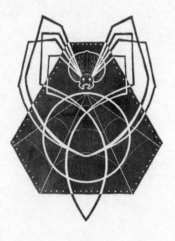

The making of a monster goes like this:
First take a shining soul and dim their light
Let hatred, pain, and fear conquer the mind
Sow seeds, let grow, then pluck the fruit when ripe
No heart takes its first beat hardened and cold
Corruption must intrude to make it so

—THE BOOK OF UNVEILING

Asla sat on the edge of her desk holding a slip of paper out to Darvyn. He crossed his arms, refusing to take it.

"You can't ignore him forever. This one might be important."

He averted his eyes, looking to the wall filled with children's drawings scribbled onto rough parchment. Asla crafted the paper from the brush surrounding the school and proudly displayed her students' work.

"This is the third telegram Aggar has sent," she said.

Darvyn had no desire to be chastised by the Keepers for deviating from the plan and coming to the school. His work on the well was nearly complete; the children and staff would have no fear of running out of water now. But he was balancing a number of complex spells and just wanted to finish his work in peace.

Asla tapped her foot, not unkindly, but damnably persistent. She was the perfect mother-figure for all of these children. Her love for them was fierce and palpable, and she had no time for nonsense from anyone no matter their age.

Darvyn sighed. "Fine, just read it and tell me what my latest transgression is. And what penance I'm likely to pay."

She scanned the coded page, the teasing light in her eyes dimming by the second. He leaned forward. "What is it?"

Asla looked up at him, horror staining her face. "You need to read this." Her hand shook as she passed the scrap of paper to him. He gripped it lightly, decoding the message in his head.

Ambush at safe house. Children recaptured. You were needed.

The borders of his heart turned to stone as Darvyn read the note again. The last sentence burned itself into his brain. Blood drained from his body to pool at his feet.

What had happened? How had the Keeper safe house been compromised?

Asla reached out for him, but he was already spinning away. Walking out of her office, out of the school building until the heat of the midday sun burned overhead. He stalked over to where the crawler was parked, out of sight of the classroom windows.

Rage and sorrow beat an insistent rhythm inside his chest. He crushed the paper in his fist and tossed it to the ground where it caught fire. The ashes heated, blazing, until a charred circle on the ground was the only thing remaining.

Tremors racked his body, but he could not allow himself to truly lose control—too much was at stake. Next to his pile of embers, a brittle bush began to smoke. He lifted a brief gust of wind to ensure no fire spread, then paced for a minute before sitting down hard on the ground. His hair was too short to tear out, but he ran his fingers across his scalp, digging his nails into his skull.

No footsteps sounded, but he felt Kyara approach. He couldn't have said how—she was still oddly and perfectly shielded from his Song—but he knew it was her before she sat down beside him.

Her soft silence was soothing. Much of the time he'd been in her presence had been spent quietly. She wasn't one to fill the space with senseless chatter, but being near her left him rested in a way he'd experienced with few others. The fog of guilt hanging over him did not feel quite as suffocating as it had moments before.

"I saw you leave Asla's office."

"Something happened," he said in a strangled tone. "Our team was ambushed at the safe house. The children we saved—they were all recaptured." His voice broke.

Kyara tensed. "How?"

He shook his head. "It was a newer safe house. I have no idea how it could have been discovered."

She stayed silent beside him.

"I should have been there." He dropped his head in his hands, squeezing. "I could have . . ." He could have stopped it. Sensed the approach of their enemies from farther than anyone else. Farron and Lizana and Navar would have tried their best, but this mission had been part of his responsibility. And he had let them all down.

"And what of your work here?" Kyara asked quietly. "I take it you felt it was just as important."

Darvyn stilled. Her gaze on him was just as tactile as her voice. The pressure made him look up. He found no pity in her stare, only grim resolve.

"You don't understand."

One of her shoulders lifted. "You're right. I don't. But I know that a single man cannot be in two places at once. Whatever responsibility you feel cannot change that fact."

She broke eye contact and turned her gaze forward to the desert. "These times we're living in—the misfortune we have to be born here, now . . . All we can do is our best, and I believe you've done yours."

She reached over and took his hand in a firm grip. A tingling heat spread where their skin touched. His awareness of her came into razor-edged focus. She squeezed gently, drawing away some of the tension coiled inside him.

"What if my best isn't good enough?"

Her grip on his hand didn't ease. "What else can you give?"

He wanted to tell her what was expected from him. Not just his best but all of the miraculous accomplishments inherent in the myth that the Shadowfox had become. He was not simply a man. Being in two places at once was not an excuse, not for him. He was expected to be so much more, so much better. He had the strange feeling that Kyara would understand.

But of course he could never tell her.

Kyara focused only on the feel of holding Darvyn's hand. Something she hadn't felt in a very long time. It was simple and honest and good. She knew she didn't deserve it but couldn't let go.

She pushed away the other awareness creeping into her mind. The one that wanted to connect certain dots in an impossible way. She wouldn't give credence to it. Not while Darvyn's hand was so warm and while he was holding onto her so tight.

He'd looked so lonely sitting on the ground alone. She'd suspected something bad had happened but the idea of all the children recaptured made even her shriveled heart bleed.

She edged closer to him, almost involuntarily, until their shoulders touched. There was strength in this—it was a rationalization, but she didn't let go of the thought. They leaned together, hand in hand, and when his head swiveled toward hers, her eyes dropped to his lips.

A taut line of awareness stretched between them. It wrapped around her chest, making her breathing shallow.

Darvyn's eyes lowered and his stare sizzled down her nerve endings.

She had little experience with this; her ignorance was visceral. What would he do? Only a small space separated them. All it would take would be to lean forward slightly—but she didn't dare. She remembered riding behind him on the horse and on the crawler. Holding onto him, strong and solid. The fear and anticipation were almost too much.

A chorus of cries rent the air, severing the invisible cord between them. Kyara and Darvyn jumped apart as the drumming of little feet thundered the ground.

"Midday break," he said, rising and dusting off his trousers, a sheepish expression crossing his face.

Asla and the other teachers led the children outside where they immediately began to run, breaking off into groups and beginning their play.

"I'm almost done with my work here. Be ready to leave in a few?"

Kyara nodded silently and watched him walk off to disappear behind the largest school building. She gulped down a breath and chuckled to herself.

"Do you think he . . . ?" She touched the tips of her fingers to her lips. "No, of course not." Shaking her head, she watched a game of carryball begin. Most of the students were out in the sun, but a group of older girls sat in the shade of one of the walkways.

Several smaller buildings were connected to the main building by the covered paths. The layout was similar to the cabal she'd grown up in but on a smaller scale. How had it been constructed all the way out here? Wherever here was . . . The Keepers would have ensured the school was well hidden, far from the highway and any military patrols, government Collectors, or wandering nomads. How did they get supplies? Rations? Water?

She opened her mind's eye, bringing the field of darkness into view around her. The adults became visible as columns of writhing light. So many dimmer lights from the eighty-plus children here, healthy and strong. Surrounding the school were the normal desert vegetation and animal life, built tough to survive the climate but with the energy of death always threaded through as it was for every living thing.

Deep roots sought out water far under the earth, and insects burrowed down. Tinier organisms lived and died almost in the blink of an eye. But behind the school was a vast area far darker than the bush surrounding them. Kyara probed further, examining the very dim glow of the decay. This was an area full of verdant life, unusual for this deep in the desert.

The world around her came back into focus as she shuttered

her inner vision. She rounded the largest building only to be startled by a sea of green. Fields stretched far into the distance, fertile soil bursting with healthy crops. Corn and wheat grew closest to the school. Nuts and small trees with white blossoms stretched out far in the distance. Though it was only a fraction of the size of the camps outside Sayya, the school's plots were abundant and vast.

Darvyn stood in the midst of the wheat, a few hundred paces away. Kyara closed her eyes and sank back into the embrace of Nethersong, seeing it all in reverse. The fertilized soil glowed dully with the presence of decayed life. But mostly, the green and beautiful field was shadowed to her inner eye.

She refocused on the visual before her, then sank back into her other sight. Darvyn was clearly standing there, but no corresponding column of light appeared in her view. She strained to find him and finally was able to sense the tiniest flicker. He held little more Nethersong than an infant.

Kyara broke off her inner vision and stumbled backward. She hadn't been aware of it before. There had always been other adults around and she hadn't scrutinized his Nether, but now, viewing him alone, it was indisputable. How could a grown man have so little death energy?

An ache began in her heart as the wound on her chest pulsed.

It shouldn't be possible. It couldn't be. She covered her mouth to suppress the sob that bubbled up. But the blood spell would not be ignored.

The pain began, starting sharply and growing more intense, recognizing Kyara's target. The spell would not be denied. It would make her capture the Shadowfox.

CHAPTER EIGHTEEN

A single candle perforates the night
Illuminating tears streaking her face
The echoes of her cries cling to her lips
But flick'ring hope gives luster to dismay
In answer to a soft whispered desire
A spark ignites and friendship catches fire

—THE BOOK OF UNVEILING

The water bucket was long empty and the stench of piss and shit was strong. So was the crying. Hours passed, a day or more? Time was stagnant. But they hadn't been beaten. That was the shiny bit under the tarnish—the bit she could grab hold of.

Zeli had almost nodded off back to sleep when a door opened. A door in the ceiling. A rickety-looking ladder was dropped down and a man's gruff voice shouted, "Boys up first!"

A key ring was dropped down onto the ground and the nearest child scrabbled over to reach it. There was just one key, but it opened all of their chains. Once unlocked, the young boys gathered together, looking suspicious, but eventually one brave soul began to climb.

With the light from the door in the ceiling, Zeli could see their surroundings better and realized the room they were in had been cut into the earth. The walls were dirt and the windows overhead were actually low to the ground from the outside.

Small faces streaked with dirt and misery blinked as at least thirty boys from five to fifteen ascended the ladder. Then the door was shut.

The key made its way to her hands and after a few tries she was able to unlock her chains. Whispers filled the space as the remaining girls chattered worriedly with one another. A small body sat next to her.

"What could be worse than this?" Ulani whispered.

Zeli reached for the little girl's hand and squeezed once she found it. "Mice gnawing at your toes. It could be freezing cold in here so our fingers turn to ice and fall off. Or burning hot as the Scald so our skin melts off."

Ulani squeezed back. "That would be worse."

"Shut up, you two," Tana grumbled. "Your little game isn't any fun."

"What else?" asked a tiny voice from across the room.

"Wild dogs pulling you by the hair to their den where they'll rip your arms off and eat them for dinner and then have your legs for first meal." Though she couldn't see clearly, she felt the rapt attention of the girls.

"A sidewinder shooting his venom into your eyeballs," Zeli said, "burning them out."

She continued to think up more and more awful things that could befall them, reasons to be grateful that they were just cold and hungry and thirsty and many had soiled themselves. They weren't dead yet and for the moment they were being left alone. She knew that one or both of those conditions were soon to change.

Their turn came about an hour later. The door in the ceiling opened again and the ladder thrown down. The same harsh voice called for the girls. As the eldest, Zeli went first, Ulani at her heels, which meant Tana was right behind her.

The unsteady rungs creaked beneath her weight but held fast. She poked her head up into a large room, close and musty, with about a dozen men scattered about. There was no sign of the boys.

The sun peeked through cracks in the mud bricks that comprised the structure. Outside, the sounds of a busy town were audible. They were near some kind of market. A whip-thin, middle-aged woman approached them, her nappy, salt-and-pepper hair coiled into a handful of thick tendrils that reached her midback.

"This way," she barked and turned back around. Zeli motioned for the younger girls to stay behind her as she followed the woman outside. They stood in a fenced-in yard with high walls. A makeshift outdoor shower was penned in the corner. It was really just a platform with a large trough overhead that could be overturned with a rope handle. The trough was fed by a pump, its pipe extended high.

"Clothes off!" the old woman said.

The girls huddled close to one another, nerves making them shiver in the heat. The woman raised a whip that Zeli hadn't seen before. Her menacing expression caused the girls to comply, tossing their foul clothing into a pile.

They took turns standing in the outdoor shower in small groups as tepid water was dumped over them. The woman tossed them two bars of soap to share. Zeli did her best to scrub the stink and other substances off her body. The dirty, wet sand beneath them soaked it all up.

When all were deemed clean, the woman passed out rough towels, tunics, and trousers. It was left to the girls to determine who could fit what. The fabric was cheap, the clothing poorly made. It abraded Zeli's skin, but she quieted the urge to scratch. She kept her hands fisted at her sides, waiting for what would come next.

"Look presentable or your heads will be shaved," the woman spat, tossing them a few combs she'd produced from her pocket. "You've got half an hour." Then she went back inside, leaving them in the open yard.

They were a pathetic lot, wet hair beginning to frizz on most of them as it dried in the scorching afternoon. The sun beat down, and the girls looked at one another blankly.

"Who knows how to braid?" Zeli asked. Over half raised their hands.

She organized the girls into groups and the braiders quickly tamed the heads of their partners with simple plaits. She patted her own head; her rows of braids weren't neat anymore, but they were still in place. It would take longer than they had to undo them and put them into some other style.

Other than the yelps of the tender-headed as kinks were combed out, the girls remained quiet. In what seemed like no time at all, the woman was back with a bucket of drinking water and each girl slaked their thirst. Then they were ushered back inside.

Now, the large room held more people. Richly hued, carefully embroidered clothing marked them all as payrollers. A handful of women were sprinkled among the men. Some had brought solemn-eyed servants with them as well.

The girls were lined up in a row from shortest to tallest. Zeli was somewhere near the middle. The woman who'd been directing them faded into the background and a shorter man with a bushy mustache and polished walking stick stepped up to greet the payrollers.

"All these whelps are strong and healthy, look for yourselves."

The payrollers walked up and down the row, inspecting the girls. *We're merchandise,* Zeli thought, clenching her jaw. They were asked to hold their hands out, show their teeth, jump up and down.

Any girl who didn't act quickly enough got a smack to the back of the head from Bushy Mustache. When Tana refused to open her mouth for one woman, his cane struck her backside. The girl's nostrils flared, but she finally complied.

One by one, the children were picked. One man took five girls, the tallest ones. He seemed like a merchant or factory type. Others seemed to be in the market for domestic servants.

"All have given tribute?" one woman asked.

Bushy Mustache eyed the row of silent children. "Certainly. We have already borne the expense of sending them to the capital so it will not be assigned to you. They're all Song-free and ready to work."

Considering the young ages of many of the girls, Zeli doubted they had all given tribute. And since none of the nabbers had bothered to ask if any of them still had their Songs, it was an empty guarantee. But once the purchasers discovered the truth, that they would have to send some of their new servants all the way to Sayya, these nabbers would be far, far away.

One man showed special interest in Ulani and Tana. His tunic was, rather ostentatiously, bordered in a colorful array of jewels. A permanent smile graced his fleshy lips, and his close attention made Zeli's skin crawl. He asked the sisters to turn around several times, peering at them closely. When he gripped Ulani's jaw to inspect her teeth, tears welled in the child's eyes. Her sister grabbed her hand tight, the veins in her hand popping out in bold relief. Zeli's stomach churned.

A voice to her left trilled prettily. "That one looks sturdy, if a bit undersized. What do you think, Kyssa-denili?"

Zeli peeled her eyes away from the man accosting the sisters to find a female payroller scrutinizing her. The woman was a bit undersized herself, thirty at most, and small-boned with a pointed chin.

"I think she will do, mideni," the servant said. She was tall and thickly built, the opposite of her mistress in just about every way. An image of Zeli standing with Devana crossed her mind briefly before she pushed it away.

The mistress nodded absently, and Kyssa approached. "Can you sew?" she asked.

Zeli nodded. "I can weave also." She held up her hand with the bracelet still attached.

Kyssa nodded, though if she wasn't from the Lake Cities, she probably didn't know anything about good-luck charms. "You come with us."

Zeli leaned forward, lowering her voice. "I'm not supposed to be here. Up until a few days ago, I was a personal servant of the Magister of Lower Faalagol. I was nabbed and brought here."

Kyssa searched her face for a moment and pursed her lips. "That may be so, but do you truly believe a Magister would have trouble replacing a servant? No doubt someone has taken your place there already."

Zeli's shoulders slumped. She was right. Devana may miss her and may resent having to train someone new, but Zeli was in no way indispensable.

Kyssa motioned toward her mistress. "Ora-mideni treats her workers well and gives opportunities for advancement. The indenture is not for a lifetime—in ten years, you could be free."

Zeli looked around the space. Of the payrollers buying children, Ora seemed the least intimidating. She had treated Kyssa with a certain amount of respect and the woman appeared well fed and uninjured.

"Yes . . . I guess you're right," Zeli said. As the woman began to turn away, she blurted, "Would you have room for my sisters as well?" She motioned to Tana and Ulani. The man who'd been inspecting them was now conferring with Bushy Mustache, several paces away. "They both sew like a dream."

Kyssa considered. "We don't really need you to sew, just have dexterous fingers."

"Look how small their fingers are," Zeli said. Both girls obligingly wiggled their appendages. "Very nimble."

"I'm not sure we need any more, and besides, I think Mengu-mideni has his eye on them." She looked over at the payroller who'd sparked such an uncomfortable reaction.

"I know," she whispered, her heart falling.

Kyssa frowned, staring at the man, a look of disgust on her face. "Give me a moment." She went to speak with her mistress. Both women looked over to where Mengu stood, then back at the girls. Ulani smiled beautifully, showing off a dimple. Even Tana managed to look pleasant. The two women bent their heads to confer.

The blood in Zeli's veins slowed as time dragged. Then Kyssa was headed her way again, face expressionless. Zeli wrung her hands, prepared to beg her case, but Kyssa gave a curt nod. The breath escaped from her lungs in a rush as the tension bunching her shoulders released. She motioned to the two younger girls who scampered to her side.

"Ora-mideni, here are your new workers," Kyssa said as her mistress sidled up.

Ora's dainty features looked upon the girls kindly. "They are such pretty things," she said. "Mengu-deni will be jealous of me, indeed." Then she spun on her heel and walked away toward the door, leaving Kyssa to complete the transaction.

Zeli's brief relief was cut short when she spied Mengu narrowing his eyes at them. Kyssa marched over, purse in her hand. She, Mengu, and Bushy Mustache were too far away to hear, but it looked like the three of them traded sharp words, likely over ownership of the girls. After a brief back and forth, Kyssa handed over a quantity of grams and Bushy Mustache smiled, greedily.

Zeli felt like she'd been riding the coach again, her body sore and taut, this time from worry. As Kyssa approached them, triumphant, Zeli took Tana's hand and pulled her closer, with Ulani on her other side. They followed Kyssa into the sunshine, and Zeli finally took a breath.

She didn't know what awaited them in the care of Ora, nor what their dexterous fingers would be needed for, but she was confident that whatever their fate entailed, it could have been much worse.

CHAPTER NINETEEN

The unfamiliar road stretched out ahead
A rocky path to walk laden with snares
The thought of a companion left her stunned
And unexpectedly, caught unawares
But bravery became her driving charge
The Scorpion embraced the waiting dark

—THE BOOK OF UNVEILING

Kyara waited in the shade of the school building, a chorus of agony singing through her veins courtesy of the wound on her chest. The pain made her eyes water, but she took it as her due.

Darvyn turned toward her, heading back to the school. He stopped at a well a few paces away and splashed his face with water from the bucket. Rivulets rolled down his cheek and neck, disappearing beneath his tunic.

"I used to wish for a different life," Kyara said, her ragged tone almost obscene paired with the laughter of the children just out of sight. "If I had any other choice, I would make it. I am so very sorry, Darvyn." Tears that hadn't made themselves known in years welled in her eyes, but they had forgotten how to fall.

Darvyn approached her, his face all concern. She couldn't take it any longer and lashed out, connecting to the Nether in the closest crops, magnifying it and relying on the residual effects to incapacitate Darvyn.

The green shoots shriveled and died. Darvyn would sicken and she could collar him and then the whole business would be done.

But when he should have bent down and vomited, he merely frowned. She reached for his Nether, so small and weak. Not enough death energy to be affected.

She didn't want to kill the entire field—the children would still need to eat—but the pain in her chest pushed her to try harder. She risked targeting him directly with her power. Pulling at the tiny wisp of Nethersong within him and enlarging it.

He clutched his stomach, wincing. What should have been a death blow for anyone else, left Darvyn only slightly pained.

The blood spell screamed for more.

Desperate, she reached for the Nether present in the scrubby, dry desert grass around the field. Darvyn simply didn't have enough Nether of his own to manipulate. The additional energy gave her enough to work with, enough to push into him and increase.

It was the reverse of what he had done to her to keep her alive. She forced Nethersong into him, struggling against his innate power and the strength of his Song. Finally, she was able to grab hold and multiply the death energy within him.

Darvyn collapsed to his hands and knees, gasping for

breath. He fought against what she was doing, and some part of her—maybe the largest part—hoped he would win. But death was inevitable. Life could not fend it off forever, no matter how strong.

He fell to his side, and his eyes involuntarily closed.

A single tear slipped down her cheek.

Even unconscious, his body fought her. She sensed no lasting damage within him, but perhaps killing him would be kinder. Whatever Ydaris and the True Father had in store would no doubt make him wish for death. However, the torment of her wound allowed only what she'd been ordered to do.

Her pain eased as she pulled the collar from the sack and moved toward him. She crouched, ready to slip the noose around his neck, when she noticed it.

Darvyn's tunic had fallen open, revealing the leather cord he wore. The collar fell from her fingertips, freeing them to pull at the cord until she could better see the pendant. Half a pendant, actually, the image of a jackal crudely emblazoned into the metal. Its legs were chaotic, mismatched and pointed in the wrong direction. The broken edge of the metal had been worn smooth with time.

A curse escaped her lips.

"Miss Kyara, what's wrong with Mister Darvyn?" a little voice behind her asked.

Kyara whipped around to find Ilynor standing there, a rag doll hanging from her fingertips.

The wound flared. Kyara's Song surged forward, menacingly.

"S-stay away from me. Don't come any closer." Kyara strangled her Song with as much control as she could muster. It wanted to complete the mission. Collar Darvyn. Prevent interruptions.

She ignored the hurt on Ilynor's face and backed away both from her and the man on the ground.

"What happened to him? Why won't he wake up?"

Another tear fell from Kyara's eye, and then another. Fire burned from the inside out as the wound made its displeasure known. She looked from Ilynor's confused concern to Darvyn and the pendant laying over his heart. Her fingers felt twice their size as she hitched the leg of her trousers and unwound a length of leather from around her ankle. Tied to the strap was a matching pendant bearing the other half of the jackal. She'd kept it there for a decade, never believing she'd find its owner.

At least there was this. A broken promise now kept.

The pain was making it hard to concentrate, and harder to keep her Song under control. Kyara spotted the diesel crawler a short dash away. The world swam and spun around her as she grew dizzy. Sweat gushed from her pores.

She tossed her pendant at Ilynor's feet. "Make sure he gets that when he wakes up." Her voice sounded hoarse.

Asla came around the corner, her ever-present smile turning to horror as she saw Darvyn sprawled on the ground and Kyara, bent over, looking close to death herself with blood now seeping through her tunic as the wound made its demands.

"What's happened? What's wrong?"

"Stay away!" Kyara shouted. "I'm not here for you."

Asla looked again to Darvyn, then to Kyara before grabbing Ilynor's shoulders to hold the girl close.

Kyara made a run for the crawler. The buzz of children's voices invaded her head, their rhythm pulsing in time to the agony on her chest. The wound saw the students as threats to her mission. She had to get out of here before she lost control.

The crawler felt like it had grown wider. She swung her leg

over the seat twice before making it. And there was Asla, screaming at her side.

"What did you do?"

The sounds of play quieted. Vaguely, Kyara was aware of the other teachers gathering the students. Kyara tried to get the engine to catch, but her hands were clumsy, her vision narrowing.

"Stay away from me. Tell them to get out of the way," she growled at Asla. When the woman went to grab her, her Song took a swing. Asla turned ashen and fell to the ground vomiting.

"There's so much I need to tell him," Kyara mumbled. Fire gnawed at her skin. It ate up almost every bit of her consciousness to withstand it. "I only wish I could."

Two male teachers approached as the crawler's engine finally roared to life. Kyara held out a hand. "I'm the Poison Flame. Now get your children out of my way."

The men froze. Kyara gripped the accelerator, and she was in motion. Students scattered as she took off.

She fought for each breath. Her vision tunneled until there was only a tiny point of light in front of her. All she had to do was get far enough away to save him, to save them all. She had kept the promise she'd made ten years earlier . . . Well, not entirely. But she'd found him and he had the other half of the pendant. Now all she had to do was get far enough away to no longer be able to cause him harm.

Soon the spell would take her mind and her breath. She would drive into the desert until she could drive no more, and then, perhaps, she could finally die.

Darvyn roused with a jolt. A lightning strike of pain fired into his head; his eyes danced open to meet dim light. He sucked down one labored breath and then another, until the stuttering in his lungs stopped and air flowed more easily. Moaning, he raised a hand to his head, attempting to stop the pounding inside.

"You're awake." A match was struck nearby, the sound releasing another crashing wave of pain to his head. Light quickly suffused the space, revealing the room he'd slept in the night before. Asla's face drew close to him, her eyes glowing in the lamplight.

Darvyn's mouth tasted like ash. He opened it, trying to speak, but Asla forced a cup of water against his lips, so he drank.

"What's happened?" he said after ending the drought in his throat.

Asla pursed her lips. "You were betrayed."

Kyara's apology came back to him, as well as the solemn look on her face and the bizarre weakness that had overtaken him just before he'd blacked out.

"Kyara?"

"The Poison Flame. You brought a viper to us, Darvyn, and almost paid the price." Her voice dropped to a whisper. "She nearly killed you."

Kyara's confidence, her poise—those things that drew him to her could also have a different explanation. But it didn't make sense. The ache in his head still pounded, scrambling his mind. His connection to Earthsong was strong, but his body was taking a long time to heal.

"Kyara is the Poison Flame? How am I alive?"

Asla's normally kind face was carved from stone. "She left this behind." She held up the ruby-red collar, and a shiver went through Darvyn. He'd seen those before but had been fortunate to never have been separated from his Song by one.

"And this." Asla opened her fist, revealing a pendant attached to a strip of leather.

Darvyn's breath stopped short. He plucked the necklace from Asla's grip, then his hand immediately went beneath his shirt, scrabbling to find his own matching pendant. He pressed the two pieces of metal together. Aside from the worn edges, they fit perfectly. An image that he'd only seen half of for decades was now whole.

The two jackals faced each other, their legs and tails intertwined. He pulled the two apart, and each jackal was just a head and a mess of limbs.

"She gave this to you?"

Asla nodded.

Darvyn struggled to sit up, causing the room to pivot around him. He feared he would vomit but forced the bile down. "What did she say? How did she get this?"

"She didn't say anything. She left on the crawler. But the way she looked, I can't imagine she made it very far."

"What do you mean?"

"She was ill. Her chest was bleeding through her tunic."

Darvyn fought his way to his feet. He swayed until the room stopped spinning. "Which direction did she go? How long ago?"

Asla stood gripping his shoulders. "She nearly killed you. Not to mention the threat she posed to every child in the school. You need to rest. Heal. Please sit down."

"You don't understand. I need to find her."

"You're being hunted by the True Father's assassin." Her words held venom.

He paused and scrutinized Asla's worried face. "She didn't harm any of the children, did she?"

Asla shook her head. He may not have known Kyara's identity, or her allegiance, but at least he'd been right about her heart.

"The Poison Flame." He shook his head. "The True Father has been after me my whole life. I'm surprised he didn't send her sooner. I know you can't understand, but . . . I need to know how she got this." He held up the pendant in his fist. "Who she really is."

"Whoever she is, it's the past. Whatever her story is won't change the future. Or what she did."

Darvyn couldn't explain it to her, he just needed to find Kyara. He couldn't go on knowing that answers to the mysteries of his life may exist and he'd missed out on them.

"She knows where we are. She could have told someone," Asla said.

He shook his head, the certainty lodged within him. "If she were going to kill me she would have. She wouldn't have left me here if she was being tracked or if there was danger." Asla's skeptical gaze bored into him. "I know it's hard for you to believe, but you have to trust me. She saved my life for a reason."

"I trust *you*. It would be foolish to trust her."

He slipped the second pendant over his head. The two pieces of metal clacked together softly against his chest.

"I need answers. For me." What did her having the pendant mean about his mother? This was the closest he'd ever come to learning what had happened to her. How could he explain that after a lifetime of wondering, the chance to find out the truth was impossible to ignore?

Asla's expression closed, her body language grew rigid, but she stood aside as he gathered his things. The effects of whatever poison Kyara had used on him made him sluggish and unsteady, but Earthsong was strengthening him minute by minute.

He walked out of the school and, by the moonlight, regarded the tracks where the crawler had smashed and flattened the bushes and tough vegetation. Following her would be easy.

"There's nothing I can say to stop you?" A frown worried Asla's normally easy features.

Darvyn went back to her and drew her into an embrace. She had always been a friend and was a born nurturer. But he'd been in danger before. When was he not?

"Take the swiftcycle, then. And be careful." She pulled away and walked back inside without another look. Darvyn felt her sorrow and worry rippling before she slammed a shield around her emotions, blocking him out.

He rounded the school to one of the smaller outbuildings that held farm equipment and wagons. The teachers always had to be ready for an evacuation on short notice if their location ever was compromised. Darvyn passed the carriages and carts until he reached a smaller vehicle. It wasn't much more than a box on wheels, thick rubber tires ensuring it could maneuver in the desert terrain. A lever jutted from the front to control the direction, and a metal pole, double his height, rose into the air with a canvas sail attached.

The swiftcycle was one of the Keepers' inventions. Meant for traversing the brush, it could only be piloted by an Earthsinger able to call the wind into the sail to propel the vehicle. Darvyn pushed it from the outbuilding and got in, holding the steering lever with one hand and the rope attached to the sail's rudder with the other.

He sang a simple spell to build the wind, gather it into the sail, and propel him forward. The swiftcycle shot out across the desert, following Kyara's tracks. Darvyn sang another spell to cover the tracks in his wake. Just in case.

The pendants clinked together when he moved, dangling close to his heart. He'd never taken his off, not since it had first been placed around his neck.

He'd awoken that night, twenty years earlier, filled with the force of his mother's sadness. It had raged inside her like a rainstorm and set him on edge. She'd been crying, but scrubbed her tears away and held him close.

"You have to go now. They're coming for you. They know what you can do," she whispered into his hair. "The Keepers will keep you safe."

"How long do I have to go for?" he asked.

She stroked his chubby cheeks. "For a while. But I will find you again." She removed the necklace she always wore and held the pendant between her thumbs. Her knuckles stretched with effort as she pressed on the round, thin circle of metal until it snapped in two. She took the half with the cord still attached and placed it over his head. "This will lead me back to you. As long as you have it, you'll know my love is never far."

A man appeared in the doorway to their tiny cottage. He was hidden in shadow, but Darvyn sensed his kindness.

"This is Turwig. He's one of the Keepers of the Promise. He's going to look after you until I can come and find you."

Mama lifted Darvyn up and deposited him in the man's arms. "And I will find you again. The Master of Jackals will be my guide. Remember, I love you more than the sun," she said as Turwig carried him outside to a waiting horse. The man climbed on, securing Darvyn against him with a heavy arm and then rode off into the night.

Darvyn no longer remembered the exact planes of his mother's face or the melodious tone of her voice. All he had of her were scraps and clouded memories—a scent that brought on a wave of nostalgia and a few bars of a lullaby that caused an ache within him.

But he'd believed her when she said she would find him. And he would never stop looking until he learned the truth of why she hadn't done what she'd promised.

No matter what Kyara had done or why, he needed to find her. He needed to hear her story.

CHAPTER TWENTY

A spirit made this world and gave it life
And veins of blood we were not meant to hoard
But growing bonds of concord must give way
To chains forged in the fires that came before
What daughter seeking love would not repay
A plea for help from one soon for the grave?

—THE BOOK OF UNVEILING

Darvyn followed Kyara's trail three hours west to the edges of the ruins of Tanagol, an ancient city lost at the beginning of the war with Elsira five hundred years ago. It was not his first time at these ruins.

He found the stolen crawler cooling on the outskirts of the city, at the base of a crumbled structure with only one sandstone wall partially intact. Kyara had made it a dozen paces beyond, but lay in a heap on the ground, her tunic coated in blood. She cried out, jerking and twitching, her body raising up and smashing back down in the midst of a seizure.

Darvyn ran to her and crouched, drawing Earthsong to him and searching in vain for a way to heal her. Her shield, or whatever it was, held strong as ever. He could not grasp hold of her life energy.

"Stay away," she shouted, surprising him. He hadn't thought she was lucid. Her pack had been flung several paces away, but her body flopped toward it, as if out of her control. She screamed, her cry tinged with pain and frustration. "No! Darvyn!"

"What's happening?"

Her head thrashed back and forth. "Don't let me touch it." Her eyes opened, and she stared right at him. Then her gaze was lost in another convulsion, strangled screams ripping out of her throat.

Her arm spasmed, rising and crashing back down onto the rock and rubble on the ground. She smashed her hand down again and again, drawing blood. A war took place inside her body. Darvyn tried to stop her, but she pulled out of his grip with incredible strength.

"She'll find you . . . Keep it away," she said between gasps.

"Who will find me? Keep what away?"

"Cantor. R-red stone." The words were drawn out of her hoarsely. She spasmed again and lurched toward her pack.

A tiny bit of rock wriggled out of the bag of its own accord. The bloodred stone jiggled and jumped like a grasshopper, moving closer and closer to Kyara's mangled hand. She wailed and drew her arm away only to have it crash down near the stone again. Darvyn picked up the vibrating rock and threw it hard enough that it sailed in a huge arc, disappearing in the ruins.

The shaking in Kyara's limbs quieted. Her head crashed to the ground, still. Darvyn fell to his knees beside her bruised and bleeding body. One side of her face was swollen unrecognizably, dirt and gravel embedded in the skin. Her right hand was a pulpy mess.

Opening himself to a rush of Earthsong, he forced it into her as he'd done before, but the energy would no longer take hold. He used more and more, flooding her, with no effect.

Her breathing slowed until the motion of her chest was barely perceptible.

She was dying.

And he couldn't save her.

Old guilt seeped from his memories to mix with this new helplessness. Regardless of what she'd done to him or whom she worked for, she needed to live.

There was only one person who could help, and as much as it pained him to call on Her after weeks free of Her interference, he had no choice.

Darvyn sat on the ground cross-legged and folded his hands in his lap. For this to work he'd have to calm down and empty his mind. His breathing slowed as he muted his Song. He didn't need the rushing energy of life around him now, only the stillness of sleep. Earthsong was too vibrant; he searched within for tranquility, the deeper link that he found only in his dreams.

Soon, he found himself in a darkened place, the sound of wind in his ears and nothing but blackness around him. He was weightless, bodiless, just a consciousness in endless space.

"You visit me, Darvyn?" a voice, honey thick, echoed all around him. "I am honored."

"I have been enjoying having my dreams to myself," Darvyn

said. His vision was still filled with black. "This is easier when I can see you."

A light materialized in front of him in the shape of a woman. Slowly, She came into focus, and the brightness of Her body dimmed. She was illuminated by no force he could ever identify, a golden glow that added to Her otherworldly quality.

"Your Majesty," he said, not bothering to put any kind of veneration in his voice.

"Darvyn." The Queen Who Sleeps smiled and inclined her head. "To what do I owe the pleasure?" Ebony hair cascaded in a riot of tight curls to Her shoulders. Her eyes flashed, dark and intense.

He had never shared with anyone his ability to contact the Queen at will. The elders would never have given him a moment's peace had they known, and it would only serve to separate him even more from the other Keepers. He hadn't sought her out in this way since he was a child. After the last time, he'd vowed never to do it again, but life humbled all men.

"Were you watching? Did you see?" he asked, impatience overtaking him.

"Yes, I did." Her voice held a smile, though Her face did not.

"Who is she? Why can't I heal her or sense her at all?"

"It is not a happy story."

"Please," he plead through clenched teeth.

The Queen clasped Her hands together and turned slightly. In front of Her, the darkness shimmered and became an image of the Living World.

A sand-colored courtyard appeared where two young girls chased one another beneath a flowering tree. Darvyn recognized the smaller of the two girls as Kyara—little and sad and fierce.

"Let's play shelter and search," the taller girl said. "You're the searcher. No peeking."

Young Kyara covered her eyes with her hands and began to count aloud. The other girl scampered off. When Kyara reached twenty, she opened her eyes and began to search.

Several women walked by. When they did, Kyara would stop her searching and stand quietly, eyes to the ground until she was passed. The women never gave her a second glance.

"What is this place?" Darvyn asked.

The Queen sighed. "One of the harem's cabals."

In the vision, a scream sounded, followed by a man's voice shouting unintelligibly. Little Kyara froze before breaking into a run. She tore down a covered path and stopped before a closed door. On the other side, something large crashed to the ground.

Shaking, Kyara opened the door and entered a dark space. She struggled to light a lamp in the entry, when suddenly every lamp in the room lit on its own.

"Earthsong," Darvyn muttered.

Light illuminated a storage room lined with shelves full of crates, jars, and pots. One shelf shook as a man in tattered clothes with matted hair attacked the taller girl.

"Ahlini!" Kyara cried out, rushing to her friend's side. She beat at the man, who had a grip around the girl's throat. Small fires bloomed on the floor and shelving. A young Earthsinger would not be able to control her power in such a situation, though Darvyn still wasn't certain if just one or both of the girls were to blame.

Kyara grabbed a clay jar and smashed it over the man's head, but it hardly affected him. He smacked her, sending her small body flying across the room. Then, suddenly, all was still.

The man collapsed. Ahlini looked lifeless as well. Darvyn leaned forward, squinting at the vision.

Fire licked up the shelves and crossed the ground, drawing nearer to the three prone bodies. Kyara sat up groggily, rubbing the back of her head. Blood came away on her fingers. Irrational relief filled Darvyn. He knew Kyara had survived this, but watching it all unfold made it seem so present.

Kyara crawled over to her friend and began to shake her. Smoke filled the room. Footsteps approached; an older woman rushed in and pulled Kyara into her arms as others raced to put out the fires. Kyara coughed and sputtered, calling out her friend's name as the older woman carried her out of the smoke.

The image froze.

Darvyn turned to the Queen who remained expressionless. "What was that? Why did you show me?"

"That is where it all began for your assassin. She killed two people without even realizing it."

Darvyn shook his head. "I don't understand. I didn't see her kill anyone."

Movement in the vision began again, revealing two armed women dressed as soldiers entering the storage room, much of which was ash now. These must be the harem guards.

"How did he get in?" one asked. The other shrugged.

The first guard knelt beside the girl, Ahlini, and pried open her eyes. The whites had turned black.

The guard hissed a curse and jumped back. "It's plague," she spat, drawing a circle on her forehead with her finger to ward off disease.

"That's not possible," the other guard responded, but both women backed away from the bodies, their fear visible.

The Queen flicked her wrist and the vision changed. It was

sometime later. Kyara was locked in a dungeon cell. She was filthy and covered in flea bites. Her arms and legs were streaked red with blood from where she'd scratched. Male guards approached her cell and opened the door. She met them with hollow eyes.

"Am I to be executed now?"

The guards didn't answer, but lifted her by shackled arms and dragged her from the cell. She hung like a rag doll between the large men. Rage swelled inside of Darvyn.

"How could she have killed with the plague? How could they die so quickly?"

The Queen said nothing, merely inclined Her head indicating he should watch.

The guards towed young Kyara up many sets of steps through the glass castle of Sayya. The walls were a deep shade of violet with just a blush of red creeping in as spring turned to summer.

She was led through a massive, elaborately carved wooden door, and onto a balcony where buckets of water were dumped on her, washing away some of the grime. Then the guards pulled her back into the room—an impressive library—where she gaped up at the towering shelves full of books. A tall woman stepped before her, shooing the guards away.

The woman was striking, dressed head to toe in a golden, jewel-encrusted gown. Her eyes were an arresting mossy green. They nearly glowed against the deep shade of her skin, giving her an otherworldly quality.

"Do you know who I am, child?" the woman cooed, coming to stand over her.

Kyara swallowed. "The Cantor."

So this was the infamous Ydaris. Darvyn had heard stories,

but had never before seen the woman responsible for so much destruction and harm.

"How did you kill that man and the girl?" the Cantor asked.

Kyara's lips quivered. "I don't know." Her voice was barely audible.

"No, I suppose you wouldn't. Come over here."

They crossed the library, passing tables laden with books and papers. One held the dissected electronic innards of a radio-phonic. Bowls and vials and powders and a startling assortment of knives lay on yet another. Ydaris led Kyara to a plain, gray stone table at the edge of the room.

"Lay down here." Her voice brooked no opposition, and Kyara complied. "You thought you were born without a Song, but you were wrong. You have a Song. It is just different from everyone else's. The *ulla* of your cabal should have brought you to me when you were born, after you killed your mother."

Kyara gasped.

"Oh, you didn't know? Well, so be it. I killed mine, too. They're rather useless creatures, mothers."

Darvyn's heart shredded as he watched the little girl buckle with the weight of sudden guilt and sorrow.

"She thought you were special," the Cantor continued. "Thought you were the answer to some sort of pagan prophecy—the *ulla*, not your mother. These superstitious heathens never cease to amaze me. Would you like to know what you are? Why your Song is impossibly deadly?"

Kyara blinked several times and managed to nod.

"First, we must be sure you don't get out of sorts and murder anyone else."

The Cantor produced a rippling white blade from the bench

next to the stone table and held it over Kyara, then cut away the
girl's ragged tunic until she lay naked.

"This may sting a bit." The Cantor closed her eyes and said a
string of words in a foreign language, gruff and guttural. Then
she lifted the blade and began carving into Kyara's chest.

It was several moments before Kyara screamed. A sympathetic pain burned Darvyn's skin as the Cantor twisted her wrist
elegantly, creating a design in blood and flesh.

"What is she doing?" Darvyn asked. He wanted to look away,
but forced himself to watch. Kyara had actually gone through it,
this was the least he could do. When she finally passed out, the
Queen's vision faded to blackness.

"Ydaris created a very powerful blood spell." The Queen's
voice held no emotion. "It forces Kyara to obey or else be tortured with a pain intense enough to kill many times over. It is
only because of her Song that she survived it for so long. Kyara is
one of those things born every few generations—an anomaly. In
my time, we killed those like her at birth. They upset the balance
of things. They are harbingers of bad times."

Darvyn had a hard time reconciling the Queen's words with
what he knew of Kyara. True, she had lied and he hadn't been
able to see it, but his own heart could not have falsified their
connection. He focused on the fact that she had tried to kill him,
willing the anger and betrayal to overcome him, but kept coming back to the desperation he'd seen in her eyes. She'd wanted
to protect him, as well. "What is she?"

"A poison. A cancer. You would do well to leave her spirit
here and allow her body to die. I have a feeling she would welcome it."

"Kyara is here? In the World Between?"

The Queen inclined Her head. "Until her body dies, she will

not be able to cross to the World After. But that is not your concern. Especially after what she did to you, what she planned. And what she did to Jaqros."

Jack. Ashamed he had not thought of his friend before, Darvyn searched his Song for the tendrils of the spell that had connected him to Jack. He could maintain a spell in his sleep, but whatever Kyara had done to him had cut him off from Earthsong completely. The thread of the spell was gone. Jack's disguise must have worn off.

"What's happened to him?"

"He lives."

Darvyn closed his eyes in relief. "But where is he? Is he hurt?"

"Your concern is a bit late, is it not? His path is set." Obsidian eyes sparkled at him. Further questions would fall on deaf ears. She had long ago warned him that Her guidance was available only for that which could be changed. Which meant whatever had happened to Jack could not be altered. Darvyn tensed, his anger and resentment toward the Queen surfacing.

He vowed to find Jack for himself. But now he sought his own answers. "I need to know why Kyara had my mother's pendant. You've never told me what happened to Mama."

"I am not omniscient, Darvyn. I see much but not all." Another evasion.

Darvyn clenched his teeth. "Can you at least tell me how to save Kyara? Her fate is not yet set."

"Why would you want to do that?"

"Will you tell me or not?"

The Queen shrugged. "It is possible Nethersong could help her. It may keep her alive. For a time. Though it is merely a stopgap. Only Ydaris can lift her spell."

"Nethersong?"

"Did you think that Earthsong was the only power that existed? Earthsong is life, but death is just as powerful. Some would argue it is more powerful. Earthsong cannot kill or harm directly, but Nethersong can. Life cleaves to life, death to death."

"So her power is . . . death? The poison comes directly from her?"

"It does."

"And death will keep her alive?"

The Queen spread Her arms. "The rules of Nethersong differ from Earthsong, but the energy of death should help her fight the blood spell. Temporarily."

"But we're in the ruins of a city. A great battle was lost here. Thousands died."

"Too long ago to be of use to her. That energy has dissipated, she needs something more recent, and in great quantities. A cemetery would do, but the Lagrimari burn their dead and the Nether scatters. A fresh battlefield would suffice or perhaps somewhere such as Serpent's Gorge."

He'd heard of the place. It was much farther north than he'd ever been. The gorge was the border between the livable part of Lagrimar and the Scald, a desert so hot that nothing could survive. The True Father used to exile his enemies to the Scald, generations ago. Now, only the Avinid pilgrims ventured there on their suicide trips.

There were other tales of Serpent's Gorge, fantastical stories he hadn't believed. Accounts of a living graveyard, with animals turned to stone just by coming near the gorge's toxic waters. If the stories were true then the place would be full of this Nethersong, the energy of death.

"It's a long way. Will she survive the trip?"

The Queen smiled enigmatically. "She already has survived far longer than she should have." The space before Her rippled until another vision appeared. This one of Kyara on the crawler, racing through the brush before she'd collapsed. She was bleary-eyed and in agony, but determined.

Darvyn's chest clenched, reacting to the sight of her obvious pain. "Then help me save her. I have done everything you've ever asked. Do this for me. Please."

The Queen sighed. "I will send her back to her body. A steady trickle of Nethersong should sustain her life until you reach the gorge."

Evidently tired of his company, She dismissed him, fading back into the darkness.

"Thank you," he said as She disappeared. He worked to calm his mind and bring himself back to consciousness. Moments later, he blinked his eyes open to find Kyara already stirring.

One side of her face was lovely and smooth, the other mangled and swollen. Her eyes fluttered beneath their lids; her mouth opened and closed. She sucked in a breath, then her hands shot to her chest. She rolled onto her side, licked her lips, and tried to speak, but no words came out.

"Death energy," he muttered to himself. "And fresh."

He extended his senses, searching the area. A new city of wildlife had moved in to take the place of Tanagol's former residents. Life bloomed all around, springing from the destruction. A lizard stuck its head out from the rocks behind him, and Darvyn grabbed it before the animal darted away.

For an Earthsinger, to cause death was torturous. He would feel every moment of the creature's agony. He thought about his mother, about the years of not knowing what happened to her, why she never came for him, and steeled himself to twist the animal's neck. Suddenly, Kyara's eyes shot open. Her hand reached out to stop him, her gaze questioning.

"You're dying. You need something dead to keep you alive," he explained.

She moved her lips, trying to speak.

"Please trust me." He looked down at the wriggling critter in his grip.

She shook her head and forced the words out. "Find . . . already . . . dead."

The effort of speaking seemed to take the last of her strength. She closed her eyes, and her body went still except for the quivering of her chest as she struggled for breath. Darvyn's heart clenched at Kyara's words. How could she be the Poison Flame? She did not even want to harm a lizard.

He released the animal, relief sagging his shoulders as it scurried back through a crack between the rocks. Kneeling next to her, he stroked the uninjured skin of her face before rising to start his search.

The wreckage of the city held an odd beauty, its stillness almost hypnotic. Toward the center, buildings stood nearly intact. The spiral streets had protected these ruins from the ravages of time and weather. A white obelisk rose from the ground, capturing his attention. It remained pristine and glowed with an unnatural light. Something about it seemed very unusual, but he dragged his gaze away and continued his quest for a freshly dead animal.

Finally, at the edge of the city, he located a suricate, a tiny furry animal known for its viciousness in contrast to its gentle appearance. The suricate had a huge snake—a desert sidewinder as thick as Darvyn's arm—in its grip and was biting through its neck.

Darvyn threw a rock at the suricate, who hissed then ran off into the bush. With the knife from his belt, Darvyn completed severing the snake's head. It was a mercy, though he still winced as death took the reptile. He carried it back to where Kyara lay.

He laid the snake's body within her reach. Her labored breathing began to stabilize, and her eyelids fluttered but did not open. She appeared to be in a peaceful slumber.

A heavy tension lifted from Darvyn's shoulders once she seemed stable. Now, he had to get her to Serpent's Gorge, hundreds of kilometers away. The swiftcycle was not designed to carry two, but the crawler's fuel tank read empty, so he had little choice. Unsure of how long the effects of the dead snake would last, he needed to hurry.

He gathered Kyara's slack form into his arms and carried her to the swiftcycle. Seated on his lap she was liable to fall off and over the side, and he needed both his hands to steer the contraption. Once again he tied a length of rope around both of their waists, securing her to him. With the addition of her weight, it would be slow-going. He wondered how many dead animals he would have to find in order to keep her alive on the trip.

CHAPTER TWENTY-ONE

The task now set, the worker takes her place
To master her bequest, her legacy
And bleed a spell that will serve to protect
The life work that had fueled her father's grief
Alone again until the work was done
The Scorpion secured the cornerstone

—THE BOOK OF UNVEILING

The noise of a bustling town greeted Zeli as she emerged from the nabbers' building. "What town is this?" she asked.

"Checkpoint Ten," Kyssa replied. Two other girls had joined their group, both newly purchased servants indentured to Kyssa's mistress.

"Ora-mideni owns a factory just outside of town. But I'll take you to the dormitory first as it's nearby."

A shiver went up Zeli's spine to think of her sleeping quarters being so close to the place where she'd been sold. But she reminded herself the nabbers didn't stay in one place for very long. Even now, they were likely clearing out, on to their next hideout. Preparing to capture more unlucky children.

"Miss Kyssa," one of the two girls who'd joined them began. She was about thirteen with a lopsided braid.

Kyssa stopped walking abruptly. "We speak High Lagrimari here, ladies. Mind your tongues."

"Sorry Kyssa-deni," the girl mumbled, swallowing whatever her question had been.

The town's spiraling main street was crowded. Kyssa kept a brisk pace, and the girls hastened to follow. They stopped at a two-story building on the outskirts of the spiral, but not so far out as to make Zeli feel unsafe. From what she could tell, this was a standard Midcountry dwelling with mud bricks and shuttered windows to keep out wind and sand.

"This is where you'll sleep and take your off-shift meals," Kyssa said, leading them inside. The home opened into a living space with a long, low table surrounded by frayed seating cushions. In the back was the kitchen, and all the other rooms appeared to be sleeping quarters. Though it was midday, many straw pallets were occupied by slumbering girls.

They didn't go upstairs, but Zeli assumed the second floor held more of the same. Once outside again after the brief tour, Kyssa began walking and talking. "You'll work twelve-hour shifts and return here when you're off duty." She led them out of town, using a well-worn path that cut through the bush. "After today, you all will draw straws to determine who works days and who works nights."

"The factory runs at night?" Zeli asked. She hadn't seen any electricity wires anywhere in town. "How will we work in the dark? And how do the machines run?"

"The factory sits atop an ether well. Ora-mideni devised her own way to funnel the gas seeping from the ground into pipes that fuel lanterns as well as the master turbine for the line shafts."

A flurry of questions rose, but before Zeli could ask, the factory became visible at the bottom of a slight hill. It was a wide structure more modern than most of the buildings in town. Constructed of smoothly hewn, golden sandstone, the long, rectangular structure looked almost majestic.

But as they drew nearer, a rhythmic whirring noise grew louder. When Kyssa led them through the door, the sheer volume inside was all Zeli could perceive for long moments. As her ears grew used to the hissing, wheezing, and slapping of machinery, she focused on what caused it.

The space was entirely open with thick columns holding up the roof. Orderly rows of wide tables held a variety of contraptions. All across the ceiling, wheels with belts wrapped around them spun. The belts were attached to more wheels and more belts and each machine on the tables below was somehow connected. All of the spinning caused the great noise that filled the air. Girls and women from five to twenty-five stood at the tables, sometimes on crates or stools, engaged in their work.

All of the new girls, including Zeli, stared wide-eyed at the enormity of the operation.

"This is one of His Majesty's three factories for munitions," Kyssa yelled. "Well, two now. One blew up a week ago because the workers weren't careful. You all will need to heed instructions very carefully or you'll share the fate of those poor souls."

A rock hardened inside Zeli's belly. How many had perished in the explosion?

They followed Kyssa down the rows like obedient ducklings. The first tables were for assembling casings. This factory made bullets and artillery shells used in the guns and massive canons the Lagrimari army brought into war. The workers didn't look up as the new girls gawked.

"Littlest fingers with me," Kyssa announced, and a girl of Ulani's size stepped forward. Ulani looked unsure at first, but moved to Kyssa's side. They were then handed off to a surly child of about ten who began instructing them on their task.

"What are they doing?" Zeli ventured to ask.

"Assembling the detonators. Lots of small fuses and springs. Tiny hands and fingers are helpful."

Zeli nodded and hastened to catch up as the woman marched on. She and Tana were offloaded at a wide table near the center of the factory floor where bullets were pressed. At one end, several girls manned narrow machines with levers that, when pulled, shaped sheets of copper into cylindrical bullet casings. Zeli was assigned the filling station and tasked with packing the casings with gunpowder. The smell of the stuff tickled her nose.

A young woman named Nedra was pulled from her own station to instruct them. She looked to be in her early twenties with eyes set far apart in a round face.

"This is what you do," she said, holding up a funnel. A tiny spoon was used to measure the black powder before pouring it through the funnel and into the casing.

"Not too much and not too little, mind you," Nedra said. "There isn't enough to spare on mistakes. Rounds from each girl are tested at random, so we'll know if you do it wrong."

After Nedra filled the casing, she placed it in a slot in a large box full of completed bullets. When the box was full, she passed it off to the next girl on the line for finishing.

"So that's all there is to it?" Zeli asked.

Nedra raised an eyebrow. "You want it to be more complicated?"

"Well, no . . . It's just that . . . we do this for twelve hours?" Filling tiny bullets with powder seemed incredibly boring.

Nedra shrugged. "That's the job. You get two five-minute breaks for the privy and thirty minutes for lunch." She dragged over a box of casings waiting for their powder and moved back to her other duties without waiting for any more questions. Zeli sighed.

The girls at her table weren't talkative. A few looked up and nodded before refocusing on their tasks. Zeli thought about how much worse things could be and determined to make the best of it.

At the end of her first shift, her feet hurt from standing, her arm hurt from pouring, and her eyes hurt from squinting to see if she'd filled the little casing up or not. Often the powder got stuck in the funnel and had to be tapped out, but that would often cause it to shake out of the bullet. Then she'd have to empty the casing and start all over again. After close to a dozen hours of this, she wanted nothing more than to eat and collapse into whatever bed was available. She could tell the other girls felt the same.

The day workers trudged back to the dormitory, passing the night workers, coming in to start their shift. There were actually several houses earmarked for the girls, and they split off into their assigned quarters. There they were fed standard rations: tough, dried meat and a porridge of some kind that had the consistency of sludge and no taste to speak of. But it didn't smell rotten and didn't make her feel sick. There was that.

At dinner, there was more conversation than there had been at work. Several of the girls chatted amiably with one another and introductions were made. Zeli wanted to ask each of them how they'd gotten there, but she suspected the stories would be too sad and so stayed quiet.

Before they left the table, Nedra, who lived in their dormitory, stood and addressed them. "Remember, eyes and ears open. Be sure to make time in your off hours to observe and report. Anyone with pertinent information is to alert your section leader."

"What does that mean?" Zeli whispered to the girl next to her, who looked to be about her age.

"Ora-mideni is upwardly bound," the girl replied. "She wants to know about anyone you may see who might not be completely loyal. She uses her workers as eyes and ears around town to get in good with the local Magister."

Zeli nodded, understanding. On her other side, Tana snorted. "So she's an informer? And she wants us to participate? No, thank you."

The girl eyed her in astonishment. "Those who give her good intel get treats. Extra rations, coffee, or even sugar." She smiled as if the thought of treats was enough to wash away the slime of the deed she was so casually discussing.

Tana looked away. "Not. Worth. It." She crossed her arms. The other teen shrugged. So their twelve hours off weren't exactly their own.

"What if we don't do it?" Zeli asked.

The girl frowned as if this option had never occurred to her. "Ora-mideni prefers if you do. If you make the mistress angry you could get sent away." She didn't specify where "away" was, but the haunted tone in her voice was telling.

"And what's to stop someone from lying?" Tana asked loudly.

Nedra turned from the woman she'd been speaking to and tilted her head, staring at Tana. "All information will be investigated by the Enforcers," she said, tightly.

But Zeli knew as well as everyone else here that truth was not a prerequisite when informing. Nudging Tana with her shoulder, she smiled at Nedra. "Of course. We'll keep our eyes and ears open." Nedra nodded and turned to head up the staircase.

Zeli turned to Tana. "You don't have to say every thought that's in your head, you know."

A mulish expression pinched the child's face. "I'm not a snitch. Do you really plan on informing on people?"

Zeli knew she wouldn't, but she couldn't stop others from it. That was how Lagrimar worked, after all. How else would the True Father know who to trust?

She shook her head quickly. She wouldn't tell on anyone, but she wouldn't call attention to herself, either. Tana, however, was digging a deep hole that she might not be able to get herself out of.

CHAPTER TWENTY-TWO

The world outside the Mountain Mother's womb
Kept secrets from the Folk incurious
With Songs now silent, quiet as a tomb
Outsiders had become injurious
Here entered a new player to the stage
An enigmatic stranger to engage

—THE BOOK OF UNVEILING

"*Again.*"

Ydaris's *voice echoed against the walls of the darkened chamber.*
Iron bars surrounded Kyara, forming a cage meant for a large animal.
Beyond the bars, the edges of the surrounding room faded into shadow.
The Cantor was out there somewhere, watching her every move.

"*No more,*" Kyara *cried, struggling to breathe. Her entire body* was a tangle of misery, her muscles were jelly, and she could barely lift her head off the cold floor.

"Again," Ydaris repeated, her voice steely. This time it held the command of the spell. Flames of pain licked out from the carving in Kyara's chest, her own skin and flesh turning against her.

"Grab hold of the scarf and this will all be over."

Kyara's vision was nearly gone, only a few spots of light marred the field of dark before her eyes. She rolled to her knees and propped herself on her forearms. The blaze in her chest quieted a fraction—it rewarded obedience.

She dragged herself across the slick brick floor, wet with sweat and blood and other bodily fluids Kyara didn't dare think of, until the bars stopped her progress. On top of the anguish of the wound's searing pain, she was hungry, sleep deprived, and caked with dirt and grime.

She pressed herself against the bars, reaching one skinny arm through. The scarf lay just out of reach, only a hairbreadth from the tips of her fingers. Try as she might, she could not reach it. The echoing of Ydaris's command pressed her to try harder, pushed her until she wedged her already torn and bloodied shoulder into the space between the bars farther and farther, regardless of the fact that it did not fit.

Resisting the spell brought pain, but even trying to obey brought no relief if she was not progressing.

"I want you to understand very clearly the consequences of your stubbornness," Ydaris said. All this because Kyara had faltered in her practice.

Her training had progressed over the past year from small animals to larger ones: insects, rats, tortoises, and a pair of captured wild dogs. She had killed them all, slowly becoming able to remain conscious and aware of how and when her power unfurled. The grief for all the creatures whose lives she'd taken was buried deep within her; she numbed herself to its bitter taste.

She'd found the pale iguana just outside her bedroom window, located next to the Cantor's library. Unsure of how it had gotten so high in the castle, she'd befriended it and fed it leaves she collected during the rare times she was allowed outside. The lizard ate directly from her hand, and she'd poured all her love into it, hoping to keep it safe.

But Ydaris had told her she would have no secrets. The Cantor found the iguana and ordered Kyara to kill it. She'd hesitated, withstanding the initial suffering, hoping maybe her little friend would sense the danger and scurry away. But Kyara could not hold out for long. Her weakness and desire to be free from the agony had won out and the iguana had gone still.

Now she was being punished. She screamed as the muscle in her shoulder tore against the rough texture of the bars. The Cantor would not accept anything less than full compliance. The unyielding pain propelled Kyara to search for a way to obey. She pushed against the rigid metal harder and harder still, until a pop sounded and the excruciating pain in her chest was replaced with one almost as severe from her dislocated shoulder. But her fingertips finally grasped hold of the scarf, curling it tight to her palm as she shuddered at the edge of consciousness.

Footsteps sounded across the floor, and the Cantor's jewel-studded shoes stopped next to Kyara's hand. The scarf was plucked from her fingertips.

"Very good," Ydaris said. "We shall try something a bit harder tomorrow."

Kyara didn't have the strength to pull herself back. She rested her forehead against the iron, her arm still bent unnaturally, shoulder out of joint, her only solace the knowledge that it would be several hours yet before her training continued.

A shroud of heat pressed against Kyara, taking with it the vestiges of the dream. She had not thought of those dark days in some time. She'd hoped to never think of them again. The sun beamed down upon her closed eyes, blinding her even in the darkness. She pressed her lids tighter, seeking relief. Suddenly something shaded the light, and she opened her eyes a fraction.

A round object floated above her head. Her mind cleared enough to name it as a parasol. She opened her mouth to try to speak, and water was promptly poured in. The liquid was warm but refreshing. She relished every drop. Her entire body was sore, as if she'd undergone a sound beating, but this was a far cry from the raging torment of her training.

She stretched her stiff limbs and blinked again. The parasol above her was purple. Odd. Where had it come from? And what was she lying on? The hard surface under her back trembled and shook. The roll of wheels vibrated below her and the clop of horses' feet kept good time.

"What do you need?" a familiar voice said from somewhere beyond her vision.

Darvyn.

She wanted to scramble away, needed to keep him safe, but she couldn't lift herself up. The best she could do was roll to the side, away from his voice, only to find three women staring at her.

Kyara's mouth hung open in surprise. Two of the women had hair streaked with gray, the third appeared closer to her own age. Their wide-eyed stares were unnerving. She painfully turned her head away only for her cheek to meet something solid and warm. Darvyn's face appeared directly above her, blocking her view of the parasol. She realized that she must be lying with her head in his lap.

Gasping out breaths, she tried to form words, but her mouth was as uncooperative as her arms and legs. All she could do was rotate her head again to find the three women still ogling her.

"Hot," was the only word she managed to eject from her lips.

"You were shivering. I wasn't sure if you were cold or not," Darvyn said. A weight was lifted from her, allowing her skin to breathe again. Her limbs felt immediately lighter, and she turned her head the other way to see Darvyn folding up a blanket.

"Who?" Her throat and tongue were still not cooperating entirely.

Darvyn's mouth settled into a grim line. She wished he would smile. "They're Avinid pilgrims. We came across their caravan, and they were kind enough to give us a ride. The swiftcycle doesn't handle two very well. We were too heavy and slow. I was afraid we wouldn't make it in time."

Kyara vaguely recalled the sound of wind beating against fabric. She must have regained consciousness briefly, but she had no idea how much time had passed or where they were even headed. "Where?"

Fortunately, Darvyn understood her monosyllabic communication. "We're heading to Serpent's Gorge."

Her head felt wobbly as confusion clouded her mind. She turned away, needing him out of her line of sight if she had any hope of concentrating on his words. Except now her vision was assaulted by the brilliant clothing of the pilgrims. The women wore the garish, multihued tunics that marked devout Avinids. Yellows, oranges, blues, greens, and purples—all mashed together in chaotic patterns, no two the same.

Brightly colored fabric was largely a frivolity reserved for payrollers. However, even their brilliantly varied wardrobes paled in comparison to the dizzying array of the Avinids. Ironic, since, judging by the intense heat, these believers were currently on their way to certain death.

While she professed familiarity with the Void, Kyara had

never quite understood the sect. Avinids met weekly in their temples, meditated, and prayed to the Void, and the very devout, once they'd reached a certain level of enlightenment, made the pilgrimage, either north to the burning Scald or to the Gelid, the frozen tundra in the south of Lagrimar. They claimed it was not a suicide trip, but no one had ever returned.

If the blood spell hadn't made suicide impossible for Kyara, she may have asked to join their one-way journey a long time ago. Would death in the burning sands of the north be more peaceful than her life had been thus far?

Darvyn's face moved into her vision again. She wanted to close her eyes against him but couldn't bring herself to. Haloed in the filtered light still coming through the parasol, he looked like some being from another world here to bring salvation. Like the men of light Nerys was always going on about.

Nerys.

Darvyn's tunic was untied at the top and the two pendants were visible lying against his chest. She reached out to them before she could stop herself, then quickly withdrew her hand.

He leaned back out of her limited range of sight. The cart rolled along, jerking and bumping over the desert terrain. The pillow of his thighs against the back of her head made her blood heat in a way that had nothing to do with the stifling temperature.

The all-over ache that had overwhelmed her when she'd awoken was melting away. "What's in Serpent's Gorge?" she finally asked once she felt she could get all the words out.

"Have you noticed anything different about your desire to kill me?"

"I'm not supposed to kill you," she muttered but noticed that her chest pulsed only with a dull ache. She was literally on top of an unrestrained and uncollared Shadowfox, yet she remained conscious and alert. She was not in agonizing pain. "What's happened?"

"I think it's starting. The closer we get, the more peaceful you've been. We're still half a day away, but you're so much better. The Nethersong is keeping the Cantor's spell at bay."

Kyara's hand shot to her breast. The wound was still there, covered with the days-old, blood-encrusted bandages. "How do you know about the spell?"

"The Queen Who Sleeps told me."

"The Queen— What?"

"It's a long story, but I can speak with Her. She told me that a place with an abundance of what She called Nethersong is the only thing that could help you. And so, Serpent's Gorge."

"And Death River?"

He leaned over her again, his face grim but not unkind. She almost asked him why he was helping her after she'd tried to capture him, but then she caught sight of the pendants again.

"Nerys," she said. "You want to know."

Darvyn froze. His gaze flicked over to the women sharing the cart.

Kyara closed her eyes, grateful for the reprieve. He deserved the full story. She had made a promise, after all.

The cart rattled on. Darvyn's voice, when it came, was weary and cautious. "The Queen showed me what happened to you. How you got the spell."

Kyara rubbed her chest, the familiar, ever-present ache just a low hum.

"I'm sorry," he said, his voice heavy.

Her eyes flew open. "No. Don't waste sympathy for me." She turned her head until the purple of the parasol was the only thing in her vision. Whatever he thought he knew was just a fraction of the whole story. If he knew the rest, he'd realize just how misplaced his compassion was. There were many who deserved his kindness, but Kyara was not one of them.

When the caravan stopped for lunch, Darvyn decided to ride up front with the wagon's driver. Watching over Kyara had grown unbearable. The unwanted pull toward her was still there under his skin, itching where he could not scratch. At least up top, gazing at the barren landscape, he could ignore her for a time.

Next to him, the driver whistled a cheerful tune. The man had introduced himself as ol-Waga—the same name every other Avinid pilgrim took. It meant "son of the Void." The women were all called ul-Waga for "daughter of the Void." Darvyn had no idea how they identified themselves more specifically, but perhaps it wasn't necessary when you were on your way to die.

He had waved the caravan down the day before, when it was clear the swiftcycle would not carry him and Kyara the distance they needed to travel. The pilgrims hadn't questioned why he was bringing an unconscious, battered woman to Serpent's Gorge. They merely agreed to transport them. The caravan would then continue west, following the twisting path of the canyon to the base of the western mountains where one could enter the Scald.

"What will you do when you arrive?" Darvyn asked during a break in the driver's whistling. This ol-Waga was a man of about forty with a salt-and-pepper beard.

"We will journey as far as we can, and then the Void will take us."

"But if you want to die, why go so far to do it? There are many ways to kill yourself."

"We do not seek death. Those who enter the World After will face the toils of life again one day when this world is ash and the next begins. What we seek is peace. And that may only be found in the emptiness beyond death."

"How do you know that the Void will take you before the Scald kills you?"

Ol-Waga smiled and lifted his face to the sun. "Faith. Our faith begs us make this pilgrimage." The man clapped Darvyn on the shoulder. "One day you will have faith in something that others cannot understand. It will not seem so strange to you then."

The man chuckled to himself and began whistling again. Darvyn looked back to Kyara, resting in the back. Perhaps he did understand.

The women and elderly rode in the open wagons. Half a dozen other men rode on horseback, bringing up the rear of the party. All were arrayed bright as peacocks, and all were on their way to die.

Try as he might, he could not tear his mind away from Kyara for long. She was growing stronger, but the closer they drew to the gorge, the less he was sure he was ready for the answers he desperately sought. The pendants pinged together with each jerk of the wagon and brought to mind his mother's voice. He could no longer picture her face, but her words were still clear: *I will find you again.* They repeated over and over in his mind.

No matter how Kyara had come into possession of the pendant, it could mean only one thing: the only place he would see his mother now would be in the World After. The hope he'd nurtured for a lifetime would take a long time to die.

As they drew closer to the gorge, the landscape began to

change. Gone were any birds flying overhead. The yellow-brown dirt deepened in color, changing to a coppery red. The mountains looked different, as though they had been worn away from something even bigger and more imposing at one time. Earthsong revealed little else alive for kilometers around. This place must truly be glutted with death energy.

The wagon stopped one hundred paces away from a great cleft in the earth. Darvyn climbed down for a closer look. Walking in this heat was like wading through waist-high sand. He reached the edge and peered over. It looked as if someone had taken a giant knife and carved a twisting shape into the terrain. The gorge went straight down, nearly two kilometers in some places, he'd heard. At its floor was a still, black river—Death River some called it. Sunlight reflected off the water, making the surface sparkle but also displaying the horrible reality of the gorge. Along its shores, animals from birds to lizards to wild dogs and bobcats stood frozen. From this distance they looked like statues, carefully carved with the meticulous detail of a skilled artist. But they weren't made of stone. No artist would have lived long enough to carve them down there.

Darvyn hadn't truly believed it. "What caused this?" he wondered aloud.

The driver of the wagon came to stand behind him. "The river is fed by the Scorned Sea, that cursed place on the border of Lagrimar, Udland, and Yaly. To drink or touch its waters is to invite death. Those animals are sentries. They've been there for hundreds of years. Petrified from the inside out from the toxic water."

"Are we safe here?"

The man nodded. "But do not attempt to descend into the gorge."

Darvyn took a step back. The wind had changed and the smell coming from the water below hit his nose. It was not the fetid stink he had imagined, but a scent both bitter and tart that coated the back of his throat.

A dozen paces away, Kyara stepped right up to the edge of the cliff. Darvyn was relieved to find her upright and looking well. She wore a rainbow-colored tunic and trousers—she must have borrowed them from one of the pilgrims—and her pack was slung across her shoulders. Part of him was relieved to see her out of her bloodstained, torn clothing.

She took in the bizarre sight below with a grim expression at odds with her colorful attire. She hadn't looked at him directly yet. Instead, she kept her distance, her body as rigid as if she had been carved from stone herself.

"We must continue our journey," a younger ol-Waga said, approaching.

Darvyn tore his attention away from Kyara to greet him properly. "Thank you for your aid." Both men bowed slightly in acknowledgment.

"We will leave you a horse so that you may make the return trip," the newcomer said.

Darvyn had not considered the fate of the horses, leading these men and women into the Scald. He wondered if the Avinids believed animals, too, were accepted into the Void. Perhaps they thought the fate a blessing for the creatures and not a senseless loss of life.

"Thank you," Darvyn said, bowing. "That is much appreciated. Best of luck on your journey."

"The Void requires no luck, my friend. It will come to those who seek it."

Both men backed away and returned to their caravan. The

horsemaster approached and handed Darvyn the reins of a black stallion. Soon the pilgrims were on their way again, headed off toward the mountains.

Once they retreated into the distance, Darvyn turned back to Kyara who was still staring off into the canyon below. The gorge had captured her attention. He took a moment to study her profile. He'd done virtually nothing but stare at her for the better part of two days on their journey north and never grew tired of her face.

Her injuries had disappeared. This Nethersong must be the cause. The power she held was fascinating. Part of him feared the unknown magic, but part of him was excited to learn of something new, even if it was lethal. He well knew the hazards encountered by someone who bore a power that few could understand. He knew how it felt to be different.

It seemed Kyara and the gorge were linked in some way, and both were absolutely captivating.

"It's a strange sort of beauty," he said. She startled, her eyes darting in his direction and then away again.

"Beautiful but deadly," she whispered. She crouched down, sifting the red dirt between her fingers as Darvyn stepped closer. "All land holds both death and life. But this place . . ."

"Earthsong is here," Darvyn finished, spreading out his senses. "But it feels different." The energy that usually felt like a rushing rapid was muted.

"It has made its peace with death here," Kyara said. "They don't struggle as they do other places."

"What do you mean?"

She stood, letting the dirt fall through her fingers, then wiped her hands on her multicolored trousers. "They're in harmony. It's like they accept each other. Perhaps Earthsong has conceded control of this place." She closed her eyes. "In other places they're at odds, there's a tension that locks them in conflict. Here, that isn't the case."

"I think I understand." Darvyn couldn't sense Nethersong at all, but he could imagine what she felt. "Is that why it recharges you?"

She shrugged. "Perhaps. For all the horror down there in that water, there is also peace."

Peace. It seemed to be what everyone was seeking.

Kyara sat again, hugging her knees to her chest and looking small and alone. He secured the horse's reins to the thick branch of a bush and sat next to her. The wind echoed a hollow melody below them.

It was a long while before Kyara began to speak.

"I met her in Checkpoint Three." Her voice sounded as hollow as the wind, like it hurt her to speak. Almost as much as it hurt him to listen.

"Nerys ul-Tahlyro. I was half-starved and she was little better. She was begging in the street by the market, speaking about men made of light to anyone who passed. The townspeople said she was touched by the stars—addled, you know?" Kyara shook her head. "When a man shoved her to the ground, I helped her up."

"When was this?"

"I was eleven. Ten years ago."

Darvyn swallowed as a shiver went through him. So long ago.

Kyara continued. "She was limping, from the fall. Was she injured when you knew her?"

He shook his head.

"I helped her back to her little cottage at the edge of the spiral."

Darvyn closed his eyes. "She was an outcast?" Only those at the edges of society lived in the outer spiral of the Midcountry towns.

"Her home shared no walls. There was nothing to protect it. The wind whipped against it something awful and sandstorms would fill the place with grit, but it was the best place I've ever lived."

He looked up to find her smiling.

"Warm and full of love. Like she was." More emotion glimmered in Kyara's eyes than he'd ever seen.

"What were you doing all alone like that?"

Her expression sobered. "You said the Queen showed you?"

"I saw what the Cantor did." His gaze dropped to her chest. "Nothing afterward."

Kyara swallowed and looked off. "I was offered the opportunity to become an assassin for the True Father. Ydaris said she could teach me to control my power. To kill only when I meant to. I said no."

Darvyn frowned. "You said no?"

She eyed him with hostility. "I was a child. Of course I said no."

He held up his hands. "And what did the Cantor do?"

"She said I was free to go."

Darvyn's eyebrows climbed to his hairline.

"Of course food, clothing, and shoes were only available to the king's employees. And so I took my ripped tunic and left. I walked out of the glass castle determined never to return."

She ran a hand across her head where Ilynor's braids were still tightly woven. "A merchant's wife took me in and hid me in her stable, kept secret from her husband. She was very kind, but when her husband found me, he beat her for wasting food on an urchin." Kyara wrapped her arms around her as if to ward off a chill.

"When I tried to stop him, he pushed me back, and I fell against the stove." Absently, she ran her fingers across an old burn scar on her arm. "I could not help what happened next."

Children had to be taught to control their Songs. Even Darvyn, who was impossibly strong virtually from birth, had had the Keepers eventually to teach him. If what the Queen had said was right about Kyara, there were no other Nethersingers to show her how to manage her power. Kyara didn't give voice to what had happened to the man and his wife, but Darvyn could guess.

"After that, I stayed to myself. When I could. When I couldn't . . . people died." She cleared her throat. "Mostly nabbers and others with bad intentions, but anyone who was close to them would get caught as well. I didn't want to stay with Nerys, I didn't want to risk hurting her, but she needed me. And we were far enough away from everyone else that I thought maybe . . ."

The thought of his mother all alone and outcast cut Darvyn deeply. He should have been there. He should have found her. "What happened to her?"

"I already told you."

Darvyn's eyes widened.

"The physician." Her words hung in the air for a moment as the sorrow that had been kept at bay by the last shred of uncertainty rushed in. "He came offering salvation, but he killed her instead."

He stood suddenly, unable to keep still. "Did she suffer?" The lump in his throat made the words sound muddy.

"Her life was full of suffering. But not at the end. I made sure of it."

"Did she tell you why?"

"Why what?" Kyara looked up at him.

"Why she never came to find me?"

Her expression softened. She stood and touched his arm. He stared at her fingers on his skin for a moment before meeting her gaze.

"She did. She searched for you. Went from town to town, wherever she heard of the works of the Keepers. She would find them and ask them about the boy she'd given up, but no one would ever tell her where he was. Then she'd stay in a place for a while—she wove baskets and sold them for money—and then be off again. Always searching. *Always*."

Her fingers rose to his chest to the pendants hanging there. "'When I am gone to the World After,' she said." Kyara's lip began to quiver. "'Promise me you will find him.' She was sick and knew she didn't have much time left. I promised I would tell you that she loved you and never forgot you. And that you brought so much light into her life. Her little sun."

Darvyn's breath stuttered.

"I-I'm only sorry that I couldn't have kept my word sooner." She rubbed her chest again and walked away.

Unable to speak, Darvyn watched her go.

CHAPTER TWENTY-THREE

A more amazing view she'd never had
Than this fey creature gleaming like the sun
With skin of fire, radiant and bright
One glimpse of him and breath swept from her lungs
The darkness of her home shunned this new sight
There was no room inside it for the light

—THE BOOK OF UNVEILING

Something nudged the corner of Kyara's mind, pushing her into wakefulness. She started and sat up. The edges of dawn had just crisped the horizon. Her back groaned with complaint; her coat made a poor bed. Next to her, Darvyn slept peacefully.

She'd returned to where he was the night before, once twilight had bloomed. But neither had spoken again while they shared a dinner of jerky before going to sleep.

Kyara's sleep had been fitful, with visions of Ahlini and Nerys filling her dreams. Hope crushed was a terrible burden and Darvyn's desire to see his mother again had been pulverized.

Now, in the light of a new day, an awareness dawned on her, one that balanced the weight of hurting Darvyn. The spell had no power over her here. She was finally free.

At the edge of the gorge where Nether filled the air, she was free. Was it possible for her to live here forever? Perhaps this was the solution? Certainly, it was unpleasantly hot and there didn't appear to be any sources for food or drinking water, but those were minor roadblocks. Ydaris's spell had no impact here, and that was all that really mattered.

The timbre of her joy was interrupted by a buzzing in her ears. She waved the air around her head, but no insect made the sound. This low vibration must have awakened her. It felt familiar somehow, but grew louder and impossible to ignore. The sound was both in her head and outside of her, coming from somewhere nearby.

The edge of the gorge curved and disappeared behind a dip in the earth to the west. That was where the buzzing was coming from.

Kyara stood. She couldn't get the sound out of her head. It was like a beetle had crawled into her ear overnight and taken residence. Once she discovered the source she could rest easy, soaking up her newly discovered liberation.

She would just go investigate quickly. No need to worry Darvyn.

Darvyn awoke to the same steady ache in his bones that had been throbbing since Kyara shared her story. He kept his eyes closed, unwilling to start the first full day of knowing his mother was dead. It was foolish, he knew. He'd berated himself for hours the night before.

He forced his eyes open, determined to take on the day. Dawn cast an orange glow on the earth. Immediately, he felt Kyara's absence. He launched to his feet, surveying the area for any sight of her.

The horse was still there, gnawing in vain on a tough olden-berry bush. Kyara couldn't have gotten very far on foot, especially with no water. He opened himself to Earthsong, forgetting that he could not sense her that way. He had always relied on his power and was not a proficient tracker, but he slowed his racing heart and concentrated on scouring the area for footprints. The hard-packed red earth disclosed nothing to his untrained eyes. Panic threatened.

Where could she have gone? And why did she leave without a word?

He mounted the horse and calmed his breathing. She had told him what he'd needed to know last night and had given him the closure he sought. His fate was not tied to hers, but she was still his last connection to his mother. He told himself that was the reason for his concern.

The land to the east was flat. Nothing moved in that direction, but to the west, a deep bend in the gorge rose into a hill that hid the land beyond from sight. He rode in that direction, following the serpentine path of the canyon to crest the rise. The sight before him caused shock to tighten his limbs, and the horse slowed to a stop as Darvyn gaped.

Nestled into a teardrop-shaped section of the earth at the edge of the gorge, a city made of glass sparkled in the morning light. Spires and towers of crystal, here in the middle of nowhere.

He urged the horse to walk downhill, his amazement growing as they drew closer. The city could perhaps more properly
be called a town, being only the size of an average Midcountry
village from what he could tell. But each building was a glass
steeple pointing to the sky. Rising out of mounds of tough, red
earth were magnificent structures, far grander and more elaborate than the towers of the glass castle in Sayya.

A thick, glass wall surrounded the tiny city, interrupted by a
gap where a gate once stood. Beyond the wall, a wide avenue cut a
path through the interior. The streets were overgrown with
tough shrubbery, having been reclaimed by the desert. Some of
the buildings leaned against one another and had begun sinking
into the dirt. Other than that, there was little sign of decay. He
sensed nothing alive within. The place had been abandoned for
ages.

Darvyn dismounted and led the horse through the entry.
There, finally, he found Kyara, her lone form standing in the center of an avenue, head tilted up, staring slack-jawed at the way
the tops of the buildings touched the sky.

She was motionless, her body rigid. His concern grew when
he reached her.

"Kyara," he called out, but her vacant expression didn't
change. He repeated her name again and again, waving his hand
in front of her eyes before pulling her hand into his own. Her eyes
remained glassy, her face blank.

Instinctively, he reached for her with Earthsong. It was second nature for him to use his power when anything was amiss.
Instead of just not being able to sense her, Darvyn felt a repel-
ling force push against him. Startled, he tried again, only to be
pushed back so vigorously that he physically stumbled.

Kyara's expression and stance did not change, but her lips moved wordlessly.

"What? What is it? Kyara?"

When she didn't respond, he cupped her face in his palms and forced her to look at him. Slowly, her eyes focused. She blinked furiously, then sagged into him, her knees buckling. He caught her around the waist and gently helped her kneel. She clutched his tunic in her fist and pressed her face to his chest. For a moment he thought she was crying, then he realized she was only gasping for breath. He rubbed her back until she'd calmed and pulled away from him, scrubbing at her eyes.

"I heard voices, whispering, chanting. They came from here," she said, her hands still covering her face.

"Voices?"

Finally, she met his eyes. "They buzzed around me in some strange language. But I could tell they wanted me to see this. I never . . ." She sat back roughly and surveyed the surrounding wonders.

He wanted to reach out to her, to comfort her again, but she felt much farther away than an arm's length. He wasn't sure his comfort would be welcome.

"I never thought it was real," she murmured.

"Me, neither. I've heard the griots speak of an ancient city of glass, but . . ." He looked around, still in awe himself.

"There are books in the Cantor's library about the early days of Lagrimar, after the Mantle's creation—forbidden books, kept by the succession of Cantors as records but hidden from the people. I read of a crystal city made by early Earthsingers opposed to the True Father. The first Keepers of the Promise broke off and came here, close to the Scald, to try to find a way to live on their own. They sang spells to create all this, spinning the sand into glass."

Earthsong was the only way Darvyn knew for such structures to exist. But he couldn't imagine creating something so elaborate and beautiful and impractical.

"What happened to them?" he asked. The griots' tales never told of the fate of the ancestors.

"The early battles." She shook her head, sadness washing over her. "The Keepers were either killed or they hid among the people, concealing their power and biding their time. At least that's what I read. Who knows if it's true . . ."

The empty, ancient city felt somehow sacred. He would ask the Queen about the place the next time She called on him.

"Maybe we should look around?" he offered.

Kyara slowly rose to her feet. Darvyn led the way down the wide, overgrown street. Unlike the other cities in Lagrimar whose outskirts bore low, scattered buildings, the tall structures began immediately beyond the wall. Some were little more than boxy glass slabs shooting out of the soil, but others bore delicate latticework, artistry apparent in their very construction. Many rose out of the ground on sturdy bases while some were lifted on thin, delicate crystal stilts.

"Do you suppose there used to be a staircase here?" Kyara mused, pointing up at a raised building with no obvious way to enter.

"The early Singers would have been far more powerful than anyone born today," Darvyn replied. He called the wind to give him a boost as he jumped, but the strange force still worked against his Song and the lift was minimal—too little to allow him to reach the platform six stories above. He flailed in the air before falling back to the ground.

Kyara laughed, the sound shattering the melancholic silence with its magical, rich tone. Her laughter flowed like the dance of a stream and bounced off the glass surrounding them like the tinkling of a bell. He stumbled, staring at her while trying to find his footing. Her eyes shone with amusement.

"What?" She sobered as he continued to gape, her discomfort apparent.

"I've never heard you laugh before," he said. The action had transformed her. Even now, with her face shuttered, the echo still reverberated.

Solemnity descended upon her like a weight on her shoulders. "You should go," she said.

"What?" He froze.

She turned away, leaving him to study her profile. He was reminded of the first time he saw her in the pub, only her nose and cheek really visible from behind her hood. She was still very much concealed from him.

"You need to go into hiding so the True Father doesn't find you. He will send others."

"Are there others like you?"

She glared at him. "No."

"He's been chasing me my entire life. I can handle myself."

She gave an exasperated sigh and marched away, down an overgrown avenue.

"Kyara!" he called, following her.

"You should get far away from me." Their voices echoed through the city. For some reason, it was cooler at the base of the massive spires than it had been beyond the glass wall. Darvyn kept pace as Kyara wended her way through a maze of streets. He reached for her hand to turn her around. She pulled out of his grip, clutching her hand to her chest as if his touch had hurt.

"I'm sorry," he said.

She shook her head. "No, I'm sorry. I'm sorry for chasing you, hurting you. But the only thing saving you from me now is the gorge and all its Nethersong. Once I leave, I won't be strong enough to resist the spell. It will push me to capture you or kill me for resisting. I do not know if I can withstand it again." Her gaze dropped to the ground. "Take the horse and go," she repeated. "Go somewhere far away. Somewhere no one can find you."

Darvyn took a deep breath and looked to the sky, unsure of what to say. A glint of color peeked through a skyline of colorless glass. It glowed a deep red against the blue overhead.

"What is that?"

She followed the path of his gaze, her brow furrowing. "I don't know," she answered before stalking off toward it.

Instead of following the spiral of the main street, they cut through the alleyways between the buildings until they reached the center of the city. A red obelisk rose from the ground. Except for its color, it was identical to the white one he'd seen in the center of the ruins of Tanagol. Overgrown streets, like the spokes of a wheel, shot out in all directions around it, but the area directly around the obelisk was clear—no dirt, or sand, or stubborn vegetation.

Just beyond, a haphazard pile of weeds lay, the roots still intact. "Someone's been here. Recently." He went to the pile and picked up a clump of beardgrass. "This is still green."

Kyara's gaze shot around, but Darvyn felt no one else nearby. Unless the visitor shared Kyara's peculiar power, they were not still here.

But what if they did share her power? The Queen had said that Nethersong was rare, but how could Kyara really be the only one? There could be someone watching them right now and he would never know.

She must have read his thoughts or seen his agitation as he searched the surrounding area, his alarm growing. "There's no one here," she said. "Unless they're an infant or like you, but then *you* would have sensed them."

At his incredulous look, she explained her Nethersong vision and how she could sense the death energy in those nearby, the same as he could sense the life. Satisfied for the moment, he looked back at the circle around the obelisk.

"How long ago do you think they were here?" Kyara asked.

"A week at most." The roots of the beardgrass were as long as his leg. The plant had adapted to the harsh environment and could store water for long periods of time. These had been pulled from the ground within the past seven days.

"Do you think it could have been an Avinid?"

Darvyn shook his head. "They're so focused on their pilgrimage. I don't think so."

She stared up at the red column while he observed its base, surrounded by a dozen concentric circles radiating outward that were etched into a dark, glassy material, like patternless marble.

He slid a finger across one of the ridges and shuddered. That same force that had bucked against him when he'd used his Song pushed at him. A sizzle, like a lightning bolt, shot through him, throwing him several paces away.

Instinctively, he grasped for Earthsong and recoiled at the state of the energy. Something about this place, this obelisk in particular, felt very wrong. His Song didn't like it, and he felt the sudden need to get away.

Kyara never turned around, not even when he was tossed

away by the invisible force. Her focus was completely taken by the obelisk. She crossed the circles, her head cocked to the side.

"I wonder . . ." She lifted her hand to the spire.

His Song howled inside him. He felt instinctively that the obelisk should be avoided. "No!" he shouted, but it was too late. When her palm hit the red glass, the circles beneath her began to ripple like water, throwing her off-balance. Cracks appeared on the surface of the undulating waves.

Darvyn met her frightened gaze a moment before the ground beneath her feet shattered with a high-pitched shriek. A scream clawed its way out of her throat, and then Kyara was falling.

The yawning sinkhole opened around the obelisk, which still stood tall and immobile. He threw himself forward to peer down, unable to see anything but blackness below. That same wrong feeling overwhelmed him, urging him to flee. Earth-song churned within him, reacting aggressively to the perceived danger.

With a deep breath, Darvyn steeled himself. Then he dove into the darkness after Kyara.

CHAPTER TWENTY-FOUR

The Scorpion was caught between two worlds
One so well-known and one beyond her grasp
For while the dark held power uneclipsed
'Twas in the light's rays that she longed to bask
The struggle was enough to rend the soul
To tear the flesh from skeleton and bone

—THE BOOK OF UNVEILING

Days at the factory passed slowly in a haze of noise, the bitter taint of gunpowder, mind-numbing boredom, and aching muscles.

Kyssa served as overseer of the entire factory, though they saw Ora pretty frequently since she kept an office in the corner of the building. The factory manager liked things to run a certain way. She liked well-kept girls in clean tunics who didn't talk back, did their work, met their quotas, and didn't cause trouble—or so Kyssa was constantly reminding them.

Zeli had no problem following the rules. She was being fed and housed and wasn't beaten. The work was easy, but tedious. Still, she had an inkling of other fates that could have befallen them, and while she missed her life in the Lake Cities, she was resigned to this new one.

For now.

But Ora wanted something more than for her factory to merely be a success. Her ambitions were clear in the way the woman dressed and in how she spoke. She had her eyes set firmly on advancement. Zeli reasoned that while Ora was technically a payroller, she was a low-ranking one, looked down upon by those who didn't have to sully themselves overseeing manual labor.

That was underscored this particular morning by the fact that the manager had called all the new workers in for a meeting. They'd been awakened early by Nedra and ordered to braid their hair afresh and appear as neatly put together as possible. Kyssa had fussed over them, ensuring their tunics had no stains or rips before leading them into a part of the factory none had yet seen.

They were led to a small corner office with glass-filled windows on one wall looking out onto an enclosed desert garden. Carefully arranged stone and rock sculptures surrounded beds of bobcat acacia, dune sunflowers, and sand heliotropes.

Ora sat behind a great wooden desk, hands clasped before her. She wore a pair of spectacles and peered over the rim at the girls lined up before her. Zeli straightened her spine under the woman's perusal. The office was quite a bit cooler than the rest of the building due to the large fans overhead, running off the line shaft belt. The walls must be thick for the noise wasn't so over-whelming in here. An eerie silence washed over the room as Ora took stock of her newest workers.

"The True Father has called for a Mercy Day to commence today at the noon hour," Ora announced.

Zeli stiffened. One of the other girls sucked in a breath. Ora continued as if there had been no reaction. "The factory will stop its operations, and you all will participate in the festivities as is required." She pursed her lips and tapped them thoughtfully.

"I have been unable to make a personal contribution to a Mercy Day in several months. And this displeases me. Since you all are new, I wanted to impress upon you the importance of re-maining vigilant. My employees are good, loyal citizens who participate and do their parts. As you go along your way today, keep your eyes open for anyone not fully enjoying the True Father's hospitality and generosity. I want names, descriptions—if you see someone, follow them and try to gather their address. Hopefully, the next time our king sees fit to benefit us with a holiday of this magnitude, I will be among those honored for their contributions to the peace."

Zeli hoped she had controlled her facial expression and not revealed the sickening sensation that had invaded her stomach. Tana stood beside her, rigid as a board.

Ora's small features broke into a shallow smile that gave a sinister gleam to her pretty face. "Girls who provide useful infor-mation will be rewarded handsomely. I'm sure Kyssa and the others have told you how grateful I can be."

While the other girls wisely held their peace regardless of how they felt about this new directive, Tana was vibrating with unchecked anger. Zeli turned to her, too late to stop it from boiling over.

"So, Ora-mideni," Tana said, a note of derision in her voice, "during this glorious day where the True Father executes those deemed disloyal, you want us to spy on the citizens of the town, looking for anyone who may be fit to receive the same fate the next time His Majesty deigns to grace us with a celebration?" Her voice took on an unusually sweet quality, but her face was cast from iron.

Ora blinked rapidly, her gaze appearing to calculate whether so small a girl could truly be quite so impertinent. After a pregnant moment in which Zeli thought her body would snap in two from the tension, Ora simply nodded and said, "Exactly. You may return to your workstations now."

The girls filed out and back to the factory floor. Kyssa remained behind, speaking in hushed tones to Ora.

Zeli nudged Tana as they went back to their table. "You shouldn't provoke her."

Tana shrugged. "It's all stupid. I'm not spying for her or anyone else."

Zeli was uncomfortable spying as well, but she wasn't going to cross the mistress in public. It wasn't wise.

The first hour of their shortened shift passed uneventfully, but then a disturbance near the main door caused the girls to look up.

A shudder wracked Zeli's body when she saw the vile payroller from the auction entering the factory with two burly guards flanking. "What is Mengu-mideni doing here?" she asked aloud.

Nedra, at the end of the table, looked up, her jaw tensing. Mengu crossed the aisles and entered the short hallway leading to Ora's office.

"Is he a frequent visitor?" Zeli asked.

Nedra stared at the door for a beat then dropped her gaze back to her work. "No. He's not. But he and Ora-mideni have a long rivalry." She continued at her machine, finishing off the filled bullets by affixing the rounded tips to them.

"It's best to stay away from him," she said after a minute. She looked up at Zeli and held her gaze, face blank. "If you encounter him in town, turn and go the other way."

Zeli swallowed. Nedra was not an emotional person, not in the few days of their acquaintance and not now, but something in her carefully disaffected demeanor gave the warning more intensity. Even without the alert, Zeli had no intention of going anywhere near the man. But somehow, a few minutes later when Kyssa approached their table, a resigned look on the woman's face, she realized she might not have much of a choice.

Kyssa stopped and everyone at the workstation held their breaths. "Tana-deni. Come with me."

Zeli's gaze shot to the younger girl, who tilted her chin up, eyes defiant. But she complied, following the tall woman back toward the manager's office.

Tana didn't look back, but across the room, Ulani stared at her sister with fear in her gaze.

Zeli's hands shook with apprehension. Whatever was going on in that office, she needed to know about it. She unhooked the belt of her machine from its wheel, disconnecting it from the line shaft's ceaseless motion.

"What do you think you're doing?" Nedra asked.

"I need the privy," Zeli answered, not looking away. She thought Nedra might challenge her, but with another look toward the office, the young woman simply nodded.

Zeli wiped off her hands and sprinted away. There were a

number of exterior doors leading to the row of privies set up in the back of the factory. Zeli chose the most roundabout route that would take her closest to Ora's office. There, she hovered in the corner, near the entrance to the short hallway. She peeked around the edge long enough to see Kyssa and Tana standing outside the office door, their backs to her. Tana's arms were crossed, her posture rigid.

"Mengu-mideni has expressed interested in acquiring additional servants for his estate. If Ora-mideni wanted, she could send you to him today, after your little display earlier." Kyssa's voice was contemptuous. "If you want to stay here, you have to play by the rules. Here is a lot better than many other places, you know."

"You sound like Zeli-deni," Tana grumbled.

"Well, Zeli-deni is correct. She has the right kind of attitude and can go far if she applies herself. You know Ora-mideni rose from almost nothing to the position she occupies today?"

"She rose by informing on her neighbors." Tana sounded venomous. "She's responsible for them being carted away to the camps or the mines or killed for things they may not have done. That's how she's gotten ahead."

Zeli heard a slapping sound and peered around to find Kyssa's hand raised and Tana holding her cheek.

"You will not speak ill of your mistress. You don't know anything about life here. Don't think I can't tell that you grew up with means. With your high and mighty attitude and self-righteousness. What right have you to judge anyone else? What did your parents do to survive, Tana-deni?"

Tana's little shoulders slumped. "Doesn't mean I have to do it, too."

"If you want to stay here, you do. If you don't have any credible information after today's Mercy Day then Ora-mideni *will* send you to Mengu-mideni's estate. She doesn't need trouble-makers. Now get back to work."

Zeli ducked her head back around the corner as Kyssa suddenly spun away. When the woman drew nearer, Zeli slipped outside to avoid being spotted eavesdropping.

She returned to her station to find Tana focused intently on her funnel and powder. The girl didn't look up or acknowledge either Zeli or the threat that had just been leveled against her in any way.

It was really none of Zeli's business. At least that's what she tried to tell herself. She'd already helped Tana and Ulani as much as she could by saving them from Mengu once. Tana's fate would be her own if she was foolish enough to provoke their mistress. If the girl didn't have a sense of self-preservation, then what was the use of Zeli getting involved?

She rubbed her remaining bracelet, wishing for a little luck right now. Because while it could easily be Tana sold to another place today, who's to say it couldn't be Ulani next, or Zeli herself? Life at the factory might not be as safe as she'd thought.

Pain was a hot needle lancing Darvyn's spine. His muscles shrieked when he attempted to move, but he forced himself up to a seated position. He reached for Earthsong, his Song seeking comfort in the familiar pathways of power, but an echoing emptiness met him.

Again he attempted to connect to the endless ocean of energy, but it was no use. Some unknown force blocked him, cutting him off from the magic as certainly as the darkness had stolen his sight.

Blackness, complete and oppressive, surrounded him. No spark or glimmer of light penetrated. Fear clawed through him.

"Kyara!" he shouted.

His voice echoed off the cavern walls. He slid a hand across the smooth ground, made of no material he could comprehend.

"Kyara!" The reverberation exacerbated his aloneness.

No response.

If she was injured somewhere, he would never know. Once again, he was helpless to save her. Without his Song, he could not even ask the Queen for guidance.

It stood to reason that the long fall would leave them near each other. Palms outstretched, he felt around methodically, trying to cover the nearby area. His voice went hoarse from calling her name over and over; his hands were rubbed raw from skimming the cavern's walls and floor.

Hours passed, and the hope of finding Kyara alive was dwindling. But if he had survived the fall without his Song, surely she would have. He did not want to give up, but hunger and exhaustion overwhelmed him, and the darkness battered his optimism. He had to find her, no matter what.

He continued moving, unwilling to stay still. As long as his body held up, he would keep going. Despair would not be allowed to overtake him.

More time flowed with no change. Not to the blackness, or the cold, or the fear in his heart that he would die in these caves without anyone ever knowing. He sidestepped a rock formation jutting up in front of him, then stopped short, staring at it.

He could see.

A faint light ahead lit the tunnel with a dull glow. He let out a whoop and jumped with a sudden burst of energy. Speeding to a run, he headed straight for the light.

The air grew fresher as he sprinted.

This tunnel must lead outside.

Ignoring the lingering aches in his limbs, he kept running until he saw daylight.

Outside, the sun shone merrily. The bitterness in the air close to the gorge smelled sweet after the damp stink of the cave. Blue sky met his grateful eyes. He'd thought he might never see it again. Then he looked down.

The entrance to the tunnel in which he stood was cut into the sheer face of a cliff. One hundred paces below, Death River flowed, its poisonous waters gently moving. This part of Serpent's Gorge was narrow, with the cliffs dropping directly into the water with no shore or riverbank to speak of.

He studied the rock face. On the other side of the gorge, the surface was a bit craggier, with possible handholds and footholds, but on his side, the canyon had been eroded to an even surface. There was no way to climb it.

With Earthsong he could have sang a spell to catch the wind in his tunic, or gouge the rock to make it climbable, even cut stairs into its sheer face, but some force still rendered him Songless.

The weight of the realization forced him to the ground. He sat, hanging his legs over the side of the tunnel's entrance, looking at freedom but not being able to grasp it.

After the endless fall, and a surprisingly soft landing, Kyara was enveloped in a womb of blackness, the heat from above replaced by the cool damp. The whispers that had awoken her this morning were louder here. The words were still unintelligible, but the emotion behind them was clear. She'd followed the voices to the crystal city, lulled into compliance by their gentle drone. Now they took on a tone of expectation. Something was waiting for her here underground.

Her hands floated against a cool, smooth surface, the darkness surrounded her, and the whispers continued. The throaty, guttural sounds made her think of the language of blood magic that Ydaris used for her spells. Kyara strained to understand, certain she was on the cusp of comprehension, but it never came.

Instead, she felt around, trying to learn about her surroundings. While the air was dense and earthy, exactly what she'd expect from a cave, her fingers slid not over dirt but strange smooth stone. She crawled forward on her hands and knees, only to knock her head against a wall.

Hissing in pain, she pulled back. Crawling the opposite way only led her to collide, more slowly, into another wall. She sat back, rubbing her forehead, as the whispered voices became more agitated. Was this what going mad felt like?

She made a quarter turn to the left and rose on wobbly legs, keeping her hands in front of her, searching for obstacles. Her forward motion was slow. She shuffled along, reaching out to forestall any more meetings with the walls. Her shin slammed against something jutting from the ground. She let out a curse and sat down heavily, rubbing her aching leg. This was ridiculous. Where was she going and how would she ever get out of here?

The voices became encouraging, murmuring cheerful, bright nonsense.

"I can't understand you!" she screamed. "Either help me or be quiet!" She dropped her head into her hands and fought the frustration and fear. She could very well die down here, wherever "here" was.

The whispers quieted, leaving her alone in the darkness. She didn't like that, either. It reminded her too much of her time locked in the cage in the dark, damp depths of the glass castle's dungeon. She'd been confined there for months during her training, as Ydaris forced her to gain control of her Song.

That was it . . .

Kyara reached for her inner vision, and the surroundings flickered to life around her. Even underground there was life and death, decay, transformation, and renewal.

Insects and tiny creatures and organisms all lived and died here. The weak glow emanating from whatever inhabited the walls around her was enough to help get a handle on her surroundings.

She'd never tried to navigate using Nethersong. Even stretching out her senses, she had a difficult time visually understanding the three dimensions so she focused only on what was directly around her. The faint gleam formed a path illuminating the rock walls and floor, lined as it was with organic life and death.

She moved forward, running her hand against the wall to keep her balance. The tunnel she was in twisted and turned and led to dozens of offshoots that created a labyrinth. Four pathways opened in front of her.

"Any ideas?" she whispered, hoping the voices hadn't abandoned her completely. As if waiting for her permission, they started up again, quieter this time, though she still couldn't understand them.

She stood in front of the first path. The tone of the whispers seemed negative, their timbre low and disapproving. She tried the next one with the same result. However, the third passageway met with an approving mumble. Kyara followed their guidance. They seemed to want something from her, which meant they would probably keep her alive. She hoped.

She continued navigating the paths this way for hours. A day, perhaps two, could have passed. Time was an impossibility. Whenever she came to an offshoot or fork, she tested the possible directions for which one made the whispers happiest.

Darvyn was never far from her mind. A desperate longing swept over her, causing her to pause. She'd wanted—no, needed— to push him away to save him, but doing so tore at her.

She swallowed against the lump in her throat and pushed forward, conscious of a glow visible to her physical eyes, not just her Nethersong sight. The caverns around her sparkled in the low light, and the outline of her arms in front of her became apparent.

As she continued down the tunnel, the light grew brighter. At the path's end, she emerged into a large open cavern—more than large, enormous. So gigantic it could have held the entire glass castle. The sides were pockmarked with darkened cave entrances, and catwalks of stone crisscrossed the open middle above and below her. She surveyed the space in awe. The sight was just as magnificent as the crystal city, and just as mysterious.

Soft light originated from below. She reached for her Song, and amid the vast field of black, five columns of light shone brighter than any she'd ever seen. Even freshly dead bodies did not display so much Nethersong.

Curiosity and dread warred with her as she tried to figure a way down to where these creatures were. Directly ahead of her, a narrow strip of the strange smooth stone crossed the gigantic cavern. One hundred paces out, a staircase descended, connecting multiple levels of footbridges. She judged herself to be at least four hundred paces from the bottom, the walkway only as wide as about four of her feet. Without railings on either side, navigating this tiny bridge would be harrowing.

She took a deep breath and stepped forward. The whispers voiced their approval, but it was of little comfort. Certainly they wanted her for something, but it could be to eat for their supper. She had no idea what she was dealing with. Still, she kept moving and reached the long staircase, allowing herself a moment of rest before climbing down.

Her legs burned by the time she made it all the way to the bottom. The light grew brighter on the way down, illuminating the cavern's interior, its stone glassy with the sparkle of minerals within.

A series of small chambers was honeycombed into the bottom level. She followed the light and heard the crackle of fire as she approached. Finally, she stood at the entrance to a small cave with a roaring fire pit. Seated around the flames were five figures.

At first she thought they were animals of some kind. Giant colorless slugs or worms. Their skin had been leached of all hue, leaving a translucent membrane protecting their muscles and organs, all of which could be seen beneath. Green-and-blue veins pulsed, and Kyara shuddered to watch their movement. Fear and revulsion locked her knees, but she forced herself forward, curiosity conquering her disgust.

The whispers were thankful, joyous, and relief tinged their foreign words. These creatures were their source, but what were they?

She was fewer than a dozen paces away when one of them stirred, unfolding itself to reveal a bald skull with two colorless eyes peering at her from an ancient face. The see-through skin sagged in bunches, but the eyes were clear. The other four figures sat up, revealing that they were indeed human, or something similar. Each appeared as old or older than the cave itself.

Kyara's hands shook as she met the stare of the first man.

Ancient, unfathomable eyes looked up at her, forcing her gaze away. None of these men wore any clothes, and two of them were actually women. Their bodies were jellylike, jiggling with every movement.

She clenched her jaw and willed bravery. Her Song had not reacted to any threat; in fact, she hadn't felt as though she was in peril at any point during this entire bizarre experience, even when she'd been certain she was going to die.

The first man who'd stirred motioned for her to sit. There was an empty place in the circle directly across from him. She swallowed and sat, still in awe at these beings.

The man spoke, his voice low and whispery as a brush on canvas. Kyara shook her head; she still could not understand the language of the whispers. He nodded, as if he knew as much and opened his fist to reveal a dark shard of glass. The sparkles embedded within marked it as a piece of the cave.

He passed the fragment to the woman on his left, who passed it to the man beside Kyara, who held it out to her. She reached for it tentatively, gasping when it hit her skin and her surroundings swirled and changed.

A man dressed in orange stands in front of the red obelisk. He turns his face and a quiver of recognition goes through Kyara. It is Raal.

She tries to shrink back, but her body is not there. She's merely watching, and this soothes her fear. Two men pull weeds from around the base of the obelisk and toss them into a pile. Each is bald with strange markings tattooed onto his head. When they clear away the last plant, they step aside, keeping their heads lowered.

Raal glides toward the spire gingerly. He runs his hand up and down the red stone, eyes ablaze with some strong emotion Kyara can't read.

A sick feeling enters her stomach, but she wants to know more.

"*Hearing cone,*" *he says, holding out his hand. She shivers at the physician's familiar voice. She's never forgotten it, not after all these years. One of the servants jumps, rummaging around in the large pack at his feet until he retrieves a small ear trumpet.*

Raal puts the cone to his ear and says a string of words in the language of blood magic. He says them quickly in a strange accent, and Kyara doesn't catch what they are. Then he is talking to an unseen person and answering as if he or she were there.

"*I have found it. It is much larger than we thought and immobile. I will do another test, but this cannot be the death stone. It is just another shrine.*"

He is quiet for a time, listening. The ear trumpet must be spelled in some way, though she has never seen a blood spell that didn't coat the object in the casing of magic-hardened blood.

"*Question the prisoners again. I have no time to chase smoke. If the father won't break, we will have to use his sons against him. They have given us nothing but lies so far. We must find the death stone quickly, and I am certain it is not here.*"

He pulls the cone from his ear and flings it to the ground. One of the servants rushes to pick it up and replace it in the bag.

Raal stalks away.

The vision faded, and Kyara opened her eyes to find five pairs of colorless ones peering back at her. The vision had leeched all the warmth from her body. She wrapped her arms around her knees and realized she no longer held the shard of rock. Wherever it had gone, she was glad to be rid of it.

"That vision was real. It happened not long ago. The physician was here, looking for something called a death stone?" Kyara asked.

The ancient man's eyes lowered. He opened his palm again to reveal a rough, red stone.

"A caldera?"

"Caldera," the man repeated and nodded.

Kyara could have sworn his palm was empty the moment before. She wondered what type of magic this was.

Once again, he passed the stone around the circle. This time, Kyara hesitated before touching it. It burned against her fingers as it flung her into another vision, much different from the first.

The entire Cavefolk assembly is gathered on the floor of the Great Cave. I feel so small, so worthless, and yet I have been given an enormous opportunity. Our shaman, Oval, sits next to me, still and solemn. When it is my time, I rise to face them. The cave grows silent with their anticipation.

My throat threatens to close, but I push forward, seeing all of them and none of them at the same time. My voice comes out, echoing across the cavern walls.

"A thousand years ago my ancestor came to this assembly and warned of the two sorcerers who would come from the sky. Many did not believe, not until the day the clouds brought forth the man and woman who transformed the Outside."

They are all looking at me, hanging on my words.

"We have lost so many to the Outside, to their curiosity about the sorcerers and their lack of respect for the old ways. We will lose more. We have protected the Folk. We have barred the Outsiders' sorcery from our caves, but more is needed. My bloodline has borne the prophecies since the beginning of time, and I have been gifted with a divination."

Shocked whispers overtake the people. Oval stands to silence them. He does not have to say a word for in moments, silence reigns again.

"Let Murmur finish," Oval says. "We must hear his words."

I clear my throat. "I have seen a future without the Folk. I have seen the three worlds at war. The living, the dead, and those in-between will battle. I cannot see the end of it, but our world as we know it will not survive."

Oval stands tall as the people begin to shout.

"The blood will protect us! The blood always has!"

"The Mother will shield us!"

Oval quiets the people again by simply raising both his hands. "The vision is many generations away. But the Folk must know. The blood will tell."

"The blood will tell," everyone intones in unison. I stumble back, glad of the weight lifted from my shoulders.

The vision changed abruptly, disorienting Kyara and throwing her out of the mind she'd been inhabiting. Murmur—that was the name of the man across from her. She had been him in the vision, young and scared. Not colorless and inhuman-looking like he was now. Just pale-skinned, with light-colored eyes that had rarely seen the world beyond the caves. Eyes terrified of the things he'd witnessed in his prophecy.

The vision settled and her own consciousness once again merged with Murmur's memories from centuries later.

The sorcerer hands the infant to me. The little girl is bundled in blankets, but fast asleep.

"Her name is Mooriah. Swear to me that she will be safe." His voice is a command, the way these Outsiders always treat those of us they call Silent, the ones born without their sorcery. As if their magic was the only in existence.

The descendants of the Folk who left the safety of the Mountain Mother to live Outside have paid a steep price. They obtained their sunlight and their rain, but now they are embroiled in a war with the sorcerers, these Earthsingers who manipulate nature as if it were clay to be molded.

But the baby before me is not an Earthsinger. She is something else.

"You are brave not to kill your daughter," I tell him. "Her Nether-song will not harm the Folk."

The sorcerer nods and looks upon the babe longingly. "I wish your mother could have seen you," he whispers and strokes the babe's cheek. Then he turns to me.

"If I do not return, raise her as your own and tell her of her legacy."

I nod before he turns and leaves the cave, to climb back down the mountain and into his world of green.

I take the babe into the darkness. The prophecy I saw as a child is still a long way off, but when that war begins, we will need soldiers to fight. Not just ones who manipulate life, but those who can alter death, as well.

"Mooriah," I say, and she stirs in my arms as if she already knows her name. She and those like her are our only hope to survive the war that will come.

Kyara let the stone drop from her hand before another vision could start. She shivered in the cool air of the cavern. The visions were from long ago, hundreds of years judging by the clothing the Earthsinger had worn. Mooriah must be long dead, unless she was somehow like these ancient creatures. But her skin was the same shade as Kyara's own—not ashen like the other Cave-folk. Did they live forever? But they were full of so much Nether-song.

"The baby . . . She was like me?" Kyara asked.

Murmur nodded.

"But she's gone now?"

Again, he nodded. And with her, Kyara's brief flare of hope for learning more about her Song. The control Ydaris had tortured into her was still tenuous. A teacher could have been the miracle Kyara always sought, but that would forever be a dream.

"Why am I here?"

"You are here because you are needed." Murmur's words now made sense. She had understood the strange, ancient language in the vision, seeing from Murmur's perspective, and that knowledge must have carried over in reality.

"I am needed for what?"

"For what is nearly upon us. The war I prophesied over five hundred years ago is beginning. We five are all that is left of the Folk. And you are here because if the living world is to survive, you will need to fight for it."

CHAPTER TWENTY-FIVE

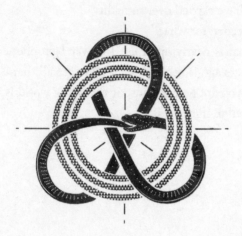

The power in the blood comes with a price
And dearer still the venom that she bore
For death is both an enemy and friend
To those for whom life leaves oft wanting more
To wield a strength that few ever conceive
Involves a struggle dire, without reprieve

—THE BOOK OF UNVEILING

"Tell me of this death stone that the physician came in search of." Kyara sat next to Murmur high in the cavern, overlooking the simple beauty below. The other Cavefolk had dispersed, back to whatever duties centuries-old underground dwellers found necessary. Murmur had asked her to follow him, leading her up several hundred stairs to reach this perch. He hadn't appeared to exert himself whatsoever on the climb, whereas Kyara felt as if her lungs were going to explode.

She was growing used to looking at him, though her gaze could not linger too long below his face as the sight of muscle and veins still made her queasy.

"When the prophecy came to me," he began, "I saw those from other lands taking sides in the war to come. Your physician wields a foreign magic. His people combine the power of the blood with elements of both Earthsong and Nethersong. The foreigners have no inborn Songs, but their magic is very advanced. He and his kind will align themselves with the dead."

Kyara shifted to cross her legs, thinking of Raal's accent, one she had barely recognized as such because there had never been foreigners in Lagrimar.

"This death stone they seek is a caldera created by a sorcerer, Mooriah's father. I met him long before she was born. I had made a mistake and sought him out so that I could make it right." Murmur's brow furrowed, and his deep breaths came slow.

"What kind of mistake?"

"A grave one, as it turns out. One that I still seek redemption for. In an effort to begin my penance, I shared some of the knowledge of our people. I showed the sorcerer how to trap one of their Songs in a caldera."

Kyara's hands flew to her mouth. "You know how to remove Songs?"

Murmur regarded her from the corner of his eye. "After Mooriah was born and her father realized her gift, he sought to trap her Song to save her life. In that time, Nethersingers were killed at birth."

"I can understand why," she said dryly.

Murmur clucked his tongue. "The sorcerer tested his plan on another infant who could call to the Nether, only it did not work as expected."

"What happened?"

"He pulled the Song from the child and stored it in a caldera. But the babe's relatives discovered what he'd done and stole the caldera." He shook his head, ancient eyes clouded over and grim. "When they touched it, they saw horrible visions and were driven mad. Even without being activated, the stone had all the potency of a powerful Nethersinger, and no one alive knew how to control it."

"Activated?"

He nodded. "The major calderas, the ones powerful enough to hold something as vast as a Song, are created with blood, but they only become active with death. The stone was dormant and still a menace. The sorcerer tried destroying the thing, but it was impossible. His only solution was to hide it where no one would ever find it."

"This caldera he hid is the death stone that Raal seeks?" she asked.

"Aye."

"And where did he hide it?"

"He sent a courier on a ship far to the west and had it thrown into the deepest part of the ocean."

"So why is the physician looking for it in Lagrimar?"

Murmur sighed. "The sorcerer queen, the one trapped in the World Between, you know of Her?"

"The Queen Who Sleeps, yes. I never believed in Her, but . . . I don't know what to believe anymore."

"Believe only the truth. She speaks to the Outsiders of the

things She sees. The World Between is thin in many places and knowledge slips through. Two years past, She sent some of Her dreamers after the death stone—a man and his twin sons—to retrieve it from the depths of the ocean. But the foreign mages—Raal's compatriots—somehow found out about the scheme and took the family captive."

"And what of the death stone?"

"The foreigners believe the family knows of its whereabouts. That they succeeded in retrieving it and hid it again before they were captured." He spread his arms to indicate he did not know the truth. "The Mountain Mother sees much, but the seas are beyond her view."

"What would happen if Raal found it?"

Murmur closed his eerie eyes. He was quiet so long that Kyara feared the ancient had fallen asleep. "His clan has chosen the wrong side in the war to come. Anything that strengthens them, harms the rest of us. Death is a powerful friend. And pure control of Nethersong is rare. The blood connects us to it, but what you do, Kyara, is very valuable and exceedingly difficult to find. They want what you have."

She gulped at a knot in her throat and hugged her arms around her. "*I* don't want what I have." A shiver went through her. "How do you know all this, anyway?"

"Mountain Mother bears witness." He rapped his knuckles on the cave floor. "And I have lived a very long time." A smile played on his lips, but it only unsettled Kyara even more.

She thought of the vision of Raal she'd had when holding the shard of glass. Only it wasn't glass, it was a piece of the cave itself. The entire interior, the smooth, sparkling substance that made up the tunnels and caves, was a caldera of sorts, she realized. The entire world of the Cavefolk held knowledge, memories of the things that happened both inside and out. A library of the world stored in the walls and floors.

A shiver rolled through her as she wondered if blood had been required to store the memories in the mountain. Blood was necessary for all calderas; could one this large be different? And if it wasn't . . . she didn't want to know.

"Kyara." Murmur's voice reclaimed her focus. "You are here because you must learn to control your Song. You have only scratched the surface of your power, and it will be needed in the days to come."

"You could take it away," she whispered, butterflies taking flight behind her rib cage. "You could take my Song and store it in a caldera. Give it to those on the right side of the war. It could be just like the death stone."

Murmur took a deep breath. She could actually see his lungs fill and struggled not to look away. "You would need to die before such a caldera would become active."

"I am willing to die. I would gladly die to be rid of my Song."

"Then you should also be willing to live."

Her fists curled involuntarily. "And what would you have me do? Using my Song means hurting people, killing them. That's all it's good for."

"That is not all." Murmur's palm opened, and another fragment of the cave appeared.

"How do you do that?" she asked as her fingers closed around it.

The vision was brief, just an image really. Darvyn sat at the edge of a tunnel, looking down into Serpent's Gorge.

She drew in a breath. "He's here. Where?"

"Use your Song. Feel the Mother's embrace around you. Sink into her knowledge and memories. Your power is greater than you know. All you have to do to master your ability is to accept it. It is part of you. Embrace it and you can control it."

Kyara clamped her lips together to keep from lashing out. She didn't want to embrace her deadly Song. She wanted to be rid of it. And Murmur knew how to help her but wouldn't. She would have to try to persuade him, but first, she needed to help Darvyn.

She glared at Murmur for a few moments before planting both her palms firmly on the cave floor and releasing her Song. It was no longer a pent-up creature surging against her strangled control. No, today it was a waiting accomplice, keen for a command. Eager to please, like a puppy.

She thought of the little lizard she'd befriended during her training. Not all beasts were monsters. Her Song could be a friend if she'd only let it.

The revelation left her shaky, but she focused on her resolve to find Darvyn. With that instruction, her Song rushed forward, showing her the map of the caves in her mind's eye. She wasn't just sensing the Nethersong in the organic life present, she was peering deep into the stone.

Nethersong was embedded in the smooth surface of the caverns. For generations, the Cavefolk's magic *had* involved blood and sacrifice. This confirmation left her uneasy, but she strengthened her resolve and fell in tune with an ancient force—a harmony that she understood to be the Mother that Murmur had mentioned.

Darvyn came into focus. Through the cave, she sensed his exhaustion, his fear and desolation. The cave prevented him from singing. It was a protection the Cavefolk had created long ago when the Outsiders—the Earthsingers—first came to this land.

She longed to comfort him, to pull him into her arms and let him find relief there. Maybe she could reach him, lead him to her through the tunnels. Her Song was eager to try this new skill.

"It's working," she whispered.

Murmur shifted beside her. "Good," he said. "Accept your Song and it will not betray you. You are capable of much more than you know."

In her vision of Darvyn, she was a presence floating beside him. The bitter scent of the poison water below irritated her nose. The steamy air outside battled with the tunnel's coolness at the cavern entrance, but the warmth of him was palpable. She reached out to touch his skin, and a blast of energy rushed past her, slamming into Darvyn and pushing him out of the tunnel.

As if in slow motion, he flailed in midair before falling to the deadly river below.

CHAPTER TWENTY-SIX

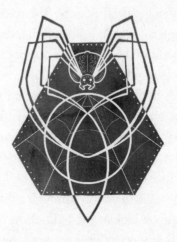

A shadow uses light to cast its shade
Consolidating two opposing foes
And if this unity causes some doubt
The shelter that they make is unopposed
The beauty of a silhouette is worth
The contradiction captured in its birth

—THE BOOK OF UNVEILING

Decorative streamers hung from lighting poles and roofs, criss-crossing the main road winding through town. Surrounded by a throng of people, Zeli stared up in awe at the elaborate designs.

She'd thought Mercy Days in the Lake Cities would be the grandest in the country, save for Sayya, so she was truly amazed at the variety of tapestries, flags, and ribbons that hung from every window and door. The displays were much, much more than what they'd done back home.

At every corner, a street urchin or elder carried a basket of wreaths woven with artificial flowers. The colors of each flower were bright enough to rival Avinid clothing, and if you were offered a wreath, tradition bound you to accept.

Zeli dutifully lowered her head to allow an old woman to lay yet another of the lightweight collars around her. Each flower was crafted from some sort of tissue paper. Somewhere there must be a factory of people doing nothing but making these wreaths for Mercy Days. Though the wreath weighed almost nothing, it hung like a noose.

As the girls wound their way through the crowded streets, Zeli got her first good look at the bulk of the town. She hadn't had much opportunity over the last week to explore. Her body was still getting used to the grueling yet tedious labor at the factory, and she spent her off hours sleeping or resting, trying to gather the strength to go back to her shift the next day. This was her first day off and despite the reason for the break, she was grateful.

The level of celebration and cheer was also much higher than what she was used to. In Laketown, everyone gathered in the market squares for free food and wine, and to witness the executions. The citizenry did their duties, smiling their strained smiles, cheering on command—surviving. But here, whether due to an edict of the local Magister or simply the culture of the Midcountry, everything was bigger, brighter, more.

The appearance of gaiety was in distinct contrast to the poverty of Checkpoint Ten; perhaps they shouted louder because they had so little else. A sense of discomfort washed over her.

She'd never liked Mercy Days—sure, the chance to sample foods she'd never be able to otherwise was exciting and the day off from work welcome, but the rest of it . . . She shivered thinking of what was to come.

They'd reached the edge of the market square. Directly across from them on the other side, a platform had been erected right in front of the statue of the True Father. Every town had at least one such statue, usually more than one, and Checkpoint Ten's was nearly identical to Laketown's. The robed and masked figure of the king had one hand up, as if in greeting, and one hand shading the place where his eyes should be on his masked face, as if looking afar. Though she couldn't see them from this distance, she knew the words EVER WISE AND EVER WATCHFUL were inscribed on the statue's base.

She stood in the center of a clutch of factory girls with Tana and Ulani right beside her. The sisters always gravitated to her whether on their walks to and from the dormitories, at meal times, or in their few free hours.

The square was quickly filling and more people streamed in behind them, pressing them closer together. While she hadn't seen Kyssa or Nedra, one of Nedra's cronies, a willowy girl whose name Zeli couldn't recall, seemed to be keeping a close eye on Tana. Her narrowed gaze was often trained in the girl's direction.

It made sense for the watchers to have watchers, but Zeli's stomach sank all the same. There had been no convincing Tana to at least appear to be playing along with Ora's edicts. The girl was resolutely opposed to even looking like she was gathering information on anyone—no sense of self-preservation, that one.

Zeli scanned the crowd around them, looking for others who

might have been assigned to keep tabs on Tana. Instead her gaze was caught by the blue domed roof of the Avinid temple, just across the square. She thought of the revival, of Devana and Kerym. Homesickness filled her, and she blinked back tears.

She tore her attention away to take in the rest of the square. Shops, inns, and stables flanked the open area that would usually have had additional merchant stalls set up. But they had been cleared away to make room for all of the people. The entire town's population would be here along with anyone passing through who needed to be witnessed participating in the mandatory holiday.

Already, volunteers had been conscripted into passing out skewers of roasted meat, fresh apples, and oranges otherwise unknown to the Midcountry, and small cups of ale. All could partake, whether payroller or peasant. The smell of delicious food made Zeli's mouth water. She wasn't used to subsisting on the rations the factory workers were given each day. So she accepted a meat skewer with no guilt whatsoever. It was Mercy Day, after all.

At first she thought Tana would refuse the food, but the girl reluctantly took the offering, showing at least a little sense. But her obstinate expression made Zeli's heart race.

As she wiped a dribble of juice from her chin that had squirted from a tender bite of goat's meat, Zeli stopped short. She noticed a telegram office wedged in between an apothecary and a leather goods shop.

She craned her neck to check the platform—still empty. The local Magister had not yet arrived to kick off the ceremony. Zeli grabbed Ulani's hand.

"Let's go over there." She motioned with her head toward the telegram office. "I think we'll have a better view."

Tana narrowed her eyes, but didn't protest and followed when Zeli led her sister away. They moved through the crowd, avoiding elbows and shoulders as best they could. Finally, they emerged just at the edge of the square, directly in front of the office.

The door to the shop was ajar. Zeli took a quick look around to see who might be watching them—no one she could identify—before approaching and peeking in. A white-haired man bustled about behind the counter.

"Wait here," she said to the younger girls before slipping inside.

The man looked up. "Closing down now. Mercy Day, you know," he said, as if it were possible for her not to know.

"Yes, of course." Zeli craned her neck to take in the small space. "But you'll stay here, right? It isn't Mercy Day everywhere, is it?" Because all production stopped during the holiday and every town couldn't be expected to have executions at the same time, Mercy Days only usually affected a handful of towns at a time. It was possible to travel the Great Highway and be waylaid by a Mercy Day on successive days in each town you passed through.

The telegram operator looked up to answer, when the machine began to whir, indicating an incoming message. He sat down and put his headphones on, listening for the coded signal that he would have to transcribe. As people in other towns would still be sending messages, someone was always needed to be on hand to receive them.

Zeli watched the man carefully, noting the two stacks of papers beside him. The words he transcribed were written on a pad to the man's left. On his right were a half-dozen slips of paper. As she stretched to see, she could tell these were outgoing messages.

An idea sprung to mind. While the operator was busy transcribing the incoming message, Zeli left the shop.

The platform was still empty, but she noticed that Nedra's nosy friend had moved closer to them. The girl stood a few paces away at the edge of the dense crowd.

"I have an idea," Zeli told the girls, quietly. "I need you two to create a distraction." Then she straightened and spoke loud enough for their spy to overhear. "I'm going to take another look at those outgoing telegrams. Could be some good intel in them for Ora-mideni."

Tana rolled her eyes, but little Ulani smiled.

"You two, go into the alley and around the back. Find the back door and rattle it or something. I need the operator to think someone is trying to break in and leave his post so I can take a look around."

Ulani grinned at her assignment and even Tana's eyes brightened, excited to be making some mischief, no doubt. When the girls scampered off, Zeli looked at their spy triumphantly. Hopefully, the news would get back to Ora that the girls were helping seek information.

Zeli went back to the office's main door. Inside, the telegraph operator was still at his desk, shuffling through his papers. Suddenly he looked up, then stood sharply before disappearing into the back.

She rushed in and leaned over the counter to rifle through the outgoing messages in case someone was somehow watching. A second pad, the one on which customers wrote their messages was just out of reach. She climbed onto the counter and grabbed for it. She had a pencil in hand and was scribbling a message to Devana in moments.

She had no money to pay for a telegram home, but she reasoned that if she slipped her message in with the others that had already been paid for, no one would be the wiser. She'd just completed the note when she heard footsteps approaching again from the back of the shop. She tapped the stack of messages to neaten them and quickly scanned the counter to ensure she hadn't upset anything.

The operator was grumbling to himself about urchins and thieves as he returned, but Zeli prowled back outside the front door before he could spot her.

Dangerous as it was, crime wasn't unheard of during Mercy Days. Just about every shop and business in town would be closed down, so it made sense. Though if you were caught thieving on such a day, it was virtually assured that the next Mercy Day would feature your execution.

Zeli met the girls back outside just in time for the Magister to take the stage. She could only hope that her actions would convince Ora to keep all of them right where they were. As for her message to Devana, she didn't even want to allow herself to hope. It was a long shot for her mistress to care enough about her to buy her back. She rubbed her single remaining bracelet. If luck was coming, now would be a good time.

We have to watch and not turn away, Ulani reminds herself. She remembers Papa drilling this into her head over and over again. No gasping or crying when the men and women are dragged onto the stage. No shutting your eyes when the ropes are draped over their necks.

The Magister drones on and on about crimes against the

Fatherland and the dutiful citizens who keep us safe with their vigilance. A gussied-up payroller preens under the attention given him. He informed on the people who are about to die.

Ulani's neck is weighed down by colorful wreaths. Thicker and lighter than the ropes the people on the platform wear. She touches the petals of one of the delicate flowers. They're pretty, but they don't feel like real flowers at all. She imagines the velvety texture of a dune sunflower, both butter soft and butter yellow. Both the vision in her head and the feel of it on her fingertips make her smile.

Her eyes are open, looking straight ahead but seeing something totally different. A green stem, slightly fuzzy but strong. Pointed green leaves. An orange center with its little fluffy bits and coming out of it, the petals, split at the ends like a fork.

Tana hits her in the shoulder, and Ulani's focus comes back to the present. The bodies on the stage are only half visible now, having fallen into the holes in the bottom. They sway slightly, heads at odd angles.

Tana kicks her foot, causing a sharp pain. Ulani looks down to see a dune sunflower growing out of the crack between paving stones just between the two of them. She wants to pick it and keep it. Once she kept a flower alive in her room for months, hidden in the jar where she stored her writing chalk. When it would wilt, she would sing it back to life, sensing its will to live and helping it along.

But Tana frowns at her now, before replacing the expression with the same splintery smile everyone around them wears. Tana slides her foot over the flower to crush it and hide it from view. Ulani knows she isn't supposed to make flowers anymore, especially not where people can see. She hadn't been trying to, but she hadn't been *not* trying to, either.

When Tana moves her foot, the little plant is gone. Not just crushed, but shriveled and brown, like all the life has been drained out of it.

Kind of how Papa looked all crumpled and empty and cold on the floor.

Ulani takes her sister's hand, threading their fingers together. She'll have to be more careful. Then again, so will Tana.

CHAPTER TWENTY-SEVEN

Fetters braided of histories entwined
Are stronger than a murmured requiem
And echoes of what was will not be hushed
They sing louder causing old wounds to mend
With whispered words breathing a truthful cry
A fuel-starved flame's denied the chance to die

—THE BOOK OF UNVEILING

Terror pummeled Kyara, forcing her out of the vision she'd been caught in and back to the cavern. The image of Darvyn falling into the poisonous waters of Death River played over and over in her mind, numbing her senses. One moment he'd been there and the next . . . "What was that? What happened?"

"Save him," Murmur said.

She scrambled to her feet, vibrating with urgency and dread. "D-did you do that? Push him off the cliff and into the river with your magic?"

"Save him." His voice was calm and thin. To her amazement, he rose and began to shuffle away.

"No! Wait!" she screamed, looking around frantically. "I can't heal. How can I save him? The water will kill him!" She raced after the ancient man, ready to strike some sense into him. An invisible force stopped her fist from flying out.

"Save him," Murmur said once more, then began moving again, quicker this time.

Kyara choked on the air entering her lungs. How could she save him when he was so far away? She would never get there in time, and if she did . . .

Her whole body shook. She kneeled, planted her palms on the ground, and released her Song again. It knew what she wanted and led her back into the arms of the Mother. She flew back through the tunnels to where Darvyn had last been. Then she was flying over Death River, viewing the sickening menagerie of petrified animals along the shallows and banks.

The river had carried Darvyn downstream to where the canyon widened. He swam with quick movements and was able to pull himself onto the shore. Kyara opened her mind's eye to find the destruction already taking root in his body. He glowed brightly, the poison doing its work.

But he was the Shadowfox. He should be able to battle the effects of the river with Earthsong.

Kyara held out this hope even as his movements slowed and he collapsed on the rocks. His limbs froze as he glowed even brighter. The river's deadly work was too fast. The Nethersong was so strong here, and his Song had been blocked before he fell. Whatever the reason, Earthsong wasn't helping him.

Tortured cries set her throat on fire and echoed through the cavern. Even her disembodied self, hovering over the river, heard them.

Darvyn stopped moving.

The Nether of the poison racing through him called to her. She prodded it as it overtook Darvyn's limbs. To her surprise, it responded, leaping to her. Kyara delved deeper, pulling the death energy from the poison and drawing it away. Just as the Nethersong of the gorge invigorated her, so did the power of the poison. In her mind's eye, the brightness coursing through Darvyn's body darkened as the Nether flowed from him to her.

It was as easy as breathing. She inhaled the Nethersong and it left his body, allowing his natural healing process to begin. His Song was now able to catch hold. Without Nether, the poison still in his blood was rendered powerless and held no destructive ability. As Darvyn continued to darken with life energy, Kyara heaved a sigh of relief.

Only once before, when she'd first tried to incapacitate Darvyn, had she been able to draw Nethersong from one place to another. Such a thing had never even occurred to her before. And once she absorbed the Nether, it was harmless. More than that, it was revitalizing. She felt giddy and energized, all fatigue gone.

A mad sort of laughter escaped her as Darvyn began to awaken. His breathing took on a deep, regular rhythm. She sagged with relief when he opened his eyes.

"Darvyn, can you hear me?"

He gave no indication that he could. She was, after all, just an intangible presence, observing him through the magic of Mountain Mother. Her body, however, cried tears of joy.

"Murmur!" Kyara stalked the corridors and bridges of the cave city, the steaming of her blood having replaced her happiness. Her voice echoed throughout the cavern, glancing over the smooth surfaces like a missile seeking its target.

Labyrinthine passageways twisted and turned around her. Hallways led to dead ends. She would never find him this way. She quieted her mind and put a hold on her anger for a moment to reach for her Song, which purred in her grasp.

Using her other sight, she navigated the maze until she found all five elders together in a torchlit chamber just off the main cavern. She raced down the staircase, arriving out of breath. Once again, they were seated in a circle on the ground.

"Murmur." She willed the man to look at her. His colorless eyes opened, and he had the nerve to raise his hairless brows.

"How could you do that to him? What would have happened if I hadn't been able to save him? Do you know how important he is?" She wanted to punch something, preferably Murmur, but any blow from her would just bounce off his magic. Plus, she couldn't very well strike a centuries-old man.

"But you did save him." His voice was infuriatingly calm.

"That is not the point."

"That is the only point," he said. "Are you ready for your next lesson?"

Her chest heaved. She rubbed the sore skin of the wound. "You're just like *her*. You only want to control me, use me in your stupid war." Her hand dropped to her side. "Well, I don't want to be used. I want to be free."

"You will only find freedom when you embrace your Song. Your friend was in no danger."

"He was *dying*."

Murmur stared back at her blankly.

She decided to try another tack. "He needs to know that I'm all right," she said. "Can you lead him here, the way you did for me?"

"The Mother does not welcome his kind."

"His kind? Earthsingers?"

"No, we are well protected from the sorcerers. It is his father's people who will never be trusted by the mountain."

Kyara had no idea who Darvyn's father was, but it was irrelevant. She wasn't going to leave him alone in the desert thinking she was dead. Especially with the True Father ruthlessly hunting him.

"I need to find him."

"You should stay. There is much to learn about your Song. Knowledge you will not find in any book. The Scorpion's memories are here with the Mother."

"The Scorpion?" she asked, her breath catching.

"Yes, that is what we called Mooriah."

"And you know her story?"

"I lived through it. I can show you."

The notion of learning from the memories of another Nethersinger, of learning the full story told in the cryptic little book gave her pause. But the image of Darvyn tossed at the mercy of the river overwhelmed her, raising her ire. She could not trust these ancients. They had their own agenda, even if she did not fully understand it yet.

If it wasn't one powerful being seeking to manipulate her, it was another.

"Prove to me that I can trust you. Take my Song. You can do what you like with it when I'm gone."

The ancients around the circle stirred. None spoke out loud, but they appeared to be communicating in some way. Finally, Murmur shook his head slowly.

"Then there is no reason for me to stay."

The fire in the torches flared, as if the Mother herself were having her say.

Murmur sucked in a deep breath, then blew it out slowly. "Be well, Kyara the Nethersinger. And remember to embrace your Song. We may yet meet again. When you choose sides, choose well."

She was surprised they were letting her go so easily, but she didn't want to stay in these caves a moment longer. The other Cavefolk sat motionless except for the movements under their skin. She left the ancients behind, uncertain if she was making the right decision. The last time she'd been given such a choice she'd chosen poorly. Ydaris and the True Father had been the lesser of evils, or at least Kyara had thought so when she was eleven. Now she believed all evil to be equal.

Standing amid the vastness of the Great Cave, she searched her Song for the fastest path to Darvyn.

A woman's voice wakes Ulani out of sleep. She bolts upright, sweat clinging to her thin nightdress.

No, the voice was in her dream. Ulani had been in the World Between again with the lady, Oola. Her warm, invisible presence had been so close. Like a hug she couldn't quite feel. And she'd sung to her again. The words of the lullaby reverberate softly in her mind.

"Wake up, little one
The time has come to go,
Make your way in haste
Don't let your feet be slow.
Let my voice serve to guide you
Don't stop 'til the race is run
For the road is waiting on you
I love you more than the sun."

Then Oola had stopped singing and with a gentle yet insistent voice she'd repeated something, over and over again. Impressing it into Ulani's mind. Only now, she can't remember.

The dream woman showed her something as well. A vision of Mengu's home. Girls and boys kept in chains. Sorrow etched into their faces. And fear.

She'd been afraid of the way the man had stared at her back at the nabber's place. Of the way he'd touched her face. She'd wanted to scrub the spot clean to remove the feeling. Tana can't be allowed to go to his home.

But that's what Kyssa had said when they'd returned to the dormitory from Mercy Day. No matter how clever Zeli had been, word had gotten back that Tana had not tried hard enough and had come back with nothing for Ora to use against any of the townsfolk.

Kyssa informed them that in the morning, Tana would be expected to report to Mengu's home. She would belong to him now.

The moon shines brightly, visible through the open window. Tana is still asleep by her side. Zeli is across the room, sharing a mattress with two other factory girls. A soft breeze moves through the room, ruffling Ulani's braids.

She wracks her brain to remember the word from the dream, then takes a deep breath, trying to calm herself.

Run.

She startles as the memory returns. Oola had told her to run.

Ulani doesn't hesitate. She inches away from her sister and stands. The bricks in the floor are cool beneath her bare toes. None of the others stir. Her tunic and trousers hang on a peg on the wall. She grabs them along with her shoes and slips out of the room and down the stairs.

The dormitories are not under guard. The girls have no money and nowhere to go—Ulani is no different. But she feels the power of the dream woman and does not doubt her at all.

She was told to run.

And so she opens the door and races out into the night.

CHAPTER TWENTY-EIGHT

The seer of the Folk was sometimes blind
To all, save what the rare visions conveyed
But what he saw was never cast in doubt
His word, once heard and questioned, was obeyed
So though the Folk would far prefer she run
They knew they yet would need the Scorpion
—THE BOOK OF UNVEILING

An urgent prodding at her shoulder forced Zeli awake. Tana's face hovered over her, ghostly lit by the moon, making the girl look like a specter. Like a death-bringing spirit on the warpath.

Zeli barely held in a gasp and grabbed Tana's arm. "What is it?" she whispered. Next to her on the mattress, another factory girl shifted and rolled over, before beginning to snore again.

"Ulani is gone."

Zeli wiped her eyes, not quite understanding what Tana was saying. When she sat up, she saw the pallet on the other side of the small room was empty.

"Maybe she's in the privy?" Zeli asked.

Tana shook her head. "Already checked."

"And the kitchen?"

"Not there, either. Her clothes are gone. She's missing."

Zeli frowned. Could someone have snuck into the room and taken the girl, or would she have left on her own? And if so, why?

She got to her feet and dressed quickly. No one else stirred. These girls slept very soundly after their long work shifts, and though she thought she saw movement in the corner, when she looked closer, that girl was out like the others.

She led Tana out of the room. They peeked into the other bedrooms on the top floor, but no one else moved. Zeli wasn't certain of the time; it must have been several hours before dawn. Once they'd ascertained for certain that Ulani was nowhere in the house, they stood together whispering downstairs in the great room.

"Do you think she would try to go back home?" Zeli asked.

Tana shook her head resolutely. "No. Not without me."

"I don't see how anyone could have taken her. Surely one of us would have woken up if there had been an intruder."

Tana firmed her lips, looking around. "She was always given to fancies. Like that whole business about the Poison Flame being at the nabber warehouse. She believes the things she imagines. Maybe she got some strange notion into her head and . . ." She shook her head.

Zeli sighed. What sort of notion would make a seven-year-old girl leave her bed *and* her sister in the middle of the night? "Well, let's get started looking for her. She can't have gone too far."

"It wouldn't be wise to leave." The voice was emotionless and familiar. Zeli turned to find Nedra facing them. She was wrapped in a thin dressing gown, a kerchief tied around her hair.

"Nedra-deni," Zeli began, her mind racing to come up with an explanation that didn't make it sound like they were abandoning their servitude. "We were just—"

"My sister had a bad dream," Tana said, cutting her off. "So I sent her outside for some cool air. That always helps her recover."

Tana stood with her hands clasped firmly in front of her, back straight. Nedra moved closer, her features coming into clearer view in the dim lighting. The weak explanation had done nothing to satisfy their supervisor.

"Aren't you due to head over to Mengu-mideni's home tomorrow?" Nedra asked.

Tana nodded her head solemnly.

Nedra sighed. "Runaways are sent to the work camps," she said, turning to Zeli. "Unlike her," she motioned to Tana, "*your* presence will be missed tomorrow. If you're not back by dawn, and Kyssa-deni discovers it, you will want to stay gone."

Zeli shivered at the thought. "I understand," she said. But did she? If she wasn't back by sunrise then she would be a fugitive for having escaped her servitude. She would be sentenced to the camps for the remainder of her allotted time with extra years added on for thievery—since Ora had paid good money for her. Zeli could be kept there the rest of her life, however short that might be considering the hard labor.

But how could she not search for Ulani? She looked at Tana, who stared at the floor. The girl was going after her sister whether Zeli came or not.

Zeli took a deep breath and faced Nedra. "I understand," she repeated more firmly. "May we greet one another again, Nedra-deni." Her voice was heavy and sad.

Nedra nodded, her gaze weary, and turned around. Halfway to the staircase she paused. "The land around the tollhouse is booby-trapped." And then she was gone on silent feet up the steps.

With a dark cloud of foreboding dogging their steps, Zeli and Tana ventured out of the dormitory's safety into the night, their thin tunics poor protection from the desert chill. The dimly lit street outside the building was quiet. Bleak and lifeless. Zeli shook off the maudlin thoughts with gratitude that there was no one else about at this hour. It was far better for Ulani to be out here alone than for her to have encountered someone unsavory.

"Into town or away from it?" Zeli wondered. Tana stared in the direction leading out, a frown on her face. For a child to head toward the Great Highway at night by herself would be terrible and foolish. But suddenly Zeli knew which way they had to go.

Tana agreed and they set off. The moon was thankfully bright, illuminating their way. They had no lantern, no money, and only the clothes on their backs. If they encountered any trouble, there would be little to do but hide.

They passed the pathway to the factory on their way out of town. Soon enough, the highway stretched out before them. The gatehouse at the toll was occupied, a lantern lit in the window. Even pedestrians were required to pay the toll, so the girls stepped off the highway to head out into the bush and go around the gate.

Zeli held up her hand, causing Tana to halt. Nedra's warning might save their lives. Zeli had forgotten about the traps set around tolls meant to catch those trying to get out of paying. Each step could hold unknown danger.

Did Ulani know? Could she have avoided the traps? Zeli's

mouth went dry. Maybe they should have checked in town after all. Still, she had to trust her gut, which assured her that they were headed in the right direction—even if that direction might result in a nasty surprise.

The moonlight allowed Zeli to thoroughly investigate the ground before she made a single step. She wished she had a walking stick or branch to prod the earth before them with, but there was nothing large enough around.

A trip wire crossed their path just ahead. She motioned to it and Tana nodded, then they each stepped carefully over. Zeli wondered what would have happened if she'd tripped over the thing, but really didn't want to know.

Tana spotted a claw trap on their path. When stepped on, its jaws would close around your foot, embedding painful serrated teeth into your flesh. A little farther along, they spotted what looked to be a pile of twigs and branches covering a hole in the ground. And farther still, Zeli almost tread on a trigger net until Tana pulled her away.

Finally, after a full five minutes had passed without them seeing any more traps, Zeli felt they might be in the clear. Unfortunately, they hadn't seen any evidence of Ulani, either.

They were approaching the highway again—this section of the roadway was paved and they'd make faster time on it than they would bushwhacking—when a horse and rider approached from the south. The girls quickly backtracked into the wilderness and hid behind the wide branches of a shrub.

They didn't move until they heard the distant toll bell ringing, marking the lifting of the gate and the rider's passage through. After that, they kept to the bush, walking alongside the main highway, and making poor time.

Tana thought they should call Ulani's name, but Zeli was

afraid of other travelers hearing them. The Father only knew what type of person could be out here with them, skulking around the bushes. But in the end, Zeli relented. What if the little girl were hurt and hiding? The risk of calling out was high but it outweighed the need for caution.

They traveled slowly along, shouting for Ulani, as a vague glow began to warm the horizon. Dawn. If they didn't find her soon and get back to the dormitory, they wouldn't be able to go back at all.

The rumble of an engine pierced the night. A diesel contraption. Far less common in the Midcountry than in the cities, its loud grinding deluged Zeli in a wave of homesickness.

"We should get off the road," Tana said, her voice wobbly. Though she masked her emotions, her fear was palpable. How far would they get on the highway having to hide from every vehicle? What would they do if they didn't find Ulani? Even if they did, without supplies and on foot, how would they survive? Even Zeli's natural optimism was no match for the terror filling her veins.

The diesel contraption drew closer, its growl vibrating the ground underfoot.

Once again the girls hid in the bush, but when the vehicle should have passed them by at speed, it slowed instead. Zeli peered around the cluster of saltbushes she was using for cover and glimpsed gleaming metal parts winking in the moonlight. The autocar was the same model the Magister owned—not cobbled together from parts, but properly imported from Yaly at astonishing expense. Zeli wondered who in this area could afford such a thing. Perhaps one of the provincial Magisters had enough wealth, though fuel was hard to come by.

The autocar continued at a crawl before stopping a few paces down the highway. The driver must, somehow, impossibly, be able to see them. The implications of that petrified Zeli's limbs. Just as she was beginning to truly panic, Tana jumped up from her hiding place.

Zeli grabbed the edge of the girl's tunic to drag her back, but Tana moved out of her reach, headed toward the autocar.

"Tana!" she whispered loudly, craning her neck to see what had made the girl abandon her caution and natural suspicion.

Zeli thought she was seeing things. There in the passenger seat, calm as you please, sat Ulani. The driver of the car peered around her to look at them. Then a grin split the man's face and recognition flooded Zeli.

"Fazar-deni?" she said, standing. "What-what are you doing here?"

"Kerym-mideni received your telegram. He borrowed the Magister's autocar and sent me out immediately. I was on my way to Ten to search for you."

Numbness stole her fear. Devana must have shared her telegram with Kerym and then he'd launched into action, sending his valet to come and find her.

"I can't believe it," she whispered.

"Aye. Told me not to come back without you, either." Fazar grinned. Kerym's valet had been a fixture in the Ephor's household for as long as Zeli could remember. He was a kind man who accompanied his master often enough to the Magister's estate that the servants all knew him.

She'd never been more glad to see anyone.

"This one flagged me down. Never so shocked in my life as to see such a little thing standing in the middle of the highway like that." He looked reprovingly at Ulani, who'd been captured by Tana in a fierce hug.

"You can't ever do that again, Ulani-yul. Promise me." Tana's voice was thick with emotion.

"I'm sorry," Ulani said. "But we had to get away."

"What on earth possessed you to do something so foolish as run away down the Great Highway?" Zeli asked.

Ulani's lip quivered and Zeli regretted her tone of voice, but she'd been so scared. "The lady in my dream told me to run."

Tana leaned back, looking ready to commit murder. Her nostrils flared, but she held herself from speaking.

Zeli moved closer. "And what made you stop Fazar-deni?"

Ulani just looked at her, but didn't answer.

"There was another rider who'd come along not long ago, did you see them?"

The girl nodded. "He felt like storm clouds," she replied. "Fazar-deni feels like the sun on your face."

Zeli was perplexed by this strange answer, but Fazar spoke up. "We'd better get started. Don't want to be on the road longer than necessary."

She realized the man was armed with a pistol at his side.

"You three get in the backseat and cover yourselves with that blanket," Fazar said. "If we come across anyone, best they not know you're here."

"You'll take us all back to Lower Faalagol?"

"Well, I certainly won't leave these children on the highway. But do you think the Magister will take them in?" Fazar asked, sounding dubious.

Zeli pursed her lips. "If I can convince Devana-mideni, then she'll insist they stay."

The girls climbed into the back and lay down with Ulani and Tana in the foot wells with Zeli curled up on the seat. Fazar turned the autocar around and they were back on their way.

"What did you mean that Fazar-deni felt like the sun on your face?" Zeli whispered. She couldn't see the other girl under the blanket, but felt a warm hand on hers.

"He just did. The way you feel like hugs."

"I don't understand."

"It's her Song," Tana answered. "It's how she talks about how she senses people with Earthsong." There was a movement from the older girl that might have been a shrug.

"Do you have your Song, too?" Zeli asked.

"No, never did. Just born wrong, I guess." Tana's affect was flat, but Zeli could only imagine what it must have been like. Though perhaps better than having had a Song and losing it.

"Ulani, no matter what the people in your dreams say, you can't just run away without telling anyone. It's very dangerous. You know that, right?" Zeli wished she could see her face.

"I know. It's just that, we had to get away from Mengu-mideni. The lady said."

After that, they rode in silence. Ulani's dream lady had led her to a positive outcome, much better than could have been expected. If Fazar had shown up in town looking for Zeli, would Ora have sold her to him? Would Zeli have been able to get the girls out as well? The situation had ended well enough, but it could have gone another way so easily.

More easily than she ever wanted to consider.

But now, after all of that, she was going home. She wasn't certain what awaited her there, but as the wheels hummed along the road, she held out hope that the future would be very shiny indeed.

CHAPTER TWENTY-NINE

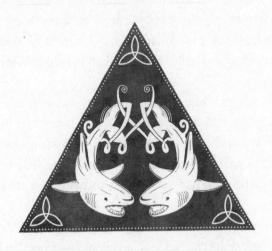

Two tunnels branch off of the traveled route
Both narrow, twisting, uncertain, and grave
One leaves behind the known for hope of more
One leads to acceptance she's always craved
Destinies converge in her direction
Hearts stand by as she makes her selection

—THE BOOK OF UNVEILING

Darvyn's climb out of the gorge was brutal. Fortunately, he had washed up at a section of the river where it turned back on itself in a horseshoe shape. The rock formation at the center of the U was rough, leaving ledges and handholds for him to grab onto as he pulled himself up. The soft earth crumbled beneath his fingers, but with his Song beginning to restore itself, he sang a spell to hold it together and support his weight. When he reached the top, he lay flat on the ground, heaving breaths.

How had he survived his fall into the river? The memories came in flashes. He'd reached out with his Song, but it had still been blocked. The waters had engulfed him as he sank below, tasting its bitter, metallic taint as it had invaded his mouth and nose.

He'd dragged himself out, still trying to catch hold of Earthsong. And then the numbness had come. His limbs had grown heavy and stopped cooperating. His consciousness had failed. Then he'd awoken, having no idea how long he'd been out, but Earthsong had thrummed through him, healing his body.

A half-remembered voice singing a familiar melody danced across his mind. Just a fragment of sound that echoed in his ears. They were probably still ringing from the fall, but it almost sounded like his mother singing a lullaby to him as he fell asleep.

A hallucination. Though it sounded so real. He took a deep breath and closed his eyes, focusing on the here and now. His parched throat. The scorching late-afternoon heat. But the strains of a sweet, sad voice singing his name as a soft lullaby lingered on.

Only it wasn't his name he heard. The song was one that mothers inserted the names of their children into in each verse, singing about the child they loved more than the sun. So why was he hallucinating someone else's name?

He sat up as the memory solidified. The Keepers had changed his name when they took him. That first night, he'd ridden off with a stranger, tears blurring his vision. That's when they'd started calling him Darvyn. There were enough Tahlyros around that they kept his surname, and he wouldn't part with the House of Jackals sigil associated with it, but his original name, the one his mother had given him, had disappeared as completely as she had.

As the song repeated in Darvyn's mind, it brought a realization. She hadn't really vanished.

Everything the Keepers had told him his whole life came into focus. They'd said she abandoned him, that they had no idea where she could be. But she'd been searching for the Keepers, had sought them out again and again. Surely word had gotten to the elders that a woman was trying to locate her son.

Anger rose within him, razor-sharp. Rage sliced at him as the desert heat seared his skin.

A torrent of power loosed itself from his hold. Lightning crackled. Winds gusted. Instead of stopping it, he leaned in, releasing the storm inside. He drew heavily from the source, pulling waves of Earthsong to him. The sky darkened as heavy clouds rolled in. With a burst of thunder, they released their loads, drenching the parched desert with rain. Hard drops stung and the Earthsong beat at him, burying him in its might.

He poured everything he had into the spell, drawing more energy than he ever had at one time, until he knew he was close to exhausting his barely restored Song.

Kyara was lost in some dark, impossible pit. He may never see her again.

He'd failed Jack and been betrayed by those who claimed to care for him.

The Keepers had instilled in him a sense of duty from the time he was four years old. His power was precious. The strongest Singer in generations. Men and women had died protecting him from the True Father's agents.

Guilt had long weighed him down, but now anger mixed with it until he was buried beneath a bitter sadness. If he had known his mother was seeking him, he would have found her. Kept her safe. No rogue physician would have ever touched her.

The storm raged on, leaving him sprawled in a sea of mud. He flopped onto his back, the mud heavy as chains binding him to the ground. The absurdity of it all struck him, and he began laughing. Nothing about this situation was humorous, but the laughter would not stop. It rose from his belly in ripples, unwilling to release him. Was this his mind breaking?

The rain died as his grasp on his Song slipped, and he laughed until there were tears in his eyes.

"What's so funny?"

That is exactly what Kyara would say if she were here. And just in that tone of voice.

And that was exactly what her face would look like if she were standing over him, frowning like he was a lunatic escaped from the asylum. The vision kneeled beside him, her brightly patterned tunic plastered to her chest, streams of water running down her face.

Darvyn sat up sharply, just missing bumping heads with her.

"Is this your idea of a joke?"

His eyes widened. It looked like her and sounded like her. He reached out and touched the soft curve of her cheek.

"Kyara?"

Her lips twisted in a wry smile. "Were you expecting someone else?"

"You're alive!" He launched himself at her, squeezing her in a hard embrace.

"Yes, and very wet." Her arms were stiff at her sides, but slowly, they came around him. "So, I guess this means you missed me."

If they had been standing he would've spun her around, but they sat there in the puddle of muck. He pulled back, his eyes hungry for her face. She was flushed, her breath short. He felt much the same way. When he cupped her cheeks in his palms, her eyes closed on a long blink.

His head still spun from the expenditure of his Song. His heart raced from exhaustion, though it might also have been from Kyara's nearness. He could blame either of those things for what he did next, but the truth was, he had wanted to do it ever since he'd first laid eyes on her.

When he pressed his lips to hers, her body went rigid, but then her hands pressed against his back, bringing him closer to her. She tilted her head like an invitation, still tentative, but curious. His tongue breached the seam of her lips and she gasped. He could not stop himself from invading her mouth, caressing her tongue and fusing their lips together.

Her hands slid under his wet tunic, warming his chilled skin. But all too soon she broke apart from him, her expression shocked. His heart pumped furiously, rattling him to the core.

Kyara swallowed. He followed the motion of her neck, longing to kiss her there. But shock turned to something else as her eyes clouded over. Something darker, more like fear. She backed away and a hollow opened inside him.

She touched her lips, tracing them the way he still wanted to even though her body language rapidly cooled the heat within him.

"Why did you do that?" she whispered.

"Did you not want me to?"

She met his eyes sharply. "I almost killed you, Darvyn."

He rubbed his forehead, then scrubbed his hands across his scalp. "But not because you wanted to."

She let out a deranged chuckle. "What does it matter? Dead is dead."

"What happened to you? Where did you end up? How did you get back here?"

"It's actually a long story."

He dried the area on which they sat. His Song was already replenishing itself so it was nothing to draw the water out of the mud, and their clothes.

Half a pace lay between them, a distance that felt vast. But once she began her story about falling into the darkness and meeting the Cavefolk, he nearly forgot the wall she was putting up.

"They wanted me to stay there with them. They said they would teach me to use my Song, but—" She pulled at a scrub of beardgrass just breaking through the earth. "I don't think I like their methods."

His tumble into the river was still very fresh in his mind. "I have to agree."

"They acted like I'm some kind of savior. There's no way I can be that." She eyed him warily. "And you should be careful of me. I'm not . . ." She looked away and took a deep breath. "What I did to you and your friend . . . you don't know what happened to him. He could be— He could be dead because of me."

Darvyn shook his head. "The Queen said he lives. And whatever happened to him is because of the True Father, not you." He shifted into her line of sight, forcing her to stop avoiding his gaze.

Her jaw was set petulantly. "I don't know if I even believe in the Queen."

"She's very real."

"And She sees us? Can She see everything?"

Kyara seemed determined to change the subject. "She can control some of what She sees," he said, "but She cannot see everything. She visits dreams at random, or maybe according to some design that only She knows. And there are a rare few in this world, like me, whom She can contact at will. I do not know the reason. If She knows, She's never shared it. Being forthcoming is not Her strong suit."

"You don't seem to like Her very much."

Twilight had fallen, and Kyara was painted in the beauty of the sun's dying light. He tried not to stare; he sensed it made her uncomfortable, but the last thing he wanted to do was talk about the Queen. Still, it was something they had in common—being controlled.

"I first had the Dream of the Queen when I was four, just after the Keepers took me in. Though I didn't tell anyone."

"Why not?"

"I was already different from the other children. Once the elders really understood the extent of my power, I was kept separate. Everything was shrouded in secrecy. I had to be protected at all costs. I didn't want one more thing to set me apart." He drew in a pained breath as the memories crashed into him. Kyara's hand settled on his arm. The light touch helped ground him.

"The Dream of the Queen kept coming, and on top of that, She showed Herself to me for some reason. It was a long time before I knew how rare that was. I've never met another Dreamer who's ever seen Her. Even then I was *special*." He spat the word out.

"And She asked me to do things. Go places, help people. I didn't mind then. I wanted to heal and feed others. To soothe all the sorrow I felt around me. To make people laugh with something funny or magical. But the things She asked me to do weren't always so benign."

"What do you mean?" Kyara's concern sounded genuine. And if anyone would understand, she would.

"The Keepers moved me every few weeks to keep ahead of the spies and the Collectors. Nowhere was safe for long." The bitterness of that realization always stung.

"I'd had the Dream a few nights before. She'd come to me and told me that we were likely to pass very near somewhere special. And that I was to follow my senses to retrieve something important for her.

"In the middle of the night, the Keepers took me from the house where I'd been staying and hid me in a wagon of straw. It itched something awful. I was scratching, trying to be quiet, when I felt something tug at my Song. I knew it's what She had warned me about. The wagon slowed at a bend in the road, and I jumped out and ran into the darkness without telling anyone. I thought that's what She'd meant when She said to follow my senses."

The memory pummeled him, strangling his voice.

"Where did you go?" Kyara asked.

He cleared his throat. "Tanagol. The same ruins where you stopped after you fled the school. That's where I felt this sensation leading me. I wandered around in the moonlight until I closed in on the source of the feeling, buried under some old crumbled bricks. A little rock, big as my fist, at the time. It was a caldera."

"Like my speaking stone."

"But ancient, and far more powerful. The Keepers tracked me down, they left the highway, braving the night in the bush and found me. But bush wranglers had seen them."

Her hand on his tightened.

"A group of them tracked us and attacked. I was distracted by the caldera and didn't give a warning. Two men died that night."

She squeezed his arm, hard. "You were just a little boy."

"I was already the Shadowfox. And people died to save me

that night. And many other nights. Too many." He pulled away from her touch. "After that I told them about the Dream. I thought maybe if I'd told them before, something could have been different."

"The Queen doesn't know the future, does She?"

"Even if She did, I doubt She'd share any more than She wanted to."

Kyara fidgeted with the bristle in her hands. Her next words were barely audible. "You blame Her?"

"I'm a game piece on a board to be moved by Her however She wants. I'm a tool for the Keepers to achieve their agenda. I'm a savior, a soldier, a hero, a legend, everything but a man. Everything but my *own* man."

Tears filled his eyes. "They lied to me about my mother, Kyara. They said they'd looked for her and never found a trace."

She frowned. "But that can't be true. Why would they say that?"

"Control." That anger bubbled up again. "Complete control."

She was quiet beside him for a long time. When she spoke, her voice was made of iron. "Well that, at least, is something you can change."

"No," Kyara said, crossing her arms. The stubborn set of her jaw caused Darvyn to flash back to their kiss the day before. He shook off the remembrance of her mouth against his before he could get lost in it. Today, she was being unreasonable.

"You can't stay here. They call it Death River for a reason."

Her eyes flashed with determination. "Once I leave the gorge, the spell will return. It will force me to try to capture you. I can die here or die resisting the spell. But I won't harm you."

"We can fight it again," he said. "We will find every carcass from here to the Breach Valley. We'll gather enough Nethersong to help you overcome the spell. I won't give up. And maybe the Keepers will have other ideas. I can speak to the elders."

She shook her head. "You can't trust them. You have a traitor in your midst giving information to the True Father. That's how I knew where to find you in the first place."

The stifling heat grew distant as a chill overtook his body. "What?"

"It's true." Her eyes softened, apologetic. "They knew the Shadowfox would be at Checkpoint Five following the nabbers. I just had to figure out which one you were and bring you to Sayya."

He ran a hand over his head. "I can't believe that one of us would turn traitor. It doesn't make sense. Only a handful knew about the mission. Why would they want me captured?" Though his feelings about the Keepers leadership were still raw, the men and women who risked their lives to fight for the freedom of their people were his family. The only one he'd truly known.

Her voice was sad. "I don't know. I wish I could tell you more."

Darvyn thought about the Keepers he'd worked with so many times before. "I should have been able to sense the deception."

"Can you feel everyone's feelings all the time?"

He shook his head.

"Even the Shadowfox is not all-powerful. Unless you asked every Keeper if they betrayed you, would you ever know?"

His jaw firmed. "I'll find out now."

"I hope so."

"And I'm not leaving you here."

Her eyes searched his. He could feel the gears churning in her mind. "If I go with you . . ." she said.

He squeezed her shoulders, joy and relief filling him.

"*If* I go with you, to help discover what happened to your friend and identify the traitor, you must promise not to allow me to harm you. Knock me out, tie me up, do what you must if the spell becomes too much for me. And then leave."

His jaw ticked; he didn't like her terms, but they made sense. He'd never felt anything like the sudden weakness that had come over him when Kyara used her power. He nodded.

"Do you promise?" she asked.

"I promise."

Kyara closed her eyes, appearing relieved, even as Darvyn's stomach churned at the thought of keeping his vow.

CHAPTER THIRTY

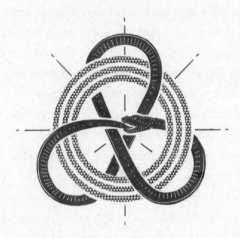

The path she trods leads only to one place
The darkness opens up, swallows her whole
Deeper into the belly of the beast
Its back she cannot break, its arms enclose
Encompassed by dutiful repentance
She accepts her orphan's inheritance

—THE BOOK OF UNVEILING

Dawn had broken on the drive from Checkpoint Eleven to Laketown. Zeli peeked around the blanket covering her to look through the window. As the mountains grew closer, her heart grew more full. With every kilometer that passed, she was able to breathe a little more deeply. The fear that they would be discovered and dragged back to the factory lessened. When they reached the Snarl and were firmly in the Magister's territory, Fazar said it was safe for them to remove the blanket.

She awakened the girls and let them sit on either side of her so they could see out the windows more easily. With the great iron gates of the city drawing up before them, Zeli felt as light as a feather.

The guard at the gate approached the vehicle and asked for their papers. Fazar pulled out a card embossed with the Magister's seal, and the gates creaked open to admit them.

Tana's and Ulani's astonished reactions to the city surprised Zeli. "Is it so different from Sayya?" she asked as their wide, open-mouthed stares became almost comical.

She recalled little of the capital city. Crowded streets, buildings pressed together in an untidy jumble, foul smells emanating from every crack and alley. But she'd seen only a small part. She tried to view the much smaller Laketown through their eyes. Grass-lined avenues with flowers growing in the center. Mountains rising up to tower overhead with their rounded peaks, some already covered in snow this early in the season.

You couldn't see the lake from the avenue they drove along, and she longed for a glimpse of its pristine, sparkling blue waters—craved it the same as she would a mouthful of water after trekking across the desert. But the effects of the long-ago transformation this region had undergone were plain.

The streets were paved with wide stones that fit together seamlessly, giving it a smooth feeling as the autocar's wheels rumbled along them. The people were not the starving stick-and-bones creatures from the towns she'd visited on her impromptu journey. Their tunics were free of dust, faces free of grime, and true smiles graced more than a few faces.

There had been a Mercy Day here as well while she'd been

away. A few stubborn streamers remained stuck, dangling overhead from electricity poles. On the streets, the engines of other diesel contraptions grumbled, along with a variety of carriages pulled by well-fed horses and ponies.

Though Tana and Ulani were the children of a wealthy capital payroller, they were astonished by the sights of Zeli's hometown. She realized just how good she'd had it her whole life. Even as a maid, she'd worked in a rich man's house. She hadn't seen and endured what many others had.

The autocar rolled up to the Magister's compound, and the sight of the sprawling connection of buildings and walkways nearly brought a tear to Zeli's eye. Vines grew up the posts between buildings and the sandstone was pristine, cleaned regularly by the gardeners. The place was a palace compared to anything she'd seen in the Midcountry.

Zeli hopped out of the vehicle and helped the girls exit. Fazar gave a wave and drove off around the circular drive. Her chest constricted. When would she be able to see Kerym and thank him for all he'd done?

As she led the girls to the kitchen entrance, she worried over how to ensure they could stay—at least until she could find somewhere else for them. Would the Magister appreciate having two more mouths to feed or would he send them away? She gripped the edge of her rough tunic and walked inside.

Gladda was there, observing the kitchen staff. She took one look at Zeli before rushing over and crushing her in strong arms. "We've all been worried sick. Devana-mideni especially. You're to see her immediately." She pulled back and noticed the two younger girls. "Now who do we have here?"

Zeli introduced them and sent a pleading glance to Gladda. "I couldn't leave them behind. Do you think it will be all right?"

Gladda firmed her lips. "That's something for the mistress to decide. Go. And I'll make sure these little ones fill their bellies." She shooed Zeli away.

Walking through the spotless halls with her road-dirty feet felt wrong. She was self-conscious about her appearance and patted her ragged braids to no avail. By the time she'd made it to Devana's rooms her heart was beating through her chest with apprehension.

She found her mistress standing at the doors to the court-yard, staring out into space.

"Devana-mideni—" The girl jumped with a screech. "I'm sorry to scare you—"

"Zeli-yul!" Devana ran over and enveloped her in a hug. The endearment she'd used was reserved for sisters and the closest of friends. "Oh, my dear. I was so worried. So long with no word! We were all beside ourselves." She didn't let go for a long time, and Zeli fought to keep her composure.

"Kerym-deni was angrier than I've ever seen him." She led them to the cushions under the window to sit. "Once he realized you were missing, he organized many of the attendees of the re-vival into a search of the area, but the nabbers were long gone by then. He considered your abduction an injury against himself personally." She shook her head. "We would have moved the skies and the earth to get you back, Zeli-yul. I'm so glad you had the presence of mind to send the telegram."

Warmth suffused Zeli's skin. She'd had no idea she would be so missed. Her memory of believing Kyssa's words that she was easily replaceable shamed her. Devana's grateful smile was genu-ine, her joy evident.

"I couldn't tell Father about the revival, of course, so when we had to return without you, I just spread the word that you were sick. But Gladda-deni knew something was up, and so I told her what really happened. Those nabbers are a scourge." She shook her head. "I know we had to dress shabbily so as not to be noticed, but the audacity of nabbing *my* servant. Something really should be done about them. Anyway, when Kerym-deni got your telegram, he made up some pretense to borrow Father's autocar and sent his man to go get you."

She smiled brilliantly, sitting back. "And now you're back. You must tell me everything that's happened. I'm sure it was awful; was it very awful?"

Nerves returned, and Zeli tried to hold them in check. "There's actually someone you should meet," she said. Devana's eyes widened and Zeli rubbed her bracelet for luck.

"Sacred seeds, they're the most adorable things I've ever seen!" Devana clapped her hands together, rushing over to sit beside Tana and Ulani. The girls looked like they were on their second or possibly third helping of stew, doled out by an undercook apparently as enamored of the girls as Devana was.

Zeli's mistress stroked the girls' hair and pinched their cheeks, cooing over them like they were kittens or dolls. Ulani grinned widely, appearing to lap up the attention, and, to her credit, Tana withstood the attention, managing not to scowl too deeply. Devana chattered on about wanting to have matching tunics made for them and debated with herself about how to style their hair. She was positively elated about the chance to show them her collection of face paints and make them up.

Whatever apprehension Zeli had harbored about the girls' presence disappeared under the onslaught of Devana's enthusiasm.

That night, Zeli resumed her duties and served dinner. Gladda had offered her the evening off but she'd refused, saying she wanted to get back to normal as soon as possible. However, the truth was slightly more complicated. Kerym was expected. And she needed to see him.

Devana's fiancé arrived a bit late, apologizing and brushing off his cloak from the sudden rain shower that had set upon the city. He took his customary seat at the head of the table and greeted first his betrothed then his future father-in-law.

The Magister had not been notified of Zeli's absence nor her return. She wasn't certain he knew who she was at all, but Yalisa had welcomed her from across the room with a warm smile. Zeli couldn't wait for the chance to speak to the woman one-on-one.

The only other guest for dinner this evening was a narrow-faced army sergeant with a healing bruise around his eye. He seemed overly preoccupied with his waxed mustache, but held the Magister's attention closely as they spoke in low tones.

After she set the first course before Devana, Kerym turned to her.

"Are you well, Tarazeli-denili?" The Magister didn't approve of using familiar suffixes with servants, so she didn't bristle at this emphasis of her position. Instead, her breath caught. Kerym's dark eyes peered at her, taking in every detail.

"I'm fine, truly. Feeling so much better now."

Anger crossed his features. "I blame myself for your situation. I should have been paying closer attention. The nerve of"—his gaze went to the man beside him still locked in conversation—"that illness."

Zeli smiled; his affront was intoxicating. She wanted to touch him. Place a hand on his shoulder to stop his guilt, but that would be inappropriate and so she held herself back.

"Please don't blame yourself, mideni. It was only the fault of . . . those careless enough to spread sickness. And thank you for responding so quickly to my entreaty. I—" A lump clogged her throat and she cleared it. "I can't tell you how much we needed help just then."

She thought of the other girls she'd left behind. Would Mengu choose another of Ora's workers? She shuddered.

Gladda passed behind her, humming softly to indicate her displeasure. Zeli shot Kerym an apologetic look and returned to her station, face hot.

After dinner, Kerym and Devana went to the game room; Devana insisted that all three of the girls come, too. They sat down to a round of zatraz. Since the game was meant for four, Tana and Ulani played as one.

Ulani was a surprisingly adept player. She moved her pieces without even consulting her sister and narrowly won, with Kerym a close second.

"Aren't they just the cutest things?" Devana said. Kerym chuckled in response. "Father already said they can stay here as long as I want. I'm going to make them both footmaids. That cow in Upper Faalagol will be so jealous."

"What's a footmaid, Devana-mideni?" Ulani's little voice rang out.

Devana wielded a gracious smile her way. "It's something of my own invention. Like a lady's maid, but smaller. Zeli-deni will show you everything you need to know."

Gone was the Zeli-yul of sisterhood, but it didn't matter. She was just glad the girls would be taken care of . . . at least while Devana's current whim remained intact. Zeli had no illusions that it would last forever. But she would have time to form a plan, somewhere for the sisters to go. She knew many servants of the favored in the city and there was no shortage of soft places for them to land.

A page came in with a message for Kerym, who left with a wink. Zeli almost imagined it was meant for her. She watched the doorway he'd disappeared through for long moments.

"You like him," an accusing voice rang in her ear. Tana had moved to sit next to her while Devana showed Ulani her *luda* in the corner of the room.

Zeli's face heated. "It's that obvious?"

Tana pursed her lips and shrugged. "I can just tell. My sister can, too."

Zeli shook her head. "He is for Devana-mideni as it should be. I would never do anything to stop that . . . even if I could," she said with a snort.

"He isn't good." Tana's words were said in her usual clipped style, but they weren't cold. Zeli scanned the girl's eyes and the normal frost was missing from her expression. She looked almost . . . apologetic.

"Did Ulani-deni tell you that? Did she sense something with her Song?"

"She said he feels like a rose with thorns. But I don't need a Song to see it. Why can't you?"

Tana stood and walked over to where Ulani was plucking at the strings of the instrument.

Her words made no sense. Kerym was noble and gentlemanly. Polite and strong and loyal. He'd gone very far out of his way to rescue a lowly servant. Besides, Ulani was very young and Tana didn't like anyone. How could a misanthrope and a small child judge a man's character?

Roses were beautiful. And the thorns, those could be cut away. Zeli brushed off the warning, quite sure that if she were to snag someone with half the good character Kerym possessed, she would have pulled off quite a feat.

CHAPTER THIRTY-ONE

A prophet failed by honor never thrives
And saviors wilt from lack of gratitude
Mistakes nourished by youth will oft take root
And wither on the vine until removed
The seedlings of dissent some cultivate
Will blossom into flowers of betrayal

—THE BOOK OF UNVEILING

Darvyn spent the first day of the journey watching Kyara closely for any sign of distress. She rode in front of him, her back pressed against his stomach, as the horse made its way south. They stopped frequently for rest and water due to the excessive heat, but she appeared to be faring well. The effects of Serpent's Gorge lingered and she hadn't tried to kill him once.

At the end of the third day, they reached Breach Valley. They made camp in the low foothills of the mountains, near where he had monitored Jack at the army base two weeks before. So much had changed in that time.

He had no binoculars with him, but stretched his senses across the area. The nearby Keeper safe house was empty. The spell that helped keep it hidden from outsiders was intact, though. He thought of Hanko and Meldi, who manned the safe house, wondering where they'd gone.

Darvyn increased his sweep. A trio of soldiers patrolled on horseback. They rode through the area between Darvyn's position and the army base. No one else was in the vicinity.

The outer reach of his range included the army base, and he honed his attention on the men gathered there. He could not pick out individuals with his Song unless he had a connection to them in the form of a spell. His thread to Jack had long since been severed, so he scanned for the injured.

The Queen had assured him Jack was alive, but she had not mentioned his condition. Darvyn's scan of the infirmary yielded only two occupants. One man had badly burned hands—perhaps a kitchen worker? Another bore a broken leg, but nothing more severe than that. The soldier's mood was rather jolly. Darvyn didn't think Jack would be so merry if he were captured and injured.

Various aches and pains, old nagging injuries and undiagnosed illnesses among the men of the base pricked Darvyn's awareness. All fit the profile of soldiers who had seen battle.

A pocket of fear, anger, and remorse snagged him. A small building at the edge of the base held half a dozen occupants. He delved deeper into their emotions and felt a familiar resonance.

He must have made a noise, for Kyara questioned him. "Have you found him?"

"No, but I think I've found Farron."

He strained the capacity of his Song, drawing even more Earthsong. He felt a young man, naturally exuberant yet cautious and angry. Even more anger emanated from an older man. It cloaked him and did not seem to have any particular motivation—it could be Aggar. Darvyn suspected that Zango and Hanko were with them along with two others. But he couldn't be sure.

He took a deep breath. He had never done what he was about to do before, but the Queen had told him of the trick often enough. It could only be done with another Singer, but it would no doubt frighten Farron half to death, if that was indeed him. Still, it was the only way to be sure of the teen's identity.

He focused on the energy of the young man and sent him a message mentally. *Farron, it's Darvyn. I'm nearby.*

The young man's heartbeat sped to a rapid pace, his body giving off the markers of shock.

I won't be able to hear you, but I can sense your body's response. Blink once if you can hear me.

Engorged as he was with Earthsong, Darvyn could feel even the slightest of motions. Farron blinked once.

Are you hurt? Once for yes, twice for no.

Two blinks.

Are Aggar, Zango, and Hanko with you?

One blink.

Are they hurt?

No.

Have you been captured?

Yes.

"They're in the base's jail," he said.

How many guards? Blink the number.

Two blinks.

Be ready to go tonight, but don't tell the others I'm coming. We may have a mole.

One blink.

Darvyn released the massive amount of Earthsong he'd been manipulating. He sagged against Kyara as the exhaustion rolled over him. The tiredness would pass. Now he and Kyara needed a way to get his fellow Keepers out of prison before he could find out what had happened to Jack.

Raucous laughter gurgled from the mess hall. A troupe of burlesque performers from the Lake Cities had entered half an hour before, drawing the attention of all who could fit inside the building. The hall lay diagonally across from the prison building at the edge of a narrow lane of one-story structures. Darvyn crouched in the shadows below a window leading to the small prison's outer chamber. The last time he'd peered in, the two guards Farron had warned him of had been seated at the metal table, playing cards.

A sharp wind blew by, ruffling the green shirt of his stolen uniform. He'd sung a concealment spell, darkening the shadows around him so if someone passed this way, they would not see him. Still, he was on alert.

Somewhere, out in the bush beyond the base, Kyara waited. He'd wanted her to stay in the abandoned safe house, but she had refused, wanting to be closer to the action in case something went wrong. Not being able to sense her out there was disconcerting, but he forced himself to focus. She could take care of herself.

Confident that no one was planning an imminent visit to the

prisoners, Darvyn reached for the energy of the two young guards. He very slowly put them to sleep so that when they awoke, they would not even be aware of anything strange. They yawned in tandem, and both heads hit the table at the same time.

Darvyn waited another five minutes to ensure the escape would remain unnoticed. Then he stood and marched into the prison as if he belonged there. His uniform marked him as a commandant. Quite laughable due to his age, but it would at least give any soldier who entered pause if they thought to question him.

He retrieved the key ring from one of the sleeping soldiers and opened the barred door to the prison cells. He didn't strictly need keys to open a lock, but his Song would damage the metal and he wanted no evidence of his presence left behind.

The door creaked on noisy hinges, making the hair on the back of his neck stand up. When neither guard stirred, Darvyn passed through into the back.

Three small cells lined both sides of the jail. The four male Keepers were stuffed into one; two women were in a cell on the opposite side.

"Darvyn!" Farron exclaimed as he rushed to the bars.

"Shh," Darvyn said, though the soldiers were in little danger of waking. "Are you all right?"

Hanko and Aggar, who were sitting on a straw mat on the ground, looked up with expressions of shock and aggravation respectively. Zango peeled himself away from the corner, a rare grin splitting his face.

"Good to see you, mate," the big man said. "Asla called in and told us what happened. A run-in with the Poison Flame?"

"I told you we couldn't trust her," Aggar grumbled.

"It's not what you think. I'll explain later," Darvyn said.

In the other cell, two female Keepers looked up at him, eyes wide. Lizana's astonishment quickly turned to joy. Meldi gaped while Darvyn tried several keys on the chain at their cell door before finding the proper one.

"You'd better close your mouth, Meldi. Or something might just fly in." He smiled as he swung the door open. She snapped her jaw shut and took the hand Lizana extended, rising to her feet.

"What happened to you all?" he asked, searching for the key to the men's door.

"They discovered the Elsiran," Hanko said, his voice scratchier than usual. Darvyn's fingers shook as the key turned in the lock. The bars whispered open, and the men came rushing out.

"Caused quite a ruckus, it did," the old man continued. "Swarms of soldiers spread out over the mountain."

"We got nabbed helping a group of women and children through the Mantle," Farron said, motioning to himself, Zango, and Lizana.

"Where's Navar?" Darvyn asked.

"On his way to Sayya," Hanko said. "One of the elders needed an Earthsinger."

"The rest of us are here because we wanted to make sure they didn't find the safe house. We all cleared out to lead the searchers away. Others are coming who'll need it." Meldi's soft voice barely carried to Darvyn's ears.

"And Jack?" Darvyn's question was for Hanko. "What happened to him?"

"Apparently, he was shot but managed to escape into the mountains. The squad he'd been with set off after him."

Darvyn peered into the outer chamber of the tiny prison house. The soldiers there were still fast asleep.

"That was nigh on a week ago," Hanko continued. "No one

has returned. Two more search teams were sent out after them, but there was a bad storm on the mountain. Both teams came back without any news, each a man down."

Darvyn took a deep breath. No news was better than bad news, but just barely. Jack was clever, and a skilled soldier to boot. All Darvyn could do now was hope for the best. The Queen had the Elsiran in Her sights. Hopefully, She would look after him and send what aid She could.

Another failure. But now wasn't the time to dwell. "Is everyone ready to run?"

"Will you be disguising us all?" Aggar asked. There was no mistaking the bitterness in his tone.

Darvyn ignored it. "No, I couldn't manage all of you. A bit of extra darkness will have to do. When we get out, go to the right, move quickly, and for feck's sake don't make any noise."

He needed to focus all of his attention on getting them to safety, though the thought that one of these people had betrayed the Keepers—betrayed him—was always at the edge of his senses, tempting him to distraction. He opened the main door, peering out and scanning with his Song. "Come on."

He rushed out with the others at his heels. Worried that Meldi wouldn't be able to keep up with her limp, he turned around, only to find that Aggar had lifted her onto his back.

The group cleared the prison building cloaked in dense, Earthsong-created shadow. The moonless night lent its aid as the Keepers moved deeper into the bush. Kyara was out here somewhere, but Darvyn was certain she would not reveal herself to them. She had told him she'd meet him near the safe house once the rescue was complete. He hadn't had time to question her further, but thoughts of her slipping away and him never seeing her again assaulted him.

He refocused on the escape, tensing when he felt a new presence approaching.

"Someone's coming fast," he whispered. "Hurry up."

The group picked up their speed. Only Darvyn could see through the gloom he'd created, but the Singers would be able to feel their way through the sparse brush and lead the Songless.

Seven unknown men advanced, sprinting directly toward the Keepers. It should not have been possible, but it was as if their pursuers could see through Darvyn's spell. His Song read their intentions. They were focused and confident. Single-minded. Were they coming for the Shadowfox?

The only way the pursuers' fast and sure movements made sense was if they were tracking him in some way. But he had no idea how that would be possible. Believing himself to be the target, he broke off from the group with a whisper to Farron to lead the rest to the safe house.

Darvyn ran east to lead the soldiers away, and sure enough, they followed. He sang a maelstrom of dust and sand to mask his movement, but the pursuers gained speed until they were nearly on top of him. Unable to understand his failure, he readied another spell, but before he could release it, a collar clamped around his neck. With the snick of a lock fitting into place, his Song was cut off from him, lifting the darkness and leaving the star-splattered night.

The glow of a lantern bloomed before him, illuminating the figures of the men who had captured him. Seven soldiers leered, panting and coated in grime from his sandstorm. Golden Flames, every one. Darvyn heaved in a breath. His shoulders sagged under the weight of the satisfaction on every face. At least the others had gotten away.

One of the taller soldiers, a clean-cut fellow with flinty

eyes, pulled back his fist and punched Darvyn in the face, knocking his head back. Seeing as they hadn't bothered to bind his hands, Darvyn seized the opportunity to hit the man back, smashing his knuckles against his cheekbone. He shook off the pain that flared in his hand. Without his Song, he would not heal, but then again, neither would the soldier fighting him. He was determined to do as much damage as he could until someone stopped this. For the moment, none of the other Flames looked ready to intervene. Their expressions bore a savage glee, happy enough to watch the fight.

The two circled around each other. The dead-eyed soldier was bulkier than Darvyn, with menace dripping off him like sweat. Darvyn used his lighter frame and greater speed to avoid the blows he could, getting in a few jabs to the man's middle. The soldier's slow patience raised an alarm in Darvyn's mind: there was no winning this fight.

He landed another punch to the man's face, then was pushed back by heavy fists ramming into his chest. His lungs faltered under the onslaught, and his knees buckled while the soldier laughed. Another punch to his head made his vision blur. He scrambled back and got to his feet, swaying.

The roar of an engine cut through the quiet night. Darvyn steeled himself as another round of blows assailed him. He landed a kidney shot but paid for it with another brain-jangling punch.

A crawler drew to a stop just at the edge of the lantern's circle of light. The look of shock on the soldier's face was so extreme that Darvyn chanced a glance over. Blood dripped into his eyes and added to his already blurry vision—he was sure he was seeing things.

It certainly looked like Kyara sitting on the vehicle, a scowl marring her beautiful face. She'd changed from the Avinid clothing into a loose-fitting green army uniform and observed the scene angrily.

"Enough! Our orders are to bring him in alive. This is pointless." She stalked over, practically snarling, beginning a staring contest with Darvyn's opponent. The man curled his lips menacingly, but it didn't appear to faze Kyara.

Then the soldier started screaming at her. "Eleven days! It's been eleven days since you've checked in!"

Kyara crossed her arms and narrowed her eyes.

"Where have you been?" Spittle flew from the soldier's mouth.

She tilted her head to avoid it. "I answer to the Cantor, not to you. I check in with *her*. I'm sorry if you've been laboring under any misconception about the chain of command, but until I hear a statement come from her lips that I am bound to obey, I don't owe you any explanations."

"Yes, you do, *Sergeant*."

"Then consider this insubordination, *Captain*. And did you bother to mention to the Cantor your little stunt in Five?"

So this captain was the same Golden Flame who had beaten her back at Checkpoint Five. Darvyn was equal parts furious with him and proud of her as she stood up to the man.

The Flame took a threatening step forward, anger rolling from him in waves. Kyara stopped him with a single finger raised between them. "If you think you are going to touch me, you're wrong. You will never lay a finger on me again." Her voice brooked no opposition.

More than one of the other Flames standing around visibly

tensed, their hands moving to their weapons. The captain eyed her, wariness tinging his features. Finally, he took a step back, growling out orders to his men.

"Tie him up! We need to get the Shadowfox to Sayya as soon as possible."

Kyara rubbed her chest unconsciously, then caught herself. She did not spare Darvyn a glance as she turned on her heel and walked off.

CHAPTER THIRTY-TWO

The night is long and cold when spent alone
And sun's rays murder sleep without a sound
Dreams die when lids open to greet the day
Their bodies burning on forsaken ground
Awaken to the truth and sleep no more
Or risk the slaying of heart's beating core

—THE BOOK OF UNVEILING

The blade separated skin from body with ease revealing solid, pale flesh. Zeli wielded the small knife expertly; flaying potatoes was an art. She and nearly a dozen other workers sat around the kitchen table, a mountain of potatoes before them. Though it wasn't her job, she'd made the mistake of entering the kitchen as the endeavor was beginning and had been roped into helping by the indomitable cook.

Outside, a steady rain fell. In one corner, water plinked into a bucket from a leak in the roof. Zeli tossed a naked potato onto the pile and picked up her next victim.

The outer door swung open revealing a soaked Gladda, who entered bearing a large, empty basket. She removed her cloak, shook it out, and hung it on a peg next to the fireplace. Then she took one look at the assembly line of peelers and ducked down the hallway.

"Smart woman," one of the grooms mumbled. No estate worker was exempt when peeling time came.

"Where does she go with all that food?" Zeli wondered out loud. The kitchen maid next to her looked at her questioningly. Fahna was a year or two older than Zeli and had penciled her eyebrows in comically large arches.

"You've never noticed Gladda taking baskets of food out of the kitchen before?"

"No." Fahna shook her head. "Then again, I always mind my business."

Zeli held back a snort. The maid was one of the biggest gossips on the entire estate, but all of the staff were very loyal to Gladda. Though curious, she was relieved that the rumor mill didn't extend to the woman's actions.

The mountain slowly shrank, and soon the cook and her assistants began the process of making potato starch. Zeli's contribution to the effort complete, she washed her hands and went off to check on Devana and the girls. The rainy day meant indoor activities, probably involving Devana's wardrobe and cosmetics.

Sure enough, she found them all in Devana's suite, both sisters seated amidst a sea of pillows and cushions, dressed and painted like delicate little dolls. Several paces away, Devana leaned into an easel, attempting to paint the girls into lifelike images. Her skill as an artist was middling at best, but as Zeli entered, she praised her mistress's effort.

"They're so . . . vibrant and colorful! How lovely."

"And look!" Devana exclaimed, beaming. "I've finally gotten my shading just right. See the way the light is hitting the little one just right? I think I've really captured it."

Zeli wasn't sure that Devana quite knew the girls' names, as she always called them "the little one" or "the bigger one." "Yes, you've done a wonderful job. How long have you been at it?"

"Oh, just a few hours," Devana said.

Zeli pursed her lips. "Maybe the girls would like a break?"

The sisters nodded emphatically, and Devana sighed. "All right, a short one. But we mustn't lose the light."

The children scampered off, likely to find a privy, and Zeli sat next to the easel.

"Have you heard?" Devana squealed.

"Heard what?"

"The guru himself will be at dinner this evening. Father told me so." She bounced up and down and clapped her hands together delightedly.

"Well, that should prove interesting. I didn't realize he ate. Isn't that too material for him?"

"Stop teasing. He's a great man."

Zeli's previous lukewarm feelings about the guru were further impacted by what had happened to her during his revival. She tried to brush off the resentment; it was irrational to blame the guru himself for the nabbers, but her unease surrounding the man persisted. Devana began to talk about how wonderful the event had been—apparently she'd been so enthralled by the lecture, she didn't even realize Zeli had been captured for quite some time. It was Kerym who'd noticed and began the search, while Devana continued to enjoy the festivities.

By dinnertime, Zeli had heard every detail of the revival's singing, dancing, speeches, and meditations. Devana's obsession with the Avinids and the guru in particular was troubling, but Zeli knew not to do more than smile and nod.

The dining hall swelled with guests eager to make the acquaintance of the "wise man of the west." Though she wouldn't have expected an Avinid to hold any rank of consequence, the old man was seated at a place of distinction at the table. The placement was doubly odd since the Magister did not profess a particular affinity for the sect. In fact, he had long been critical of the group, but he must have had a change of heart, for he greeted the elder like a long-lost friend.

Kerym entered with the other Ephors. Zeli's gaze lingered on him no matter how hard she tried not to look. He was dashing in a formal, royal blue tunic with silver thread. When she managed to look away it was to find Yalisa's smirking face silently mocking her. Zeli ducked her head and busied herself with her duties.

A griot had been invited to the occasion and was set up in the center of the room with her *luda*. She began with a story of a race between the Master of Bobcats and the Mistress of Horses. It was light and comical and kept the guests laughing in their seats.

Next she sang an epic song about the Poison Flame. "From Laketown to Checkpoint Eight to One and back again," she crooned, "from Scald to Gelid ere she roams to spread her deadly plan. From mountain west to mountain east, you cannot hide or flee. There is no place of safety once she sets her sights on thee. She'll stop your heart without a care, best grab the shovel and sack. The Poison Flame will burn you up, your eyes will fade to black."

A bit morbid for dinner perhaps, and the subject matter adhered a little too near to what had happened at the last big gathering for Zeli's liking—the Poison Flame only came for payrollers the True Father had issue with—but the guests seemed to enjoy it.

Just after the main course was served, movement behind the columns leading to the courtyard caught her attention. She took the long way around the hall to investigate and was not surprised at all to find Tana and Ulani spying on the meal from their poorly concealed hiding place.

Zeli squatted down behind the girls, unnoticed at first because they were arguing.

"It *was* her," Ulani hissed, expression fierce. "I know you don't believe me, but the Poison Flame killed Papa and also saved us from the nabbers."

"Just like an invisible dream woman told you to run away from the factory dormitory?" Tana said, exasperated. "And remember when you said a man who shone with light like the sun visited you and you gave him the pomegranate we'd gotten at Mercy Day? Papa blamed me for eating it and I got whipped. You're too old to keep telling these stories, Ulani-yul. One day these fanciful tales will get you into real trouble."

Ulani crossed her arms and pouted, looking away. Zeli wasn't sure what to say to comfort her. Tana was right: listening to these dreams, or whatever they were, would lead to terrible consequences one day.

"No matter what you see or hear, you must promise not to run off again without telling anyone, Ulani-deni. Can you promise?" Zeli said.

Ulani glanced at Zeli from the corner of her eye, lips still protruding. Finally, she relented. "I promise."

"Thank you. And whether it was the Poison Flame or not who saved you from the first nabbers, you're not supposed to be here. Devana-mideni might not mind, but her father would. The Magister is a stickler for propriety."

"But we want to see." This time it was Tana who pouted.

"You can listen from the courtyard and peer in around the curtains, but that's all. Now hurry before Gladda-deni finds you. You won't have apple cake for a week if she catches you where you're not supposed to be."

The threat of missing dessert got the sisters moving. The two crept into the courtyard through the open door, where Zeli hoped they would remain out of sight. Devana's indulgences aside, the girls were servants now and needed to learn what was expected of them.

When Zeli stood, one of the butlers caught her eye and pointed to the stack of soiled napkins on his tray. Zeli nodded her understanding and mouthed that she would go get fresh ones as she was nearest the hallway leading to the cabinet where they were stored.

She'd just retrieved a stack of clean, cloth napkins, when voices in a dark alcove just down the hall rose to greet her. Two men were speaking, but she couldn't make out exactly what was being said. She closed the cabinet door quietly and peered down into the gloomy passageway, trying to identify the speakers.

The voices remained quiet, and she tiptoed forward. If she was discovered, she had a ready excuse stacked in her arms for being here.

"The time is now," an older man said—she did not recognize the voice. "Everything is in place for this change to happen."

"Are you certain? I don't have the support of the other Ephors." Zeli's ears perked up. That was Kerym's voice.

"Trust me," the older man said. "The breach is nearly upon us. The king will be otherwise occupied with the war, and will be grateful for the speedy squelching of any unrest in this area. If you can truly unify this region, there are those more powerful than the Ephors who will back you."

Kerym took a deep breath. "All right. I'll put my plan into place."

"With that foolish child?"

"No, I'll need her. And I'll thank you not to encourage her attentions. I have someone else in mind."

"Faith is faith," the older man said mildly. "I do not control who is moved by the truth I speak."

Kerym snorted.

The man continued. "Just remember you must strike quickly like a viper or be bitten like one."

A door slamming shut at the other end of the corridor made Zeli jerk. She turned and rushed back to the dining hall. When Kerym strode back in a few minutes later, she was delivering napkins to the guests in preparation for the dessert course. She scanned the table and found the only other person missing was the guru.

The voice in the hall hadn't sounded like Waga-nedri's, it had been strong and robust where the guru always spoke in a soft and reedy tone. But who else could it have been? And what in the Father's name had they been talking about?

Zeli knocked on Yalisa's door and waited for the woman to call her in. As she entered, the sweet scent of vanilla filled her nostrils.

It reminded her of warm nights in front of Yalisa's fire. Of dressing up in the woman's tunics and jewelry the way Devana had never let her do. Of imagining a better, more comfortable life where she was adored and cherished.

Though the Magister didn't show it in public, behind closed doors he was very tender toward Yalisa. And for her part, the woman seemed to truly care for him. If the small smile she wore when she spoke of him were any indication.

At the moment though, she had cream all over her face, one of her mysterious concoctions that banished wrinkles and kept skin smooth and supple.

"Zeli-yul, I'm glad you came to see me. We have not had time to chat since you returned. And no matter what Devana-deni said, I knew you weren't holed up somewhere sick. Tell me everything."

They sat together amidst a cascade of silken pillows while Zeli recounted her tale of being nabbed. She told Yalisa what she hadn't told Devana—of the dread that weighed more than the chains, of her hopelessness and desperation. Of trying to help the girls and keep the spirits up of the others in the factory. Of Mengu and the cold fear she'd had when he was near.

Yalisa listened quietly and held Zeli when she cried. "There, there, *uli*," she said. "You did the right thing. And it was very nice of Kerym-deni to send his man for you. Why do you think he did it?" Her voice was soft and comforting, but the question was asked a little too innocently.

"I-I'm not sure. I'd thought Devana-mideni begged him to. She couldn't very well ask her father for help without telling him that she snuck away in the first place. But now, I'm not so sure. She didn't even realize I was gone until Kerym-mideni told her.

And she said *he* brought *her* the telegram, when I'd sent it to her in the first place. How would he have gotten it?"

"You'll find that Kerym-deni sees everything and knows much that you wouldn't expect." Her words had an edge to them. "Don't let your feelings for him cloud your judgement, *uli*."

"I'm not daft. I know he isn't meant for me, it's just—" How could she explain it? "He is noble and good and kind. Is that not how the Magister acts with you? I think that maybe if I have his favor, he would not be opposed to one of his friends elevating me, the way the Magister did with you."

Yalisa's smile was strained. "Don't you want more for yourself than to be a rich man's whore?"

Zeli flinched, blinking rapidly. "That's, that's not . . . You're not . . ." She couldn't believe Yalisa would call herself such.

"What is the difference between the True Father's harems and what the favored do? That man who wanted the little girls, do you not think he was trying to emulate the king's harems? Isn't that what the Magister is doing with me?" She chuckled. "At least he's never looked at a child that way."

"But he has only you." Disbelief strained her vision.

Yalisa shook her head, eyes heavy. "No, I'm the only one with the privilege of living here. He shows me off at his dinners like a jewel or a fancy new contraption he's acquired, but there are others. Always others."

"Yes, but as you say, you live here. Your rooms are fine and you wear beautiful clothes and don't have to serve—"

"You think I don't serve?" She laughed harshly. "I have done you a disservice all these years. I've allowed you to think that this life was full of glamour because I couldn't stand to crush your dreams or see you disappointed." She stroked her cheek. "Please forgive me. You imagine that my life is something it's not. There are many ways to serve, and being one of the favored is stepping into a nest of hornets."

Her gaze grew distant. "You may survive for a while, but it's only a matter of time before you are stung."

The hushed words of the guru in the hall came to mind. *Strike like a viper or be bitten like one.*

Yalisa focused on Zeli again. "They backstab and fight one another for the king's favor. None of us are truly safe."

"But I'm not safe now. A servant can be tossed aside like common trash. Doesn't the fact that Kerym-mideni sent for me mean that I have a chance for more?"

Yalisa held her close to her chest, in an embrace that reminded her of her mama's. "*More* is what I'm worried about, little swan. More is not always better."

Zeli held on as tightly as she dared, still not quite believing Yalisa's words. If she didn't dream of more, then she'd have to accept that her whole life would be spent as a lowly maid. She couldn't do that.

As Yalisa continued to rock her, the last remaining bracelet on Zeli's wrist fell away, crumbling onto the satin pillow.

CHAPTER THIRTY-THREE

Pain floods the senses, tearing shrieks from throats
The lancing agony overwhelms fear
And though she has a calculating hand
She's pushed further than she can ever bear
The wolf and prey are now one and the same
In tragedy she is the one to blame

—THE BOOK OF UNVEILING

"Where is she?" Aren's voice boomed through the Cantor's empty library in the glass castle, making the hairs on the back of Kyara's neck stand up. How had she survived even one night with him? Something was truly wrong with her.

The young guard manning the door made the mistake of showing fear. Aren was like a wild animal; any weakness shown only served to rile him up even more.

"The T-true Father called the C-cantor away on an errand," the guard stammered. "She's to return tomorrow or the next day."

"Tomorrow or the next day?" Aren roared, incredulous. Kyara bit back a sigh of relief. There was time yet. Time to do the impossible.

Aren's temper had grown with each passing kilometer of the journey across the Grand Highway, reaching a fever pitch when they'd dragged Darvyn to the library. Ydaris's absence only made it worse. Kyara knew this was partially her fault for having not answered any of his questions about her whereabouts for the past week and a half. But his suspicions about her behavior meant little; he was not the one she had to convince.

"Let's drop him in the dungeon. I'm hungry," she said, carefully schooling her voice to boredom. She could not look at Darvyn. Not just yet. Especially not when Aren took his frustration out on him with another blow to the head. Kyara clenched her fist so tight, her short nails broke through the skin on her palm.

"I don't think so. I can start this interrogation myself," Aren said.

He couldn't be serious. "Do you even know what Ydaris wanted to question him about? I think this is above both our pay grades."

Aren looked back at her with murder in his eyes. She shut her mouth, the frustration of not being able to strike out at him coursing through her. Her wound was as it had always been, a dull ache of pain irritated by the touch of her tunic. The rush of power from days at Serpent's Gorge had finally ended shortly before Aren's ambush of the Keepers, reinstating the full weight of the spell that controlled her.

Aren hauled Darvyn over to the dreaded stone table. There were no words in the Lagrimari tongue to describe her hatred for that table. The thing was made only to run red with blood.

Darvyn's head knocked against the stone as he was pushed onto the surface. Kyara gritted her teeth to keep from screaming. His eyes never met hers. She was glad of it. If he had looked directly at her she might not have been able to keep her composure. The urge to do Aren bodily harm was so strong that her Song buzzed in her chest, clamoring for release. She clamped down on it, holding every muscle in her body taut. The destruction simmering within, longing to break free, had never been so fierce.

Aren perused the display of sharp instruments Ydaris kept nearby. He had a cruel streak a hundred paces wide. She may commit the acts of a monster, but he was worse. He enjoyed every horrible act. He *was* a monster.

She used all of her resolve to stand still as Aren ripped open Darvyn's shirt, exposing his chest. The firm, sculpted muscle there was perfect and unmarred. It would not be that way for long.

The tool Aren picked up—a curved scythe about the size of her fist—made the bile rise to her throat once again. Aren laughed wickedly and then put it down.

"Since you can't heal yourself, we can't have too much fun. I do need you to be conscious when Ydaris returns."

Aren ran his fingers over the metal instruments, stopping at a small, cruel scalpel. Darvyn's face was impassive as the Flame approached, wielding the blade with flair, seeking a reaction. When he didn't get it, the savage smile Kyara knew too well appeared. Aren poised the tip of the blade over Darvyn's chest.

She tried to bring herself to watch but couldn't. Instead, her vision blanked as she thought of all the men she'd killed. The fear in their eyes, the pain. Fathers and husbands, sons and friends. Some had been brutal and deserving of death while others had just been on the wrong side of the True Father's fragile ego. Some had been suspected of being Keepers—a few likely were. Kyara had given most of them swift deaths, a gentle passing from this world to the World After.

What Aren did was messy and horrific. He loved every moment of it. Kyara planted her feet and made herself stay, even when she wanted to run and find a place to vomit or bawl her eyes out.

Her resolve lasted as long as Darvyn's did. She began to crumble when his screams rent the air. He was strong, so strong, but still human, and Aren was sick and twisted.

Though her eyes were open, her vision had glazed over. When she blinked and took in Darvyn's blood-soaked chest and mangled fingers, she stepped forward to Aren's side.

It was as if she were outside herself looking down from above at the body she admired, the skin she'd longed to run her fingers across, now bruised and battered. Ribbons had been sliced into his chest and abdomen.

Aren watched him carefully, a gleam in his eyes. There was so much further Aren could take it, but Kyara could not stand any more. She grasped hold of Darvyn's Nether, now strong and bright within him. She accelerated it, pushing it further, filling him, and bringing him past unconsciousness to the very brink of death. At the last moment, she pulled back, in shock of having nearly lost control.

His heart still beat, his lungs still expanded and contracted. He lived, barely, but his suffering was over for the moment.

Her eyes flew shut, and she stifled a gasp upon realizing what she'd done. Aren and the other Flames in the room were close enough to bear the brunt of the spell. She darted a glance toward them, expecting them to be passed out or vomiting, but none had been affected. They all stood, eyes transfixed on Darvyn's unmoving body.

Was this because the blood spell prevented her from harming them? But it hadn't given her so much as a twinge when she had been lost in Darvyn's Nether. In the past, merely accessing her Song while in the presence of those she was forbidden to harm would cause pain.

Kyara's sole focus had been on Darvyn, and she had manipulated his Nether with pinpoint accuracy. Maybe the blood spell hadn't kicked in because Aren and the others had never been in danger from her. Had she finally controlled her Song? And could she do it again?

The scalpel clattered to the ground as Aren's self-satisfied expression transformed into one of fear. She wished she *had* tried to hurt him.

Aren felt Darvyn's neck for a pulse. His shoulders loosened once he confirmed the prisoner still lived.

"Not so strong as all that," he said, his lips twisting in disdain. Of course he thought *he'd* caused Darvyn to pass out.

"Thank the Void for that," Kyara said, her voice monotone. "I was tired of hearing him scream." She stalked out of the library. Once she was out of view of the guards, she ran all the way to her room. Only there did the dam break and the tears fell. Darvyn lived, but she hadn't been able to truly protect him.

Ydaris's summons came in the morning. She must have called for Kyara as soon as she'd returned to the castle. According to the guards, Darvyn was still unconscious. Without his Song to heal him, the damage Kyara had done, on top of Aren's sadism, had taken its toll.

She'd tried to visit his cell, using some pretense, but Ydaris had issued instructions prohibiting any visitors. At least that had kept him safe from Aren.

Kyara walked rigidly toward the library. The time had come for her to answer for her disappearance and failure to respond to Ydaris's call with the speaking stone. Aren had cornered her repeatedly since they'd returned, and each time she had refused to answer any of his questions, stating that she would speak only to the Cantor. Now the time had come, and she still wasn't sure what to say.

She could not lie to Ydaris—the Cantor was an Earthsinger, after all—but the truth would earn her a swift death. The World After held no fear for her. She had longed for death many times. But if she died today, what would become of Darvyn?

Standing outside the double doors, she held her breath. She could choose her words carefully, saying only true things, but all Ydaris needed to do was issue a command and the blood spell would force her lips to speak candidly. Could she resist again? What would happen if she just ran away?

"Kyara-denili!" Ydaris called. "Are you going to stand in the hall all day?"

She pushed open the doors and entered. Each step felt like she was moving toward the gallows. The deep red of the glass walls bathed the room in an ominous light. Ydaris sat at one of her long tables, each side piled high with books. Today, the woman had a pinched and harried look about her. The gown she wore was far simpler than the elaborate creations she normally favored, and the wrap holding back her hair had been hastily tied.

Kyara had never known Ydaris to be anything other than impeccably put together. She'd never seen the woman in anything less than immaculate makeup and a perfectly tailored gown. Her current appearance was alarming.

"Come here," she said. Her hand moved quickly, scribbling out words on a sheaf of paper. She did not look up. From across the table, Kyara couldn't read the writing. Ydaris wrote for a moment longer before placing the page in a pile and starting a new one.

"Our guest has awakened. He is being brought up now for my questioning. Would you care to enlighten me as to what happened out there? Why you didn't respond to my call?"

Kyara swallowed and stared at Ydaris's bent head. Only the truth. "The speaking stone. It was lost." Brevity seemed her best option.

Ydaris's hand did not pause its movement across the page. She dipped her fountain pen into the inkwell and began a new line.

"That's all? You lost it? And were you searching for it for the rest of the week?"

Kyara took a deep breath. "I've never been given a capture mission before." Again, true. "And you know the power of the Shadowfox. It was not easy. I had it under control before Aren arrived."

"Under so much control that you allowed the escape of a group of Keepers just before the Shadowfox's capture."

"They weren't the mission."

For a few moments, the scratching of pen against paper was the only sound in the room. "And his current condition?"

"What about it?"

"Aren believes his ministrations were responsible, but I am not certain."

Kyara pressed her lips together. There had been no question asked. Suddenly, Ydaris's green gaze pinned her in place. She stacked the pages before her neatly, then pushed them to the side and clasped her hands on the table. "He certainly is attractive. I would not fault you for bedding him."

Kyara's breath stuttered to a stop. Her eyes blinked furiously.

"Even despite Aren's handiwork"—Ydaris sneered at this—"it's clear the young man is a fine specimen. And it's about time you began using your feminine wiles. I'd expect one so dedicated as he would have taken some time to wear down. Honestly, I didn't think you had it in you."

With a gasp, breath returned to Kyara's body. Ydaris looked upon her, something like pride in her eyes. Clearly she had created her own version of what had happened over the past week. Kyara certainly wasn't going to contradict her mistress.

"He would make a far better bedmate than Aren-denili, at any rate. A little brain can trump a pound of brawn. By the way, what happened in Five with the Golden Flames has come to my attention. I need all of you focused, so I'm modifying your binding. You may retaliate against one of the soldiers in the castle for the purposes of self-defense. I don't need infighting distracting any of you from the task at hand. The True Father is putting entirely too much pressure on me, and I can't afford these kinds of disturbances."

Kyara's wound flared with the new command. Some of the tightness left her body, and she stood straighter as Ydaris's gaze raked over her. "Have you gotten your dalliance with our prisoner out of your system?"

Her relief was short-lived. Ydaris had asked a question, and her eyebrows rose high, waiting for Kyara's response.

Had she gotten Darvyn out of her system? Not by a long shot. But Ydaris's indulgence would certainly not include Kyara's true feelings. It went beyond the promise she made to Nerys, beyond finding comfort in the arms of a man. Darvyn had pierced her heart, an organ made tough and cold through training and inattention.

But what could she tell Ydaris? The lie was ready on her tongue. She was prepared to say with a dispassionate affect that Darvyn meant nothing to her. But the doors slammed open and two guards hauled in the man in question. Several other Golden Flames followed, and Ydaris stood, her attention completely taken with her prisoner. Kyara's voice never came, nor would it, once she saw Darvyn dragged back onto that table.

CHAPTER THIRTY-FOUR

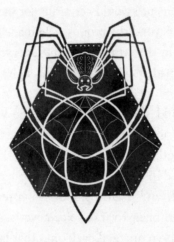

Nether removed can fan the dying flames
And sparks will reclaim ashes growing cold
Venom, so deadly, can be drawn from veins
To save a soul from death's unyielding hold
But for the clinging twilight to retire
A lambent, brilliant power will be required
—THE BOOK OF UNVEILING

Darvyn didn't bother to struggle as he was hauled into the Cantor's library and strapped to the same stone table as before. Exhaustion made his bones heavy. He searched the men surrounding him, looking for Kyara's face, but instead found only scowls from the Golden Flames. Aren's vicious gaze stabbed him.

He'd lost time, at least a day. At one point he'd thought himself in the World Between, but his recollection was fuzzy and he had not seen the Queen. Maybe without access to his Song, She was beyond his reach? Could She see him? For as long as he'd desired to be free from Her control, he ironically now wished for Her intervention. Otherwise, there was little hope for a rescue.

The Cantor approached, her unnerving gaze focused on him. He couldn't tear his eyes away. She was imposing and ageless—terrifying, if he was being honest. Not as terrifying as the Queen, but a close second. She also wasn't as powerful as the Queen, he reminded himself. She scrutinized him while running her hand down his body. It took every ounce of his control not to wince as she pressed the still-healing flesh on his chest and abdomen.

"It seems Aren was a bit overenthusiastic." She shot Aren a biting glare. "Thankfully, Kyara stopped him before he rendered you completely useless." Aren frowned and looked over his shoulder to where Darvyn guessed Kyara was standing. So she was here. Darvyn exhaled softly. He would rather she be present than locked in the dungeon along with him. It appeared her true loyalties had not been discovered.

Withstanding what was to come felt more bearable knowing she was safe. Part of her was lodged inside him, immoveable. More so, he did not want her gone.

Above him, everything faded from his vision except the Cantor's shrewd stare.

"The True Father needs answers quickly, so I don't have time for the usual tactics."

She produced a knife from her side, different from the one Aren had used on him. This one was longer and white, with an ornately carved handle. She held it respectfully, stroking its blade almost as she would a lover.

Darvyn's chest was bare but already covered in lacerations

and cuts—the result of Aren's attentions. The Cantor tsked as she looked down at him, then ran her hand down his thigh, dangerously close to his manhood.

"What a shame," she said. A dark fear pierced him, but she simply used the knife to cut off his trousers and brushed away the fabric. "I need unmarked skin for this."

She gripped the knife with both hands and uttered a string of words in a foreign language, low and guttural. The invocation made the collar at his neck ache even more as unfamiliar magic settled over him, holding him in place. She lowered the knife to his thigh and began to carve.

His jaw clenched against the pain, not as bad now as the last time he'd lain on this table. In the corner of his eye, Kyara came into view. He turned his head to take her in. The assassin's gaze, hardened and cold, stared back at him. He locked onto her until his vision was blocked by the Cantor's body when she shifted position. Done with the spell, she rested the bloody knife back on the bench with the other instruments of torture.

A scraping across the carpet sounded as she pulled a chair close. Then she sat and stroked his head. He flinched from her touch, but she kept at it. She appeared far wearier than she had a few minutes ago. Her breathing was heavy. The spell had taken some toll.

"All right, lovely, now you'll tell me what I want to know."

Kyara stepped to the side, into his line of sight again. He watched her hands, fisted, the skin at her knuckles taut.

"You will tell me where the caldera is," the Cantor said. Her voice was mellifluous, calming. Darvyn's mouth opened of its own accord. He did not want to answer but felt his will bent by a powerful force. Pain erupted on his thigh when he tried to remain silent. So this was what Kyara endured, what she suffered each time a command was given, and what had nearly killed her as she fought it to keep him alive. His respect for her redoubled.

"What caldera?" he said, his voice cracking from the pain.

She revealed sharp, white teeth. "The one you found at Tanagol. The one the Keepers of the Promise have been hiding for twenty years."

"How do you know about that?" The Keepers had long suspected the True Father knew of the stone Darvyn had found in the ruins as a boy, and had taken great pains to keep it from him.

A haze covered his vision. Kyara was so much stronger than he was. His Song had healed him quickly his whole life. Without it, misery overwhelmed him. How had she held on for so long?

"Whispers here and there. You hear much if you listen hard enough," the Cantor said with a brittle smile.

No one who had survived Tanagol that day would have spoken of it, but the gleam in the woman's eyes was feral. The pain in his thigh exploded, pulsing with agony in time to his heartbeat. Darvyn's lips opened, even though he fought against it. But he was exhausted, half-starved, bloodied, and torn. He prayed to lose consciousness and not be forced to speak. The Cantor only stared at him harder. The pain was so great he could not even move his eyes to find Kyara, so he shut them.

"Open your eyes." They flew open immediately. "Tell. Me."

He could resist no longer. "It's in Elsira."

"With whom?"

"The refugees. I don't know which one." For which he was grateful. The plan was for his mentor, Turwig, to take it out of the country, traveling with some of the other elders. Darvyn thought they should try to get the caldera into the Elsiran palace where the body of the Queen Who Sleeps had been resting for five centuries. The Queen had not told him exactly what the caldera would do. All She had said was that it was needed in Elsira and would help end the war. The faith of the elders propelled them forward even when She had no more answers to give. But they needed a chance to succeed, and Darvyn hoped his weakness had not doomed them.

"And what do they plan to do with it in Elsira?" the Cantor purred.

"I don't know. Await a sign from the Queen." The torment searing him faded to an ache. His attention centered on making his lungs work as Kyara's face came into focus above him.

Is she gone? he mouthed.

Kyara nodded.

"She raced out of here like her skirt was on fire." Aren's voice made Kyara's solemn expression tense. Darvyn longed to stroke away the worry line from her brow, if he could only move his limbs. "I guess we don't need him anymore," the Flame said.

Kyara produced a switchblade from somewhere—one minute her hands had been empty and the next the handle of the blade twirled across her fingers in an impressive dance.

"He belongs to the True Father now," she said. "Imagine what a tribute he will be. Only then can he die. And if anyone is going to kill him, it will be me. He was my assignment."

Aren snorted. "An assignment you barely completed. What was your plan?"

His voice dripped with suspicion. Kyara smiled wickedly, looking wild and unhinged. Darvyn smiled through his pain. That dangerous confidence of hers affected him like nothing else.

Kyara moved closer to Aren. The man had the good sense to take a step back. "Blood spells can be changed. If you outlive your usefulness to His Majesty, maybe one day *you'll* be my assignment." Her smile turned sweet, but the Flame's expression froze in horror.

The man's fist clenched, and he moved as if to strike her. The switchblade in Kyara's hand shot up, pointed at his chest. "I believe you've been expressly forbidden from harming me, have you not?"

Aren's heavy breathing slowed; he unfurled his fingers. Kyara clicked the blade closed and spun on her heel.

"Guards, get the prisoner back to the dungeon. He's bleeding on the Cantor's floors," she said.

Aren snarled and stalked from the room, passing the two soldiers who came in. The guards unbound Darvyn and hustled him off the table, dragging him past Kyara, whose blank eyes met his.

The callous mask broke for an instant, long enough to lay bare the torment she was going through. It took almost no effort for Darvyn to grin and wink at her. He must have looked grotesque with the state his face was in, but the corners of her mouth curved a fraction, such a tiny amount that it could have been his imagination. He leveled a promise to her in his gaze. There was still breath in his body. That meant there was still a way out of this.

Kyara had been staring at the same page for an hour, but her sight was overtaken by the vision of Darvyn's flesh sliced by a pale blade. His will shattering as Ydaris pried secrets from his lips.

Invisible bugs crawled over Kyara's skin; she felt ill. She needed to find a way to free Darvyn. To save him before the

True Father drained his Song, increasing the king's terrible power.

She shivered, trying to force the images of Darvyn's pain from her mind, when her Song lurched forcefully the way it did when there was an imminent threat. But she sat in her tiny bedroom—there was no danger here.

Kyara dipped into her second sight, and still nothing seemed amiss. She searched for a reason as her Song continued to strain. Spreading her senses to their limit, she finally recognized it. Far below, in the depths of the glass castle, the Nethersong of a fresh death called to her.

She was on her feet and out the door in a heartbeat. She drew in the Nether, and as she descended long staircases and grew closer to its source, a sizzling invigoration electrified her. The energy almost crackled from her fingertips, bringing a smile to her face.

The scowls of the dungeon guards fell away as she tugged on their Nethersong. Instantly, they collapsed. She managed to control her power enough to not kill them and simply remove their consciousness.

The power thrumming through her veins made her giddy. She took out every guard she encountered, the Nether making it easy to defy the blood spell. Her wound didn't so much as tickle.

She sped through the dank, icy hallways searching for Darvyn. The dungeon hadn't changed in the past eleven years. It was still rotten and fetid, each cell lined with moldy, insect-infested straw. Aside from her footsteps, the only sounds were the defeated moans of the inhabitants and the scurrying of critters best left in the dark.

She found Darvyn, motionless in a corner cell. The flickering lamp in the corridor illuminated his battered form. He was out cold, lying on the floor, encrusted with blood and grime.

The iron door to his chamber was barred, but the last guard she'd disabled had a ring of keys attached to his belt. Kyara retrieved them and after several tries, found the matching key. The rusted lock complained, but she pushed the heavy door open and rushed inside.

"Darvyn," she said, kneeling beside him. She lifted his head and cursed, realizing she had no water or cloth with which to clean him off.

The collar around his neck needed to be dealt with, but the ring of keys did not hold one small enough to fit the tiny padlock. Ydaris would have it, but there was no time to head all the way back to the Cantor's library to retrieve it. She wasn't sure how long the Nethersong from a single dead body would last, and she needed to get Darvyn out of here.

She patted his face gently until he roused.

"Kyara?" His eyes were unfocused, but her name on his lips made her heart jump. "What? How?"

"Shh." She brushed a finger over his mouth. "Can you stand?"

He rose unsteadily to his feet. She placed an arm around him to support much of his weight as he stumbled out of the cell.

They made it down the row and past the cell holding the dead man. Dozens of shallow cuts covered the prisoner's emaciated body. One of Yaris's projects?

"May you find serenity in the World After," Kyara mumbled.

Darvyn stared at the downed guards curiously but was having a hard time keeping his head upright and remaining on his feet. She needed to remove the collar so he could heal.

"Wherearewegoing?" His tongue sounded swollen.

Kyara nearly stopped when she realized she had no idea. "Any suggestions?"

His breathing was heavy and slow. "Keeper . . . safe . . . house."

She shook her head. "The Keepers are compromised. One of them turned you in."

"No choice." He lifted his shoulders in an attempt at a shrug and groaned. "Need to . . . find . . . who." He sighed and his head pitched forward, hanging limply from his neck. Kyara took on even more of his weight.

Of course Darvyn would want to know who betrayed him. But heading into that pit of vipers made no sense. However . . .

The Keeper informer hadn't given the True Father anything more than the Shadowfox's location. He or she could have easily revealed the location of any number of safe houses or identities of their members, but hadn't. Could Kyara risk betting on the fact that whoever had betrayed Darvyn didn't want to betray the rest of the group and that the safe house would stay safe?

She shook her head. "I don't like it."

"Please." Darvyn's wheezing turned into a prolonged cough. "Need to know."

He stumbled, and she righted him then continued hustling through the dark hallways toward the exit.

"You want to trust the Keepers even though we know we can't trust them?" She sighed. "Fine. Where's the safe house?"

"Low End . . . Monarch's Reign Boulevard. Fifth house . . . from the wall." He coughed again and then rasped out the rest. "Knock four times . . . Code is: 'Denmar seven-oh-three.'"

An unconscious soldier lay in front of the thick wooden door leading out of the dungeon. Kyara propped Darvyn against the wall so she could move the body out of their way. On the other side of the door was a little-used staircase leading to a side entrance of the castle.

She retrieved Daryvn and began the long climb up. His heavy breathing indicated how difficult the task was for him, though he never complained and never gave up. Supporting much of his weight was draining, but they kept going.

At the top of the steps, she paused to catch her breath and extended her second sight to scan the area. She motioned for Darvyn to keep silent as a column of light passed by the outer door. When it was gone, she cracked open the door and ventured a glance out.

Empty.

She tugged on Darvyn and they entered the antechamber, hoping that their luck would hold.

The castle's outer door was right in front of them. Once outside, they just had to cross the courtyard and slip out of the gate in the castle's border wall. From there they could disappear onto the busy Avenue of Kings and hire a ride across the city to Low End.

They headed out into the blazing sunshine, the red of the castle walls lending the afternoon a sinister quality. Kyara dipped back into her second sight to find three glowing columns of light approaching from the south.

She picked up the pace, crossing an open courtyard devoid of any vegetation that could hide them. Darvyn stumbled, his feet unsteady, blood now soaking his leg where some wound must have reopened.

Kyara was grateful Ydaris had made no lasting commands of Darvyn using his blood spell. Such magic was draining and the Cantor had been so harried, she must not have wanted to attempt it. A small mercy that the True Father had Ydaris working on something big that was taking the bulk of her attention and resources.

They had almost reached the gate when a voice called out from behind.

"Kyara!"

Shite. She shot a glance over her shoulder to find Aren racing toward her. Part of her was afraid to use her power with Darvyn clinging to her, but if she didn't they were both dead.

She took a deep breath, pulling in the last of the dead prisoner's Nethersong, drawing it deeply into her until there was none left. She turned and eyed Aren who, along with his two favorite henchmen, was running toward them. The men were twenty paces away.

Kyara targeted their Nethersong and they dropped to the ground, their forward momentum making them crash face-first. Next to her, Darvyn went limp.

Shite, shite, shite.

She checked his pulse—he was out cold, but there was no getting him up again, not until that collar was removed. She scanned the area—empty for the moment. It took all of her strength to maneuver Darvyn's dead weight onto her shoulders and lift him. He hung across her back like a human yoke. She staggered to the gate and leaned her weight against it, praying to any god in any land to make it open.

Blessedly it did, on quiet hinges. The chaos of the city enveloped her as she stepped onto the busy avenue. Rickshaws, carts, horses, wagons, and diesel contraptions congested the wide street. People filled the sidewalks. They parted for her, a young woman carrying a grown man on her shoulders, but no one commented or gave her a second look. This was Sayya after all and people only paid attention to what concerned them.

Kyara flagged down a rickshaw and dumped Darvyn into the carriage before climbing in beside him.

"Monarch's Reign Boulevard, fast as you can," she said, and the man took off running.

She rested Darvyn's head on her shoulder and stroked his hair as they were whisked through the city.

CHAPTER THIRTY-FIVE

What would you do for someone that you love?
Bury your pride, no matter what the cost?
Help right a wrong that causes them such pain
And in so doing guarantee your loss?
A stranger once and future paid this price
To gift a rival with the light of life

—THE BOOK OF UNVEILING

Zeli entered Devana's suite that morning, surprised to find her mistress packing. "Are we headed on another trip?" she asked, anxiety quickening her heartbeat.

Devana turned, her expression unusually placid. "No. You're staying here to cover for me. If anyone asks, I'm in the bath, or painting my nails, or at the spa and not to be disturbed."

Zeli froze. "For how long?"

"Until I'm too far away to catch."

She blinked rapidly, sorting through the torrent of questions bubbling up. "Where are you going, by yourself, that you don't want to be caught?"

Devana leaned in, more grave than Zeli had ever seen. "I'm going with the guru. He and I had a long talk late last night and he imparted so much wisdom to me. I'm going to follow him as one of his acolytes. Travel the land and help teach others about the Void."

"H-he invited you?"

"Well, not exactly." Devana frowned. "But his caravan leaves in an hour and once I stow away, he won't very well send me back."

A few moments passed before Zeli could speak. She couldn't banish the vision of the guru conspiring with Kerym in a dark corner. She knew the old man was quite a bit more than he appeared. Fear for Devana gripped her.

"The Magister will find out eventually. When he does—"

Devana waved her off. "Father will have a few moments of heartache, to be sure, but I'm following a spiritual mission. He's going to have to respect that."

Zeli wasn't so sure. "And what about Kerym-mideni?"

Devana looked down, her mouth drawn. "Kerym-deni is a wonderful man. I would have loved being married to him. He'll be the next Magister, you know?" A fleeting look of longing crossed her face before the determination set in again. "But I've got to follow my heart."

A wave of dizziness crashed into Zeli. She swayed in place for a moment while Devana turned back to her packing. The girl had never packed her own bag in her life, and yet here she was, resolved to live a life of independence.

Zeli wanted to be proud. Devana had always been stubborn, but she'd grown up so privileged. For however long this lasted, the desire to aid others and be a part of something bigger than herself could be a good thing. But Zeli's natural optimism warred with her knowledge of her mistress. And more so, her suspicions about the guru.

Who knew what sort of man he was really, under the veneer of spirituality and peace? The words she recalled him speaking to Kerym stank of a greater political involvement than the Avinids were known for.

Devana was nearly ready to go. Amazingly, she'd kept the bag light; it would be easily manageable on her own. She was only taking her simplest tunics—which would no doubt be replaced by garishly colorful ones—sturdy shoes, and a warm coat. No jewels or face paints or other non-essentials. Her mind was made up and no amount of pleading on Zeli's part could change it.

Devana faced her, holding her shoulders. "You've been a great friend to me, Tarazeli-deni. I wish you peace and the pursuit of the Void. This is a higher calling," she said solemnly, and Zeli couldn't protest. She managed a half-smile as Devana hoisted the bag to her shoulder.

The two girls stared at one another, one last time. "May we greet one another again," Zeli whispered.

Devana repeated the words of leave-taking and then she was gone. Out the door to the courtyard and down the covered passageway to the shadowy side door out of the estate. Zeli wondered where her journey would lead; Devana had always wanted to have adventures.

Zeli stood in the courtyard watching the door, just in case the girl decided to come back, when a scream rent the air. It wasn't particularly close, but it lingered, intensifying with blood-curdling potency.

Zeli ran toward the sound, which seemed to be coming from the kitchen. There she found Fahna, the gossipy kitchen maid, standing in the center of the room, holding one hand in another, blood dripping from her fisted palm. The cook and under-cook had backed themselves into a corner and all three were staring at a desert sidewinder slithering across the brick floor.

The deadly snake darted toward the doorway Zeli had just run through, attracted to her movement. She grabbed the first thing she saw, a large, empty basket next to the door and upended it over the snake, trapping it inside. Then she sat on the basket, trying to catch her breath.

"Are you all right?" she asked Fahna.

The girl had turned ashen, gray undertones cooling her warm skin tone. "When I saw it, my hand slipped." She motioned to the knife and cutting board on the counter, blood pooling around the onions she'd been chopping.

She began to sway on her feet as a handful of other servants rushed in through the opposite door. The cook recovered quickly and ordered Fahna to sit down.

"Keep your hand fisted. Hold it tight," the woman com-manded. "Everyone else, out!" Though her voice was harsh and usually obeyed, this time nobody moved.

Ulani rushed in from the courtyard and peeked her head be-tween two footmen, before creeping to Fahna's side. The cook didn't appear to notice the little girl, fussing as she was with the injured woman's hand. Ulani stood silently and closed her eyes. When she opened them moments later, she touched Fahna's shoulder.

"It's okay now," the girl said.

A look of shock on her face, Fahna opened her hand. Blood still coated it, but she flexed and tensed, and then took a deep breath, laughing nervously. "It is. The wound is gone."

The other servants looked on in wonder.

With a touch of envy, Zeli remembered the feeling of Earthsong bubbling inside her. How it felt to connect with the flow of energy and pull it into herself, to hold it inside her Song. The familiar emptiness that had replaced her power after the True Father had taken her Song throbbed now, pulsing with pain and regret.

Normally it didn't bother her. She could go whole weeks without feeling that hollow sensation within. But it always came back. She shook herself and focused on the scene before her. Gladda had appeared, pulling Ulani into a half-embrace and talking sternly to the staff.

"No one mentions this, not to the Magister or anyone else. You two, clean up the blood." She motioned to a pair of maids. "Fahna-deni, go lay down for a bit, you've had quite a shock. Cook, finish the morning meal. Not one word."

Gladda's instructions were followed with alacrity. She led Ulani into the corner and squatted down before her. "It's dangerous to show your power like that, you know?"

Ulani frowned. "Papa said I wouldn't have to give tribute until I was older," she whispered. "He said he liked having a Singer in the household." Tana had moved in next to her, fists clenched, her face severe. Judging by her scarred body, it was clear that Ulani had not often been allowed to heal her sister.

"I know you wanted to help," Gladda said, "and I'm sure Fahna-deni is grateful, but the Magister doesn't like Earthsong. Tributes are given early in this household. If he hears of this, you'll be sent away to Sayya to see the king, you understand?"

Ulani nodded, shuddering. Gladda drew her close and wrapped her in an embrace. "It's all right, child," she cooed. "Just be very careful from now on, all right?" She drew Tana into the hug, and the girl didn't protest.

Zeli took that moment to slide a board under the basket to trap the snake and then turn the whole thing over, shut the lid, and secure it.

"I'll take this down to the market," she announced, though no one was paying attention to her. Sidewinder venom was used by apothecaries in many of their cures. They paid well for live specimens, which they could milk. Though she shivered at the thought, leaving now had the added benefit of putting off any questioning she might encounter about Devana's where-abouts.

She hefted the large basket into her arms and rushed out the door.

At this early hour, the market was still waking up for the day. Vendors were rolling back awnings and opening shutters. Zeli walked with no great speed toward the side of the square that held the largest apothecary. As she crossed the street, her way was blocked by a middle-aged woman with closely cut hair and deep circles under her eyes.

Zeli stepped back warily. The woman was dressed plainly, but didn't appear to be a beggar.

"Did Gladda send you?" the woman asked. At Zeli's con-fused expression, she motioned to the basket.

Zeli looked down, realizing this was the same painted basket that Gladda often disappeared with. She pulled back sharply and shook her head, then scrutinized the woman more carefully. Her oval face held kind eyes, a slightly crooked nose, and a wide mouth, which broadened into a grin.

"You're Yarrink and Sefa's child, aren't you?" the woman asked.

Shock stole Zeli's vocal cords for a moment. "Y-you knew my parents?"

"Of course." She looked around, her gaze taking in the entire square in seconds. Though the market was still largely empty, more people were beginning to arrive. "Tell Gladda that Fakera says there are only two days left."

"Two days left?" Zeli repeated, dumbly.

Fakera nodded, then turned and disappeared. A gust of wind came out of nowhere, kicking up a torrent of dust. But it didn't reach Zeli's nose or mouth as she would have expected. And then the wind and dust died down just as fast as they'd come.

Only an Earthsinger could do something like that.

Zeli stood with her feet glued to the paving stones. What was happening for two more days?

What was Gladda up to?

When Zeli returned to the estate, Gladda was nowhere to be found. Oddly relieved by that, she retreated to Devana's suite to hide. Fortunately, the Magister had been invited to a dinner at one of the Ephor's homes. Devana would not have attended had she been here, so Zeli would be blessedly saved from questions about her mistress's whereabouts for at least a night.

Or so she'd thought.

An hour before bedtime, a page boy rapped on the door leading to the courtyard. Zeli opened the door a crack and peeked out.

"Kerym-mideni is here for Devana-mideni," the boy said.

Zeli's shoulders slumped. She should have known it wouldn't be so easy. She followed the page to the same side door that Devana had left out of that morning.

Kerym stood in the archway, illuminated by moonlight. His eyes twinkled merrily, and he gripped a bouquet of lavender, red, and yellow coneflowers in his fist. They were Devana's favorite.

Zeli sighed. "She was not expecting you," she said, her voice small.

"Well, no," he said, laughing. "That's why it's called a surprise. Besides, I know the Magister will be away until the early morning. What better time for a visit?"

If Devana had been there, she would have welcomed him and praised his clever timing. Zeli would have spent the evening on her crowded bed, imagining what the two of them were getting up to all alone. But Devana was not here.

"I'm sorry, but Devana-mideni is . . . indisposed. One of her . . . twelve-hour beauty treatments. She cannot be disturbed."

Kerym narrowed his eyes and stepped through the doorway, bringing him closer to her. Zeli took a small step back.

"You know you're a terrible liar, Zeli-deni, I don't know why Devana-deni would ask you to. Where is she really?"

Zeli kept her mouth closed. She crossed her arms over her chest, pressing tightly. Kerym's gaze dropped, whether to her arms or her breasts, which had been raised by the motion, she wasn't sure, but the very thought made her cheeks flame.

"When will she be back?" He took another step closer, and she moved back again. But she didn't respond, sealing her lips shut into a firm line. She *was* a bad liar and had no desire to lie to him anyway. It had been nearly a full day; was that long enough for Devana to get away?

Kerym sighed and leaned a shoulder against the wall, flowers

held casually. The action put a few needed breaths of space between them. "Has she done something stupid?"

Her face must have betrayed some emotion for Kerym
shook his head and sighed. "Tell me so I can fix it."

"There's nothing to fix," she said. Devana had made her choice.

Kerym ran a hand across his forehead, breathing deeply. "I
suppose you're right. Whatever she's done, we'll simply have to
deal with it." He smiled, revealing sharp, white teeth. "I just
wish she were half as sensible as you."

Zeli's breath jerked. Kerym was staring at her, looking
thoughtful. She swallowed and willed her heart to stop racing.

"Is she in danger? Can you tell me that at least?" he pleaded.

"I hope not." Her mouth snapped shut, horrified that she'd let
even that much slip out.

Kerym stood to his full height, towering over her, and held
the flowers out. "Shame for these to go to waste then."

Zeli shook her head, hands itching for the bouquet, but
knowing it wasn't proper. "I-I couldn't."

"Please take them. Otherwise they'll just go in the trash."
His eyes were lit from within with hope. Did she dare?

Against her will, her hand reached forward to grasp the
flowers' stems. She brushed Kerym's fingertips as he passed them
off to her, and her skin burned from the contact.

She'd never received flowers before. Even those meant for
another. Her imagination would run wild, dreaming up scenar-
ios in which these beautiful blossoms had been really destined
for her all along. Her dreams would be sweet for a week.

"May we greet one another again, Zeli-deni," Kerym said
with a short bow, walking backward to the door and then out
into the night.

Forgetting her desire to avoid everyone in the house, Zeli ran straight to Yalisa's room, flowers clutched like a trophy in her hand. She knocked on the woman's door and when she received no response, knocked again.

Finally, she peeked in, to find the room dark. Perhaps she'd gone with the Magister to dinner? It was unusual for him to escort her off of the estate, but not unprecedented. Zeli had wanted to share what had just happened and ask about Yalisa's method of keeping flowers fresh. It involved dipping the cut stems into hot and cold water, but she couldn't remember the order or duration. But she would just have to make do.

She ran back to Devana's room eager to admire the bouquet and go to bed early so she could dream of Kerym.

CHAPTER THIRTY-SIX

The Scorpion surrendered to her grief
Shunning all praise, she faltered in acclaim
She knew the beating of the drum now meant
An existence forever to be changed
The life she had fought so hard to protect
Looked dull and dim with no light to reflect

—THE BOOK OF UNVEILING

Darvyn's Song beat at his consciousness, pushing him toward wakefulness. The afterglow of healing felt like butterflies humming just under his skin, knitting him back together from the inside out. He stretched kinked and tired limbs, relieved to no longer be in agony.

The ceiling was cracked, forming broken lines like someone

had taken a hammer to it. He struggled to a sitting position, taking in the dim room, lit only from the gaps around the woven mat covering the doorway. He sat on a low cot, the air heavy with bitter incense.

Low End. The safe house. Kyara. It all rushed back to him.

He made a mental inventory of his body. Not only was he healed and clean of the muck of the dungeons, his Song was at full strength. Gone were the rags he'd worn while imprisoned. Someone had dressed him in a loose-fitting tunic and trousers.

Not more than a few hours had gone by, judging by the tenderness of his thigh where Ydaris had carved him. The skin there felt new and fresh.

He sensed two people approaching and rose when the mat was pushed back. Aggar entered with Meldi on his heels.

"So you're awake then." Aggar reeked of barely contained rage. Meldi frowned up at Darvyn, concern spiking through her.

"Did you have a pleasant nap?" the bearded man asked, a jagged edge to his voice.

"Where's Kyara?"

Meldi's eyes widened; Aggar snorted. "How could you bring the Poison Flame here? How could you dare?"

Darvyn stepped toward Aggar, menace suffusing him. "Where. Is. She?"

"Where she belongs." Aggar turned and stomped out of the room.

"How could you betray all of us?"

He turned to find Meldi's eyes round and wet.

"I didn't." He reached for her hands, gripping them. She was unusually cold, her bones so delicate. "Kyara isn't what you think. She saved my life—twice now. I owe her everything."

Meldi pulled out of his grasp, her face crumpling. "She's being kept under guard." She rushed for the door, her limp more pronounced than usual.

Darvyn followed her out of the tiny room and down a dimly lit hall. This safe house was nestled in the heart of Low End, one of the poorest areas of the city. Here, the structures were built narrow and tall. Upper floors were impossibly hot and the buildings teetered, often dangerously, higher than the wall dividing the neighborhood from the river.

Meldi negotiated her way down two claustrophobic sets of uneven staircases. Darvyn held his breath behind her, afraid she would fall at any moment. Daylight pierced the cracks in the walls.

They emerged in a main room that took up the entire level. A dozen Keepers sat on low padded benches or cushions. Tension clouded the air along with the incense. All conversation stopped when Darvyn appeared. Hanko, Lizana, Navar, Zango, and Farron were all present. They'd all come to Sayya. For him? Aggar stood in the corner, arms folded, scowl firmly in place. They had all been on the nabber mission and were the only ones who knew that Darvyn would be at Checkpoint Five that day. One of them had given him up to the True Father.

Zango had been his friend since Darvyn broke him out of a mine prison. The man had been by his side on nearly every mission from that day on. Darvyn remembered when Farron was born. His parents had risked their lives hiding a Keeper they didn't know from a group of soldiers. Lizana and Navar had worked by his side for years, and he'd always thought of Hanko as a mentor. And though Aggar and Darvyn had a painful history, the Keeper had always been devoted to the cause.

When Darvyn had first been taken from his mother, Aggar's home had been a favorite among the many he was shuffled between. His parents had treated him like family.

How could any of them betray the Keepers in such a spectacular way? A scan of their emotions revealed no one with a heart of treachery, merely confusion, dismay, and fear. He would have to ask them each to see if they lied to him.

He did a double take at the figure he finally saw sitting in the corner, arms and legs tied with rope. Kyara.

His chest constricted. Kyara met his eyes, and where he expected fury, he found only resignation. Her fiery spirit was dimmed—that made him want to lash out. Blood heated in his veins like water in a kettle.

Every eye in the room tracked his movements. Two elders were present, Hanko and a woman named Talida with whom Darvyn had barely had contact as his missions rarely brought him to Sayya. Both scrutinized him with heavy suspicion. He straightened his shoulders and stood tall.

A storm was about to hit. He would brave it to gain the answers he sought. And to find a way to spare Kyara the wrath of the Keepers.

Hanko sighed gravely. "I'm glad to see you are well. But Darvyn . . ." He pursed his lips and shot an annoyed look at Talida sitting next to him. "You have transgressed."

A transgression was the worst offense a Keeper could commit. Each member pledged an oath when they joined, not only to keep the Promise to the Queen Who Sleeps, but to protect each other. All they had was their word and their honor, and each Keeper risked his or her life for this cause. So when one broke his oath, justice was swift and severe.

Darvyn scanned the room again, taking its temperature. "There are only two elders present to judge me. Are not three required?"

Aggar stepped forward, a smug expression contorting his face. He sank into the open seat next to Talida.

"Aggar has been promoted to the rank of elder," Hanko announced. Darvyn ground his teeth. Aggar was only five years older than him.

Hanko continued. "Our numbers are low due to the efforts in the west. We are all needed there, yet we traveled here to find a way to save the Shadowfox. Little did we know that he had thrown in his lot with an agent of the enemy." The elder's gaze was accusatory. "Darvyn ul-Tahlyro. The charges against you are dereliction of duty and perfidy. How do you answer them?"

"I've done no wrong." Darvyn's voice was resolute. The room hummed with the murmurs of the others.

Aggar's eyes narrowed. "You disobeyed a direct order and left your mission. You brought an operative of the True Father to a classified location and put dozens of young ones at risk. And then you brought her *here*. Gave her a valid pass code so that she was in our midst before we knew what had happened." His voice rose with each charge. Talida put a hand on his arm to try to calm him.

In the corner, Kyara appeared to wilt.

Darvyn could rail at them, hurl accusations about all of the Keepers' lies to him over the years, but forced himself to keep his head.

"Aggar, did you betray me?" He drew energy into his Song and focused on the man's emotions. Aggar's fury was pure. It did not have the sense of betrayal around the edges.

"Betray you?" Spittle flew from the man's mouth. His eyebrows rose. "It is you who have betrayed us!"

For all his flaws, the man was straightforward and honest. If he wanted Darvyn dead, he would have tried to kill him himself, not rely on the True Father.

"All of my actions have been justified," Darvyn said. "I can defend everything I've done. I wonder if everyone present can say the same."

Scornful mumbles rippled through the Keepers. Hanko's brow furrowed, while Aggar scoffed. Darvyn turned his attention to the elder whose voice instantly quieted the room.

"You feel you were justified in bringing the Poison Flame, the lead assassin in the king's deadly arsenal, here?" Hanko's eyes bugged almost comically.

"I trust her. She saved my life." He glanced at Kyara, who stared at the floor, her face a mask. "And she didn't choose her path—the True Father forced her."

The elder sighed deeply.

"Hanko, did you betray me?" Darvyn asked, his chest tight.

Hanko sputtered. "What is this nonsense? It is not I who am being questioned, it's you." Nothing but disappointment and duty colored the man's emotions. Though he didn't answer, no guilt pushed through, either.

Meldi stepped forward. "How could you be more loyal to her than to us? We're the ones fighting against this tyranny. Whatever grip the king has on her is strong enough to make her kill. In cold blood. How could you risk us all?"

Darvyn dropped his head into his hands. He couldn't be angry at Meldi; she was simply saying what the others thought. "My entire life has been about loyalty. How dare any of you question it? I've given *everything*. Every day I give my all. No one has exhausted their Song more than I have for this cause. For freedom. If I tell you she can be trusted, why do I not get the benefit of the doubt?"

Meldi shook her head. "You are not infallible, Shadowfox." She limped to the side of the room and took a seat, appearing exhausted.

"Meldi, I'm sorry I couldn't save your parents. That you were hurt when the soldiers came searching for me and burned the house. That I wasn't there to heal you. Aggar lost his family, too, defending me. Many of you have lost people to this cause." He turned in a circle, meeting the eyes of everyone in the room.

"You're right, I'm not infallible. I can't save everyone, much as I want to, but I am loyal. Every loss has gutted me. Stolen something precious from deep inside. I have given this group far more loyalty than it has ever given me."

Hanko stared at Darvyn with rheumy eyes. "All who transgress the code of the Keepers must be questioned. Even the Shadowfox. As for the Poison Flame, she will be interrogated for any intelligence she can provide. And then she will be executed for crimes against the people."

Darvyn's chest cracked open. "I won't let you do that." His voice was low. A promise, a warning, a threat.

"Darvyn." Kyara's plea was soft but desperate. He caught her gaze, and a million emotions swam in her eyes. Regret. Sorrow. Something more, or was that just wishful thinking?

Inside him, everything clicked into place. The confusion of the past days. The longing. Mixed in with the desperation and fear of being in the True Father's clutches had been a shining truth. Darvyn didn't regret any of the events that had brought Kyara to him. He loved her, deadly Song and all. And he would keep her safe.

His Song swelled, pulling in enough Earthsong to fill him. Aggar rushed to his feet and the two locked eyes.

"Navar, now," Aggar commanded, and Darvyn felt movement behind him. He turned, pulling the focus of his Song back just in time to feel Navar's intention. But too late to stop the man from clamping the bloodred collar around his neck.

A scream tore from Kyara's chest when the padlock snicked into place. Three men held Darvyn—two pinned his arms to his sides, one held his legs while he writhed and kicked and shouted like a rabid animal.

"Darvyn, stop!" she yelled. Amazingly, the room quieted. Darvyn quit struggling and stared at her. She'd never seen him so fierce and feral. It filled her heart with gratitude and pain. He would fight his own people to free her. He would destroy the only life he knew, the only family he had left.

All for her. And she couldn't let him.

"You don't know the whole story," she said, unable to tear her gaze away from him. "I'm not worth this."

"Kyara, I won't let them kill you. I—"

"The only reason I'm here is because I choose to be." Her voice echoed across the walls. Fear shone in the eyes of those who looked at her.

She swallowed, determined to come clean at last. "It's true the blood spell controls me. But I chose to become the Poison Flame. I gave up my freedom and chose this life."

Darvyn frowned. "What do you mean?"

She closed her eyes to press back the pain so she could speak. No one moved or made a sound. The shock of the Shadowfox in a collar allowed her to tell her tale.

She raised her bound hands to pull at her tunic, revealing the top of her bandaged chest. "When I was eleven years old, the Cantor gave me this wound, this blood spell, and forbade me from harming anyone in the glass castle. When I refused to become the True Father's assassin, she let me go."

"And you wandered through the Midcountry. You met"—Darvyn's voice wavered—"Nerys."

Kyara's lips curved. "Yes. And after she died, I was on my own again. I traveled and met people who wanted to hurt me. Those people would die. But not just them, everyone around them. Their horses, their neighbors, the vegetation around them. Others started to notice."

Though the room was full of people, she spoke only to him. "One day, I was in a town, a small one between checkpoints. A man on horseback had passed me on the road the day before. When he saw me at the market, buying bread with stolen money, he called for the constable. Told of how he'd seen the damage I created up and down the Great Highway. He said after I left a town, days later plague would take dozens of lives."

Darvyn tilted his head. "Days later? That wasn't you."

"No. But it didn't matter. The townsfolk latched onto his story and the crowd grew agitated. The plague must have been because the physician—Raal—was taking the same route I was, but of course I couldn't prove it. The constable made a big show of questioning me, right there on the street. People nearby called to their friends. The crowd grew so quickly. Someone threw a rock and my Song . . ." Her gaze held his and clung to the understanding shining back at her.

"I had to get away from there. There were so many people surrounding me. Women and children. They kept throwing rocks and I knew I had to leave before . . . before they all died."

Sounds of confusion and shock filtered throughout the room, but Darvyn's was the only face she saw.

"I ran. I pushed through them, dodging the hands that

grabbed for me. I tried to escape, and they chased me. They wanted blood. They didn't understand the danger they were in."

Kyara dropped her head, remembering the fear and the urgency. The tight grip she'd held on her Song, but she knew it wasn't tight enough.

"I hid—crawled through an alley to the next street. I thought maybe I'd lost them, but there *she* was."

"Who?" Darvyn asked.

"Ydaris. She was waiting for me."

The horseless carriage had gleamed in the sun. Sparkling chrome and red metal. A rich man's contraption in a poor man's town. And the sound of the approaching mob thundered, coming down the street. Determined.

The castle welcomes you back any time, Kyara, the Cantor had said. Her voice had been so kind, so soothing.

"She told me she could teach me to control my Song." *Or would you rather kill everyone in this town?*

"I could hear the mob coming; they were just out of sight. I knew I wouldn't be able to get away from them fast enough on foot, and my Song was clawing and tearing at me. It was nearly beyond my ability to hold it back anymore. Then they came into view, a group of little boys out in front and I—" A spasm shook her voice as she remembered how they'd looked. Scared children who didn't know how terrified they should really be.

"Ydaris started her engine and began driving away. The mob just got closer and closer." Kyara closed her eyes.

"So you went with her." Darvyn's voice was resigned.

Kyara nodded, feeling spent. She couldn't look at him again, couldn't stand to see the disappointment and disgust on his face.

"Kyara—"

The old man who appeared to be in charge finally spoke up. "Zango, take her downstairs," he barked.

She opened her eyes to find the enormous miner she'd met earlier looming above her. His hand grasped her upper arm, surprisingly gentle. She didn't fight him when he urged her to stand. Keeping her eyes on the ground to avoid the sight of Darvyn, she headed for the stairs.

Whispers followed her down.

"She must be deranged."

"How can a Song kill?"

"Madness!"

The bottom floor of the safe house was several degrees cooler. A short, wiry fellow stood smoking a cigar, guarding the same door she'd dragged an unconscious Darvyn through several hours before. Zango nodded at the him. "I've got this. Head upstairs if you want."

With a dirty look in her direction, the guard pushed off the wall. He blew smoke in her face as he passed, before disappearing up the stairs.

Zango waited a few moments before turning her around to face him. She took a step back, finding him wielding a slim knife. Her knife, the one he'd taken from her boot after he'd patted her down earlier at Aggar's insistence. He twirled the knife on his thumb and then neatly cut through the ropes binding her hands.

With another flip of the knife, he presented it to her handle first. She grabbed it, then backed away to slice the rope around her ankles. Rubbing her chafed wrists, she peered at him.

"Why are you helping me?"

"He gave you his code." Zango's voice rumbled low and

thunderous. Kyara glowered, not understanding. "Each Keeper has two identification codes. If you'd forced or coerced him, he would have given the other one. Darvyn trusts you. That's enough for me."

She wanted to smile, but the thought of Darvyn collared sobered her. "What will they do to him?"

Zango crossed his arms and leaned back against the opposite wall. "We need the Shadowfox now more than ever. They're just trying to scare him. Get him back where he was before."

"Under their thumb?"

He blinked, surprised, before nodding.

"It won't work," Kyara said. "Not now." Darvyn's eyes had been opened to the truth about the Keepers. He wouldn't be blinded again.

She looked the big man up and down. "Do you trust them?"

His eyebrows raised. "Most. Why?"

"At least one of them told the True Father exactly where I could find the Shadowfox. That he would be in Checkpoint Five following the nabbers."

The slight flaring of Zango's nostrils was his only reaction.

"That's why he's asking all of you if you betrayed him." She watched him carefully for any sign of guilt. Zango stood up taller and stuck out his chest.

"He'll hear the truth in my voice. I have nothing to hide. You have a Song, you can tell. I would never betray him."

Kyara narrowed her eyes. No point in telling him her Song didn't work like that. Darvyn would be able to find the informer; maybe he already had. Besides, she believed Zango. She'd looked enough snakes in the eyes over the years to recognize a good man.

"He needs his Song back."

Zango nodded. "I'm on it." He took a step toward the staircase before pausing. "He'll want to know where you went."

Kyara stopped at the door, already spreading her senses to determine if anyone was out there lying in wait. "It's better if he doesn't."

She opened the door and slipped out into the dusk.

Darvyn seethed, his breathing heavy in the quiet room. Kyara's story had left the other Keepers bewildered. More than one gazed at the collar around his neck with visible horror. The same fecking collar the Golden Flames had used to capture and torture him. Placed by his own people.

Navar had wisely stepped out of reach after clicking the lock into place. Darvyn almost felt sorry for the man, broken as he had been by his time in the Wailers. Was he so far gone that he'd betrayed Darvyn to the True Father? Darvyn should have tested him before losing access to his Song.

"Is that really necessary?" Lizana asked.

"You know his power," Aggar snapped. "You heard him threaten us."

"I heard no such thing."

Hanko raised a hand. "We all need to be calm. Darvyn is not the threat here."

Darvyn rolled his head, hating the way the collar chafed him. "I'll be the worst nightmare of anyone who hurts Kyara." Somehow she'd thought telling him of her awful choice would make him turn away from her. But it only made his heart all the more hers.

Aggar raised his arms as if to say *this is what I mean*. Darvyn wanted to throw something at him.

Heavy footfalls sounded on the steps from below. Zango had taken Kyara away and nothing made sense. Darvyn hated not knowing who he could trust. He would have staked his life on being able to rely on Zango at least—could he be so wrong about everyone?

"Who's guarding the prisoner?" Talida asked, alarm making her voice shrill.

Darvyn felt Zango come up behind him and whipped around to face him. But that left Navar at his back, which he didn't want, either. Navar's Song wasn't terribly powerful—he definitely couldn't put Darvyn to sleep, but now the threat was everywhere and he couldn't be faulted for being paranoid.

Zango remained silent, but grabbed Darvyn by his neck and held him in place with incredible strength. A growl sounded in Darvyn's throat as he was manhandled. For pip's sake, this was his closest friend, or so he'd thought. Several Keepers stood, to help or not, he wasn't sure.

Then the snick of a lock unbolting rattled his ear, and his Song was within his control once more. Darvyn sucked in Earthsong until he was almost light-headed, so glad to have his connection back.

Aggar rushed to his feet, neither as tall or as wide as Zango, for all his menace. "What do you think you're doing?"

"I'm doing what all of you should have done the moment this monstrosity went on his neck." Zango dropped the collar and stomped on it, cracking the hard covering to reveal a bit of wire inside the red casing. "And no, I did not betray you."

The tightness in Darvyn's shoulders eased. Zango spoke the

truth. There was no treachery in his heart. He wanted to grab him in a hug, but settled for a smile. Zango answered with a nod.

The energy in the room thickened. Relief warred with apprehension among the Keepers.

"Where's Kyara?" Darvyn whispered to Zango.

"Gone."

Relief won out, and Darvyn faced off against the elders. He rubbed his neck as Zango stood beside him, cracking his knuckles. Aggar's expression would have sheared the shell off a beetle. Hanko and Talida were grim.

Pain struck Darvyn's heart. "Again and again, the people I relied on—those who called themselves my family have betrayed me." He turned to Navar. "Before today, did you betray me?"

Shame and regret oozed from him. "No," he answered quietly. The man was pliable, certainly, and lived to follow orders, even those he hated. He was telling the truth.

A heavy weight descended on Darvyn's heart. He turned in a circle. "I've given my entire life, every day, for you, all of you. And in return you gave me lies."

Talida frowned. "What are you talking about? What lies?"

"You said my mother abandoned me. That she never came to look for me. I know she did."

Hanko's eyebrows climbed in surprise.

"Why?" Darvyn's voice was a whisper.

For a moment, Hanko's mouth opened and closed. "We needed you focused on the mission," Hanko finally said. "Free from distractions."

Darvyn's fists tightened. "My mother was not a distraction. You could have at least taken care of her. She lived in poverty, all alone at the end of the spiral where the dogs and the storms and the bandits could have killed her. You could have done something for her! But you just left her to rot!"

Even Aggar had the decency to looked ashamed. Darvyn tore his gaze from the elder to scan the room.

"Lizana?"

The tall Keeper's eyes were filled with tears. She shook her head. "I did not betray you."

Darvyn nodded. She was not the informer.

Hanko's voice was brittle when he spoke. "We are not perfect, Darvyn, but we did our best. You were a difficult child to control. Your power made you more dangerous than you realize. And you clung to her memory so earnestly. When she first came looking, it was too soon. We had just begun to make progress." He shook his head. "There was so much at stake."

Darvyn shook with restrained anger. He thought his knuckles might burst from his skin. "And what was it all for? So you could lead a group who would one day betray me?"

"None of us betrayed you!" Aggar bellowed. "No matter the mistakes that were made, *you* brought the Poison Flame to our midst."

"And one of *you* sold me out to the True Father!" His roar matched Aggar's.

Shock, thick and viscous, permeated the room.

"None of us would ever." Hanko's face took on a gray pallor.

"One of you did. That is how the Poison Flame found me outside Checkpoint Five. She knew exactly where I was going to be. What my mission was."

The elder shook his head. "But the only ones who knew about the mission were those of you who took part."

Darvyn looked around the room again. Where was Farron? He'd been here a moment ago, but was now missing.

Hanko looked as sick as Darvyn felt, like he'd aged a decade in the past minute. The elder's gaze flicked to his granddaughter and back as if scared to look at her.

Heart sinking slowly to his feet, Darvyn turned to Meldi sitting in the corner.

He hadn't asked her. She shouldn't have known about the mission at all. But Hanko always had a soft spot for her, stuck in safe houses, unable to go on assignments. Stomach churning, Darvyn arrowed the power of his Song in her direction. She flinched as if she could feel the intrusion.

Her emotions were quiet. There was neither the guilt he expected to find in a traitor nor the shame. Instead he felt her satisfaction. She stood, jutting her chin into the air.

"I didn't betray the Keepers, Grandfather. Everything I did, I did for us all."

Hanko rose, horror pulling at the corners of his eyes and mouth. "What did you do?"

"I used the Flames' radio frequency to send the messages. To tell them where the Shadowfox would be, how they could find him. You have to understand, you relied on him too much and he makes mistakes. So many mistakes."

She turned to Aggar whose jaw was slack. Tears welled in the man's eyes.

She moved closer to him. "You told me yourself how irresponsible he was. Always wanting to go off on his own, not taking orders. Look what happened when he rushed off to the school."

"The children . . ." Aggar whispered, incredulous.

Meldi nodded, thinking he was agreeing with her. "Those poor children you saved were recaptured because he ran off."

Aggar shook his head.

"Meldi, that doesn't make any sense," Darvyn said. "The children were recaptured because the Golden Flames followed our team. Because you told them about the mission in the first place."

She frowned, looking down as if confused, then pointed to him. "Everything can't depend on you. People who depend on you die, or worse." She hitched up the leg of her trousers to reveal her mangled leg. Burn scars had misshapen the muscle and twisted her flesh.

Her voice shook. "You were my friend. You were supposed to save me. Save my parents. They would have done anything for you. But they depended on you and they're gone now."

She looked around wildly. "We have to free ourselves from him. It can't all be about one man. The Keepers are bigger than one man."

Darvyn's eyes stung. A dense silence hung over the room. He backed away, heart feeling like lead in his chest. Meldi's breathing was shallow, her skin flushed. "I did it for the Keepers," she said. "I did it to help us all."

Hanko moved to her side and wrapped her in an embrace. He pressed his cheek against the top of her head. "Meldi ul-Darnikor. My darling girl. You have transgressed."

Darvyn closed his Song against the despondency in the room. He thought of the smiling girl he'd known since he was five years old. A part of him was shattered. He needed air. He needed space. He needed to get out of there.

Slipping away from the chaos was easy. Those who observed his exit said nothing. He bound down the steps and into the twilight. The desert heat was stifling, but not as bad as inside the safe house had been.

A familiar whistle caught his ear from the alley. Farron. Darvyn hustled into the shadows to meet him.

"What happened?" Farron asked, taking in Darvyn's expression.

Darvyn gripped the back of his neck, exhaling hard enough to empty his lungs. He shook his head, unable to form the words.

Farron frowned, looking over at the safe house. Before long, he would learn what Darvyn couldn't say.

"I need to find Kyara," Darvyn murmured, looking down the dusky street.

Farron's eyes brightened. "I thought you might say that."

CHAPTER THIRTY-SEVEN

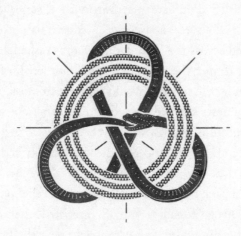

She fled beyond the mountain's stifling arms
Her loyalty a chain that was secure
She long wished for an ironclad embrace
An unconditional love that endured
The cornerstone her father made would bind
A heart rent open by thwarted desire

—THE BOOK OF UNVEILING

The skies over Lower Faalagol were overcast and an uncharacteristically chilly wind had blown in. Zeli sat in the courtyard, her back against a tree, wondering if the clouds would unload and drench them all. She flinched anytime footsteps sounded along one of the covered walkways connecting the buildings.

From her position here, she couldn't be seen by most passersby, but she wasn't so foolish as to imagine herself hidden. There was nowhere she could hide.

The Magister was back.

He'd returned in late morning with a series of shouted orders that had set the household on edge. His powerful stride had pounded across the tiled floors. Doors crashed and shutters rattled. His dinner the night before had not left him in a jovial mood and now the servants would suffer. Zeli most of all.

The summons she had been dreading came not a half hour later. Her bottom had grown numb on the cold ground and while the clouds kept their peace, the wind had kicked up significantly. She'd been watching the boughs above her teeter and sway when a page boy found her. The look of relief on his face at completing his task made a stab of regret strike her. She'd contemplated running away, but who would bear the brunt of that decision?

Devana had run away without a care about how it would affect anyone else. Zeli could not do the same. Even if she'd had somewhere to go.

She stood slowly, gathering her strength. Lying to a Magister, to any representative of the True Father, was punishable by death. Why had Devana asked her to do such a thing? Had she cared so little for Zeli's life that her own wants and needs were always more important? Of course they were. She was raised the only child of a powerful man. And Zeli was just a servant, after all. Replaceable. Unneeded now that Devana was no longer here. And if the girl never reappeared and Zeli somehow escaped the noose, would she be sent away? Was another factory, or worse, in her future?

Her steps were languid as she approached the Magister's suite—a small building of its own set in the corner of the estate.

She knocked on the carved wooden door, solid and unforgiving under her knuckles, and waited for the gruff voice to bid her to enter.

She set foot in a room that appeared to be an office. On the far end, seated on a long, low couch, the Magister sat rigidly. He set aside the lap desk on which he'd been writing and gave his full attention to Zeli. Her limbs numbed under his gaze.

"You are my daughter's personal maid?" His voice was low and dangerous.

"Yes, mideni."

"And where *is* my daughter?" He clasped his hands in his lap, fixing her with a piercing stare that flayed skin from muscle.

Zeli gripped her tunic in tight fists, took a deep breath, and decided the only thing she could do to spare her life was tell the truth. "She left with the guru Waga-nedri, mideni."

The Magister did not move. He didn't so much as blink. The scar bisecting his eyebrow and leading down his cheek seemed to twitch, but that may have been her imagination. "When?" was his response.

"Yesterday morning." She swallowed.

"And why did you not stop her?"

Zeli dropped her head. "She is my mistress."

He sighed, as if talking to a simpleton. "Why did you not inform someone then?"

"She forbade me. I could not—"

"So you just let her go?" he roared, rising to his feet. Zeli's knees quaked, threatening to fail her. "Allowed my daughter to run off with some ancient scheming charlatan? The Father only knows what he'll do with her to spite me."

He began pacing before her. With her head still lowered, she saw only his boots, polished to a high shine as they tread the tiled floor. "I should have tied the little idiot down when that cunning old cur stepped foot on this estate. Of course he would try something like this."

He abruptly stopped before her and grabbed her chin with powerful fingers, wrenching her head up roughly. "Your duties are to serve my daughter, not give in to her every inane whim. I should have you hanged for this."

A lump swelled in her throat and tears burned her eyes. His grip on her chin was painful, but she tried to swallow the discomfort.

"Ah!" he muttered and shoved her away, returning to his couch. "The silly chit. So foolish and headstrong." He wiped a hand over his face and leaned forward to rest his elbows on his thighs.

"Kurron!" he bellowed, foregoing any politeness, as was his way. The Magister's valet appeared soundlessly in the doorway.

"Twenty lashes for this child and get her out of my sight."

Zeli was led away with a coarse hand on her upper arm, her legs barely supporting her weight. She would live, but after a beating from Kurron, she would likely wish she was dead.

Ulani found her on the ground in the yard behind the stable, back bloodied and torn, unable to move. At least none of the staff had been forced to watch her punishment, but likewise, none had helped, for fear of drawing the master's ire. Eventually, Gladda would send someone, when the Magister was distracted with a meal or a visitor, but Zeli hadn't expected help for quite some time.

So she startled when Ulani sat down wordlessly beside her and picked up her hand. In moments, the tingling sensation of

WHISPERS OF SHADOW & FLAME

Earthsong washed over Zeli's body. The searing pain on her back lessened until she could take a full, deep breath. Kurron had done his duty with gusto, using a thickly corded whip that she was certain had also broken one of her ribs. Under Ulani's ministrations, the bones moved back into place, knitting together inside her. Flesh mended and ravaged skin smoothed, becoming whole again.

Before she could thank the girl, a deep voice pierced the quiet afternoon. "Zeli-deni, I heard what happened. I—"

Zeli turned her head, still on the ground, recognizing Kerym standing over her. Well, she recognized his voice and shoes; she couldn't see much more of him than that. But she imagined what had cut him off midsentence. Her, laying there in the dirt, bloody and half-naked, but with no wounds.

He crouched next to her, bringing his face into her sightline, then looked over at Ulani. "The child has her Song?" His voice had gone low and strange.

Zeli closed her eyes and rested her forehead on the cool ground. She wished there was some way she could get Ulani away from here. Somewhere safe. Somewhere far away.

"She should give tribute," Kerym said. "You know the True Father has been collecting power in larger numbers. She's not quite of age yet, but—"

"Kerym-mideni." She struggled to her knees, clutching what was left of her tunic to her chest. The pain was gone, but exhaustion from both the experience and the healing kept her movements sluggish. And concern for Ulani caused any self-consciousness she would normally have had to flee. "She is only seven. Far too young to be sent by herself across the country to be stripped of her Song. Please have mercy on her. Just until she's older. The Magister doesn't know about her."

Kerym's face turned grim. "It's our duty to provide the king with the power he needs to rule."

"I know, and she will. But the minimum age for tributes used to be fourteen. It's been getting younger and younger and . . ." She turned toward Ulani, whose eyes were wide. "Please, mideni. I beg you."

When she looked back, the severity in his handsome features had softened. "You have a big heart, Zeli-deni," he said, cupping her cheek. "I will think about it."

A gust of air escaped her lungs and she dropped her head. Kerym helped her stand with a hand at her elbow, but the knowledge of her current state of undress, plus the blood still covering her, made her suddenly shy.

"I should go and clean up," she said quickly. "Thank you, again."

He surprised her by reaching for her hand and plucking it away from its iron grip across her chest to place a kiss on the back of her palm. Confusion, desire, and awe played chords within her.

She backed away. Unwilling to give him another view of her back, but unable to meet his eyes. She was afraid to know what sort of emotion they held.

"Come, Ulani-deni," she said, and headed away from him.

Zeli rinsed herself at the spigot outside the stable, crouching down to fit her body under its stream. She didn't want to force herself or any of the other maids to have to clean the blood and grime from the servant washroom. A clean towel and tunic had appeared on the ledge beside her and she spun around to find Gladda standing there, face grim.

"So it's true, then?" the woman asked.

"Is what true?" Zeli replied, quickly rubbing her skin dry.

"Kerym-mideni knows about Ulani-yul's Song?"

Zeli slipped the tunic over her head, nodding sadly. "Yes, he saw her heal me."

Gladda cursed.

"But he might not report it to the Magister."

The older woman shot Zeli an incredulous look, much as if she'd said the horses would sprout wings and take to the air.

"H-he said he would think about not telling the Magister. I asked him not to. Begged him really, and he said he'd consider it."

"Oh, child," Gladda said, pulling her into a hug. "You are so trusting."

First, Kerym had called her good-hearted and now Gladda thought her too trusting. She prickled inside the warm embrace.

"He will disappoint you, *uli*," Gladda said.

Zeli pulled away. "How could he disappoint me? I have no expectations of him. But he is good, and honorable and . . ." She trailed off, recalling his voice in the darkness as he spoke to the guru. Plotting something. But all the favored had their plots and plans. And he'd sent his servant to save her when she'd needed help. She wasn't quite sure what to feel.

Now dressed, she turned toward to the path leading to the courtyard.

"Where are you going?" Gladda asked.

"I want to talk to Yalisa. Ask her what she thinks the Magister will do with me now. She's the one who knows him best. She may be able to influence him." Before she took another step, she looked back at Gladda. "And what's so wrong about wanting what she has? She was just like me, but the Magister saw something more in her. Something good and worthy that could be cultivated. You don't think it's possible for Kerym-mideni to see something in me?"

Gladda's gaze was sad. She looked off toward the mountains but didn't respond.

Zeli chuckled humorously. "I met Fakera-deni at the market."

The older woman's eyes widened, almost in warning.

"She said to tell you there are only two days left. What does that mean, I wonder? Or maybe I shouldn't wonder. Maybe I shouldn't ask why you've been taking food out of the Magister's kitchen and delivering it to some . . . some . . ." *Earthsinger.* But she couldn't say the word aloud. Not here. No matter how aggravated she was with Gladda. An adult Earthsinger was nearly synonymous with rebel.

Gladda brushed her hand along her tunic, smoothing invisible wrinkles. "The master has always given food to the poor."

Her words were true but Zeli shook her head. "She knew my parents. Perhaps too well. You must be careful, Gladda-deni. We must all be more careful." The last words were whispered, regretful.

She moved down the walkway, knowing Gladda would not reply. Her footsteps were solemn and sadness draped her. She longed for Yalisa's wisdom. She wouldn't reveal Gladda's actions, the thought of informing on anyone still rubbed her wrong, but she needed some reassurance.

However, when she reached the woman's room, two footmen were carrying out armloads of clothes.

"What's going on here?"

One man shrugged. "We were ordered to clean this room out."

"Yalisa-deni is gone."

Zeli spun around to find Fahna behind her, a basket of linen in her arms. The maid's hand was perfectly healed now and she hadn't missed more than a few hours of work in her recovery.

"Gone? Where?"

Fahna drew closer, expression subdued, but still obviously eager to share her gossip. "To the work camps. Apparently, the guru and Kerym-mideni found out she was selling citizenship documents to people in the Snarl."

"Yalisa-mideni?" Zeli was stunned. "Selling citizenships? That makes no sense!"

Fahna nodded sagely. "The Magister stores the documents in his office. She had access to all parts of the estate and the Ephors verified that more people than normal have been allowed entry into the city. Kerym-mideni was certain it was her, and the guru confirmed it."

"And so the Magister sent her to the *camps*?"

"Oh, he was none too pleased about it. But he couldn't deny two esteemed sources. When another Ephor confirmed it last night he had no other choice."

Fahna shook her head and continued down the walkway, while Zeli's blood chilled.

Strike quickly like a viper or be bitten like one. Was this what they'd been plotting over? But why? Why get rid of Yalisa? Zeli was certain the woman would not risk her position with something as silly as selling citizenship.

She'd had a good life. A stable one, or so Zeli had thought.

She leaned against the wall, feeling deflated. All it took was one voice, a single accusation and everything could be taken away. Gone like mist in morning.

Almost as if it never had been.

CHAPTER THIRTY-EIGHT

Reverberations from a life endure
In silence they may hide until their time
Then ride on fissures, causing hairline cracks
Fracturing certainty and peace of mind
In her own spell she faced the truth she'd fought
Her destiny and future now she sought

—THE BOOK OF UNVEILING

Kyara crept through the shadows in the alleys. After attacking
Aren while rescuing Darvyn, she knew there was a hunt on for
her. Each time a group of soldiers marched by, shining their
lamps, searching for the fugitives, she attempted to melt into the
darkness. She wasn't sure if Ydaris could change the parameters
of her spell and try to force Kyara out of hiding. She suspected
the magic needed her to be within earshot of the commands;

that's how it had always been. But she did not know for sure and her life now depended on it.

She followed the Morladyn River from Low End to the warehouse district, a neighborhood full of dark streets and buildings that would be empty at this hour. Plenty of places to hide.

A barge passed on its way to Checkpoint One; the rumble of its engine made her chest vibrate. An odd feeling of awareness had been tugging at her since she'd left the safe house. Somewhere out there, something was calling her.

It reminded her of the whispering voices that had led her to the crystal city, but this compulsion was different. There were no voices this time, only a strong desire that drew her like a magnet until she could ignore it no longer. She crossed the street, staying out of the pools cast by the gaslights.

Warehouses lined the road, most filled with goods from Yaly, Lagrimar's only trading partner. Unmanned chain boats came through Morladyn's Pass from the neighboring country. Goods were unloaded here and packaged before being sent to the rest of Lagrimar.

The only vehicle on the street was a covered rickshaw in front of one such nondescript warehouse on the corner. A rickshaw was an odd luxury in this part of the city. The driver stood at attention, ever at the ready.

Kyara hid herself in the shadows of a building across the street. What had pulled her toward this particular property? She had only been waiting a few minutes when the door opened and a shrouded figure wearing a funeral veil emerged and climbed into the carriage. Not a sliver of the person's skin was visible, but Kyara knew that purposeful walk anywhere. Ydaris.

What business did the Cantor have here?

In seconds, the driver perked up and took off. But a man

remained in the warehouse doorway. Kyara caught a glimpse of mud-brown trousers and a gray tunic—workmen's clothes—but gasped when she caught sight of his face before he shut the door.

Raal.

Kyara's blood ran cold. She backed against the bricks on shaking legs, relying on the wall to support her. What was he doing here?

She waited, watching the warehouse and the rest of the street for soldiers, worry gnawing at her insides. Evening passed to night, but she could not bring herself to move. Ydaris being here with Raal could not be a coincidence.

She freed her Song, sinking into her other vision only to be blinded by the sheer quantity of Nethersong filling the warehouse. Short of Serpent's Gorge, she had never seen such a concentrated cache of the energy. She reached for it, seeking the invigoration it supplied, but something blocked her. A shield or ward of some kind kept the Nethersong in place and out of her reach. Her curiosity was piqued. She needed to get inside.

Just then, the physician emerged. Gone was his signature hat; his bald pate gleamed in the lamplight, and a dark cloak covered his clothes. He took off down the street and disappeared into an alley. Kyara had just moved to follow him when he appeared again, this time on horseback, and galloped away toward the main avenue.

Due to the overwhelming Nethersong, she could not tell if anyone else was in the warehouse. She had not yet seen the two servants Raal had had in the vision she'd seen of him at the crystal city. The men could very well be inside.

Going in blind was a risk, but she needed to investigate. She must have been led here for a reason, and the same feeling that had drawn her here continued to pull her toward the warehouse.

After checking her surroundings to make sure no one was showing her undue attention—if an alert had gone out, a layperson could give her up just as easily as a soldier—Kyara crossed the street and pushed against the front door. It was unlocked. Her caution doubled. She remembered something the *ulla* used to say. People who didn't lock their doors had either nothing to hide or should be hidden from, and Raal was definitely hiding something.

Thick, stale air clogged her lungs. The dim interior was heavy and oppressive. When her eyes adjusted to the meager light, she found herself in an old storeroom. Tables stacked with junk lay covered in dust, and shipping crates, jars, and pallets cluttered the floor.

Nethersong swirled around her, intense and forceful. How could this place hold so much death?

A single wooden door stood on the opposite wall. Unlike the front entry, this one was locked. Urgency bit at her heels. She had no skill at lock picking so it took only a split second to decide to kick in the door. If she had to fight someone on the other side, so be it.

Her first kick merely caused the door to creak. She readied herself for another try when she felt the tug of Nethersong in the dead wood of the door.

This was new. She cocked her head to the side, focusing. With only a nudge from her Song, the dead wood splintered into shards. She jumped back in surprise. The Nethersong here was concentrated and potent. The same heady intoxication from Serpent's Gorge filled her.

Beyond the ruined door, a huge room spread out before her. High windows from the second story let in filtered light. A metal lattice catwalk edged the interior, just below the windows. Kyara's breath caught as her gaze tracked down.

Laid out in orderly rows on the floor were white cloths—hundreds of them—taking up the entire vast space. Each cloth covered a lumpy but recognizable form. Kyara knelt next to the nearest sheet and lifted it, her heart in her throat.

The sightless eyes of a corpse stared back at her, the whites darkened to black. She checked the gums, as well, though she knew what she would find.

She jerked the sheet off to view the dead man's body. Grisly wounds marked the neck, wrists, and thighs over the thickest arteries. Other corpses featured the same. Ydaris's handiwork. She must be working on a spell of unprecedented magnitude to need this much blood.

Kyara sank back into her mind's eye. Brilliant flashes of Nether whirled and eddied. But something else hung in the spaces between the dancing lights. It was different from the darkness of Earthsong. Smokelike and empty, she could only describe it as visual static. Then a word came to her: Void.

Trying to focus her sight on the Void was like trying to capture the wind in a bottle. Its movements were at once random and graceful, but ever elusive even to her inner vision.

Kyara grabbed hold of the Nethersong of the nearest body and pulled it to her the way she had with the Death River poison that had filled Darvyn. As it swirled into her Song, hazy waves of the Void settled onto the corpse, taking the place of the Nether. She had never observed this before, though it began to make sense. The dead held no Earthsong, but when their Nethersong was siphoned, the Void replaced it.

But the Void was inconstant. No sooner had it moved into the body than a glimmer of Nethersong flickered to life, growing quickly to displace the vacuous emptiness.

She was reminded of the balance she'd felt at Serpent's Gorge. Earthsong and Nethersong waxing and waning in a steady equilibrium. She hadn't seen the Void then, but she hadn't known what to look for. The Void could be easy to miss, like a shadow cast by a single candle in a dark room.

"What is this place?" she whispered to herself.

"Think of it like a giant battery."

She whipped around and stumbled as she came face-to-face with Raal. She took a step back, ready to lash out at him. He held his hands out, trying to appear harmless.

"Kyara, I can help you."

"If you move, I'll stop your heart." Kyara's voice was deadly calm even as fear consumed her. She grabbed hold of the Nether in Raal's body. He was far older than he looked but healthy.

He smiled, ignoring her threat. "I know. Isn't it amazing?"

She paused. The possibility that he might be insane hadn't crossed her mind before.

"Your power is magnificent, Kyara. And yet you want to get rid of it."

"How do you know that?"

He raised his eyebrows slightly.

"I can help you," he repeated. His words sent a chill of intrigue through her. At the same time, common sense countered that he would say anything to spare his life.

"You took someone from me. You've killed so many people." She swept her arm to indicate the warehouse.

"I didn't kill these people. This is Ydaris's work."

"Why so many?" she murmured.

"The True Father has given her quite a task. She must create a spell strong enough to tear down the Mantle. Something like that requires a fair amount of blood."

Kyara felt sick to her stomach. All those people. No wonder the nabbers had been grabbing children like never before to replace the workforce. Entire neighborhoods or villages must have given their lives for this spell.

"And what's your excuse?" she asked.

"You say I took someone from you?"

"You don't remember meeting me before?" She cocked her head to the side.

His brow furrowed, and Kyara let out a deranged laugh. "It's just as well. I suppose a madman crossing the country spreading the plague wouldn't remember every little girl he came across."

Hands still raised, he took a step forward. She tightened the grip on his Nethersong, sending a jolt of nausea through him that made him stop short. Sweat beaded across his forehead.

"I said don't move."

"All right, all right. Then just listen. I am sorry if my experiments took someone you love. But I can help you achieve your goal."

"Your experiments? What exactly are you, and what do you want?"

"In Yaly, we are known as Physicks, and our magic is called amalgam. It takes the life magic of Earthsong, the death magic of Nethersong, the spirit magic of the blood, and combines it with material objects to create amalgamations." His eyes shone with excitement. "If you'll allow me to show you?"

Kyara's mind raced, but she could not discard her curiosity. She nodded. "As long as no one is harmed," she cautioned. Raal reached into the pocket of his tunic and produced a pair of spectacles. He held them out to her.

She inched closer until she could grasp them from his hand. "What are these?"

"Put them on."

She glared at him.

"I vow to you I am not here to harm you or anyone else."

"Your vow means nothing, murderer."

"If murdering you was my objective, it would have already been done." His tone was pleasant, but a layer of ice covered his green eyes.

She didn't unfold the prongs of the spectacles, unwilling to fully put them on. Instead she held them up to one eye, so she could still watch Raal with the other. Through the glass, the warehouse changed. Nethersong shone, similar to how it did in her mind's eye, but instead of bright columns of light, it was rendered as red clouds. The walls of the warehouse were outlined in a blue glow—the shield she'd sensed from outside. Beyond the building, tiny pulses of green dotted the surrounding area.

"What is the green?"

"Those are Earthsingers. Children, most likely, who haven't yet given tribute."

Kyara turned the lens to Raal himself. He had no color, but blotches of yellow could be seen on his person.

"And the yellow?" she asked.

"Other amalgamations. A pocket watch that reminds you of your appointments and warns you if you're late. A pen that translates your writing into other languages. A compass for traveling. A coin that shifts to any currency."

"If these objects are made with blood magic, why are they not covered in the red stone the way calderas are?"

"That is the benefit of amalgam. Blood spells mesh the three magics but in a primitive way. The creation of a caldera does not imbue the actual object with any power, it merely serves as a container to hold magic. With amalgam, we create spelled objects that are far more powerful."

Kyara had to admit she had never seen anything like these spectacles, and the other objects he mentioned sounded fantastical.

"What do the Physicks want?" she asked, lowering the glasses.

"For a thousand years, we have sought one thing and one thing only: immortality."

Kyara took an instinctive step back. "You will live forever in the World After."

"Are you certain? We have only old stories and misguided faith to tell us this. The Living World, however, is proven. Think of all you could do with eternity to play with right here."

"It hasn't done the True Father any good."

Raal sneered. "His long life is due only to stolen magic. The thieving corrupts it. What we seek is something else, something more." His face transformed into a glorious smile. "And I believe that you can help us."

She took another step back. "Me? How?"

"Your Song . . . It is so rare. To find an adult Nethersinger is unheard of. If you truly want to remove your Song, we can help. In Yaly, the Physicks can safely divest you of it. You would be free of your servitude to the immortal king. Is that not what you seek?"

She was certain she could not trust this man. His hands were even bloodier than her own. "The True Father would never let me go."

Raal shrugged. "He would not have to know."

"And what would you do with my Song, once you had it?"

His smile thinned. "We would keep it, of course. But you would not be harmed at all."

So Raal wanted a death stone . . . Wasn't that merely the Song of a Nethersinger trapped in a caldera? And with the ancient death stone lost, of course the Physicks would seek to use her to create a new one.

But he was lying when he'd said she wouldn't be harmed if she went with him to Yaly and allowed him to experiment on her. Murmur had said she would have to die in order for any caldera made of her Song to be useful.

And what then? Would that begin the war that Murmur had spoken of?

She shook her head and tossed the spectacles back to him.

"Think over my offer," Raal said. "When we next meet, you may be more inclined to accept."

He smiled again and stepped to the side, clearing her way to leave.

Her skin crawled as she eased past him and picked up speed to get as far away as possible.

CHAPTER THIRTY-NINE

Reborn from rock and stone her path was cleared
To journey forth where others dared not tread
The voice whose call she heeded was unknown
Yet beat familiar rhythms in her head
She hummed an ans'ring melody to keep
The solitude at bay, and hidden deep

—THE BOOK OF UNVEILING

Water sluiced over Zeli's skin as she sank deeper into the tub in Devana's bathing room. She normally would never have dared to partake in such a luxury—even while Devana was away—but tonight was different. She was heartbroken, exhausted, bereft. If she was whipped again for stealing a bath, then so be it, but the Magister never stepped foot in his daughter's suite, and none of the other servants had reason to now.

Her head rested on the copper rim. The aroma of fragrant oils wafted up, and Zeli breathed deeply, closing her eyes, trying to soak away the memory of the past weeks. Images came to her one after another: the cramped coach ride, the masses gathered at the revival, her head being covered by a sack, bouncing around while chained to the wagon, being frightened out of her mind. Neither the relaxing water nor the aromatic oils could erase her reality.

She opened her eyes, caught sight of a figure just in front of her, and screamed.

Kerym stood at the entrance to the bathing room, leaning against the doorway. Zeli splashed, trying to find something to cover herself with. She crossed her arms over her chest and raised her knees, curling up against the far corner of the large tub.

Kerym held up his hands and smiled; the same smile she'd always thought noble and kind now appeared forbidding in the low lighting. He pulled a towel off the rack and crossed to the tub, sitting at its edge and handing the plush cloth to her.

She wasn't sure what to do and so pulled the towel into the water, covering herself. He'd seen her partially clothed twice today. Her face burned and heart raced, but this time with growing fear.

"Kerym-mideni, what are you doing here?"

His smile slipped as he leaned forward. With nowhere to go, she pressed her back into the metal. Kerym stroked her cheek, then slowly pressed his lips to hers.

Shock froze her in place. Was this some sort of dream? Could the warmth and comfort of the bath have lulled her into sleep? But his lips were solid against hers. Firm and unyielding. She'd never been kissed before and felt she wasn't doing it right, but wasn't sure what to do. It was nothing like she'd always dreamt of.

Finally, he leaned back, palm still cupping her face. "You're so lovely. I've wanted to do that for quite some time."

The heated tub chilled around her. She raised a shaking hand to touch her lips. "You have?"

He nodded and grabbed her hand, rubbing her knuckles with his thumb. "When Devana returns and she and I are married, you will have a position of favor in our household. Is that something you would want?"

His eyes drank her in and she couldn't look away, but her mouth and vocal cords refused to work.

"It would be a great honor, would it not, to be the first mistress of the Magister?" he asked.

"First . . . mistress?" Her voice was more croak than whisper.

"Yes," he said, eyes alight. "When I am Magister, I will unite the Lake Cities and rule them as one. All of this petty squabbling will end. I'll become indispensable to the True Father, a favored lieutenant." His gaze was fevered; he squeezed her hand even tighter.

"I will be expected to embody the lifestyle the king promotes, but no matter how many mistresses I have, even if I one day have my own harem, you will always have a place of distinction as the first among them."

Zeli blinked rapidly, her breath struggling for purchase.

"You will have the finest silks." His fingertips ran down her neck and skated across her collarbone. She pressed the towel tighter with her free hand. "Jewelry. Entertainment. Anything you want."

His hand snaked behind her neck and pressed her forward to meet his lips again. Zeli tried her best to respond to the kiss, but the light in her chest that usually sparked when he was near had gone out.

Shouldn't she be rejoicing? This was what she'd longed for—what she hadn't even had the courage to dream of. Obtaining status and rank, fine things, a life of ease. She would finally be like Yalisa.

Yalisa. Her throat constricted. How easy was the woman's life now?

"Th-that is a long way off, mideni. The Magister is not an old man."

"He's not a young man, either. And he has many enemies." Kerym eased back, fingertips still grazing her skin. He looked at her adoringly—or was it lustfully? She held herself very still, not wanting to do anything to provoke him. This was not at all what she'd thought it would be.

"Why would you do this for me?" she whispered.

One finger lifted her chin as his thumb caressed her lower lip. "You are sensible, loyal, discreet. You remind me of a baby dove. Small and soft." He chuckled. "Besides, you manage Devana as well as can be expected. That will be a benefit. You know she won't last long on this journey of hers. The guru will end up a great disappointment. He will tire of her quickly and send her back. And the comforts of life afforded her here are not easily given up."

He seemed so confident. So certain, but Zeli was not. His hand went to her hair, tracing the braids that hugged close to her scalp.

"I want you to know that your place is secure here. No matter what happens over the next few days. You are very special to me. One of the many things I've been looking forward to for quite some time." His gaze dropped to the wet towel covering her. Zeli held her breath.

But Kerym shifted back, pulling his arm away and looking around at the bathing room. "These rooms can be yours, you know. And we will modernize them. This entire estate is so outdated, I'll want to make some changes around here."

He tapped his hand on the tub's edge, preparing to rise. "But we can't have Earthsingers on the staff. The little girl must give tribute. Then she will return and you all can dress her up or do whatever you like with her." He smiled graciously. "That's just the way it must be."

Zeli stared at him and nodded. He winked at her. "You will have a happy life, Tarazeli-yul. Trust me."

He leaned forward again for a last kiss that was so brief it might have been imagined, then rose and left the room, as quietly and ghostlike as he'd entered.

She sat in the chilled water, towel pressed against her until she was certain he wouldn't return.

After running through the dark streets of Sayya, Farron showed Darvyn the warehouse he'd followed Kyara to after she left the safe house.

"I saw her head in there, then I went back to find you," the teen said.

"Thank you." Darvyn peered at the nondescript building, hoping she was still inside. With soldiers searching for them, the likelihood was good. She wouldn't want to be on the street any more than she had to until she had some kind of plan.

"What happens now?" Farron asked.

"What do you mean?"

"You were willing to take on every Keeper there for her." He searched Darvyn's eyes. "Are you in love with her?"

Darvyn swallowed. "I don't know what happens now. The soldiers will be searching for us. We'll have to find a way out of the city somehow."

"I'll stand guard while you go in to find her."

"No." Darvyn gripped Farron's shoulder. "Go back. Get Zango. Kyara and I will find a way out. Monitor the gold frequency, and I'll get a message to you, okay?"

Stubbornness tightened Farron's mouth.

Darvyn lowered his voice. "Please."

Farron exhaled slowly, his shoulders slumping. "Okay."

"Thank you." Darvyn watched the boy's retreat. He was grateful for his friend's loyalty, but the hole formed from discovering Meldi's treachery caused him to rethink his instincts. What if Darvyn really was undependable? Farron shouldn't have to pay the price for that.

Across the street, the warehouse door flew open. Kyara raced out like she was being chased by wild dogs. She sprinted across the road and nearly slammed into him before recognizing him. Her eyes rounded; she clutched him tight for a moment, then backed away.

"What are you doing here?" She looked over her shoulder. Darvyn hadn't seen her like this before. She was afraid.

"What happened?"

"Come on, we have to get away from here, now." She grabbed hold of his hand and took off. She darted into an alley, but stopped at the other end.

Darvyn peeked around the corner. Soldiers on crawlers drove slowly down the street, necks on a swivel. Half a block up, men were going door-to-door in pairs.

"Any chance they're looking for someone else?" Darvyn asked.

She snorted. "'Fraid not. Do you think they know about the safe house?"

Darvyn thought for a moment, then shook his head. "She wouldn't have risked her grandfather."

"You found the traitor?"

"Meldi." He choked on her name.

Kyara's gaze was sad. She reached for him, then changed her mind at the last moment. "I think they'll expect us to find a hiding place somewhere in Low End. They'll probably spend all night searching every building."

"Makes sense. Not like we could find shelter in Windy Hill with the payrollers."

Kyara froze. A slow smile spread across her face. "Actually, I think we could."

Darvyn's eyebrows climbed, but he followed her into the darkness.

CHAPTER FORTY

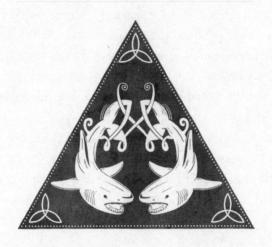

The dream she once thought slaughtered by the morn
Pierced by the dawn's zealous march toward day
Was a resilient thing, this reverie
It beckoned bright and built for her a way
To find that which she'd long been in search of
A sheltered place to fall, a time to love

—THE BOOK OF UNVEILING

The town house was majestic on the outside; inside it had obviously been targeted by sackers. Once plush, luxurious finishes had been stripped down to nothing.

"Whose house was this?" he asked.

"Someone who made a lot of money placating the True Father until the king grew tired of him."

The hardness of her voice set off an alarm in Darvyn's head. "One of your assignments?"

She nodded, her lips pressed into a grim line. He wouldn't ask any more about it. But she was right, no one would expect to find an escaped prisoner and a rogue soldier in this neighborhood. They hadn't even seen any search parties since they'd entered Windy Hill.

"We should be safe here," she said, but uneasiness crept through him.

She moved around the living room, checking the window shutters, but he sensed she was really keeping space between them. She found a half-burned candle in a pile of debris in the corner and set it on an empty shelf. When she searched her pockets for something to light it with and came up empty, Darvyn lit the wick with Earthsong.

Kyara faced away from him, her head hanging. "He was there. In the warehouse." Her voice was like fluttering dust.

"Who was?"

"The man who killed your mother."

She turned around slowly, but wouldn't meet his eyes. Instead, she stared at the floor while she told of the mass gravesite she'd stumbled onto, and her strange meeting with Raal.

Darvyn's throat thickened; fear strangled him. What was the physician's endgame? Darvyn knew as well as Kyara did the man couldn't be trusted, and now he wielded another new type of magic Darvyn didn't understand. He felt helpless in his ignorance.

"I should have killed him," Kyara said. "I'm so sorry, Darvyn."

He shook his head. "You don't have to apologize for that."

Her voice hardened. "I should have killed the man who

stole your mother's life and not allowed his words to cause me to stray."

"Do you believe he could do as he says? Remove your Song?"

Her face crumpled. "It seems so. I've never heard of his sort of power before. I don't know what else it is capable of, but from the little I've seen, it's not to be trifled with. And he wants something from me."

"Then it's good you kept him alive until you can learn more." Her eyes were round with shock when she finally looked up at him.

"You aren't mad? I made a vow to kill him. I essentially stabbed you in the back."

An enormous weight was pressing down on him. He gave in to it and stretched out on the floor. "That's the least backstabbing anyone has done to me today. If the physician's people are after you, it's best to know why. If you killed him, they would just send others."

She sat, leaving a good distance between them, her face marred by a scowl. He wished he could make her understand—his heart was too heavy to hold anger at her. It already carried more sorrow than he could take.

They were each lost in their thoughts for a long time. Darvyn searched his memory for what he could have done differently.

"You're thinking of her?" Kyara asked. "Meldi." She answered his questioning look.

He sighed deeply. "I was thirteen when her parents died and she was hurt in that fire. The soldiers came in the middle of the night for me, but I'd been moved the day before. She blames me as she should. If I'd been there, I could have saved them."

Kyara reached over and grabbed his hand. "Stop it. You

saved many, many lives many, many times. What she wants is impossible. She wants perfection. Are you listening to yourself? You were *thirteen*."

"And I had a responsibility—"

"One placed on your shoulders long before it was right. Listen to me: this is not your fault. Her betrayal is her burden to bear, not yours." She squeezed him tighter, forcing him to stay connected. "Nerys is not your burden, either. That's not why she asked me to find you. And that's not why she gave you to the Keepers."

Tears stung his eyes as he remembered his mother.

"You have to forgive yourself, Darvyn. Your mother never blamed you. She wouldn't want you to blame yourself."

He shut his eyes, but her words penetrated. He wasn't sure what was true anymore, what was right for him to feel. He was locked in a never-ending whirlwind of guilt and helplessness.

Kyara's soft voice filled the darkness, singing a familiar lullaby. *His* lullaby. The one his mother had sung so often about how she loved him more than the sun.

He curled into a ball and cried for all he'd lost. A family. A childhood. But he'd gained much as well. Loyal friends. Purpose in his life. And if he could convince Kyara to let down her walls—maybe more.

She moved closer and wrapped her arms around him as she sang. He sank into her embrace.

After the last notes of the song had faded, he whispered to her. "You have to do it, too. Forgive yourself. You didn't choose to become the Poison Flame. That day your choice was to save the lives of every innocent person in that town."

Her body grew rigid. "It isn't the same."

"Yes, it is."

His arms snaked around her until they were holding each other, wrapped up in one another. Little by little, she relaxed.

"I've killed ninety-three men," she whispered. "Eight women. And three children . . . that I know of. I don't know the number of animals." Her voice was a storm of sorrow. "Seventy-one of those kills were done in the service of the True Father."

He drew in a jagged breath, and this time he pulled her so close he felt her heart beat through his own chest. It was like they were fused together. Heart to heart, beating in time together.

Kyara awakened to a cage of safety surrounding her. Darvyn's arms trapped her in place against him. They'd fallen asleep like this. His breathing was soft and steady; the warmth of his breath heated her ear. No sunlight peeked through the gaps around the shutters, but her internal clock told her that dawn was near.

She held herself still, inhaling him, enjoying the feel of his arms tight around her. Lingering incense mixed with his skin's unique scent. Goose bumps pebbled her skin, although she was warm. If she could have nothing else but this—exist for all time in his embrace—she would be forever satisfied.

She closed her eyes, committing the feel of him to memory. The heaviness of his arm. The solid wall of his chest against her back. Scared even to move, lest the moment be taken from her.

His even breaths made her think he was asleep, but his arms tightened, drawing her closer. Behind her, his head shifted and then lips grazed her neck, light as the tip of a paintbrush. She shivered.

Tingles flickered to life along the path his mouth took. Kyara closed her eyes to focus on the sensation and everything his gentle touch did to her body.

Darvyn's hand was splayed across her abdomen. He dipped his fingers underneath the hem of her tunic, which had ridden up during the night. She gasped at the shock that rippled through her. Electricity raced across her skin, chasing his fingers. Vibrations from the small touch sank into her bones and radiated outward.

His lips firmed to press a kiss where her neck met her shoulder at the same time as his fingertips swept up to brush the underside of her breast. Her body quaked with each stroke.

Last night, she had wanted to keep a healthy distance between them. It would be better for him to stay away from her—she was poison, after all. But seeing as he had no intention of doing so, she allowed herself the indulgence of desire.

So few things were within her grasp, but here they were, not a sliver of daylight between them and him seeking more, gently, as was his way.

All the reasons they couldn't be together flew from her mind. She covered his hand with hers and shifted it higher, boldly inviting him to caress her breast.

When he froze, his body rigid, she thought that he'd finally come to his senses. Of course she would ruin this with her eagerness. She had no regrets though, even if he was preparing to retreat. Instead, he rolled her to her back and moved over her, hovering, one hand on her breast, the other grabbing her braids. His lips descended, soft at first, then eager, consuming, bruising. He drank her in as if dying of thirst.

She was ravenous for him, as well. They collided, desperation erasing any hesitancy or doubt. A flurry of movement ensued—

arms, legs, teeth. Fabric tore as he rushed to pull off her tunic. His fully healed chest was bared to her. She ran her hands across him, dipping into the ridges, skating across the coiled hair of his lower abdomen.

He tugged at the tie to his trousers, then slid hers down her legs in a fluid motion. She was bare, bathed in the early morning glow now filtering around the shutters. Darvyn's eyes glittered with promise and admiration.

Kyara was not even self-conscious about her bandages, or of him possibly seeing the raw flesh on her mangled chest. His fingers grazed her breasts but were soon replaced by his mouth, first on one rigid peak and then the other. He licked a trail across them and back again. Her skin was so sensitive out in the open.

She shivered and clamped her legs together. Need, urgent and unfamiliar, beat a rhythm within. As though he knew exactly what she needed, Darvyn skimmed her side to grip her hip. He kneaded it gently as he suckled her breast and then slid his fingers between her thighs. She unclenched her muscles, allowing her legs to fall apart. He teased her there, not dipping in, just skirting her edges.

She ground her teeth together to keep from begging and then released all pride. "Please," she said on a gasp, arching into his mouth, trying to urge his fingers inside her.

Very slowly, he complied, sliding into her. The anticipation was excruciating, too much and yet not nearly enough.

"More," she said, rocking against his hand.

His chuckle was muffled by the presence of her breast in his mouth, but he did not draw back. Another finger joined the first, and the two worked together, building the tension to greater heights. She moaned, then bit her lip, trying to contain the pleasure.

His mouth traced up her neck to suck at her jaw. She tilted her head down until her lips found his and kissed him with explosive longing. His fingers worked furiously, manipulating the coiled tension within her, changing its direction, bunching it up and then releasing. She came against his hand, her cries smothered by his mouth on hers, his tongue delving deep inside.

As the potency of her orgasm waned, she still felt achy and needy. Her hands grazed the muscles of his backside, then went around to stroke him. Feeling his hardness magnified her desire.

Part of her wanted to take her time and feel the entire silken length, but the larger part was far more impatient. She positioned him, wrapped her legs around his back, and pushed.

He hissed as he sunk into her. The slight burn of the invasion eased quickly, and Kyara threw her head back, lost in the motion of their bodies. His mouth roamed across her jaw to nip at her ear. He tilted her, then lifted her with hands firmly gripping the globes of her ass. The position left only her shoulders on the mat, and Darvyn controlled her motions completely, picking up speed. She surrendered. Letting him take control was no hardship.

Sweat dripped from both of them as they came together. He shifted positions yet again, which triggered a wave of bliss to roll through her. It expanded, then lingered, lasting longer than her first orgasm. Darvyn sank back on his heels and, to her surprise, flipped her over so she was on her hands and knees. Then he was inside her again, taking and giving, forcing the breath from her body as she gasped with pleasure.

Every motion was like a flame singeing her, and her sweat did nothing to cool the inferno beneath her skin. Her fingers scrabbled on the floorboards, searching for something to hold onto as the world rocked around her. Her body was a bundle of nerves, and she could feel Darvyn on every part of her skin. He squeezed her waist hard enough to bruise, and then he tensed, nearly collapsing onto her back. His release sparked another from her. Bright spots laced her vision as she collapsed, too, his weight on top of her.

Her body hummed with the aftershocks. She could not have moved if one hundred venomous serpents had been chasing her. He lifted off her, and dragged her close to his side. Their breaths mingled as they panted for air. Tucking her against his chest, he wrapped her in his loving embrace. She closed her eyes, letting the memory sink into every part of her being.

CHAPTER FORTY-ONE

The sands of time are not lost when they pass
Those tiny granules one day flow again
And seers know and prove to all who doubt
The power held inside one tiny grain
Whether your life's water or wine, just wait
The glass will turn again by hands of fate

—THE BOOK OF UNVEILING

Zeli left the estate, walking out into the night, eager to be away from the confines of its walls. She'd once felt so safe there, welcomed as a child after enduring days of terror, but now everything from the dark presence of the trees in the courtyard, to the flickering shadows formed by the lanterns made her itch inside her skin.

Kerym's visit replayed in her mind. His soft words of praise, his touch, his kiss. She wrapped her cloak around herself tighter to beat away the chill that accompanied the memory. She had not stopped shaking since climbing out of the bath.

When she'd started down the hill, it had been with a vague notion of going to Lake Faala. To sit along its placid shores and watch the moon reflected off the water. Perhaps listen to the owls calling to one another from their places nestled in the surrounding trees. But her two feet had minds of their own and soon she found herself at the outer wall of the city.

The guards were far more concerned with keeping people out than in. So no one stopped her, or even looked twice, as she walked out of the gate and into another world.

While the city slept, the community that had sprung up outside of it was alive. Globe lights with candles had been strung up along the main pathway and larger pit fires raged every few hundred paces. The night was chilly and the earth damp, but that did not slow anyone down.

Everywhere there were singers singing and dancers dancing; laughter peppered the darkness as did the rowdy cheers of the drunk and raucous. Zeli had thought the Magister's political dinners were wild when some of the Ephors imbibed too heartily on wine and spirits, but she revised her opinion. She'd never seen anything inside the city even a fraction as unrestrained as this.

Life was lived out here in the margins of respectability, at least by the standards of the favored. She walked the makeshift streets in awe. Artists painted and crafted by firelight. A female blacksmith hammered on a square of dark metal. Jewelry makers hawked their wares and she even spotted someone selling handwoven bracelets, much like the ones she made.

There were far more women than men, and many more children than she'd realized. The younger ones scampered around in small gangs, while adolescents apprenticed at the food carts and pottery makers and cartwrights. These people were poor, but industrious, crafting something out of nothing in the most surprising ways.

As she walked along with no destination in mind, she passed several musicians, but a familiar voice drew her closer to one of them. A griot, the same woman who'd been at the Magister's the other night, sat near a fire pit, capturing the attention of her rapt audience. She sat with her *luda* on her lap, strumming a fast, jaunty melody, her silvery voice, bell-clear and full-throated.

> "Well the Shadowfox came into my town, to see what he could see,
>> He saw the dry grass, the fields burned to ash,
>> But he won't see a hair of me, no, no,
>> He won't see a hair of me."

Listeners smiled, clapped, and nodded along, many mouthing along with the words. Griots would often change familiar songs to make them their own, though many of the lines were kept the same.

> "The Shadowfox knelt down in the dirt, the soil was yellow-brown,
>> I watched him dip down, deep into the ground,
>> And pull the salt right into his hand, yes, yes,
>> He pulled the salt right into his hand."

Zeli had heard this one. Usually, she turned away whenever it was sung, unwilling to be a part of such a subversive act as listening to a song about the Keepers. The old pain of her parents' deaths had never left her, it simply made a home just below the surface and emerged at inopportune times.

> "Magister came around the next day, he heard the echoed cries,
> Now the people rejoiced, their joy had a voice
> And they sang on into the night, oh, how,
> They sang on into the night."

This storyteller didn't know the Shadowfox, had no idea what kind of man he was. Probably didn't personally know any Keepers at all. But Zeli remembered the quiet boy her parents had sheltered for a few days. Two elders had come to the door late one night, a sharp-cheeked boy in tow. Zeli had been roused from her bed, had given it up to their visitor, and slept between her parents until the elders returned and spirited him away again.

Her parents hadn't confirmed the boy's identity, but whispers that the Shadowfox had planted a field just outside the Snarl arose after he'd left. She'd put two and two together, surprised at the time that someone so powerful could be so young. Just a teenager. A few months later, her home received another late-night visit.

This time, instead of soft-voice elders, it was Enforcers kicking in the door. Screaming, guns pointed, chains and ropes binding her. Her future never the same.

Her chest panged, the emptiness of the space where her Song should be was more pronounced tonight.

Did she blame the Keepers? The Shadowfox? Well, why shouldn't she? Whether it was sheltering him that had brought her family down or some other treasonous act, it didn't matter.

Her parents had chosen their revolution, their stupid, stupid rebellion over her.

She looked up, startled to find tears streaming down her cheeks. The griot went on and on, with verse after verse of how the Shadowfox healed people, saved them from tribute, and was in turn rewarded by the love of the people. Many would seek to pay him back by setting out food and drink for him that would be gone in the morning, or leaving blankets and spare clothing in a barn or stable. The song made him sound like a mythical spirit, not a man at all. When the singer finished, the crowd applauded.

Zeli tried to imagine the heroic figure the others saw, but couldn't. All she could see was the door smashed in and her mother screaming wildly.

"What about the ones who get caught?" Startled faces turned Zeli's way and she realized she was the one who'd spoken.

The griot peered at her silently, head tilted to the side in question.

"Do you have any songs about the Keepers who are sent to the platform on Mercy Day? Ropes draped around their necks. The ones punished for their crimes. The families torn apart by the Keepers' selfishness? Ripped out of their mothers' arms in the middle of the night?"

Zeli backed away from the crowd, heart drumming wildly. "Sing about that, why don't you? Sing something that means something."

Many in the audience looked at her pitifully, others with anger. She'd broken an unspoken rule in their land, talked of the misery that everyone gathered here was desperately trying to forget. Broken her own rule, actually, pushed over the edge by emotions she couldn't name or control. But the anger simmering beneath the surface had finally found a way to break free.

Two older men approached her, their expressions menacing. Shakily, she stepped back again, fear bleeding through the rage. She was all alone in a strange place with unfriendly people.

She stumbled, legs unsteady, vision blurry. From behind, arms reached for her—she flashed back to the revival, the hand around her ankle, her struggling in vain. Her limbs hardened to iron, ready to fight, ready to die if she had to rather than be captured again. She wished she had the strength to stop others from manhandling her—from handling her at all.

But strong hands turned her around. She tensed until she found herself staring up into the grim face of Fakera, the woman she'd met in the market.

"Come with me child," Fakera said. She gathered Zeli close, gently this time, and sent a glare behind her, to the men who'd formed a barrier between them and the crowd.

Numb now and pliable, Zeli allowed Fakera to lead her all the way back to a covered wagon near the wall. No one followed. Inside, the space was warm and bright, with no source of heat or light visible. Woven tapestries hung on the walls and thick, worn cushions padded the floor.

A teakettle sat on a square of metal in the corner. Baskets and clay pots lined the floor.

"Drink this," she said, holding out a steaming cup of tea. There was no stove or fire, and Zeli looked at it suspiciously.

"You think I'd poison you, *uli*? Drink it."

She reluctantly accepted. The brew was sweet and felt good going down her throat. A soft tingle swept over her, and she felt her raw emotions soothe.

"No spells," Zeli said, defensive. "I don't want it."

Fakera shrugged. "You worked yourself into a frenzy. You need to calm down." But the tingling residue of magic stopped.

Zeli took a deep breath. "Thank you."

The woman nodded, her heavy eyes looking even more weighed down than the first time they'd met. No one spoke for a long time. Not until Zeli finished her tea did she break the silence again. "You knew my parents?"

Fakera's lips curved sadly. "We all did. Brave people. Highly respected. They accepted dangerous assignments because they believed that resistance is the only way to truly live." She shook her head. "When they were gone, Gladda took on the job of keeping an eye on you. For their sake. Yarrink and Sefa saved my life. Saved many lives. More than once. You should know that."

"Not my life," Zeli breathed. "They left me behind. They chose the Keepers over me."

Fakera swallowed, her expression tormented. "This path is one of sacrifice. Sometimes we give up more than we expect."

The words did nothing to assuage Zeli's pain. It was a cold, hard ball surrounding her heart.

"Gladda-deni brings you food. Why?"

The woman's gaze sharpened. "The Magister's food stores hold more than he needs. The excess is distributed. Some to those here, some to those going over the mountains."

"Why would you tell me this? You don't know me enough to trust."

"Don't I?" Fakera raised her hand and the kettle moved, under its own power, across the room to her side. She refilled her cup and raised her eyebrows at Zeli, who shook her head.

"How do you do that?"

"Air currents," she said simply.

Zeli didn't recall having been able to control air currents using her Song. Or heat tea. Perhaps she hadn't been very strong. "Gladda didn't trust me." She crossed her arms.

"She didn't tell you what you weren't ready to hear."

"And now I'm ready to hear it?"

"Why did you come out here tonight? It's quite a long way from your estate."

Zeli's lips snapped shut. The thought of the estate eroded whatever calm she'd begun to feel here. "This world is a lie," she muttered.

Fakera leaned forward, a strange glint in her eye. "Yes, yes, it is." At Zeli's surprise, she snorted. "Did you think I would disagree with you? All of this, everything the True Father has built here *is* a lie. A very old and very entrenched one. And once your eyes are opened"—she turned her hand palm up to reveal a glowing ball of light hovering over it—"it's very hard to close them again."

"I don't know what to do now."

"What do you want to do?"

She thought of Kerym's offer, her dream. Without it, what did she have left? And even if she accepted, what was to keep her from being sent away to the work camps for some manufactured crime? She was lost without a shiny side to find under all the tarnish.

But there was still hope for the girls. "You're helping lead people over the mountain? Through the cracks in the Mantle?"

Fakera nodded.

"What kind of people?"

"Anyone who wants to go." She tilted her head. "Do you . . . ?"

"No, not me," she said emphatically. She still couldn't fathom life in a foreign land. "But . . . there's a girl. Two girls really. One still has her Song. Maybe . . ." She looked down.

"Our last group is headed over at dawn. If you get the children ready, Gladda will know how to find us. We've helped many to keep their Songs. And we've helped many without them." She looked at Zeli significantly.

Zeli mulled over the idea of leaving Lagrimar and taking a chance on the unknown in Elsira. The hard little ball around her heart felt like a weight she'd never be able to shed.

Tana and Ulani slept in a tiny alcove just outside of Devana's suite, out of the way of the business of the rest of the estate. Zeli crept up and shook Tana.

The girl sat up sharply, appearing instantly awake. "What's wrong?" Her hands were curled into fists, gripping the pallet they slept on.

"Nothing, everything's all right. But you two must come with me."

"We're leaving?" Ulani asked, groggily wiping her eyes.

"Yes. Kerym-mideni is planning to tell the Magister about your Song and . . ." Zeli shook her head in frustration. She couldn't put into words exactly why it was so important for this one girl to keep her Song. Whether it was the old pain of losing hers or the terrifying journey to the capital, she wasn't sure. But she couldn't bear it if Ulani was stripped of her power.

"Grab your things and let's go," she said.

The girls donned their tunics quickly. Neither had anything more they wanted to bring although Devana had gifted them a number of beautiful things.

"Are you sure you want to leave the clothing and jewelry behind?" Zeli asked.

"We didn't want them," Ulani said.

"They're hers, not ours," Tana added, voice clipped.

Zeli shrugged and led them into the courtyard, walking slowly and quietly. This late at night it was doubtful they would run into anyone, but just in case, explaining what they were all doing would be difficult.

They entered the kitchen, which was lit only by the glow of embers shining through the grates in the oven door. Seeing the normally bustling room so silent and empty was eerie. Zeli's fear ratcheted up a notch when the shadows in the corner began to move. She moved in front of the girls protectively, then relaxed as Gladda's face became visible.

"Are you all ready?" the woman whispered.

"Where are we going?" Ulani asked.

Zeli crouched down to speak to her. "Gladda-deni knows the Keepers. They will take you two over the mountains and into Elsira. Many people are fleeing Lagrimar, seeking better lives. Your Song will be safe there. I've heard the whole land is like Laketown, green and beautiful." Her eyes stung but she was determined not to cry.

"You're not coming with us?" Ulani said, her lip beginning to quiver.

"No, *uli*," she said, pulling her in for a hug. "I . . . There's nothing there for me. But you will both be safe."

Tana bristled. "What do you mean there's nothing there for you? What's *here* for you?"

Zeli swallowed, unwilling to meet the girl's eye. "Kerym-mideni has offered . . ." She cleared her throat. "I'll have a position here. He says Devana-mideni will return, and I think he's right. One day he will be Magister and he is . . . He's said he will take care of me."

She finally drew her head up to face Tana, whose dark eyes flashed. "He's a liar."

"You don't understand—"

"We're not going without you." Ulani crossed her arms, for once looking as stubborn as her sister. Tana mimicked the action, glaring.

"You both need to leave here. You won't be alone, the Keepers will protect you."

"We won't be alone because you're coming with us," Tana said, with more steel in her voice than an eleven-year-old should be capable of.

"It's safer for you if I stay. I don't think they'll look for you, but just in case—"

"Do you love him?" Ulani asked, looking up at her guilelessly.

Zeli sank back on her heels. A chill went through her at the memory of Kerym's kiss. "No."

"Then why stay for him?"

She shook her head. How could she explain to them what she was feeling? The uncertainty, the terror, the longing for something more? Then she looked into Ulani's questioning gaze and Tana's young-old eyes and realized the truth. These two, young as they were, could understand.

"I'm scared," she admitted, voice quivering. "This is all I've ever known. I don't have . . ." She motioned between the two of them. "I don't have anyone watching out for me." Tears streamed down her face.

Gladda's warm hand clamped down on her shoulder, then

slid to her back, rubbing soothing circles. "You've always had people watching out for you."

Zeli wiped her eyes. "You are all braver than me."

Ulani reached for her hand and squeezed. "We can be brave enough for you, too."

Zeli's heart hurt. The pain radiated out in rippling waves. She couldn't break down now, they didn't have the time, but a pull started, weak at first and then stronger. A pull toward the unknown. "I—"

"Shh." Gladda raised a finger to her lips. Outside the door, soft footsteps crunched lightly on the walkway. She must have ears like a bat to have been able to hear it.

Gladda tiptoed to the window and peeked through the break in the shutter. Zeli eased to her side.

"Kerym-mideni," the woman mouthed, and ice froze Zeli's veins.

Was he looking for her again? What else would he be doing at this time of night? And what would he do if he didn't find her? When the footsteps passed, she turned to the others. "You all, go. Now. If Kerym-mideni is looking for me and thinks something is wrong he could start searching."

"I doubt he'd awaken the household in the middle of the night," Gladda said, frowning.

"We don't know why he's here," Zeli insisted. "You all *must* leave. Now."

Gladda nodded, worry creasing her brow, but Zeli couldn't go along if she thought Kerym might be looking for her. Or even worse, what if he discovered Gladda and the girls leaving in the middle of the night? No, she had to stay and distract him, or at least make sure he didn't discover the others before they were safe.

The thought made her convulse with dread, but it was more important that the girls get away.

Gladda looked grim. "Fine. We're taking the path around the lake to meet up with my contact at dawn. Then the Keepers will take us all over the mountain."

"You're going with them?" Zeli asked, encouraged.

"Yes, it's time to leave this place. Nothing good can come from staying." Her words were pointed. "I expect to see you at dawn."

Zeli pursed her lips then looked back to the girls. They both appeared poised to protest, so she relented. "Fine, I'll be there by dawn."

"Do you promise?" Ulani asked.

Regret and shame filled her. "I promise," she said, and shooed them all on their way. She hated to lie, but saw no other option.

What was it Fakera had said about sacrifice? *Sometimes we give up more than we expect.* Maybe she was more like her parents than she ever thought. She wondered if they would be proud.

CHAPTER FORTY-TWO

The Scorpion foretasted happiness
Like vengeance it's a meal best eaten cold
And for her faith she paid a pretty price
A bargain which few knew, and fewer told
Our promises were made for us to keep
A debt's due even if the cost is steep

—THE BOOK OF UNVEILING

Early morning sunshine stabbed through the shutters illuminating the planes of Darvyn's face. Kyara traced the edges of his lips, humming in satisfaction.

He smiled under her fingertips, and she laughed—a sound so unfamiliar. A weight had been lifted from her. Happiness was lighter than she'd ever imagined. The moment was breached by the growling of her stomach. They had spent hours in each other's arms, but now practical matters needed to be addressed.

"What are the chances that the sackers left any food behind?" Darvyn asked.

"None. But the market is close. I'll go and bring us something back."

Darvyn sat up, his easy smile fading. "I'll go with you."

She shook her head. "The soldiers are looking—"

"For both of us. They're looking for both of us. And after what you did to Aren when we escaped the castle, you may be a higher priority than me now."

She snorted. "I didn't know you were conscious for that."

"Barely." His smile returned; he cupped her cheek. "We go together."

She leaned forward until her forehead met his. "Fine. But you should disguise yourself."

She kept stealing looks at him from the corner of her eye. Her handsome, diamond-eyed rebel had become a shadow of his former self. Darvyn had transformed into a man of the same height and weight, but that's where the similarities ended.

Deep acne scars pockmarked his face. His eyes were small and deep set beneath a heavy brow ridge. A single eyebrow connected in the middle. He was frankly horrifying. She was having a hard time tearing her eyes away.

They'd liberated an elaborately embroidered mourning veil from the laundry line of a Windy Hill payroller. The fabric and lace hid Kyara completely from view. It also kept her remarkably cool in the stifling heat.

The market was clogged with shoppers. Men and women shouted, haggled, and jostled one another, trading grams or ration tokens for their supplies.

An old woman's fry cart was Darvyn and Kyara's first stop. They purchased two hand pies each—fresh from the vat of oil bubbling on the portable grill. Kyara burned her fingertips when she tried to steal a taste. Darvyn laughed as she blew on her fingers. But he sobered quickly, gazing through the crowd.

A flash of black amidst a sea of earth tones hardened Kyara's spine. Golden Flames.

"I know he's nearby." Aren's voice made her stomach roil. The appetizing smell of the pies was now repulsive. "Search every stall, every alleyway until you find him."

How had Aren found them so quickly?

Black-clad figures spread like insects through the rows of merchants. Darvyn grabbed her hand and squeezed. All they had to do was act naturally. She and Darvyn just needed to not call attention to themselves and make their escape calmly.

The rows of vendors surrounded a small square of dirt where a towering statue of the True Father stood, looming. These statues were everywhere in Sayya, a reminder that the immortal king was always watching.

Aren climbed the base of the statue—a defacement usually punishable by death. But the additional height allowed him to peer down at the marketplace. He pulled something from his pocket, and Kyara cursed.

"What is it?" Darvyn asked.

"He's got a pair of spectacles. We have to get you out of here now."

She grabbed his arm and turned on her heel, pulling him

down the row. Other shoppers had the same idea and were all heading away now, fleeing the market. The sight of Golden Flames was enough to make them abandon their shopping.

Ydaris's presence at the warehouse the night before became more clear. She must be getting these amalgamation objects from Raal and had given one to Aren. That was how he'd captured Darvyn at the army base.

Half a dozen stalls ahead of them, the path was blocked by two Flames Kyara recognized. She reached for her Song, knowing it was useless. With this many people around and without a huge store of Nethersong, she wouldn't be able to control it. If she used her power, she wasn't sure she could pull back and keep from killing whoever was closest to her in the crowd, including Darvyn.

Suddenly, both soldiers dropped. She looked at Darvyn with surprise and he grinned. Of course, the Shadowfox could take care of himself.

"Bring the prisoners," Aren yelled, his voice amplified. Kyara chanced a glance over her shoulder to find Aren holding a speaking trumpet to his lips.

When a small figure was pushed up onto the statue's base, Darvyn jerked to a stop. Aren grabbed the young woman's bound hands before she wobbled and fell.

"Meldi," Darvyn whispered.

Squinting, Kyara recognized the woman from the Keeper's safe house. "She's the one who betrayed you?"

Though Darvyn's face was foreign, she was very familiar with the expression he wore—hard eyes glittering, jaw locked, mouth firmed.

"Would the Keepers have turned her in?" Kyara wondered.

"No. Our justice is our own. She must have been caught

somehow." His voice was unemotional, but pain flashed in his eyes.

Aren's voice sounded tinny through the metal device pressed to his lips. "The Shadowfox cannot resist aiding a cripple."

A smug satisfaction grew in Kyara. They were trying to appeal to Shadowfox's loyalty; little did they know it had been destroyed. At least where Meldi was concerned.

She continued moving, pulling Darvyn forward. They were only steps from the end of the row when Aren's taunting voice called out again. "Or perhaps this youth will tug on the fugitive's heartstrings."

Something told her not to look. Not to let Darvyn look. But she could stop neither of them. The sight of the second prisoner brought to the platform made her blood freeze.

Farron stood, held in the clutches of Aren's lackey, Dalgo. The boy's lip was split and his eye blackened. The ruby red of a collar glinted around his neck.

Darvyn's grip on her hand tightened. She wrenched his arm back, trying to drag him away. "You go. I'll get Farron," she said through clenched teeth. But he shook his head. "Darvyn, if you get caught—"

Aren's maniacal laugh tore her gaze back to the platform. Now he was looking right at them, the glass from the spectacles glinting in the sun.

"How powerful is the Shadowfox now?"

Slowly, Aren raised his pistol to Meldi's head. The woman's eyes grew wide; tears leaked down her cheeks, but Kyara felt no sympathy.

Darvyn responded to Aren's threat by straightening his shoulders. He raised his chin as his disguise fell away, revealing a scowl.

Kyara's Song paced its cage, sensing the danger and eager to be let out. The blood spell no longer prevented her from harming Aren, but there were so many innocents here. She had never been able to control her power in a crowd. Too many people, too close together. She removed her veil, taking a stand with Darvyn out in the open even as dread made her heartbeat stutter.

Farron searched the crowd. When he caught sight of Darvyn, he glared, shaking his head. Dalgo freed his pistol and held it to the boy's head, a perverse smile bending the soldier's lips.

A dark part of Kyara hoped that Aren shot Meldi, releasing a store of Nethersong that would let her control her Song. When Meldi pitched forward, for a moment Kyara thought her malicious wish had been granted, but no Nethersong flooded her. The traitor had just fainted.

Aren huffed in annoyance. He dropped Meldi and pushed Dalgo out of the way before pointing his pistol at Farron. Darvyn grew more rigid beside her. Meldi would be no great loss, but Farron was another story. Kyara, too, had a soft spot for the teen.

Her fingers itched for the knife in her boot. She needed Nethersong, and there were two Golden Flames coming toward them, pacing down the row. No one would miss either of them. Once they were within striking distance, she could act.

Darvyn took a step forward as Farron struggled against his bonds.

"No!" Farron cried. "The True Father will get your Song. You can't let him!"

Kyara's heart tore as sorrow filled Darvyn's eyes. "I can't watch you die for me," he called out to Farron. "I won't."

Aren pressed the barrel of the gun hard against Farron's temple.

"Put Aren to sleep," she whispered, trying not to move her lips.

Darvyn shook his head and jerked his chin up toward the rooftops surrounding the market square. She'd been so focused on the prisoners, she hadn't noticed a ring of soldiers had surrounded them, rifles trained on the market.

"You know the playbook, Kyara," Aren's voice rang out. "If either of you use your power against me or my men, the snipers will start shooting. They'll target the civilians first."

Cowering shoppers and vendors around them gasped. Fear made the air stink.

Once again Kyara considered her power. With a single death, could she lash out more quickly than a bullet? A few casualties of war could save them all. Would the losses be worth it, to save the Shadowfox?

"No, Kyara," Darvyn said, as if he could read her thoughts. "Nobody else dies for me."

Her lip quivered at the finality in his voice. She shook her head. She was the Poison Flame. There were songs sung about her deadliness. And now, when it mattered, could she let the one man she cared about sacrifice everything?

His jaw was hard, but his eyes pleaded with her. The guilt in them called her name. Was she strong enough to give him this? Did she love him enough to respect his wish?

The thought of losing him shook her. He squeezed her hand, wanting her agreement.

Finally she exhaled a ragged breath. "No one else dies."

He nodded once, then released her. She was bereft without his touch.

He stalked forward as the crowd parted. Did they know who

they were making way for? Did they know how many times this man had saved them?

She followed in his wake, feeling out of her body, like she was watching from high above and these were other people headed toward their doom. People she didn't care about. People she didn't love.

The thought made her knees feel like jelly. Her heart shook just as hard.

Darvyn approached the statue, ignoring Farron's cries for him to run and save himself. When he was close enough, Dalgo raised a collar and snapped it around his neck.

Kyara fell to her knees, a scream shredding her throat.

Two Flames bound Darvyn's hands behind him. Aren jumped from the platform and punched him in the face, a feral gleam in his eye. Then he pulled a tiny red stone from his pocket and wiped it in the blood seeping from Darvyn's split lip.

"Speak." Ydaris's voice was clear and impatient.

"It's done. We have them both."

"Kyara ul-Lagrimar." Kyara's wound pulsed at the voice. "Return to the castle immediately and harm no one on your way here."

The pain flared, and Kyara's head fell. No shackles or chains were needed to bind her. The manacles holding Darvyn were enough.

She wasn't sure she had anything left to fight for.

CHAPTER FORTY-THREE

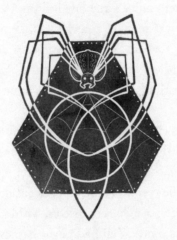

Surrendering desire for duty's yoke
Marks those whose characters others will heed
When making wishes on faraway stars
An open heart will transmit every need
And though the long separation will burn
A stranger is a friend when they return

—THE BOOK OF UNVEILING

Zeli ran across the dimly lit pathways that were as familiar to her as her own skin. She was headed to Devana's suite, where Kerym had found her last, hoping to head him off, when she saw one of the two doors in the Magister's building cracked open, light spilling out.

That was an odd enough sight that she froze, listening for

anything that didn't fit. A creak sounded, and she slipped behind a support post, cloaking herself in shadow.

Kerym ran out of the Magister's building, through the door next to the master's office—the one leading to his bedchamber. The young man was moving as swiftly and quietly as a cat. Instead of heading toward Devana's rooms, he darted away from them, back toward the kitchen and, presumably, the estate's exit. Zeli held her breath hoping Gladda had gotten the girls away in time.

For Kerym to visit the Magister's personal chamber was unheard of. Especially in the middle of the night. He hadn't been there long enough to chat, and the Magister never left his door open like that. She crept forward to peek inside, the strange series of events plucking strings of discord within her.

Much like his office, Zeli had never had cause to be in the Magister's chamber before. The large space was illuminated by candles, instead of electric lighting. Papers were spread over an enormous bed in the center of the room, a four-posted monstrosity, which took up most of the space. Apparently he'd been reading. And now?

Now, he lay gasping for breath, the handle of a knife protruding from his chest.

Zeli's lungs emptied. She covered her mouth with a shaking hand and wobbled on her feet, air rushing in her ears.

The Magister's broad chest was bare; blood poured across it, mingling with the tightly coiled hair. For the first time, he seemed human. Perhaps because he was dying.

The blade had been plunged into his left side. His gasping breaths began to quiet as the life flowed out of him. The gateway to the World After was very close. Zeli blinked rapidly, her feet unable to move forward or back.

A small figure streaked past, darting into the room. Zeli startled as Ulani raced to the Magister's bedside.

"Ulani, no!" Zeli whispered, holding a hand out as if to stop her, but remaining rooted in place, still horrified by the sight before her. The girl climbed up on the large mattress and placed one hand on the man's chest, the other on the knife handle. She pulled, but the thing wouldn't budge.

She looked back, eyes wide and pleading for help. Zeli shook the shock off and approached cautiously. Ulani was going to try and heal him. Perhaps it wasn't too late. That possibility loosened the grip of terror and shock.

She rushed forward and gripped the knife handle, adding her strength to the effort to remove it. The blade was stuck, perhaps in bone, but they kept pulling. Finally, it gave and slipped out, the wound gushing over with blood.

And just as quickly, the flow ended. The gaping wound closed before her eyes. The Magister's quiet, ragged breathing normalized. His eyes slowly fluttered open.

Ulani sat back, breathing heavily, a sheen of sweat on her brow. For the first time, Zeli realized how strong the girl's Song must be. Healing a mortal wound was a difficult task for any Singer, much less a small child, barely trained.

The Magister sat up, running a hand over his chest. Blood still slicked his skin; he looked at his red palm with wonder. Zeli held her breath; here she sat next to the most powerful man in the city, his blood still covering her hands.

His stunned gaze went first to Zeli, and then Ulani. The angry scar over his eye was pronounced in the flickering candle-light. Did he know what had happened? And if not, would they be able to outrun his rage?

He opened his mouth then closed it, looking unsure of

himself for the first time, maybe ever. Finally, he bowed his head and took a deep breath.

"You used Earthsong to heal me?" His voice was a deep growl.

Ulani's eyes widened. She looked at Zeli with panic.

"Yes, mideni," Zeli replied, wrapping a protective arm around the girl. She readied herself to run.

He raised his head, gaze solemn. "You have my gratitude. Both of you."

Relief overwhelmed her. She wasn't sure how much he'd been conscious of as he lay dying, but at least he knew that neither of them had tried to kill him.

The Magister picked up the knife at his side and inspected it. "Stabbed by my own blade." He snorted. Rough fingers skated over the engravings in the blade's hilt, a detailed design portraying the lake and trees.

"I admired the young man's ambition, but I should have been more wary of it. Yalisa tried to warn me." He chuckled humorlessly. "And look where it got her. You saw him? Kerym?"

Zeli nodded. Her whole body still felt shaky and loose.

"Well, you will be the last person who ever shall, besides me," he said through a low rumble in his chest.

A small piece of her heart cracked knowing that Kerym would not survive this night. But a new, cynical voice in her head whispered this was the last of her innocence chipping away. She would have to leave behind childish dreams now and keep her feet firmly planted. She would have to save herself.

The Magister abruptly stood, towering over the both of them. Zeli got to her feet, pulling Ulani with her. "Your actions have saved my life," he said. "I owe you a debt."

Zeli was incredulous. "N-no need, mideni."

"You have shown loyalty to my family, to my daughter—misguided as she is—and to myself. I have elevated men to favored status for far less worthy reasons."

She couldn't believe it. He was offering to elevate her? And not even as a mistress, but in her own right. Everything she'd ever dreamed. It was right here, in front of her fingertips.

Ulani squeezed her hand. Zeli looked down into round, two-toned brown eyes full of hope and something more . . . Trust.

Zeli swallowed and bowed her head again. "You are gracious, mideni. But I ask nothing in return. Life is sacred and it was not your time to meet the World After. May we greet one another again." She folded herself into a bow, and Ulani did as well. Then they left the room, hand in hand, walking swiftly away from the bloodied warrior preparing his revenge.

Outside, they quickened their pace to a near run until they had breached the estate's gate.

"How did you know to come?" she asked Ulani.

"You cannot lie to an Earthsinger, Zeli-yul," the girl said sweetly.

Zeli shook her head, and they raced into the night to where Gladda and Tana were waiting.

"Where to now?" Darvyn asked. The Golden Flames had shuttled him to the glass castle, where a pair of royal guards had taken over. He didn't expect either of the grim-faced men to answer, but the one on his left surprised him.

"Tribute," he said, something close to an apology in his voice.

The Keepers had feared this day since they discovered the true extent of Darvyn's power. What would the True Father do after stealing Darvyn's Song? Once the Mantle fell, he could easily take over the world. The king had not displayed his power in many years, relying instead on the Cantor's magic for daily operations. Instead, it was believed he hoarded power, preferring to have rather than use the stolen Songs.

The people were effectively cowed by the terrors the king had once wrought on the populace. There were enough old stories to maintain their submission. The army and the Collectors, the tributes and rations merely kept the people downtrodden. Tales whispered with fearful voices reminded them that life could be so much worse.

But Darvyn could only live with so much loss. He was not sure he could have recovered from being responsible for Farron's death. A broken Shadowfox was of no help to his people. Then again, neither was one without his Song, and no one had ever escaped a tribute.

They stopped before a nondescript door at the end of a narrow hallway. Both guards tensed, looking on Darvyn with pity. They had once been in his position, standing before this door, waiting, the same as most other adult Lagrimari.

The guard who'd spoken to him rapped on the door three times. It opened, apparently by its own force, revealing a small, dimly lit room. The only furniture inside was a low, stone table. With a nudge, Darvyn was pushed across the threshold and the door closed behind him.

A sharp-faced attendant in a floor-length white robe stood facing Darvyn in the tribute room. The man's hair matched his robe, and the uncombed white tufts stuck out, giving him a comical appearance not at all in line with his grim expression.

"Lie on the table," the man said, his voice creaking with age.

Even collared, Darvyn was certain he could overpower the

elder, but then what? Armed guards awaited him on the other side of the door. Another door stood on the opposite side of the room. Carved into it was a man-sized spider hanging from the limb of a tree. The spider's eyes were rubies, glittering in the lamplight. Looking on them gave him a strange feeling, like the gems could see him, or perhaps someone was watching through them. But the door had no handle.

"On the table," the elderly attendant repeated as he placed a firm hand on Darvyn's shoulder.

He shook the hand off, unwilling to make this run smoothly.

The man simply shrugged. "You will sleep now." Darvyn jerked as the attendant produced a vial from the billowing sleeve of his robe and uncorked it. Almost immediately, Darvyn's body slackened, overcome with exhaustion. He collapsed onto the floor, his limbs too heavy to lift.

He fought against the unconsciousness, knowing that on the other side of this laid the end of his Song.

Forever.

Just before his vision faded and the dim glow of the room was lost, his Song broke free of its bonds. It surged inside him, eager and relieved like a long-lost friend coming home. The collar was gone. The old man must have removed it, believing Darvyn to be asleep. But his newly freed Song immediately began fighting against the sleeping drug, counteracting its effects.

He was trapped at the edge of consciousness—his body not yet under his control, but his mind clear. Clear enough to hear the carved door scrape open. The footsteps of the attendant shuffled out of the room, and new footsteps replaced them, crossing to where Darvyn lay.

He struggled to pry his eyelids apart so he could see what was happening, but was still not in full control of his Song or his body. Earthsong controlled by someone else lifted his body onto the table.

"Your Song is mighty, Darvyn ol-Tahlyro." The voice sounded from over the top of his head. Its rasp was like the fall of leaves onto jagged blades. "I have not had one so strong in many years." Smug satisfaction echoed through the king's abrading tone.

Darvyn willed his muscles to move, but they would not obey. His connection to Earthsong was there, but he had never before faced such an obstacle. This went beyond the drug that he should have been able to fight off easily. Something far more powerful was determined to bend Darvyn's senses to its will. The thunderous presence tried to draw him under.

How could Earthsong be used in such a way? It shouldn't have been possible. Some corruption had to have taken hold—the True Father's power was tainted. Darvyn felt as though he were being toyed with, batted around like a cat with a mouse. At any moment he could be crushed.

A brush of air whispered over Darvyn's bare chest. He managed to pry one eye open just enough to see a glittering, gloved hand bearing a white blade—just like Ydaris's—hovering above his chest. The point of the knife descended slowly until it pierced his skin.

He could not control his mouth or throat in order to scream. He could only watch as the knife plunged into his body.

CHAPTER FORTY-FOUR

Sufficient motivation moves all men,
And women struggle no less for their woes.
When faced with threats to keenly guarded joy,
both find the strength to battle hated foes.
The warrior who fights for love is bound
by no impediment heretofore found

—THE BOOK OF UNVEILING

Aren's grip on Kyara's arm was meant to hurt. He led her through the castle and to the dungeon himself instead of tasking one of the guards. She was sure he had something horrible and painful in store once she was locked in the cell; she only hoped the numbness that had started in her heart and spread to all her extremities would hold.

Ydaris's command for her not to harm anyone held. If she could lash out at anyone, Aren would be the perfect victim.

A vein bulged in his forehead as he dragged her down the steps. Some sense of self-preservation awoke in her and had her paying attention to the surroundings. She couldn't let herself get caught alone with Aren. The dungeon guards would ignore her screams and whatever he planned would be, judging by the mad glint in his eye, long and brutal.

They turned the corner into a dim hallway lined with iron bars. Aren jerked to a stop at the figure blocking his way.

"Mistress." He dropped his head deferentially at Ydaris's cool stare.

"Thank you, Aren. I'll take it from here." Her voice was ice.

Kyara nearly gasped in relief when Aren's merciless fingers left her arm. He shot her a glare full of daggers before stomping away.

Ydaris made no move to open a cell. Kyara looked around finding it odd that there were no guards present. No prisoners, either, at least not in this row.

"He's being taken to tribute," the Cantor said in a voice almost too low to hear.

"No," Kyara whispered, the last of her numbness fading away into heartache.

"I have waited fifty years for this day, moving all the pieces into place, and I will not see all of my efforts spoiled because of one man. I am getting out of this backwater borough, and you are going to help me."

Kyara swallowed as a chill went through her. Ydaris's anger was usually a calm thing, her cruelty unemotional, but today she was different. Rage bubbled beneath the surface.

"The keystone is now complete. The Mantle will be destroyed tomorrow at dawn. Once the True Father siphons your rebel's Song and crosses the breach into Elsira, he will easily overwhelm any force arrayed against him. He will have enough power to conquer this continent."

Ydaris's fingers worried the neckline of her gown, skimming across her collarbone to the necklace she wore. "I would stop him myself, but . . ." A rueful smile crossed her lips. She pulled down the top of her dress to reveal a twisted mass of scarring on her breastbone. As Kyara had long suspected, the Cantor also bore a blood spell. "While he is in power, I am still bound."

"Y-you want me to stop the True Father?" Kyara's voice wavered, the impossibility of going against the immortal king locking her in place. "How?"

"With this." She unclasped the gold chain at her neck and pulled off one of two pendants that hung there. The small, bronze medallion she kept, but removed an oval golden locket. Once she'd reaffixed her chain, Ydaris fished a length of cord from a pocket and held both locket and cord to Kyara.

"It's an amalgam. It holds Nethersong. Enough for you to save your rebel."

Kyara was drawn to the necklace. It called to her, whispering of power in the same way the warehouse had. She plucked it from Ydaris's hand and immediately felt the Nethersong within energizing her. The ache of the wound disappeared as a raw force flowed through her veins. It was a potent drug, like the bitter herbs the women of the cabal smoked in pipes. Only Kyara felt electric and vibrant, not lazy and dull. Accepting a gift of this kind from Ydaris felt wrong, but Kyara had no wish to give the locket back.

"Do whatever you must, but do not allow the Shadowfox to give tribute," Ydaris said. "Save him."

She echoed the words Murmur had used not long ago. Save Darvyn. Of course Kyara wanted to save him, she would do anything for him, but how could she single-handedly stop the True Father?

When Kyara would have questioned her, Ydaris leveled her with a gaze. "We do not have much time."

Kyara's petrified limbs came to life. She tied the cord around her neck with jerky movements, uncertain of how to accomplish the monumental task before her.

"Now!" Ydaris screamed.

Kyara took off running from the dungeon. She raced up the steps spurred on by Ydaris's urgency. The hallways were quiet, but when she encountered a couple of guards, she knocked them out with little more than a thought. The exhilaration of the locket thrilled her.

She came upon another pair of guards, this time bearing a prisoner. They moved slowly to accommodate the young woman's limping gait. Meldi, the traitor. When the lead man noticed her, Kyara felt no qualms about rendering the entire party unconscious. They fell to the ground in a heap as she ran on.

However, the next duo of guards she encountered gave her pause. They held Farron between them, chained and defiant. Kyara let out the barest trickle of power and the older guards bent over, vomiting. Farron winced and grabbed his stomach, but thanks to his youth, whatever he'd eaten today stayed put.

"Grab their keys," she hissed. Looking a bit green, Farron complied and kicked one of the men into a pool of his own sick before handing her the key ring.

"Find the Keepers you trust," she said, unlocking his shackles. "I'm going to go free Darvyn."

"I can help!"

"No." She grabbed his wrist. "I can't risk having you too near my power. Trust me. But if I get him out of this, we'll need a way out of the city. Find help and meet near the West Gate as soon as you can. You have to hurry."

He nodded and turned to go, then looked back. "*When* you get him out. Not if." He held her gaze for a moment before taking off at a sprint.

Kyara rubbed a hand down her face and began running again until she reached the feared place where the Lagrimari citizens were drained of their Songs. Tribute days were usually solemn affairs, with dozens of bound Earthsingers led inside for the mysterious process. None remembered what happened in the room, but all who left were haunted by it for the rest of their lives.

Two more guards stood at attention outside the room. She flooded them with enough Nethersong to leave them unconscious for hours, then raced forward as they sagged to the floor. She kneeled before the door, opening her other sight to sense the room's occupants. Dread seized her to find the seething column of power embodying the True Father already there.

She had never before used her other vision in the king's presence. Seeing the force twisting inside him was terrifying. She had never seen color in her mind's eye before, but a tornado of rainbow light represented the True Father.

Kyara crouched, taken aback. Any fantasy she'd had over the years of latching onto the True Father's centuries-old Nether and killing him melted away. It was impossible. There were so many energies, so much perversion of the energies, she wasn't sure she could handle any of it.

Her focus shifted to the other light in the room, very dim but growing steadily brighter. Nether was filling this person quickly—Darvyn.

Instinctively she reached for his Nether, pulling it to her just as she'd done with the poison of Death River. It responded to her immediately, drawing out of him and into her. Earthsong rushed in to fill him, but she could also see the Void waiting in the pockets between energies, seeping in to pick up the slack.

A war took place among the three forces struggling inside Darvyn. Kyara kept drawing the Nethersong that steadily filled him, while Earthsong sought to replenish him, and the Void exerted itself for an unknown purpose.

The presence of Earthsong meant that the True Father had not yet stolen Darvyn's Song, but Kyara had no idea if what she was doing could stop it.

A savage wind tore at Darvyn, seeking to rip his skin from his bones. He was enclosed in a wall of sound that overpowered his ability to comprehend. Extreme heat and cold hit him at once. He was sightless, yet surrounded by color. Every sense was battered, overwhelmed, overloaded. Thought was impossible as he struggled to withstand the onslaught.

Then, as if someone flipped a switch, calm took over. Gentle hands pulled him from the storm and settled him somewhere dark and warm. His vision returned, but around him were only blurry shadows.

A familiar presence surrounded him. "Kyara?"

A woman sighed. Not Kyara.

"Where am I?" he asked.

"Open your eyes."

He nearly told the woman that his eyes were open, but then he opened them again and found himself in an endless darkness, sitting next to the Queen Who Sleeps. As usual, She appeared to glow from within, but Her face was unusually taut with worry.

"Am I dead?"

"Not yet."

"He is stealing my Song."

"He is trying. But he cannot complete the spell while Kyara helps you."

"She's helping? I thought I felt her. How?"

"He needs the Nethersong created by stabbing you in order to take your Song. But Kyara is stealing it from him." Something close to a smile pulled at Her lips. "He was not expecting that."

"She's in danger."

"Yes, she will always be in danger. Go back and free yourself."

Darvyn's mind raced. He had no idea how to free himself, though the Queen seemed to think it possible. "How? He's much more powerful than me."

"When was the last time he used his power? Truly used it." Her words echoed as she began to fade away. "Free yourself, Darvyn. And then run. You may be able to startle him, but you are not strong enough to defeat him."

Blackness descended. He felt himself sink back into his physical body, this time in control. Pain screamed from the center of his chest where the knife was embedded. The True Father was still standing over him, repeating a string of foreign words. The language spoken in the king's ruined voice made the hairs on the back of Darvyn's neck stand up. He withstood the pain, steadying his body until he was certain it would respond to him. Then he reared up, head-butting the king and throwing him off-balance.

Darvyn rolled off the table and pulled the dagger from his breast. He stretched his Song as wide as he could, allowing torrents of Earthsong to flood him. He would burn out quickly, but he needed every scrap of strength he could muster to fight off the True Father.

The staggering king righted himself. His mood, before confused and impatient, grew irate. He didn't bother with a shield for his Song. Every emotion poured into Darvyn, who barely resisted the urge to bend over and retch the dark flood of feeling from his consciousness.

Darvyn pulled down a shield to block himself, but the overwhelming emotions threatened to paralyze him. The stone table he'd been lying on a moment earlier hurtled against the wall and exploded into a thousand splinters on impact. The air around him charged and changed, hardening into a force that picked him up and tossed him.

He sang a spell to form a cushion of air to catch him before he smashed into the wall. A fireball hurtled toward him, and Darvyn deflected it with a gust of wind. The small room thundered with the fury of the spell-charged air.

The True Father's attack was clumsy. The Queen was right, it seemed as though he wasn't used to singing defensively or offensively. When was the last time he'd had any direct opposition? The people had been cowed for years and there had been no Singer strong enough to challenge him for far longer. Darvyn used his old trick of darkness to cloak the room, then blasted the king with the shards of the destroyed table, propelling them with great enough force to pin his long, bejeweled tunic to the glass floor.

Darvyn raced for the door he'd entered through. Still reaching for the handle, a heavy gust blew him upward and smashed him into the ceiling. The force of the impact left him seeing stars. With just as much gusto, the spell forced him to the ground, but he caught himself on a pillow of air just before his face collided with the floor. The king replaced Darvyn's darkness spell with brilliant circles of fire swirling around the ceiling. Darvyn bounced on the ground and rolled over, only to find the king flying, slicing through the air toward him.

Sharp bits of glass tore from the walls and attacked Darvyn. The spell he sang to blow them away lobbed them toward the True Father, who simply batted them back. Dozens, then hundreds, then thousands of razor-sharp shards flew back and forth through the air.

Darvyn's concentration was scattered as the glass twisted and turned, seeking a way through his defenses. When he maneuvered them away, they shattered, multiplying, and even more splintered off the walls and floor. His Song was on the cusp of burning out, leaving him to be impaled by the debris.

Several fragments broke through the cyclone he'd sung to keep them out and nicked him, drawing blood across his chest and arms. None of the True Father's skin was visible, but a few of the slivers had pierced his outer tunic, revealing another layer of clothing beneath it. The king was well-protected. Were his stolen Songs near the point of exhaustion, as well?

Darvyn tried one final gambit. He latched onto the ragged glass beneath the True Father's feet and rapidly raised the temperature. He pulled deep from his Song to melt it, then forced the thick molten liquid around the king's feet to lick at his ankles. With the last of his power, Darvyn dropped the temperature of the glass, cooling and hardening it.

It would be a small annoyance for the True Father but left Darvyn enough time to launch himself at the door to the hallway.

It disintegrated with the force of his attack, sending him sprawling. He fell at the feet of a startled Kyara whose wide eyes looked down on him.

"Run!" he rasped out, scrambling to his feet. She grabbed his hand and pulled him forward down the long corridor.

CHAPTER FORTY-FIVE

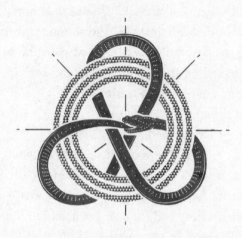

Our sacrifices are a burden grave
When heavy hands hold secrets to their breast
Just one decision can lead to the grave
One all-consuming choice conquers the rest
This legacy yet haunts the world today
The cost so long deferred, but all will pay

——THE BOOK OF UNVEILING

As they raced through the castle, Kyara looked over her shoulder again and again, expecting pursuers, but none appeared. She had rendered virtually everyone unconscious, thanks to the locket. Soldiers would have to be brought from other posts in the city to give chase. The True Father would not let the Shadowfox slip away so easily.

The sun was high in the sky as they ran through the main gates and down the long path leading to the Avenue of Majesty. A shrill wailing tore through the air.

"That's the alarm," Kyara said. "We need to hurry."

They passed through the castle gate unmolested and ran onto the bustling avenue, which was clogged with the usual traffic. Darvyn stumbled on the sidewalk, tripping over his own feet. Kyara shot out a hand to steady him.

"Are you all right?" she asked.

"My Song—I'm drained."

She wasn't surprised after what she'd heard going on in the tribute room. It was a wonder he was moving at all. Though his physical injuries had healed, his exhaustion was evident. The True Father's whirling eddy of energies had been dim as well at the end; could the fight have weakened the king?

Still, Darvyn moved forward with determination. Spotting an opening in the flow of traffic, Kyara darted into the street. An angry cyclist ran his thumb across his nose in an offensive gesture as he darted around her.

"Whore's son," she cursed. Darvyn snorted.

The West Gate was half a dozen blocks away. But between them and the gate was a problem. Six Golden Flames riding crawlers, three on each side of the street, monitored the passing traffic with eagle eyes. Kyara growled when she noticed Aren was one of them.

She pressed Darvyn back against the window of a shop, hidden under its awning. Since he was drained, the spectacles Aren wore would be of no use in finding someone with a brightly lit Song. But Darvyn couldn't disguise himself, either. There was no way to get out of the city this way, and each gate would likely be the same.

A low whistling tune rang out amidst the din of the street. Darvyn perked up beside her and whistled an answering melody.

The first whistle sounded again, and Darvyn tilted his head. "This way," he said, moving down the walkway toward the Flames.

Kyara kept her eyes on the soldiers as she and Darvyn moved with the flow of pedestrian traffic.

"Here," he said, ducking into an alley. The narrow space dead-ended in a pile of rubbish and what smelled like an overflowing sewer pipe. An enormous bald man stood with his arms crossed and Kyara had never been so glad to be in such a foul-smelling place.

Zango grinned and stepped to the side to reveal Farron behind him. The men hugged, relief spilling from them.

"Did they—" Farron swallowed. "Did they take your Song?"

"No, thankfully Kyara got there in time." Darvyn smiled, but his eyes were still haunted from his encounter with the True Father. Kyara longed to know what had really happened in the tribute room.

"In time to do what?" Farron's eyes were wide and round.

She shook her head. "Don't ask me how I was able to stop the tribute, I don't know."

"But you . . . saw the True Father?"

Darvyn stared at Farron for a moment, before nodding. Kyara grabbed his hand and squeezed. The others regarded them in silence.

Shifting on his feet, Darvyn cleared his throat. "There will be time to recount my meeting with the king later; now we need a plan to get out of here. My Song won't regenerate fully before nightfall." He stifled a yawn that no one missed.

"We have to draw them away somehow," Zango said.

"Where are the others?" Kyara asked.

Farron's expression hardened. "Aggar forbade anyone else from coming to Darvyn's aid."

"He said we weren't Keepers anymore if we left." The big man shrugged.

"Thank you," Kyara said. Both of them had sacrificed much for their friend. She turned to Darvyn, but found his eyes closed, his breathing steady. He was sleeping on his feet.

"If he's drained, he'll need sleep," Zango said. "That's the best way to get his Song back."

Kyara nodded. "I'll draw off the Flames, and you get him through the gate. Let's meet at the Avinid temple just outside the city."

Zango's brows descended. He shot a worried glance at Darvyn, who was sure to veto the plan. If he was awake. Now his face was slack and peaceful. Kyara longed to kiss him one more time. She wanted to tell him everything she felt, but was scared to say. But she would get the chance when they met up again.

Her chest heaved as she backed down the alley. She gave Darvyn one last look before disappearing around the corner, her heart on fire.

The street was even more crowded than minutes before. The Flames were still spread out, checking the backs of wagons and inside rickshaws.

With steps steady and will unshakeable, she approached her former colleagues. She felt it in her marrow when Aren spotted her. His gaze was frost on her soul. They locked eyes for a pregnant moment before she took off running in the opposite direction, away from the West Gate, begging him to give chase.

The strength of the locket made her almost giddy. She left the sidewalk, darting through the middle of the street, dodging carts and bicycles and contraptions.

A horse snorted in her direction, maybe reacting to the swirl of power within her, now begging to be released. She tightened her hold on her Song and hopped onto the opposite curb.

The Golden Flames, unable to use their crawlers due to the traffic, fanned out across the street on foot, giving chase. That should allow Darvyn and the others to get out of Sayya.

Kyara raced toward an intersection where vehicles were stopped, waiting for the traffic changer to flip his sign.

A shot rang out. The woman helming the rickshaw next to her fell, blood spurting from her neck. Kyara twisted around to find Aren, standing on the back of an open wagon twenty paces away, staring down the sight of his rifle at her.

His smile was cruel. He was an excellent shot, so she knew he had missed her on purpose, probably wanting to draw this out. She had no time to mourn the innocent woman, but the Nethersong from her death combined with the power of the locket would make this showdown between her and Aren end very differently.

Kyara walked toward Aren and his rifle, leaning in to his malicious gaze.

"No!" a familiar voice shouted. She turned in horror to find Darvyn barreling down the street toward her, pushing people out of the way. Zango was hot on his heels, with Farron behind.

Kyara met Aren's gaze across the barrel of the rifle, his finger hovering over the trigger. She quieted her mind and reached for her other sight, filtering through all the energies of the people surrounding her to focus on his.

This would be a death blow, and she needed to make sure she

was precise. Even with the locket and all the Nethersong giving her control, she had never dared to use her power amidst a crowd. She couldn't afford to make a mistake.

Aren shifted, turning to point the rifle at Darvyn.

Kyara wasn't ready. She focused her Song, preparing to strike.

Aren's finger squeezed the trigger.

Time slowed.

The shot sounded.

The force of the blast lifted Darvyn off his feet. Nethersong mushroomed inside him.

Kyara broke.

Her leash dissolved and her Song escaped, stronger than ever before. Rabid and keening, it ran wild, rushing out for the Nethersong present in every living thing surrounding her. Somewhere, from high above, she watched, but exerted no control over the beast that had broken out of its cage.

Aren fell, the rifle dropping from his hands like a stone. Darvyn hit the ground, and Zango, and Farron. The man on the sidewalk who'd been carrying a bundle of newsprint crumpled. The woman in the carriage next to her dropped the reins and keeled over. The horse went down. People collapsed in a growing circle around her, spreading out. She watched, helpless to stop it, numbed by the swirling eddy of Nethersong rushing through her.

The circle of her spell expanded even farther. It hit the pub, the buildings, the vehicles. Out one hundred paces, two hundred paces. People and animals fell where they stood.

"Enough," a voice said sharply, though she wasn't sure where it came from. She could feel the spell's connection to her, could sense the Nethersong using her as a conduit. There were no barriers, no ends to her ability. More and more people throughout the city of Sayya fell.

"Enough!" The voice jarred her. A slap across the face brought her back to herself. She seized control of her Song and leashed it.

Two pairs of green eyes stared at her.

Kyara sucked in a breath. She, Raal, and Ydaris were the only people alive as far as she could tell.

Destruction surrounded them. Bicycles and rickshaws had toppled over. Horses caught in their harnesses, carriages flipped. People were sprawled everywhere. Birds littered the ground from where they'd dropped from the sky.

Kyara let out a desperate sob and sank to her knees. Darvyn's motionless body was just out of reach. Her hand covered her mouth. All feeling drained away.

"You shouldn't have tried to hide her from us, Ydaris," Raal was saying. His voice sounded far away, as if he were speaking underwater. "All this could have been avoided if she had been properly trained. So much waste." He tsked under his breath as her hearing cleared.

"She was my best bargaining chip. You would have done the same."

"I will leave you to clean this up, then."

Ydaris made a noise of protest. Then Kyara felt a tug on her arm, pulling her to a standing position. Her brain was a fog as she tried to comprehend what she had done.

"I think she's in shock," Raal said.

"Such a delicate little thing. Best take her now. When she comes out of it she won't be nearly as pliable."

"Hmm." He seemed to consider this.

Kyara was jostled, still floating outside of her body. Everything was emptiness. There was no room even for grief.

She heard a rustling, and then Raal's voice speaking in the language of the blood magic. So similar to the language Murmur and the Cavefolk had spoken. Through the haze of her mind, it took a moment to realize. Her vision swam as her body grew lighter than air. The boulevard faded, and wind rushed her ears.

Recognition set in as she understood the word he'd spoken. *Home.*

Ydaris grasped the compass Raal had handed her before he left with the girl. With it, she could finally return to the land of her birth. She had spent decades in this godsforsaken country, scheming and planning her way back. And more than that, a way to return home on top, not at the bottom, not crawling on her hands and knees the way she'd left.

She was not the same child who'd killed her lying, thieving, whoring mother. Nor was she the urchin who had escaped the Physick-run reformatory with a stolen and very powerful amalgam medallion and had hidden in a shipment of silk on its way to Lagrimar.

No, she was the Royal Cantor, second-in-command only to an immortal madman. She had fooled an entire country into believing she was an Earthsinger. And one little Nethersinger was all she needed to return to the good graces of the Physicks. Imagine what she could do outside of this dilapidated desert and in civilization once more.

But first, she had to clean up the mess the girl had made. The sight made her wince. So much power, so little control. It had not been in Ydaris's best interest to teach the girl to manage her

Song properly, though over the years she'd wondered if just a touch more mastery would have proven useful. Still, she had done what she'd needed to, and it had all worked out in the end.

Ten years ago, when she'd first discovered Kyara's rare gift, Ydaris had approached the Physick who had been infiltrating Lagrimar with his pesky experiments. But Raal had insulted her and hadn't stayed long enough to hear her out. So she had rethought her plan. A trained Nethersinger, even one as barely competent as Kyara, would give her a stronger bargaining position. So she'd bided her time. Waited until the Physicks were on the cusp of desperation. When Raal returned to the country, she hadn't allowed his snobbery to affect her. And the deal had been made.

Now she just had one more task to accomplish and she could return to Yaly. She grasped hold of the medallion around her neck and took a deep breath. It would take a great deal of Earthsong to reverse Kyara's love-addled chaos. Perhaps it would be easier if Ydaris had a true Song as the Lagrimari did, but the medallion she'd stolen mimicked one effectively. It had held up quite well over the years, regardless of the strain the idiot king had put on it.

She whispered the words to activate the medallion and draw Earthsong into it. Another spoken spell released the energy into all the bodies within the range of damage that Kyara had wrought. In the girl's tantrum, she had pulled the Nethersong out of her victims, allowing the Void to fill them. They weren't dead, merely on the cusp. An infusion of Earthsong was all they needed to awaken. This was fortunate for Ydaris as a thousand dead bodies would have been quite inconvenient to bury, and she no longer required the Nethersong they would have produced. Though she did expend a regrettable amount of time and energy rousing everyone.

Everyone except Aren. It seemed Kyara did have some level of subconscious control.

The Cantor shrugged. Good riddance. Her job here was done. She opened the compass Raal had given her and whispered the words that would take her home again.

Darvyn rose, rubbing his aching head. He had no idea what had just happened. One minute, he'd been running toward Kyara, the next, he was on the ground, confusion swarming around him.

Dozens of crashed vehicles littered the street, but no one appeared injured. He scanned those around him and found them all perfectly healthy.

Among the oddities he noted: his Song was restored, but not yet at full strength. The sun was considerably lower in the sky than before. A hole marred the front of his tunic, burnt around the edges like a bullet hole, yet he didn't recall being shot. But most importantly, Kyara was nowhere to be found.

Aren, however, lay dead where he had been standing.

Darvyn hoped the man met every person he'd ever wronged in the World After.

Zango and Farron brushed themselves off beside him. "Where is she?" Farron asked.

Darvyn rubbed his head again. "I don't know. She was right there."

Everyone else on the street appeared as discombobulated as he was. He reached out his senses to search for Kyara, though he knew it was useless. He couldn't feel her even when she was right next to him; there was no way he could find her with his Song.

"Do you think she was captured?" Farron asked.

Darvyn looked around once more. The other Flames who'd been monitoring the street were rousing with the rest of the crowd. "No, I don't." But what had become of her? Why would she have left him?

"Maybe something happened and she'll meet us at the temple like she said." Farron's voice was hopeful.

Darvyn didn't want to contradict his optimism, but he had a bad feeling.

As the Flames began to regroup, Zango clapped him on the shoulder. "You know she can take care of herself, mate. Are you up for a row?" His voice was low, and he eyed the soldiers warily.

With Darvyn's Song still recovering, he'd rather not get into a fight. Especially not in the open like this.

"Let's go wait at the temple," he said.

Zango held his eye and nodded. They disappeared into the turmoil of the crowd.

CHAPTER FORTY-SIX

And now, I fear, my tale is incomplete
Though I have writ the words my father told
The lies we tell, the secrets that we keep
Though fires of old memories grow cold
The future that she sought is still to be
It approaches with fate's own certainty

—THE BOOK OF UNVEILING

The walk through the mountains is harder than Ulani thought it would be, though, honestly, she's never spent a great deal of time thinking about walking through mountains. The group led by the Keepers has only just started on the path that winds over ancient peaks dusted with a cold, white substance Gladda tells her is called "snow," when Ulani feels something change.

A sensation ripples through her, thrumming against her Song like the hard pluck of a *luda*'s strings. Tana is walking a little ahead of her so Ulani tugs on Zeli's tunic.

"It's gone," she whispers.

Zeli frowns down at her. "What's gone?"

"The Mantle."

"What do you mean?"

The lady who feels like soft summer rain, the one they call Fakera, looks back at her and tilts her head. Then she nods. "She's right. I don't feel the Mantle anymore. It's gone."

Everyone in the group stops and stares at the mountains rising overhead as if searching for a visible difference. Only the Earthsingers can sense that the Mantle, which was there just a moment ago, now isn't.

"Will Elsira still be safe for us?" a lady asks.

"No matter what, it will be safer than staying here," Gladda says. Others murmur in agreement. And so they keep moving up and up again, over rocky paths and over boulders. Past darkened cave openings that echo with a bleak wrongness so strong, the yawning mouths make Ulani cringe. They climb up into air so cold it's like being locked in the icebox back home. But she doesn't complain.

She does, however, wonder about the lady in her dream. Each night since the last time she saw her, Ulani has hoped for another visit, but never again found herself in that dark place with her body more of a suggestion than a reality and the lovely, rainbow voice from the woman who called herself Oola.

Even still, she thinks she'll see her again.

At night, around their campfire, one of the women in the group sings. She's the same griot who performed at the Magister's house a few days ago. The one who sang about the Poison Flame. Her voice makes Ulani think of drops of water on eyelashes and the warm grass of the courtyard under her feet.

When they stop tonight, after finishing their evening meal, the griot will look at Tana and announce that she will sing a new song, one she hasn't sung in a long time. One her mother and her mother's mother taught her.

"It's been passed down in our branch of the House of Eagles for generations," she'll say.

"Why haven't you sung it in so long?" Ulani will ask.

"Because it wasn't time then. But I think the time is now."

The griot will strum her *luda* and begin singing about a different animal. One with no house Ulani has ever heard about. A scorpion.

Sometimes it will seem like she's singing the song just for Tana. Her gaze will drift to the girl, eyes shining, like she's found the missing piece to a puzzle. Ulani will wonder aloud why there aren't more scorpions.

"We don't have scorpions in Lagrimar," one of the old women sitting around the fire will say.

"Don't we?" the griot will respond, her gaze tracking Tana. "I think there may be one or two around."

Dawn broke over the peaks of eastern mountains. Darvyn paced back and forth on the narrow walkway surrounding the dome of the Avinid temple. He'd been up all night waiting and worrying.

Sayya's West Gate loomed less than a kilometer away. If she was coming, she would have been there already. Not only his heart, but his Song was disturbed.

He maintained a connection to Earthsong to check for soldiers approaching, but the source energy was in flux. Something very powerful strained the energy before it reverted back to normal. His head snapped over to the west, sensing the source of the disturbance lay there.

He couldn't shake the feeling that something massive had just changed. Silence reigned over the endless desert, but chaos approached, he just knew it.

Not long after, Farron ran up the steps and climbed onto the roof. "Darvyn! You'll never guess what's happened!"

"The Mantle has fallen." Recognition hit him as the words left his mouth.

Farron's shock was almost comical. "How did you know?"

Darvyn rubbed his chest. "I felt it."

"Not only did the Mantle fall, but the Queen is arisen." He spoke in a hush, eyes alight with excitement. Darvyn wished he could match Farron's enthusiasm, but his emotions were empty.

"A transmission went out from the border on all our frequencies," Farron continued. "It said that a half-Lagrimari girl awakened the Queen using the caldera you sent with Turwig and the others."

Farron chattered away about how the True Father had been there, too, and had challenged the newly awakened Queen Who Sleeps, but the Lagrimari girl had attacked him and with the Queen's help, drained him of his Song.

"He's powerless, Darvyn. The True Father is going to rot in an Elsiran prison." He tapered off and stared out at the desert along with Darvyn. "We're free." Disbelief and awe colored his voice.

"Free," Darvyn repeated. The word tasted strange on his

tongue. It was what he'd worked for his entire life, yet the victory was bittersweet.

Joy, melancholy, hope, fear, and regret all danced within him. Farron's emotions echoed the same steps.

"Should it feel different?" Farron whispered.

"I don't know."

Just past midday, Zango joined them to watch the caravan approaching from the west. A dust cloud heralded the arrival of the motorized vehicles, all far larger than diesel crawlers. The conveyances were foreign to Lagrimar. Long and short, open topped and closed, every single one of them was filled with brown-clad Elsiran soldiers. Sunlight glinted off the chrome of the vehicles.

"They must have driven half the day to get here," Farron said with wonder in his voice.

"They're headed for Sayya," Zango said. "Do you think our soldiers will resist?"

"If the True Father is really gone, what would they have to fight for?" Darvyn replied.

Elsirans streamed across the highway for hours. And as the day limped on, more and more Lagrimari citizens began to head the other way. People had packed whatever meager belongings they could carry, loaded them into carts, onto mules and horses or on their backs and immediately begun the trip west.

Something like hope bubbled up within him. The Mantle coming down meant they were no longer locked behind the borders of this country. He could travel, visit other lands, and meet other people. Long-suppressed dreams were now a possibility—except, he wasn't going anywhere without Kyara. Her absence caused an emptiness to yawn inside him.

Gripping the railing before him, he regarded the foreign

soldiers still heading in. Even from the roof, he could hear the murmured whispers working their way through both the Lagrimari leaving and the Elsirans entering the city. Everyone began looking up and pointing.

A white comet of light arced slowly across the sky, capturing the attention of those on the ground. Wariness thrummed in Darvyn's veins. That light felt familiar. He ducked through the door into the temple and raced down three levels of staircases to reach the bottom floor.

Once outside again, he found the light hovering above a crowd who had stopped to stare. Soon it became clear that the spectacle was not a light after all, but a glowing woman. She floated above them, a swirl of wind playing with Her white dress, whipping it around. Dark, curling tresses haloed Her head like a cloud. Her skin shone with the same light as She'd had in the World Between, which soon dimmed to a dull shine.

The people clogging the road gaped, open-mouthed, at the site of Her, wild hair blowing in the invented breeze, crackles of Earthsong radiating from Her essence.

The Queen Who Sleeps had found him.

To the Lagrimari who had not joined the ranks of the Keepers of the Promise, *Her* promise, She was merely a legend. But Darvyn knew better.

Your Majesty. Darvyn sent his thoughts to Her, bowing his head slightly, mostly to hide his aggravation.

Darvyn. Her voice in his head was amused. She looked the same as always, but larger than life now. More like a goddess. The only difference was the pendant around Her neck, one he'd never seen before. Its stark twisting and folding lines formed a long-legged insect. The sigil of the House of Spiders.

You do not appear to be happy, She said.

We are truly free?

You are.

And what of Jack?

Her eyes smiled, though it didn't make it to Her lips. *He is well. He will be king of our new land.*

Relief filled part of the void within him. Jack was all right, and he would make a good king. Somehow, Darvyn wasn't even surprised. *And the True Father?*

The Queen's eyes flashed, but not in anger, as he'd expected. In sadness. The emotion passed so quickly that Darvyn thought he might have imagined it.

Powerless. Mortal again. His stolen Songs have been removed from him. For now he is imprisoned, but I will deal with him in time.

Then this is truly a happy day. Part of him meant it. A very large part.

And yet?

Could She not feel that a chunk of him was missing? Darvyn swallowed. *Do you know what's happened to Kyara?*

The Queen tilted Her head as if listening for Kyara's location. The hope ballooning in his chest collapsed when She settled her cold attention back on him.

You must go west. You will aid the new king and queen, Jaqros and Jasminda.

No. Darvyn shook his head. *I need to find her.*

Now is not the time for you and her. I owe the new queen a debt, and it must be paid. Family is all that matters now. And it is high time Jasminda's family came home.

Darvyn stared in disbelief.

Instead of explaining Her cryptic statements, She rose into the air and disappeared into the blue of the sky.

He dropped his head into his hands and squatted down, suddenly unable to breathe. Farron crouched beside him. No one but Darvyn had heard the Queen's speech, but they had all seen the face-off between him and the goddess.

"So that's Her," Farron said, ignoring the silent tears streaming down Darvyn's cheeks. Whatever Her agenda was would be difficult to ignore, but he was through being Her—or anyone else's—pawn.

"She's wrong," Darvyn whispered. "I will make my own promise. A new promise."

Farron looked at him curiously. Darvyn balled his hands into fists and pressed them together to seal his vow. "I will find her. I won't rest until I do. And then I'm never letting her go. This, I vow."

The promise rang through his Song, imprinting itself onto his being. He clutched his head in his hands again, battling the rising pressure.

He *would* find Kyara.

EPILOGUE

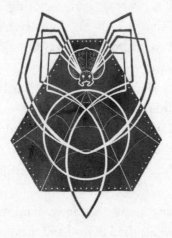

Death comes to all, it heeds not bad nor good
Our lives are candles, reaching for the flame
The scales, when balanced, measure out our time
But who's to say we cannot live again?
A glimpse beyond the veil once sealed her fate
And in that dark tomb is now where she waits

—THE BOOK OF UNVEILING

Elsiran women in blue robes marched down the aisles of the city
of white tents, each bearing a crate with supplies of some kind.
Aside from the few soldiers who kept their distance from the refugees, these women were the only Elsirans Zeli had seen.

The older Lagrimari men who spoke Elsiran and served as
translators called the women "sisters." It took a while for Zeli to
understand that they were not all part of an enormous family,

but a religious order of some kind. Like Avinids, but not. The women were kind, helpful, and, as it turned out, responsible for the well-being of the hundreds of refugees who'd poured into the country before the Mantle fell, and the thousands entering since then.

They worshipped the newly awakened Elsiran goddess, a woman who, like their new queen, both looked and spoke Lagrimari, according to those who'd seen both of them. Zeli hadn't, and cared little about who ruled this land—anyone was better than the True Father she thought, surprising herself. But such thoughts were no longer treason, not when he'd been arrested and locked away in an Elsiran prison.

And what sort of place were so many of her countrymen entering? The land was green and fertile, much like the Lake Cities, but everything here looked fresh and modern. She'd thought the Magister's estate such a beautiful, serene place but it was a hovel compared to the structures in the towns they'd passed in their journey west across Elsira.

The tents in which they were now housed were simple, but kept out the rain and chill. Zeli stayed with Tana, Ulani, and three other motherless children, and Gladda stopped by every day to check on them.

The Keepers had set up a school in the camp for the children, and Zeli had offered to help teach the younger ones. She was on her way there, but had stopped to watch the progression of the blue-clad Sisters, distributing supplies.

Something about their serenity and clarity of purpose called to her. A Sister with a rippling burn scar on one side of her face caught her staring and smiled. Zeli smiled back.

As she headed toward the grassy area being used as the school, her attention snagged on a cluster of long-bladed grass shooting up in tufts. She stooped down for a closer look. This wasn't hispid blade, but it was similar. She reached out and felt the strength of each little leaf between her fingers.

She could make something of this. With enough of them she could weave a bracelet. Something for luck.

She tilted her face to the sky and smiled.

Kyara opened her eyes, huffing in breaths as the dream receded. She had been in the World After, having come face-to-face with all the people she'd killed. Every single one of them had accused her, laying the blame squarely at her feet.

Where it belonged.

She clutched at her chest. The wound was still there, though the locket was missing. Where was she?

Polished chrome bars filled her vision. Another cage.

She sat up, finding herself on a thick, divinely soft mattress. What a thing to sleep on, especially in a prison. She nudged it, alarmed at how it sprang back into place.

"It's filled with feathers."

She turned sharply to find a teenaged boy peering at her from the cell next to hers. His shock of ginger hair and amber eyes marked him as an Elsiran. Freckles peppered his nose. He sat on another feather mattress, and just beyond him, an identical boy stared at her, as well.

"You speak Lagrimari." It was the first thought that had entered her mind. The boys' strange golden eyes blinked back at her.

"So do you," the second twin said, mockingly.

Kyara frowned. "But you're Elsiran."

Both boys shrugged. Another in the cell stirred, rising from his spot on the floor to stand. He was Lagrimari, middle-aged but strong.

"I taught my children Lagrimari so they would know where they come from," the man said.

Kyara's gaze fell from the man to the two boys and back again. Something stirred in her memory, but she was too shocked to access it. "Your children?"

She had a million questions all vying for position in the front of her brain. But first things first. "Where are we?"

The man's face grew solemn, and the boys both looked away.

"Very far from home," the man said.

"Yaly," the closest twin said.

She sank back onto the unlikely comfort of her mattress and sighed.

Raal. Of course.

"You all have been here for some time?" she asked.

The father nodded sadly. "Years."

She bit back a gasp. Years? She could very well be here the rest of her life.

"What do they want with you?" the surly twin asked.

"My Song. My twisted, deadly, hateful Song. They think it will make them immortal somehow, but it will probably just start a war among the three worlds and wind up ending humanity as we know it."

No one spoke in the cell next door. Kyara rolled over to look at them. "Sounds crazy, right?"

Their solemn faces spoke volumes. None of them thought it sounded crazy at all.

No one spoke after that.

Kyara's eyes eventually fluttered closed and images of Darvyn filled her mind. She would have gladly traded her

Song, and anything else her enemies wanted, to go back in time and tell Darvyn she loved him.

An outer door opened, and footsteps came toward the cells. Raal entered with Ydaris at his heels.

Both twins rose from their mattresses to stand next to their father. They were tall, perhaps sixteen or seventeen, and sturdy. They eyed the two Yalyish with open contempt.

"I see you're awake, my dear," Ydaris said, her voice dripping with false care. "Good."

The door to Kyara's cell opened with the help of no mechanism that she could see. She did not move from her delightful mattress.

"We're ready to begin."

ACKNOWLEDGMENTS

My deepest thanks to my editor, Monique Patterson, who can move mountains. And to everyone at St. Martin's Press whose hard work made this possible.

To my agent, Sara Megibow, whose firm belief in our world domination is constantly inspiring.

To Nakeesha and Cerece, for putting up with all the crazy and being ports of calm in the storm.

To my family who has always supported me and without whom I couldn't do this.

I'm very grateful to my original beta readers: Mom, Paul, Andy Palmer, Gina Boyer, Kaia Danielle, Lynette Leong, Melissa McShane, Ines Johnson, Rebecca Roanhorse, and Rebecca Rivard.

Once again, a huge thanks to Danielle Rose Poiesz, who fights the good fight with the manuscripts I send her and inevitably makes them better.

And to Jared, who's always ready to dive into a bottomless pit after me.

ABOUT THE AUTHOR

Valerie Bey

L. PENELOPE has been writing since she could hold a pen and loves getting lost in the worlds in her head. She is an award-winning author of new adult, fantasy, and paranormal romance. She lives in Maryland with her husband and their furry dependents. Her books include the Earthsinger Chronicles (*Song of Blood & Stone, Whispers of Shadow & Flame*).